Acclaim for

CALOR

"From the moment I started *Calor*, I could not put it down. I found the magic system fascinating, the plot captured my thoughts when I wasn't reading, but most of all I loved the characters. They were individual and unique, a welcome change from the usual fantasy variety. This is an excellent story that needs to be on the list of every fantasy reader."

— MORGAN L. BUSSE, award-winning author of The Ravenwood Saga

"From the very beginning, Fischer's gift of words summons beauty through the chill of a desolate world, bringing Sephone's and Dorian's search for courage, truth, and hope to life. It's a world studded with gems of truth, a sparkling story, the sort of book that I don't want to put down and stays with me long after I finish. *Calor* has become a new favorite, and the second book in The Nightingale Trilogy cannot come soon enough!"

— CATHY MCCRUMB, author of the Children of the Consortium series

"J.J. Fischer has penned a stirring new take on the Persephone story. *Calor* captivated me, and I can't wait to follow her team of well-drawn, heartstring-plucking characters into the next installment!"

— LINDSAY A. FRANKLIN, Carol Award-winning author of *The Story Peddler*

"[A] unique twist on classical tales. Fischer brings intriguing characters to life in this slow-burn romance that pulls you deeper into the dangerous world of mystical powers and unrelenting suspense and leaves you wanting more. Can't wait to find out what happens next!"

— SANDRA FERNANDEZ RHOADS, award-winning author of *Mortal Sight*

"*Calor* is a thrilling fantasy adventure that tugs on your heartstrings the whole way through. Crafted with compelling characters, unique and sensational magical abilities, hints of romance, looming dangers, and a whole lot of heart, *Calor* reminds the reader that some things are too precious to sacrifice, even if that means confronting life's painful memories. This magical novel will captivate readers from beginning to end and leave them craving the next chapter."

— ASHLEY BUSTAMANTE, author of *Vivid*

CALOR

Books by J. J. Fischer

The Darcentaria Duology
The Sword in His Hand
The Secret of Fire

The Nightingale Trilogy
Calor
Lumen

CALOR

THE NIGHTINGALE TRILOGY | BOOK 1

J. J. FISCHER

Calor
Copyright © 2023 by J. J. Fischer

Published by Enclave Publishing, an imprint of Oasis Family Media, LLC.

Carol Stream, Illinois, USA.
www.enclavepublishing.com

ISBN: 979-8-88605-022-6 (hardback)
ISBN: 979-8-88605-023-3 (printed softcover)
ISBN: 979-8-88605-025-7 (ebook)

Cover design by Kirk DouPonce, www.DogEaredDesign.com
Typesetting by Jamie Foley, www.JamieFoley.com

Printed in the United States of America.

For anyone who ever wanted to save the world
and discovered they couldn't.

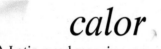

calor

A Latin word meaning *warmth* or *heat*.

"The whole world knows what I possess better than I do myself."

— THE EMPEROR, *THE NIGHTINGALE*
BY HANS CHRISTIAN ANDERSEN (1843)

"It does not do to dwell on dreams and forget to live."

— ALBUS DUMBLEDORE, *HARRY POTTER
AND THE PHILOSOPHER'S STONE* BY J. K. ROWLING

His father might be in the middle of saving the world, but Dorian was still bored. Nulla was about as close to the apocalypse as a place could get, and that was saying something, because the world had already ended once. It was certainly no place for a fourteen-year-old boy to spend the best days of the summer.

Not that Nulla had any concept of summer. The canals were still frozen solid, and the streets laden with a fresh fall of snow—if you could call it fresh, since the sickly gray color made the sky's latest offering look like a mourning shroud. Even the air stung. While his father was holed up in meeting after meeting with the lord of Nulla—an unpleasant-looking fellow by the name of Lord Guerin—Dorian had gone exploring, but the city's breezes were needling, mischievous things that seemed to have minds and wills of their own, and he'd soon returned to the inn.

He pried open the window of the third-story room and leaned on the sill, wishing he could inhale the fresh mountain air of Maera instead. It wasn't much warmer there in summer, but there was sunshine, at least, and sunshine tended to help a body forget it was cold. There was his gift, of course, but that was no more useful to him than snowshoes for a bear—gifts were always for other people. Restless, he looked down at the bustling city sprawled below his window.

It was sometime around mid-afternoon, though it might have been night for the oppressive weight of the sky. Dark-looking clouds knotted so closely together they seemed about to burst at their seams. Below and to his right, a street peddler, clutching the arms of the cart that displayed his wares, cowered before two larger men beneath the grimy awning of a nearby shopfront. A pitiful, blubbering sound drifted upward. As Dorian stared in their direction, the familiar heat building inside his chest, the peddler abruptly straightened to his full height, his bristling chin jutting out, and looked them full in the face.

Dorian quickly shifted away. Apparently, his gift worked at a considerable distance. After a moment, he dared to look down again, this time watching as a well-dressed man and woman walked past, arm in arm. A little girl darted around the pair, white-blond hair streaming behind her like a kite, heading for the main canal.

Maybe she's going ice skating, Dorian thought to himself. But there were few children in Nulla, and the idea that any of the existing ones would indulge in such a carefree leisure activity was ludicrous. He hadn't heard a laugh or seen a smile in the three days since he and his father had arrived. The seam folk were a melancholy bunch.

A few moments later, a scream jolted him from his reverie, followed by several shouts. A crowd had formed at the rim of the canal, and several people were pointing into the middle of the frozen passage. Dorian looked beyond them, and his stomach twisted. There was a hole in the ice, exposing choppy black water beneath. Someone was thrashing in it—he caught the occasional flailing of a pale arm and the bobbing of a fair head. Who would be foolish enough to try to cross the canal when the ice was so dangerously thin?

Though by now a large crowd had gathered beside the canal, not one of the townsfolk attempted to help the person. Indignation blazed in Dorian's chest once more, and he left the window, crossed the room in several long strides, and flung open the door. Not stopping to close it again, he took the stairs two or three at a time. In seconds, he was outside, and in less than a minute, he had reached the canal.

The crowd parted to let him through. Pale, hollow faces watched him curiously as he knelt at the edge of the canal, testing his weight on the brittle surface. It was thicker nearer the edges, and he thought it would support him, but what about when he neared the middle?

There was no time left to wonder. The water was still churning, but he could no longer see a head or an arm. Bubbles rose to the surface. He lowered himself until he was lying on his stomach, arms and legs spread out. Then he inched himself forward, as quickly as he could without straining the ice, making for the hole that now loomed ahead of him. It felt like miles away instead of mere yards.

By the time he made it, his heart was hammering painfully. Whoever had fallen through the ice had made it to the middle of the canal before being plunged into the filthy depths below. There were several broken fragments around the lip of the hole; he had to go around a way until he could safely reach the edge. He raised himself on his elbows and peered into the water. Nothing? Had they already drowned? He plunged his hand beneath the surface over and over again, like a bear fishing, shivering as the cold sliced into his skin.

Come on. He summoned every last vestige of strength. *Come on.*

The next time he submerged his arm, he felt it—a small hand brushing against him. Tiny fingers closed weakly around his wrist. He latched onto them immediately.

By all the old gods, it's a child!

He reached for his gift, pouring everything he could into the tenuous contact. In response, the child gripped harder. He braced himself and pulled. The child wasn't heavy, and he used both hands to drag her onto the ice fragment beside him.

"I've got you," he breathed. "I've got you safe and sound." Then he noticed the dripping, white-blond hair.

It was the same girl he'd seen running before, the one he'd imagined might be going ice skating. Where were her parents? And why had no one attempted to save her? She couldn't be any more than four years old. What kind of people were content to watch a child drown?

Though she'd gripped his hand tightly before, she was unconscious now. Had she ingested too much water? A slight movement caught his attention and he glanced back. Someone had thrown them a rope. He quickly tied it about her torso, watching as a strapping lad with a dirt-smeared apron dragged her to the edge of the canal, her sopping clothes bleeding water in her wake. A few seconds later, a second rope landed beside him. He gripped it tightly as the lad tugged him to safety.

He had never been more grateful for solid ground in his life. His teeth chattered and his body trembled—and he hadn't even been the one to fall through the ice. He got to his feet and looked around for the girl.

They had laid her on the very rim of the canal, atop the stone cobbles. She was completely soaked, and yet not one of them seemed to have tried to warm her.

He muttered beneath his breath as the crowds parted to let him through once more, curious, but doing nothing to aid him. He knelt beside her and pulled her into his arms. "Little miss!" he said urgently, gently slapping her cheeks to wake her. "Little miss!"

"She isn't breathing, lad."

Ignoring the man who'd spoken, he laid her on her back. She was ghostly white, her lips tinged with blue. There was only one thing he could think to do. He wove his fingers together and laid them over her small chest, then pressed down hard in a steady rhythm that mimicked the thumping of a heart. Every now and then, he blew a breath into her lifeless mouth, occasionally touching the back of her hand in the vain hope that his gift might rouse her.

"Stay with me," he whispered. "Stay with me, little one."

The crowd murmured around him, restless and growing bolder. "She's too far gone," said a yellow-haired woman in Lethean, with a decisive shake of her head.

"No thanks to any of you," Dorian retorted in her native tongue and kept working, not waiting for the woman's exclamation of surprise.

He had almost given up when the girl finally stirred. His pulse leaped as she took a shuddering, shallow breath. He turned her on her side so that she could expel the canal water from her lungs—hopefully not as toxic as it looked—and then held her close to warm her.

"Are you all right, little miss? For a while there, you weren't breathing. I thought for sure I'd lost you . . ."

Her head turned, and brown eyes locked with his. Though she was small, an awareness in her eyes made her appear years older than she was.

"Where's your father, little one? I'll take you to him if you can point me in the right direction."

"Sephone!" came a voice from behind the crowd.

Her hand latched onto his wrist again, brown eyes widening. She was still afraid—and no wonder, for she had very nearly died. He reached for his gift once more.

Still holding the girl, he stood and looked around as he addressed the crowd. "Where are her parents? Do you know her mother? Or her father?" He had to get her to her family. They would be beside themselves with worry. And if she didn't get warm soon, she would likely die. But the townspeople only stared at him blankly.

The crowd parted a third time, and a man with a shaven head appeared. His eyes found the little girl immediately and filled with relief. "Sephone!"

Dorian sighed with a little relief of his own, even though the girl still clung to him like an oyster. The child's father. Surely she would be safe and return to a home as loving as his own.

And just like that, his summer had become a little less boring.

17 YEARS LATER

"Are you sure you can handle this, Miss Winter?"

If it had been any other person asking the question, I might have laughed. A whole-body-seizing, muscle-spasm-in-your-belly, temporarily paralyzing kind of laugh. It was not the sort of question you put to a girl who had watched the end of the world more times than she could count. A girl who'd seen her first corpse before she was old enough to understand that the body concerned was not merely *playing* at being dead.

But one did not laugh at the lord of Nulla.

I bowed my head so the lord would only perceive the contempt in my eyes if he relocated his bulky frame to the floor—an impossibility on several fronts.

"Aye, my lord," I replied crisply. "I can handle it."

Perching on the edge of the faded, high-backed armchair stationed opposite his, I peeled off my long, close-fitting gloves and draped them carefully over the armrest. Though he would be a head taller than me when standing, and likely outweighed me by fifty pounds, the elderly Lord Guerin eyed my bare hands as if he expected me to throttle him then and there. One of his advisors—a tall man with hardly any lips and a peaky face—hovered behind his shoulder, shooting pointed glances at the two guards stationed beside the door. A clear warning not to exceed my earlier instructions.

Finally, the advisor pinned me with a steely glare. "You may proceed, Miss Winter."

As if I waited for his approval. But I nodded anyway. It was never wise to test the upper crust, no matter how flaky and insubstantial it appeared. Either of these men could have me before an execution squad faster than a snap frost, and I could hardly use my gift at such a distance. Not even Cutter could intervene if Lord Guerin decided I had exhausted my usefulness, though, credit where credit was due, he would likely try. He had to protect his greatest asset, after all.

But I had certain reassurances. If I were executed, the lord's best hope for a peaceable afternoon nap—if not an untroubled retirement—would die with me. For who else was able to keep his hideous nightmares at bay?

I leaned forward and was once again struck by the lord's nervous manner. I wondered, as I had since the first time I entered his mind, whether he was truly sane. His head darted around like a small bird's, snapping from side to side with rapid, truncated movements, studying me from behind a half-lidded gaze that displayed more of the black of his eyes than the white. Such obvious unease was odd coming from a man who, after the war, had enjoyed wielding power like it was going out of fashion. Though his iron grip on his city had eased in recent years.

All that, of course, I knew to keep to myself.

I reached for his craggy face, letting my hand hover over a temple that boasted more intersecting threads than a weaver's loom. He flinched at my touch, but the coldness of his mind was a far greater affront than the faint brush of calloused fingertips against sandpaper skin. As I drew on my gift, the familiar black tendrils leaped from my fingers, wreathing my hand in inky wisps finer than spider silk, awaiting my wordless command. I gave a mental nod, and the wisps scattered and sank beneath the lord's weathered skin as easily as dew melting into the ground.

The lord groaned and I hid a scowl. The procedure itself was completely painless—for him, at least. The only pain would come from his own recollections, and that was the reason for my presence in the first place.

The room shimmered and then vanished altogether, and I dodged the now-familiar assault of memories, a kaleidoscope of mental chaos more lethal than a dozen assassin's knives hurled in the dark. The first time I had entered the lord's slippery, festering mind, I had whimpered,

forced to traverse the house of horrors memory by memory, each more
hideous than the last—a jumble of starving children and missing limbs
and abscessed wounds and violated women.

All that Lord Guerin had witnessed, and for some of it, he was
directly responsible. It was the reason he had summoned me to his
manor house almost the very moment he had heard about Cutter's
powerful new *mem*. Apart from me, he'd never again be able to close
his eyes without being prodded and stabbed by his conscience.

If not for Cutter, I would have gladly let the lord bleed out from his
wounds. As it was, I had lost many a precious meal in the early years
of my service. These days, I had a stronger stomach. I had learned
to shield my mind from the worst of the onslaught, to thumb idly
through the images in the same way an illiterate slave might peruse his
master's accounting books—without any real comprehension of what
he viewed. There was no need to look closely at each memory, for in
the end, they were all the stuff of nightmares. I did not need to know
the why or the how—only the what.

After all, one does not need to understand the past in order to
neutralize it.

In time, I had discovered the true potential of my gift: that I could
not only watch Lord Guerin's life unfold before my eyes like a tragic,
gory play, but I could make subtle changes. Not to the memories
themselves—for the past could not, or perhaps *would* not, be changed.
But it could be edited. I could shine a spotlight on one memory—a
pleasant memory, for example—while carefully shrouding another. A
blunted edge here, a sharp ache eased there. A mental game of smoke
and mirrors. What could not be concealed was easily anesthetized.

And though I'd never experienced it myself, the after-effects
were deemed pleasant. Some compared it to the sweet oblivion of
intoxication without the headache, though it would, much like stiff
drink, not last forever. A couple of days at most, and for some, their
memories were so strong that the numbing effect would only prevent
the horrors from intruding for a few hours. Some of those had found
comfort in the glaze of the bottle as well as in my gift.

The mind-bleeding, it was called by most Calderans, after the
blood-letting procedures of the ancient times. But it was a poor name

for what actually took place—for nothing remotely resembling blood ever escaped those invisible wounds. In my own mind, I called it the soul-letting. For though the effects of my gift were temporary, I had begun to notice—

"What are you waiting for, Miss Winter?" This time, it was the lord's voice which sliced through my thoughts. "Proceed." He shifted uncomfortably in his chair, evidently not wanting to be in contact with me longer than necessary.

The feeling was mutual.

I closed my eyes to concentrate. The lord's mind shuddered, and I kept a firm grip on the grotesque specters shifting restlessly in the mental earthquake. It would be worse for us both if I lost my hold on him and had to start again. Abruptly, I found the memory which disturbed him the most, the one I had numbed at least a dozen times before. If it had taken physical form, it would have been as black as his eyes, a black so complete it consumed every bit of light it touched. It was as familiar to me as the back of my own hand.

Carefully, I moved to examine it, choking down the accompanying surge of bile. I never got used to this one. It was the memory of a massacre, one Lord Guerin himself had ordered, though he was only a young man when it had taken place—a little older than myself. Sixty years ago, perhaps. The countries of Memosine and Lethe, each in their infancy, bickering like children, while Marianthe was toddling in the south on unsteady legs, having not yet found her way to the sea.

As relations between Lethe and Memosine disintegrated, Lord Guerin's men, fighting for Lethe in those days, had been driven mad by the threat of starvation to the point of bloodlust. I felt a fleeting prick of pity on viewing their desperation in the lord's mind. But since I had seen scarecrow limbs and hollowed cheeks aplenty on both sides, what happened next was inexcusable. And it was not merely food they had demanded from the terrified villagers to sate their hunger.

Aye, Lord Guerin and his men deserved their subsequent exile into the no-man's-land between the walls. For not even Lethe would lay claim to what they'd done, and Lethe, more than any of the fledgling nations, was good at forgetting.

Lord Guerin flinched as I came across the tenderest memory—a

young woman who had been torn apart, as by a beast. Her child . . .
Now, *I* flinched, opening my eyes. A tiny shard of the memory had
come loose from the main mass, found its way through my mental
connection with Lord Guerin, and lodged itself in my mind. Memory
splinters, they were called, and I inwardly groaned. They were almost
impossible to remove.

Plucking it from my conscious mind, I blunted the sharpest edges
and compressed the rest of the horror the only way I knew how: into
a tight, prickly ball, which I forced from my throat into my stomach,
tamping it down until I could no longer feel its thorns. I would never
forget the massacred child, even though he had been dead for sixty
years, but it could be worse. Some of the memories had thorns which
were poisonous, and they could not be swallowed.

Now, to business. My hand grew colder as my gift stirred to life,
and the black tendrils swirling beneath the pads of my fingers wriggled
and danced, undaunted by the frigid temperature. As the cold spread
from my fingers to the lord's skin, the memory of the massacre cooled
and turned to ice, the worst parts sizzling and hissing as the flames
were extinguished. Though it was fanciful, I imagined a veneer of
delicate crystals forming like lace across the surface of the memory.
Thinking of myself as an artisan, leaving beauty in place of savagery,
made the business of memory manipulation more tolerable. Later, the
ice would thaw, and nothing of my careful handiwork would remain.
But for now, it was enough.

Lord Guerin expelled a long breath, more sigh than exhale, and
his tense body loosened. His head fell back against the taut, padded
fabric of the armchair, his eyes lidding shut as a swath of bone-white
hair fell across his lined forehead. The nervous, hyperattentive bird
was gone. Grateful the worst was over, I quickly located the remaining
memories and numbed them, too, being careful to avoid any more
memory splinters. The lord would sleep now—the sleep of the blissfully
unaware, if not the blessedly untroubled.

For when he woke, he would remember everything.

I retrieved my hand and pulled away.

The thin-lipped advisor watched me closely. "You have a rare gift,
Miss Winter."

Sephone, I would have insisted if I glimpsed anything resembling kindness in his face, but he was hawk-nosed and assessing, much like Cutter. Instead, I busied myself, pulling on my elbow-length gloves.

The advisor waved a hand in a flippant gesture, and the two guards disappeared, closing the door behind them. He continued his observation. "You perform a great service for Lord Guerin. Yet, it would seem that the effects of the mind-bleeding are significantly less . . . enduring . . . than when you were first summoned here some years ago."

The tone was faintly threatening, and I drew myself upright. As with Lord Guerin, I hardly came up to the advisor's collarbone, but I could shoot splintery glances with the best of them.

After all, I had been raised by Cutter, whose most genuine smiles could curdle a pint of milk. And not even in a useful way.

"I warned you from the first, sir, that the numbing effect would diminish with time. The past always finds a way to assert itself. And Lord Guerin's past is more . . ." I hesitated. It would not do to offend the advisor, even if the lord was practically unconscious. ". . . unforgettable than most."

There. I could be tactful. An iron fist in a velvet glove, Cutter always said. It was one of his more useful pieces of advice.

"Perhaps your gift is still developing, as it has been since you were a child." He looked me over, his subsequent sniff reeking of condescension.

"I'm nearly twenty-one years old, Mister Tr—"

"*Lord* Traemore, Miss Winter."

I retreated a step into the half of the room yet to be warmed by the spluttering hearth fire. Was Traemore more than Lord Guerin's advisor, then? But I had known the man since the first time I came to the manor house. It was Traemore who had introduced Cutter and me to the lord of Nulla. Not that Cutter accompanied me to the manor house anymore.

Traemore sniffed again, wrinkling his nose, as if he suddenly found himself allergic to the dank room. "I recently inherited my father's title, Miss Winter. Insignificant as it is without an allotment of land to accompany it."

The curse of those living in the pockets of no-man's-land between the thick walls of the seam. How fortunate, then, that men like Traemore did not require land to make their fortune.

"Happily," he droned on, "since my father was also Traemore, I am permitted to keep the name I am known by."

"Congratulations, my lord," I said quickly, with a clumsy bow in place of the expected curtsey. I was no lady, and both of us knew it. Better he thought me rustic and simple-minded, malleable beneath his control. It would give me time to work out why he had detained me.

"As I was saying, my lord, I am nearly twenty-one. My gift will not likely change in nature or strength from this point on. And all *mems* warn of the diminishing effects of the mind-bleeding. Our power is not without its limits. It is to be expected."

What was not expected was the effect of the mind-bleeding on those who had it performed regularly. Memories which were repeatedly numbed tended to fade in intensity, like a garment washed too many times, becoming leached of all color and emotion, even affecting surrounding memories. It was as if the soul of the person departed fiber by fiber, leaving behind an empty husk of a being, more a wraith than a flesh-and-blood human. Yet the pain of the original memory always remained or found expression in another way. Memories, after all, could never be permanently erased.

Was Lord Traemore aware Lord Guerin wasn't the same man I had first met as a child? Or could an elderly, cerebrally compromised lord of Nulla be part of his plans?

"Aye, some diminishing is to be expected, Miss Winter. And yet you are stronger than any *mem* who has passed through Nulla to date." He eyed the copper bracelets encircling my partially bare upper arms below my sleeveless dress. "Cutter was fortunate in his adoption of you."

"*Adoption*?" I barely contained the instinctive snarl at the mention of those early years. At least Traemore knew better than to pretend Cutter went by anything so proper as a last name. "My parents are dead. It was more an acquisition than an adoption. He has papers to prove it."

Lord Traemore raised a thin eyebrow, his hooked beak of a nose twitching, and I cursed my impulsive tongue. He would not think me simple-minded now. "Then you are unhappy in your present situation, Miss Winter?"

I shrugged. "A slave is not permitted to be unhappy. It's against the rules."

Lord Traemore expelled a mirthless chuckle, one with more bark than bite. "Ah, but your obvious intelligence is wasted on that boorish fellow, Miss—may I call you Sephone?"

I would rather he called his guards to escort me out, since it would be getting dark soon, but I nodded anyway. Better to suffer the advisor's company than those darkening the doorways of Cutter's tavern-shop.

"*Sephone*, then," Traemore continued briskly. "Slave or nay, you have great potential. You are a custodian of sacred memories, a caretaker of the past."

So Cutter liked to call us. But sacred? Traemore had clearly never seen inside Lord Guerin's mind.

"There are those who would be willing to pay good money in order to free you."

"Money, my lord?" Though a form of coinage was used in the rest of Caldera, Nulla's merchants had discovered a far more valuable currency.

He waved an impatient hand. "Or the equivalent."

Memories, he meant. Nostalgia. The other half of Nulla's thriving economy, and the bulk of Cutter's business. While men like Lord Guerin sought to surrender their past, many others would give anything to remember. And not just their own memories, either, but the memories which, once upon a time, had belonged exclusively to others. A first kiss in summer rain. The birth of a healthy firstborn child. The mastery of a greatly prized skill. A delicious meal made from rare ingredients. The hearing of a masterful symphony for the first time. Even a wedding night.

The first experience of anything pleasurable was always considered exceedingly valuable.

Some of the memories Cutter traded were old, older even than Lord Guerin, like fine wines cellared until their labels became dusty and peeling. But Cutter kept track of them all. The most expensive were memories of the time before the end of the world. The golden age of what we called the world-that-was—its true name was forbidden to be spoken aloud—when there was peace and plenty, and people knew with near certainty that they would survive from one winter to the next. Barring, of course, accidental death or sudden illness.

Though I had seen those things with my own eyes—far more than even Lord Traemore could fathom—I could not help doubting. Surely nothing was so perfect. For while the world was always changing, people usually stayed the same. It was an interesting illusion, much like a river that looks familiar year after year, even though the water that flows through it is completely different.

Lord Traemore's voice broke into my thoughts. "You are very quiet, Sephone. Do you not value your freedom?"

I stilled at the question. Freedom. It was a dangerous word to dangle in front of a slave. As Lord Traemore's eyes grazed my face, I thought of my jaw-length hair and the arm bands that chafed at my skin even after so many years.

Cutter's promise danced behind my eyes: *Before your parents died from fever, they gave you one last memory, Sephone. They made me promise not to give it to you before you were old enough to understand. I have it hidden safely away, waiting for you. On the day you turn twenty-one, you will have it for your own.*

The words were sweeter than pollen to a bee. They had kept me alive through two childhood fevers of my own—one of which had nearly taken me. As a young girl, I had lain awake in the formless dark of the night, wondering what it would be like to be loved the way I'd seen in the memories of others. I imagined it would feel like the honey mead Cutter saved for his most valued guests, of which I'd once stolen a gulp when I was twelve. A spreading warmth with a pleasant sensation of burning deep in my insides. I craved that warmth more than anything. For even when he claimed me, there had been nothing like it in Cutter's barren mind, and I had known from the first touch of his skin that he was an orphan too.

Two weeks. Two weeks, and I would consume that memory, sipping it slowly at first, so as to savor their love. I would feel their affection across the expanse of seventeen years of lonely grief. They hadn't known Cutter would take me as a slave rather than a daughter. I was sure of it. They had loved me.

I would find my way back to that love again, even if it no longer existed in real life.

"Aye, my lord," I said at last, fighting against the moisture in my eyes. "I value freedom." Freedom in love, at least.

Lord Traemore's stony expression boasted not even a hairline fracture. "It grows late, Sephone, so I won't detain you further. But think on our conversation. You have much to offer. There are those who would wish to give you what you truly deserve."

Such gentle words from so unfeeling a man. Still, they sank into me with no more resistance than my black wisps had encountered from the lord's skin, and I blinked the impending tears away. It was a dangerous man who could see so easily what others wanted, especially if he knew how to make them want it more. Cutter was a case in point. And since I had not peered into Lord Traemore's mind, I was at a distinct disadvantage. Likely, he was one of the few who would never allow me close, not even for the sake of an untroubled repose.

Leaving Lord Guerin now snoring noisily in his chair, Lord Traemore escorted me to the door. His guards flanked me the rest of the way to the manor house's entry hall and parlor. It was a fine space, far more impressive than the dimly lit study where I was usually summoned for the mind-bleeding. But then, given I was a frequent visitor to this house as well as to its master's mind, Lord Guerin likely knew that such pretenses at civility were unnecessary. There was, after all, no point in making the study presentable when most chambers of the lord's mind were stacked to the ceiling with bodies. If nothing else, I shared Lord Guerin's pragmatism.

Outside, a winter wind was ready to fling its own array of knives with deadly accuracy. I took my satchel from the guard and hastily donned my sleeveless cloak, pulling the rabbit fur-lined hood and collar snug around my exposed face and neck. Though my upper arms were bare, the cloak completely covered the thin woolen dress beneath. My toes curled inside my knee-high leather boots.

At least I had boots. Boots without holes were another bonus of being Cutter's most prized slave. He might be mercenary-minded, but in some things at least, he shared his good fortune.

It was more than I could say for Lord Guerin. Though the light was fading fast as the door closed behind me, I took my time returning to the canal, looking from side to side to survey the lord's finely manicured gardens, which had only last week been covered with a light fall of snow. Towering trees, of a height I'd never seen elsewhere—at least with my own eyes—lined the path I traversed. They were naked now, their fallen mantles carefully raked into piles and borne away by the lord's dutiful gardeners. Not for the first time, I wished I remembered more of the four years before Cutter. All I could remember were mountains, and Caldera had mountains aplenty.

I fumbled beneath my cloak for the necklace which, thankfully, had been too worthless for Cutter to ever consider selling. He had always been permissive of sentiment, so long as it was affordable. Warmed by my skin, my prized charm rested in my palm at the end of a tarnished chain long enough for me to stuff beneath my shirt or the collar of my dress. Not a locket, though I had often probed the metal backing, looking for a hidden catch that might spring open to reveal a precious rendering of my dead parents, or even a photograph—although these days, such things were impossibly rare.

But it was just a plain, unadorned oval with a thin, curving border scratched into the metal a fraction from the edge. The real beauty resided in the center of the charm: a tiny clutch of four pressed white flowers, no longer than my thumbnail from stem to petal, captured forever in their spring glory beneath a smooth, outwardly curved window of clear resin. In my sweetest daydreams, my father had given it to my mother as a token of his love, along with a proposal of marriage. Of course, they would tell me the entire story in the memory potion they'd made for me.

My boots crunched on the gravel, and a lick of wind found the bare patch of skin I'd exposed to ponder my necklace. I allowed a brief interlude of mental self-flagellation for entertaining such whimsical notions, then forced myself onward. In the clutch of such memories, even Lord Guerin's beautiful garden had lost its charm. Wondering if Traemore watched me daydreaming from the manor house, I found the small, wrought iron gate set into the thick stone wall, unlatched it, and slipped through, closing it firmly behind me. I could not afford to daydream. Not when my actual business lay in the stuff of nightmares.

A foul odor wafted on the breeze as I descended the small flight of stone stairs and hurried to the boat tied up at the canal's edge, my boots thumping on the wooden planks of the jetty. Animal refuse, or possibly human. How many times had I seen chamber pots emptied into the canals, along with all manner of other things?

Untying the knotted rope and holding the sides carefully to ensure I didn't unbalance the craft, I swung onto the seat, stashed my satchel safely behind me, and reached for the oars lying on the bottom of the boat. Maneuvering them into the oarlocks, I glanced behind me before dipping the wooden paddles into the canal. As usual, I tried not to inhale the scent of the water too deeply. It was one of many lessons a child quickly grasped growing up in Nulla—how to breathe with only half the capacity of your lungs. A familiar weight tugged at my chest, and I forced my thoughts away from dreamy contemplations of fresh, abundant mountain air.

Two weeks.

If the sun had been visible, it would have just dipped below the horizon. After the war, and the first years of the fog-smoke we called *the gray*, Calderans had learned to tell apart the different shades from dawn to dusk. But I had experienced real sunlight in Lord Guerin's mind, and our idea of a sunset was to the actual thing as a toddler's mud pie is to the local baker's prize-winning creation. The joy of witnessing such effortless beauty—such impossible, shining warmth— was one of the few things that made my weekly forays into Lord Guerin's mind bearable.

Few traversed the canals at this late hour, and I spied only the usual narrowboats tethered to their moorings, along with a trader or two steering their heavily laden crafts, and two figures manning what looked like a fishing boat, one older and the other younger—a man and his adult son, perhaps. I dragged my hood more firmly over my hair. No point arousing more interest than a woman alone usually did, though those who knew me knew better than to detain me against my will.

The stench of the waterway became more pervasive the closer I drew to the city center. Something nearby smelled like the memory Cutter had opened last week, only to find it had spoiled. A string of choice cusswords had ensued, and I made sure to stay out of his way. Not all memories cellared well.

As the canal grew more crowded, I was careful not to splash the oars. One never knew what foul things bobbed in the canals, or far beneath the surface where nightmarish creatures haunted the sucking mud. With water so precious, it was hard to stay clean. The only time I could touch it was when it froze in the coldest weeks of winter. Ice, as usual, seemed to cleanse everything.

I shivered. I had a long history with ice. Despite my gift, I'd had a healthy fear of it ever since that fateful encounter seventeen years ago. I pulled my collar more snugly around my neck. If not for *him*, I would have drowned or frozen to death, my soul slipping soundlessly beneath the fragile surface of the ice to commune with the wraiths below.

Since then, I had preferred snow to its firmer counterpart. I thought of the gleaming white coat covering Lord Guerin's garden. So fresh, so pure, so unsullied. Nothing like the dirty slush the street children kicked around and tossed at each other.

I reached the main canal thoroughfare, the wide tributary dividing Nulla into a city of two halves and feeding an elaborate network of smaller canals, which serviced the outer edges of the city. Even at the late hour, it was crowded with boats and workers going about their business. A young lad of around fifteen hollered to a man who looked to be his brother, and the two hefted a long crate from beside the canal onto the main deck of a large, flat-bottomed boat that was maneuvered with poles.

Stubble-cheeked men were beginning to eye the tall buildings on one side of the elongated city square, lank hair barely drifting in the wind, their gnarled hands fisted around tiny bottles. Some were empty, some halfway to becoming so. Cutter would welcome anyone who had something to trade.

I came alongside the main dock, where the canal opened into a broad, rectangular shaped passage, tapering at the neck and waist, where two bridges straddled the thinnest sections of the widened canal. Grabbing my satchel, I made short work of tying up the boat, aware of those watching me from several paces away. I hadn't yet discovered what they feared most: my gift, or the man who was so well-known he didn't need anything as superfluous as a last name.

Probably both.

Keeping the hood secure over my hair, I straightened, stepped to the edge of the wooden platform, and climbed the stairs to the only properly paved street in the whole of Nulla. The main street was intersected by the central canal at right angles, effectively splitting it into two halves connected via the stone bridges.

On the east side lay Cutter's tavern-shop and an assortment of similar establishments—the buildings the men looked at so longingly at the end of the working day. On the west side, the more respectable businesses congregated: a couple of bakeries, a fishmonger, three butchers, a draper's shop, and several inns, outfitted accordingly for guests from Memosine or Lethe, or even Marianthe, though it was said that they preferred hammocks to proper beds and could rarely fall asleep without the distant crashing of the sea.

There were several buildings I'd heard about but never seen, including one with a stern façade, polished floors, and burnished door handles, which oversaw matters of government, trade, and respectable business. Lord Guerin, as the ruling lord of Nulla, spent much of his time there—when he was not confined to his manor house on the edge of the city, mentally corralling reminders of the horrific events which had led to his assumption of power and Nulla's creation. All the men of his ilk would pretend Nulla didn't depend on anything so common as memories. But even if they never came to the east side, they would make sure it came to them.

I was proof of that.

Ignoring the curious glances straying my way, I squared my shoulders and hurried in the direction of Cutter's tavern-shop. Vials clinked in my satchel, and it was nearly impossible not to mutter *two weeks* beneath my breath. Adrenaline surged through my veins, devouring any lingering unease. What would my parents look like? Would I have my mother's hair or my father's eyes? Might there be other family members—

"Please—help."

I skidded to a halt and glanced to my left. Leaning against the wall of a dilapidated shop was an elderly man, his hair even whiter than my own. A threadbare blanket covered his lap, the chin of a mangy mutt resting against it. Worn, liver-spotted fingers entwined with the dog's fur, stroking gently. Though it was undoubtedly the old man who had spoken, he did not meet my eyes.

I hesitated. From the beginning, Cutter had warned me to stay away from the men slumped against the walls of narrow alleys or crouching in alcoves—of which there were plenty, especially at night. Noses in their potions, caught up in a memory, it was difficult to predict how they would react to the intrusion of the present.

And I was already late. Cutter would reprimand me for stalling. I could not tell him that Traemore had detained me to make cryptic hints regarding my promising future, since I doubted any of his plans were intended to work in Cutter's favor.

But the man was old, and his coat was too thin to put up much of an affront to the wind. A stiff breeze could likely push him over, perhaps even roll him all the way to the canal like a piece of chaff.

Besides, I liked his dog.

Both man and mutt opened their eyes as I stepped closer. An unclouded, forget-me-not blue beckoned me from both, so different to what I'd seen in Lord Guerin's gaze that I momentarily lowered my guard.

"Pardon me, sir, but did you say something?"

"'Sir?'" He gave a slight chuckle and shifted his weight beneath the blanket, enough for me to see that both of his legs ended just above the knees—or rather, where his knees would have been. "Aye, miss, I'll answer to sir, though it has been many years since I was addressed so politely."

He patted the mutt's head with such fondness I could not help smiling. I had always liked dogs—at least, the historical dogs I had learned about in the minds of those who had once kept them as pets. This soft-hearted mutt seemed more kin to those loyal hounds than the curs I'd seen prowling the city in packs, who would sooner amputate a man's limb than relax beneath its comforting touch.

"What's his name?"

"This young pup?"

I nodded, suppressing a laugh as the dog rearranged arthritic-looking forelegs while studying me dolefully. Young pup, indeed. At least age hadn't stolen his dignity.

"This is Felix."

"He looks . . . kind."

The old man nodded sagely, as if he knew as well as I did how rare a commodity that was these days. "Aye, he is a good soul. It is for him that I called to you, miss." He patted the dog's flank. "His coat is thin, of late."

"His?" I repeated, glancing pointedly at the man's threadbare covering. Though he was about as old as Lord Guerin, he had none of the usual comforts to ease his last days. How did he move about? And though I knew every alley and alcove in Nulla, I had never once seen him.

"Aye, *his* coat." He stroked the dog's ears—ears that looked soft and not flea-bitten, despite the matted fur. "He finds it difficult to move."

I pushed back my hood.

"And when it is cold, the wind goes straight through his bones."

I sank into a crouch before him as the oil lamps stirred to life around us.

"And his eyesight is not what it used to be."

A tear hovered at the corner of the old man's wrinkled eyes, though it did naught to cloud the blue—a blue which was somehow visible even in the faded light. A sigh went through his body, but the dog's head only nestled more into the man's lap.

"I'm away from home," I said, stirred by the poignant picture they made, "and though my master does not abide unpaying visitors, I will return as soon as I can with blankets and food for you both." I would take them from my own bed if I had to. The desperation of Nulla's inhabitants had moved me before, but never had I been so stirred by such selfless loyalty. Oh, that they might slip away together one night, the hurts of life eased in the gentle embrace of death.

"In the meantime, *sir*," I said with a smile, "I have something for you." It would help him to pass the time until I returned.

I flicked open the satchel Cutter never let me leave the tavern without—not one to waste any opportunity for peddling—and withdrew a single slender vial from the half-dozen or so carefully packaged therein. I set the satchel to one side.

"This is for you. Free of charge."

Hopefully Cutter wouldn't notice it missing, though he had proven himself eagle-eyed in his accounting before.

The man eyed the label pasted on the vial, and though I believed he was only pretending to read, remarked a moment later, "Strawberries, hmm?"

"Aye." In this domain at least, I could take some pride. Few *mems* were capable of extracting memories of such quality. "The mixture even tastes and smells like strawberries."

"Have you ever tasted strawberries, young lady?"

I paused. Of course not. Nothing so fine would ever be given to a slave, even if such a thing could be procured. But I had tasted them a hundred times as I dallied in the minds of others, savoring the tart sweetness on my tongue, mingled with the rich fullness of whipped cream, which was impossible to put to words, since milk was rarely had, and sugar was a luxury.

Wasn't it the same?

The old man was watching me with something like pity. "I thought as much."

He uncorked the vial of glossy red liquid, eyed it suspiciously for one long moment, sniffed the contents, then tossed it back, his throat convulsing as he swallowed. His eyes lidded, and I imagined him savoring the memory of a bowl of small, sweet strawberries, picked fresh from the mother plant and sprinkled with sugar. I had extracted and preserved the memory myself. It was of particularly fine quality, like everything Cutter dealt in. He always selected his donors carefully. And they were willing, which was not always true of the donors used by other merchants.

"It is good," he said at last. His blue eyes fixed on mine again. "But nothing like the real thing."

He must have seen my frown, for he smiled gently.

"I thank you, of course. You are a gifted *mem,* young lady. But it is only a memory of a memory." Keeping one hand on the dog, he reached out to touch my gloved forearm. I tried not to flinch. "Do you want to see it?"

"See what?" What could this man show me that I had not already seen?

"The real thing."

"The taste of strawberries?" I whispered.

"Aye." He studied my face. "Something like that. You have naught to fear from me, lady, I assure you."

For the second time that day, I nearly laughed. First, because of the undeserved address of *lady*. Second, because of his reassurances. Of course I had nothing to fear from this surprisingly well-spoken, oddly literate homeless man. I was the *mem*, after all, able to take charge of his mind with only the barest touch of his skin.

"Are you not afraid of me, sir?"

He looked down at the shaggy-haired dog. "Felix is an excellent judge of these kinds of things. I knew the shape of you before I called to you."

Again, I hesitated. This man was old enough to have seen the world-that-was. Very few could lay claim to that many years, and Lord Guerin was the only one whose mind I had regularly perused. Certainly, he had never tasted strawberries—or had not remembered doing so. His pleasures had been of a more sinister sort.

The old man was right. These days, many memories were second- or even third-hand, passed down like treasured heirlooms as a generational inheritance. Memories of the war and the world-that-was were often distorted by their carriers, who held differing perspectives on their actions in the conflict. The war hero of one man's memory was frequently a villain in the memory of another.

But in Nulla, few among the wealthy cared to dredge the atrocities of the past when they could share in its pleasures. The poor traded their finest memories in exchange for the basic necessities. After all, who held on to a memory of sugared, sweet fruit when one was starving to death?

I began peeling off my glove, but the old man stopped me. His hand found the edge of my glove, near my elbow. I had expected his touch to be cold. But his skin hummed with a strange warmth, even through the fabric.

"Watch carefully," he said. "Listen. Nothing is ever as it seems." His fingers encircled my bare skin.

I felt myself fall forward, as if I'd toppled over into a body of water. But this water was as warm as a freshly drawn bath, and clear, unlike any mind I'd ever entered. His inner world instantly surrounded me, a rapid sequence of images rather than the legible script of thoughts, which was what people assumed I saw.

Though the old man couldn't have been aware of my movements through his mind, he guided me through his memories as effortlessly as a mother might have once shown her children pictures of departed relatives from an album. Casually, he handed me the memory of strawberries, and *oh!* I tasted it like I had never tasted anything in my life. Tart, but so tart it shot invisible needles of delight into my tongue and wrinkled my nose. Sweet, but so sweet I wanted to savor every bite. Like a man consuming his final earthly meal whose every sense is heightened, I inhaled a strawberry's woodsy fragrance, fingering the rich, ruby-red of the pitted surface and the deep, slightly rough green of the stem and leaves.

"Do you see?" I heard him say and felt myself sigh in answer.

He showed me other memories, too, things I had never seen in full. The world-that-was before the war, with its expansive cities and busy streets. The yeasty warmth of freshly baked bread. The heat of the sun in all its unveiled glory, undiluted by clouds or fog or smoke. It had all come to a sudden end when he was only a boy, and he had journeyed to Caldera with the rest, eventually becoming a soldier. There was no hint of how he had lost his legs. If it had been Lord Guerin's mind, such a horror would have leaped out at me the moment I opened the album of memories, a grotesque skeleton in the closet waiting to spring at unwitting intruders.

I circled back to the strawberries, wanting to taste them again.

"Even this, Sephone," the old man said as if, impossibly, he knew my intentions, "is only a shadow of the real thing."

Sephone? How did he know my name?

I came back to myself, pulling my arm from the old man's gentle hold. Immediately, I felt bereft, as if I had lost something too intangible to describe in words. The dog, Felix, raised his shaggy head to look at me. Again, both man and mutt seemed to gaze into my soul.

"I have to go."

I fought the shiver that had stolen over me, pebbling my skin. It was the wind, of course. I'd lingered too long. Any person who endured a winter in Nulla knew the way the cold stole into the bones.

"I'll come back," I said, grabbing my satchel and jumping to my feet, not even bothering to hitch the strap over my shoulder. "I promise."

I spun away, heading for Cutter's tavern, the remaining vials clinking in the satchel. Hopefully they wouldn't be broken in my rapid flight.

Two weeks.

Once again, I shut my mind to the reminder. It was only when I reached the tavern, closed the door behind me, and leaned back against it, that I caught my breath . . . and the thought struck me. Though the old man's mind felt different to any I had yet encountered, I had forgotten to ask his name.

And yet, somehow, he had known mine.

"Where have you been?" Cutter's voice grated. Still leaning against the door, I blinked twice and looked up to find him scowling at me.

I stole a furtive glance at the room behind him. Thankfully, it was already crowded with customers, or Cutter might have been significantly less polite. He had never struck me—being as wary of touching me as was everyone else—even though that meant he was unable to use his gift on me. But he could just as easily slice me into tiny pieces with his words. I'd always thought him suitably named.

"I'm sorry, Cutter. A big shipment came through the main canal, and they closed it briefly. I came as soon as I could."

Could he see the lie in my eyes? He watched my lungs heave, as if I really had sprinted home, and I inwardly blessed the breathlessness I had rued a moment before. Besides, the event I'd named as reason for my delay was not so uncommon an occurrence. If Cutter asked no questions, he'd be none the wiser. I could slip out and return to the old man before the night was over. This time, I would ask his name.

The scowl's potency diminished by about half. "Customers are waiting, girl."

I moved to obey the unspoken command, but his fingers closed around my gloved wrist. He pulled on my arm, and both of us leaned forward. I grimaced at his fetid breath, puffing from between cracked lips at the level of my forehead. Impossible to recall those strawberries now.

"Your hair's getting long again. Cut it."

I felt a flicker of dismay. That very morning, I had relished the fact that it had finally reached my jaw. A cause for triumph, especially when Cutter had several times hacked it off nearly to the scalp, beginning when I was only four years old. Though he shaved his own head in an attempt to hide the silver hair which marked his abilities, no one would ever mistake me for his daughter, just as they would never take Regis, with his hip-length braid, to be his son. I was as forbidden to grow my hair as Reg was to cut his.

But to cut it again? A second time, I inwardly grumbled over his perfectly suited name. Outwardly, I pasted on a veneer of dutiful obedience and nodded. "Aye, Cutter."

"Aye, *master*. Now get going." He swung around as a voice from the corner bellowed his name, heading toward the call with a dutiful smile of his own.

Since he'd shoved me in the direction of the shop, I went that way, glad to escape the busy tavern with its crowded tables and glassy-eyed, loose-handed men. Cutter's shop was only a small chamber abutting his much larger tavern, lined on three sides with tall shelves from floor to ceiling and connected to the tavern via a small door. A long counter separated shopkeeper from customer, while a selection of comfortable stools on the customer side housed those who deliberated over their purchases rather than ordering from the tavern menu or relying on Cutter's supposedly "tailored" recommendations. Sometimes, customers came in with something in mind. Most times, they just wanted to be elsewhere. Elsewhere was Cutter's favorite commission.

Everything was kept spotlessly clean—the dust permitted to linger only on the most expensive memories from Cutter's locked cabinet, and then only for showmanship's sake. Cutter had cleverly arranged his lanterns and sconces so the colored glass bottles appeared to glow from within, and he had worked some magic with carefully placed mirrors to make the existing merchandise appear not as hundreds of flasks, but thousands. When the lanterns and candles were lit, as they usually were, the display gave the impression of stained glass windows, a thousand bolts of liquid color shining down as if the whole of Cutter's operation was blessed from on high.

Mercifully, the shop was empty except for Regis, who glanced up as I approached.

"Where have you been, Seph? I've been worrying after you." There was no mention of Cutter or the verbal lashings Reg must have endured in my absence. I smiled at him, though I pretended not to see the hand he extended to touch my arm, slipping past him to dump my satchel on the counter.

He flicked his braid over his shoulder and turned, following me with his eyes. He lowered his voice. "Did they truly close the main canal?"

So he had been listening behind the door again. If Cutter caught him, he'd be in for a whipping, for Cutter's so-called chivalry only extended to the one slave he had no desire to touch, not even to make use of his most prized gift. The two times he'd attempted to had been enough for the both of us.

"Of course they didn't close the canal. Lord Traemore kept me back to talk nonsense." I couldn't mention the old man and the strawberry potion, not even to Reg. If Cutter discovered I'd given away a potion for free, and Reg had been aware of it, he'd suffer a far worse punishment than me.

"*Lord* Traemore?"

"Aye, he recently inherited a title."

"Then he's set his sights on becoming lord of Nulla?"

I tossed a barbed glance his way. Cutter forbade any talk of government in his tavern, but Reg followed the stench of politics the way a starving man's nose tracked the aroma of roasting meat. Still, I gave in to his insatiable hunger for news. "Lord Guerin is very old. It can't be long now."

"It can't be long? Seph, you've read his mind. Surely you know more than anyone how much time he has."

"I told you before, I don't read minds. Not like a book, anyway. It's more like flicking through a series of pictures. And the pictures don't always make sense."

"It's the same thing."

"Nay, it isn't. I've told you before, Reg, I can't read your every thought. I wouldn't know what you were thinking right now unless it formed a very clear image—or sequence of images—in your mind."

He gave a wry smile. "Like wanting to strangle Cutter with my bare hands. Watching the life drain out of his eyes. Standing beside his grave, looking down at his cold, gray body."

"Aye, something like that." I glanced at his bronzed hands—large and bare, since Reg wasn't a *mem*, or even an *alter*, the generic name given to those who were gifted. It was far easier to page through memories than discern future intent, which was why my gift had proven so valuable to a merchant like Cutter. Still, I could usually see what someone desired, or snatch a hazy glimpse of their dreams and aspirations. After all, memories, especially the older ones, were gilded with emotions.

Early in my girlhood, I had nurtured a secret passion for the idealistic and fiercely protective Regis. Though, unlike most childhood crushes, I had the means of ascertaining whether or not my ardent affection was returned. To my disappointment, a casual touch of his arm confirmed what I had then refused to accept, capsizing my most elaborately constructed fantasies: Reg saw me only as a little sister. More than that, he pined for the butcher's middle daughter.

He still did.

His hand alighted between my shoulder blades, and I flinched. "I'm sorry," he murmured, pulling his hand away, lantern light bouncing off the metal cuff at his wrist. "I always forget."

"It's no matter." Bestowing casual touches was as natural to Reg as avoiding them was to me. I turned to face him, watching the sorrow trickling into his steady gaze, dampening the silver and gold motes in his honey-brown irises. "Two weeks, and it will all be worth it."

"Worth seventeen years of slavery, Seph?"

I shrugged out of my cloak. "Aye."

"For five minutes of freedom?"

"Of course." What did he expect? All the memory potions were like that. Some, like the vial I'd given to the old man, only lasted a few seconds. Others—some of the larger bottles Cutter sold—lasted perhaps half an hour or more.

Once they were consumed, they could be extracted again, but no memory potion was as potent the second time around. As with the mind-bleeding, they had diminishing returns. And a third-hand memory was not nearly as valuable as a first-hand one. For that reason,

Cutter frequently paid for donors to come to Nulla for the extraction procedure. Memory couriers were as rare as the *mems* themselves.

Reg shook his head. "Be wary of your dreams, Seph. The world may not be so kind in reality as it appears in your imagination."

A fine one he was to talk of such things. Was not all politics a hankering after flimsy ideals? "You're a slave too, Reg. Don't you have dreams?"

"Aye." His gaze turned faraway, and I knew he was thinking of the butcher's daughter. "I have dreams." Then the molten longing in his eyes hardened to black, and his shoulders sagged. "But reality has a way of draining the life from everything."

As if to punctuate that grim conclusion, a loud voice barked from the doorway. "Tell me. Do I merely give commands for my own amusement?" Cutter stood there, meaty hands propped on narrow hips, glaring between us.

Regis swiveled and paled to the color he had after being whipped for some trifling offense.

I intervened. "It was my fault. I detained him."

Cutter strode forward, and though Regis topped him by a head at least, the younger man seemed to shrink. I would have liked to call Cutter weasel-faced, but for the fact that most would consider him a man of agreeable appearance—at least, those who had not seen the shambles of his teeth, more tightly packed and disorderly than his tavern guests, some of them leaning over to indulge in idle conversation with the adjacent fellow, and many of them appearing jaundiced above the gums. Still, if he kept his mouth closed—which he almost never did—he would appear pleasant-looking.

Cutter dismissed Regis with a flick of his wrist, glanced at the few bottles Regis had yet to polish, then turned to me. "Finish here, then come find me." His cloudy gray eyes narrowed. "Remember, girl. Two weeks. I would hate to withhold your parents' final legacy because of disobedience."

I stilled. Surely, he would not—

He would.

I looked into his face, watching his growing pleasure as I realized my powerlessness. Until that potion was mine, I would remain under his control. Only then could I consider what Regis had talked about for years: running away from the neutral ground with him and the butcher's daughter to Marianthe and the sea. Only then could I weigh the cost of defiance.

Before then, any thrashing around in Cutter's trap would only hurt the limb by which he had me pinned. Or, worse, it could hurt Regis. Which Cutter knew.

And so, for perhaps the thousandth time, I swallowed my defiance and nodded.

"Aye . . . master."

Two weeks. It had become my mantra, a mindless chant intended to consume every corner of my head not required for the performance of my usual tasks. I fed from its hope, no better than Regis with his talk of politics, blind to all else. Still, my brain churned, thinking of the old man and his strawberries. Reg and his dreams.

Cutter.

Hoping to erase his earlier displeasure, I obeyed his every instruction to the letter. Cutter could be cruel, but he was generally fair. At least to me. Everyone else lived in fear of his gift.

According to his wishes, I kept my arm cuffs visible and my hair uncovered. I would cut it later, even if Cutter wanted me as bald as he was. Whatever it took to get my hands on that memory potion. Stuffed beneath the collar of my sleeveless dress, I felt the resin necklace warm, absorbing the heat from my skin. I had survived seventeen years of subservience. I could survive a few more days.

I wove between the tables with practiced ease, wishing Regis had not been banished to the cellar to unload supplies. His formidable presence was usually a deterrent to too much familiarity from Cutter's customers—those who failed to recognize that I was an *alter*—even if they knew a slave could never lay a hand on them.

I drew on evasive maneuvers instead, taking the long route to the bar to avoid a reaching hand that would have pulled me down into a stranger's lap, and skirting around a stray chair to shield myself from a particularly boisterous group of canal workers. Cutter dealt in normal liquor as well as liquid memories, and both offerings proved equally popular, though this particular crowd mostly preferred the common stuff.

It was the men under the influence of the past who were the greater cause for evasion, and they arrived at all times of the day—and night. Usually, they were solitary guests and kept to themselves. Slumped in one of the corner booths Cutter had designed for the private nursing of drinks, they worked their way through glass vials until they didn't know their right hand from their left, let alone a free woman from a slave—or an *altered* person from an ordinary one.

But Cutter always remained on the floor, supervising my delivery of various drinks and potions, and he allowed no mistreatment of his slaves on his watch. It was better than I could say for many of the taverns on this side of the city, which blurred the line between past and present more deliberately, much to the dismay of the women involved.

As the night's customers finally dwindled and Cutter gestured across the room in silent dismissal from the main floor, I retreated behind the bar—a slightly larger sibling to the one in the shop—and propped my elbows against the pitted wood. I released a heavy sigh as I traced the mottled stain left by a spilt potion that had been verdant green.

"You have a very interesting city."

I glanced up at the bar's sole occupant, a dark-haired man perched on a stool across from me perusing one of Cutter's menus. How had I not seen him come in? His hair was roughly chopped, as if it had recently been cut, and not by an experienced hand, either. His barber appeared to have suffered from some kind of violent tremor.

"It's not my city," I replied without thinking. Nulla was no one's property, not even Lord Guerin's. It was a legacy from the war, sandwiched between Memosine and Lethe, but belonging to neither.

Rather like myself.

The stranger glanced up and grinned. His eyes seemed to take my measure in one sweep, lingering on my gloves and arm cuffs. "What's with all the canals everywhere? It seems a strange way to do business."

He had a strong accent, even speaking the common tongue. All clipped and staccato, a contrast to the earthy, almost sensuous speech of those who hailed from Memosine, or the crisp, formal tones of the Letheans. Marianthean? I hadn't met enough representatives of that country to say so with any certainty. Still, what Calderan was unfamiliar with the story of the neutral ground?

I chanced a look at Cutter. He was looking away. But he would want me to be friendly to a potential customer. "They're from the war," I finally said. "When they were fighting over borders, Memosine and Lethe dug their defenses in what is now known as the neutral ground. Holes and trenches and the like. By the end of the war, it was a mess, what with each trying to sabotage the other's fortifications. I guess someone thought to take advantage of the natural course of the river and the ruined landscape as it was and turn it into a city."

"Someone? Then you aren't under the control of the arch-lord? Or some king of your own appointing?"

I shook my head. "We in Nulla live only for ourselves." Kings were a memory belonging to the world-that-was. And Lord Guerin's leadership was hardly worth mentioning.

He smiled, rather ruefully. "It is much the same in the rest of the world."

It might have been a trick of the light—a lantern illuminating shafts of color from the clusters of empty glass bottles strewn between us—but I could have sworn that as I'd spoken, ribbons of vibrant green light had crept along the bench toward me, thicker than the delicate wisps that comprised my gift, coming from the person of the stranger and tangling with each other like vines. I stepped back. Was he an *alter*? I looked toward Cutter again. But the stranger's long torso and his voluminous black cloak would conceal any unusual phenomena from the rest of the room.

As if he hadn't noticed anything odd, the stranger closed the menu with a snap. "Tantalizing promises of rare dishes and unseen glimpses of the world-that-was. As I said, this is a very interesting place." He leaned back to study me again. "I've heard a great deal about this tavern. Tell me: what's in these potions of yours?"

They're not my *potions.* I swallowed the instinctive reply. "Shall I summon my master for you?" I preferred Cutter to be the one who did the lying.

"You'll do just as well, miss."

"Cutter is the expert."

I wasn't imagining things. The ribbons still scattered along the counter abruptly thickened and turned to black, and the stranger frowned. "I think not." He edged closer, a nearby lantern throwing half of his face into sharp relief, shadows clinging to the upper half. He was young, not older than twenty-five, but his skin was weatherworn, as if he'd spent most of his youth exposed to the elements. A briny smell lifted from his cloak. From Marianthe, then. I thought of Regis and tried to ignore the snakelike ribbons of light tangling between us. Perhaps this stranger would have news of his country.

I suppressed a sigh. "The potions are made using the water from the upper reaches of the River Memosine. The water has magical qualities, the nature of which we do not yet understand. The memories themselves are extracted by a *mem*, and the essence of the memory is combined with the water to form a liquid that can be consumed, thus preserving the memory."

"Like a jam."

"More like a syrup. The water takes on some of the properties of the memory itself. For example, taste and smell."

Not a lie, exactly. But I could not tell this stranger the whole truth: that Cutter, unscrupulous as he was, also added another ingredient to his most popular potions. A banned substance that would ensure his customers would not soon forget the taste of whatever memory they'd consumed. And that they would return for more.

The ribbons turned green again, though a thin vein of black ran through the largest of the strands. This time, the stranger studied it, then me, carefully. "A *mem*, you say? A memory manipulator?"

"Aye." The green streams of light twisted and veered in my direction.

"And Nulla has many of these?"

"Very few. There are others, though, elsewhere in Memosine and Lethe. I would imagine in Marianthe, too."

The green remained green, and I released a breath I'd not known I was holding. Somehow, this stranger knew whether or not I was telling the truth.

He tapped his finger on the wooden counter. He, too, was wearing gloves, though his were made of black leather and reached only to his wrists. "How many *mems* do you have here?"

"One."

Black ribbons.

"Well, two."

Green.

I fought panic. I had to disengage from this conversation lest I unwittingly divulge every one of Cutter's secrets. No one but Regis and I knew Cutter had some ability as a *mem*, though for reasons unknown, he had told no one about the secondary gift. Although he could extract basic memories, his powers were far weaker than my own, and he mostly employed his abilities to view the memories I'd procured before valuing them carefully. That, and bestowing casual touches on the shoulders of unsuspecting customers to learn what they wanted. They called his knack for knowing what one craved uncanny. I knew better.

I shuddered at the thought of his retribution. I'd only experienced it twice, but his primary gift was far stronger and altogether more horrifying. It was the reason Regis had meekly removed himself to the cellar instead of challenging him.

As I turned, the stranger abruptly smiled. A smile some women might consider heart-stopping.

"Sorry for the interrogation, miss. I'm new to these parts and anxious to get the lay of the land." He thrust out a hand toward me, scattering the ribbons of light. "It's a pleasure to meet you."

What further mischief might he be able to work if I shook his hand? Still, we both wore gloves. The ribbons of light seemed harmless enough. And he had far more to fear from me than I did from him. Hesitantly, I grasped his hand. His grip was firm. No soft-pawed hold fearful of crushing a woman's delicate fingers. Perhaps he didn't know I was a *mem*.

"The pleasure is mine," I ventured.

The ribbons reappeared, quickly turning obsidian black.

The stranger grinned knowingly.

I drew back and fidgeted with my gloves. "You're an *alter*, then?"

"You recognize your own kind."

I began to nod, then realized my mistake. I'd attempted to corner him, and instead, I'd ensnared myself. Then again, it was no secret I was a *mem*. He would discover the truth eventually.

Folding his arms, he moved fully into the light. I bit down a gasp, for the man could not be described by any word besides *beautiful*. His hair was a thick, glossy black, but not *just* black. Like a rooster's tail, it captured the light then reflected it in unearthly, impossible flashes of green and even purple. His eyes were an iridescent blue-green, the hue of a sea grotto caught in the first rays of dawn. He held my gaze the entire time I studied him, as if he didn't care to hide his appearance from the rest of the room. He had the self-assured smile of a man who knows he is handsome enough to break female hearts with the bestowing or withdrawing of a single glance.

He casually retrieved the menu again and pretended to study it. "What do you recommend, then?"

This part, I could do in my sleep. "Do you have a favorite type of memory? A food, perhaps? An experience? A skill you've always wanted to learn?"

Dimly, I was aware of Cutter's attention from the other side of the room. At last, he had seen the *alter*. He took a purposeful stride in our direction before being stalled by another customer.

The stranger kept his attention on me. "Strawberries are a longtime favorite."

I nearly startled, thinking of the old veteran, though the preference was common enough. But the sweet fruit did not grow well without sunlight. And sunlight was one of many things Caldera lacked.

"And I enjoy mingling with the fairer sex."

Of course you do. I ignored the stranger's flirtatious wink. Still, I found myself drawn to his stunning eyes. Surely he wouldn't dabble in the pleasures all men seemed to dabble in.

Inwardly, I cursed my naïveté. Was I so desperate for affection I would mull over every glance a handsome stranger cast my way? This man would be like all the rest. Besides Regis and the old man, I'd only ever touched one mind which was different. But that one had been merely passing through Nulla. I doubted he would return.

The stranger set the menu down as Cutter approached. I expected my master's face to be a mask of pleasantry and deference, as it usually was when customers were present, but instead he wore a tight expression.

"You are welcome here, sir. I'll be with you in a moment." To me, he hissed, "Two weeks, Sephone. Have you forgotten our bargain?" Something shifted in his eyes, and I felt a prickle of fear down my spine. I had conversed too long with the stranger. Did Cutter think I was asking questions about Marianthe? But there was something in the way he said *two weeks* that felt different. As if he knew we both danced on the edge of a knife.

As an idea occurred to me, I glanced at the stranger who was looking between us curiously. "Aye. Two weeks, Cutter, and you'll give me the memory potion my parents made for me."

Cutter stared at me like my hair had turned blue. "Aye, of course. Now get going, girl, before I—"

Black ribbons swirled in the wake of his words, emanating from the stranger and lunging toward Cutter. My heart contracted as my stomach went into freefall. My worst fear had been realized.

He was lying.

Cutter's face purpled, as if he had guessed what the stranger was and the nature of the ploy I'd used to test his word. Coming around the counter, he seized my gloved wrist, dragging me away from the bar.

The stranger got up from his stool. "I do believe you're hurting the girl, sir."

I tried to wrench my wrist from his grip. The stranger had naught to worry about; Cutter wouldn't touch me. Not after the last two times. But Cutter's lips curved into a snarl, and he gripped my upper arm with his bare, calloused hand.

I instantly stilled.

Like the other two occasions, time seemed to hold its breath. Even the stranger looked as if he had frozen, half-reaching for us, half-desiring to mind his business. A clawing dread fought its way down my throat and settled into an immovable lump, harder than coal and more bitter than gall. Barbed wire raked at my insides, the bloody mess churning like a maelstrom in the pit of my stomach. My blood turned to ice, and I went rigid in Cutter's hold, unable to move. My heart pounded a frantic rhythm, a tight whirling in my chest that skipped more pirouettes than it executed. Every breath was guttural and painful. There was no room for thought.

Only the fear.

At last, Cutter released my arm, though he still held onto my gloved wrist. The rest of the room stirred to life around us, though only the stranger still watched us. To my dim satisfaction, Cutter looked pale and drained; though, stunned by the increased potency of his gift, I'd made no attempt to enter his mind this time.

But the warning in his eyes was clear. Should I speak against him, he would not hesitate to punish me again.

A warning wasn't necessary. I couldn't move, despite the fact that his grip on my wrist had loosened. There was no way I would be able to talk.

"That man is a *lumen*, girl," Cutter hissed into my ear. "Believe naught that comes from his mouth. He's in the business of lies."

"Actually, miss," the stranger winked at me again, though the rest of his face had grown somber, "I mostly find myself in the business of truth."

Cutter jerked me around and dragged me from the room. Neither the stranger with his insatiable curiosity nor anyone else made any attempt to follow us. He didn't stop until he had propelled me into the tiny, windowless room he used for the punishment of those who disobeyed him. By then, I had found my tongue.

"You lied," I said as he stood in the doorway, his heavyset frame smudged by the murky shadows. "You were never going to give me the memory potion, were you?" At that thought, the dread that settled in my gut was far worse than the one with which Cutter had briefly controlled me.

"Did you sell it, then?"

His eyes flashed, and he took two long strides before striking me across the face. Gasping, I clutched my nose, which was already streaming blood. The ruby-red liquid dripped down the front of my dress and splashed onto the floor. But the brief contact with his wretched hide had been enough to see the truth.

"There was never any potion. Was there?"

Cutter pinned me with a steely look, smothering a hollow cough with his grimy hand. "Careful, girl."

"How could you, Cutter?"

"I warned you. Oppose me again, and you'll lose more than a pathetic potion."

What else did I have to lose? "I'll oppose you till the day I die."

Cutter raised his hand, but when I didn't flinch, he lowered it again. "You think you're indispensable, girl? You are *nothing*. I could sell you in an instant and make a fortune from you. And not all masters are as generous or patient as I am."

I suppressed a shiver, because as despicable as he was, he was right. "If I am nothing," I ground out, "why am I worth a fortune?"

"Careful, girl," he repeated, backing out of the room. "Careful."

The final word was laced with a threat.

For two days, he kept me locked in the room, denied water and food. It was bitterly cold at night, but I could only think of the old man and his mutt, waiting for comforts that would never arrive. Had other passersby taken pity on them? Regis, perhaps?

Why did Regis not come? Usually, he was able to sneak me a flask of water or a crust of bread. One time, he had even smuggled in a blanket. I did the same for him when he was punished. We looked out for each other that way.

When Cutter finally released me, it was with a faint smirk. His anger had vanished, replaced with a good humor that pitted my stomach. It was not long before I realized the reason for his smug manner.

Regis, my only friend in all the world, was gone.

The old man and his dog had also disappeared. Had they died in the two days I had been locked in that room, their bodies cremated in the streets or dragged away to the crude cemetery outside the city? But when I asked after them, no one had seen them, or even known of their existence in the first place. Perhaps everyone else was as blind as I had been.

I could still feel the sweet tang of strawberries on my tongue. All memories were like that, leaving behind a trace of themselves. A faint aroma or taste of what had been, the way one recalls the spices in a favorite stew or the key garnish in a prized dish. Some declared that memories left behind an artificial taste, like a child who has consumed too much candy and temporarily finds real food unpleasant, though before meeting the old veteran, I had always thought the comparison foolish.

Pleasant memories could be extracted from their donors almost in full, but that, too, often left behind a memory shadow—a cold, emotionless set of details that would forever remind the donor of the memory they'd surrendered. Unpleasant memories were far more resistant to extraction and could only be numbed or dimmed. Those tasked with that vile business were vulnerable not only to splinters, but the shadows of those memories, the worst of which haunted them too, stalking every waking hour. Many a *mem* had been driven mad from the exposure and become a fractured, rambling mess.

I would never forget the coldness of Cutter's mind the first time I'd touched it, nor the horrors lurking in Lord Guerin's. As the most skilled *mem* in Nulla, I carried at least half of the city's nightmares in my pocket. And many of their secrets besides. It was the reason no one acknowledged me, at least openly, averting their eyes when they passed me on the street though I had traveled alongside the darkest undercurrents of their mind, ferrying them safely to the other side of their terrors. Even if I had not been a slave, I would have been shunned by polite society. Did they think I would steal their secrets? Had I not proven myself worthy of their trust?

The world may not be so kind in reality as it appears in your imagination . . .

Perhaps Regis was—or had been—right. Where was he now? Was he truly sold, as Cutter said? Or had he escaped at last? If he had, why had he left me behind?

Finally freed from my prison, I walked down the main street of Nulla, my satchel slapping against my hip, hardly caring if I was late for Cutter. It was well after dark, and the wind had brought a light rain that pebbled even the more sheltered canals, seeping through my cloak. I had answered another summons from Lord Guerin, but when I had entered the manor house, Traemore had announced that the lord had been detained by the unexpected arrival of an important visitor. Some haughty lord from Memosine or Lethe, no doubt. When the visit had stretched to hours, Traemore had dismissed me, promising to send for me again.

I paused near the place where I had met the old veteran and his hound. There was nothing there; no indication we had ever sheltered from the wind's chill together and spoken so intensely of strawberries.

As I stared at the shopfront, I caught a flicker of movement. A small bird was perched on the window ledge, drab and brown, with a buff-and-white chest, a reddish tail, and slender legs. I studied it, fascinated. Nulla typically boasted more ravens than songbirds, their harsh calls well-suited to the ugly city.

The bird opened its mouth and sang: an exquisite sequence of delicate trills, whistles, and gurgles that, at times, caused it to open its beak impossibly wide. A simple combination of notes, and yet something about them stirred the deep places inside of me, the parts

that had seemed all but buried when I learned I would never see my
parents again.

I raked through my memories, searching for its name. *There.* It
was a nightingale, and I had heard its song. Before Memosine and
Lethe had established their uneasy peace—before the birth of Caldera,
even—nightingales had once been common, their songs prized for
their power, purity, and beauty. The male sang to attract his mate,
while the female remained mute. But I had never seen the bird myself.
Had the songbirds come back at last?

I compared my memories, all secondhand, to the call of the bird
before me. The old man was right: there was no substituting it. The
memory was no more accurate a depiction of the rich, pure notes than
ash is an honest representation of fire.

Brown and white flashed again as the bird flitted away. I watched
him go, feeling oddly bereft. Should I have offered him food? Crumbs,
perhaps, from the slice of bread crammed into my satchel? I didn't
want to see him starve. Whether humans or animals, those on their
own without currency or resources would be exposed to the ravages
of hunger, unshielded from the merciless bite of the elements.

Or so Cutter often reminded me.

At the thought of Cutter, a strange thrill pierced me. Could I not
do it? Could I not escape on my own? I had always longed to see
beyond the walls which enclosed Nulla in a stone tomb. Closing my
eyes, I imagined inhaling mountain air instead of the stench of a canal-
bound city. The fresh, briny tang of the sea instead of grimy sludge.
The earthy scent of heather—if it was truly as earthy as it seemed in
the memories of Lord Guerin. A whole field of flowers like the ones
in my necklace.

I tamped down the pinpricks of fear, reaching—nay, clutching—for
the few remaining straws of courage I possessed. A plan began to take
shape in my mind, a bare skeleton I would need to clothe with sinew,
muscle, and eventually flesh.

For Cutter had done the very opposite of what he had intended. In
selling Regis, he thought to frighten me into staying in my cage.

Instead, he had clipped the last tether that bound me to his side.

He had set me free.

The dark-haired stranger had not returned to the tavern. A *lumen,* Cutter had called him: a truth-teller, or not exactly, since they were capable of speaking untruths without consequence in the course of a conversation, even if their listeners were not. I had heard of them before, but never met one. They were enigmas, no one knowing exactly how their gift worked. What had the *lumen* been doing in Cutter's tavern, of all places?

It was a quiet night. I kept to the shadows where I could, mindful of the bruise Cutter's hand had left on my cheekbone. Wind sheeted beneath the door and rattled the closed shutters, howling like a pack of wolves seeking admittance. The large hearth fire could never quite take the edge off the chill, though Cutter kept it well-fed. He often grumbled about the shabbiness of the premises and talked about moving to another city, though he knew as well as I did that Nulla was exceptionally well-placed for its trading.

In the past, on nights like this, after the customers had gone home or at least stumbled out into the cold to other elsewheres, I would steal one of Cutter's ledgers and climb the stairs to Regis's attic bedroom where he painstakingly taught me, then a girl of six or seven, how to read. He had not been a slave his whole life, but was indentured after his merchant father fell into heavy debt, the principal creditor being Cutter himself. Since Regis's father had taken his life shortly after learning the news, it would take Reg a lifetime of servitude to repay the debt, but he was determined to return to his family in Marianthe, freeing the two brothers who had been indentured alongside himself.

The hollow growl of my stomach was nearly audible. Not a hunger for food, as was the usual custom, but a yearning for finer things. For Regis and me both.

You deserved better, Reg.

The tavern door opened, and a blast of wind nearly knocked me over, even standing as I was on the other side of the room. I set down the tray of used glasses I was carrying, which had rattled in the onslaught, and turned. A tall man stepped over the threshold, his broad shoulders dusted with a light fall of snow. He shoved back his similarly covered hood, but instead of tossing his head the way the other men did, like a dog shaking out wet fur, he merely scraped his fingers through his hair, smoothing it down. As near as I could tell, it was golden-brown and curling slightly at the ends.

Cutter materialized from nowhere, drawn like a moth to a naked flame, for the man was obviously wealthy. His boots were brown leather, but molded to his calves as if they'd been made for him. Given the size of his feet, they likely had been. He carried himself with a dignified poise I'd not seen from Lord Guerin or Traemore. A thane, perhaps—one of the lords elected to rule over the largest cities. Was he of Memosine or Lethe? Inhabitants of both countries frequented Cutter's tavern, though for very different reasons.

Though I couldn't see the rest of the lord's clothes beneath his dark blue mantle, the garment was lined with a velvety material and collared with black fur—bear, or maybe mountain lion. The edges had been hemmed with a skillful needle and embroidered with an elaborate design of interlocking silver circles and triangles, while a delicate brass brooch secured the cloak below the column of his throat. I stepped closer. The ring was fashioned in the shape of a circular shield, inlaid with colored stones, while the pin resembled a crossbow bolt piercing the metal.

"Miss." An empty mug banged the table near me, drawing my attention. A disgruntled face met mine. "How long were you planning on leaving this mess here?"

"I apologize, sir," I said quickly and whisked the dirty dishes away to the kitchen. Maude, the woman who usually served as Cutter's cook—not that guests really came for the food—was resting at home, apparently covered with "ten thousand itchy spots from head to toe." There was naught to do but fill the tub with the water heating over the kitchen fire and plunge my own hands, sans gloves, into the lukewarm suds.

What could a thane want from a man like Cutter? Usually, the rich summoned us to their manor houses rather than making the laborious trip in person. Could this be the fine guest Traemore had mentioned?

Since there were few customers to tend to, and Cutter could handle their orders on his own, I busied myself ferrying dishes to and from the kitchen in Maude's place. Cutter had seated the lord in the booth closest to the fire and hovered nearby, but surprisingly, the man had only ordered ale. As the hours stretched by, he made no attempt to pick up the menu of memory potions. Cutter would be livid at the man's moderation.

I shot a hasty glance in the lord's direction. He was staring into his drink as if he sought to conjure a demon from the depths. Shadows bunched around his tall frame—not even the well-stoked fire allowed a good view of his features—and he pursed his lips as if he continually bit down on curse words. What reason could he possibly have to feel sorry for himself? By the looks of it, the man had everything, young as he was—not much above thirty.

The next time I looked at him, his eyes were on Cutter, narrow and assessing. I frowned. A man of his stature could procure far better ale without leaving his fancy accommodation close to the middle of the night. The lord glanced around, catching me staring at him, and I hastily turned my focus back to my chores.

Little by little, the tavern emptied. Sometimes the slow nights were also the longest, since those who had finally defrosted themselves by the fire were reluctant to re-enter the frozen, barren expanse of the outside world. The lord was the last to leave, and when I emerged from the kitchen with a tower of clean glasses, his booth was empty, a tidy stack of coins next to the half-full mug. Cutter glided forward and began counting them.

"Least he was generous," he muttered.

I put the glasses away, slipped on my gloves again, and reached for a broom. Tucking the coins into his pocket, Cutter moved about the tavern, straightening chairs and tables, then bent to stoke the fire so the room would be warm come morning. When he was done, he turned his glare on my handiwork.

"Is the kitchen in order?"

I nodded.

Casting a final glance around the room, and finding nothing else to critique, he finally returned his attention to me. "Your hair is still long."

"I'll cut it tomorrow." I kept my gaze lowered, as I'd done with Lord Guerin. *Let him think me afraid of him.* Razor-sharp as he was, not even Cutter would know the plans I was rapidly forming.

There was no nod, only a returning scowl. The door rattled once as he tested the bolt and then padded away, heading for the creaking staircase that led to his second-floor bedroom. The hearth there would already be lit by another of his slaves, unlike the tiny, cold, third-floor room assigned to me. Setting aside the broom, I lingered next to the fire for a moment before wandering to the shop.

Devoid of its usual adornments, the chamber was lit by only a single lantern which remained atop the counter, waiting for my ascension of the stairs. I sighed. Everything felt different without Regis. Even the vast shelves, lined with bottles of every shape and color and size—a sight which had always entranced me—no longer held any charm. Was it because I now knew that not one of those bottles belonged to me?

I bit down on a prickle of hope. If ever my parents' memory potion had existed, it was long gone now. People had appetites for the strangest things, and Cutter would have found a buyer. It was my parents' final goodbye. And the last of anything was sometimes considered as valuable as the first of it.

I had trusted him—foolishly—when I, more than anyone, knew what he was.

Reaching out for the lantern, I heard the scuff of boots behind me. I turned and saw the frame of a tall man occupying the doorway, approaching me with upraised hands. The thane. Where had he come from?

I opened my mouth to scream. His eyes filled with alarm, and he bounded forward, clapping his ungloved hand over my lips. His skin was warm and calloused, and panic knifed my stomach. What kind of man dared to touch me?

His mind was exposed, and I was as drawn to it as Cutter had been to the coins in the thane's purse. If the story of his life had been a book, only one image would populate the cover: a young woman with waist-length blond hair and piercing blue eyes. The thane was wildly in love with his wife, and no wonder, for she was a rare beauty. Then the image shuddered and changed, and the woman was lying on the ground, her legs tangled and her lovely dress bloodied. Blood pooled around her head in a garish halo. I felt the man's anguish as my own.

She was dead, then. The wife this man longed for was dead. Was he one of those who, discontented with the artificiality of Cutter's potions, sought the real thing? I had learned, early on, how to deal with such men.

I shoved against his chest, which achieved little, since he was athletically built and steady on his feet. I brought my knee up, but perhaps he possessed some mental foreknowledge of his own, for he quickly twisted away. He spun me, pulling my back against his chest. One arm wrapped around my waist while the other pressed against my mouth. Firmly, but not cruelly. There was, of course, another way to free myself, but until I knew the nature of this man, I would not use it.

"I mean you no harm, miss," he said in an undertone. "I only want to speak with you."

His voice was deep, his accent earthy and full. A thane of Memosine, then. I saw his city in my mind: Maera, deep in the Jackal Mountains. A beautiful city, carved from stone and possessing sweet mountain air, redolent of history and memory.

Didn't he know who he held? I took the opportunity to probe deeper. He flinched as if he felt my assault. Impossible. I didn't need to venture far to prove the thane was telling the truth: he intended no evil toward me. Certainly not the kind I had feared. But he had come to see me. And every manner of nameless horror snapped at his heels.

I searched for his name, then gave a start. I had touched this mind once before. I was certain of it. How? When? I had never met him until today.

And then I saw it. That day on the ice. Lost to his conscious awareness—he'd likely forgotten the memory even existed. He had been only a boy, then.

But it was him.

I swallowed. This stranger, at least, I knew.

And I knew why he had come back.

4

DORIAN

The tavern was empty. The oily mannered merchant had gone upstairs, leaving the serving maid alone to finish her chores. Now was his chance to question her out from under the watchful eye of her master.

Her cruel master. Dorian had seen the vivid bruise on her cheek and observed the brusque way the merchant treated his slaves. There was no point questioning the merchant about the *mem* who worked for him. The only currencies the man understood were memories and fear.

But Dorian had frightened the maid, too. He had not meant to startle her, though he guessed that any guest who hid himself behind a door in an attempt to interrogate the servants after hours would terrify a woman alone. He had acted on instinct, not wanting the entire household to come running. Of course she had struggled. She was surprisingly strong for such a small creature. He had saved himself from the attempted unmanning, chiding himself for his ungallant use of a man's strength against a slighter woman. Lida would be ashamed of him.

Lida . . .

Following his hasty reassurances, the girl had gone still in his hold. Was it merely pretense in the hope he would let his guard down, so she could scream for help? Or had he truly won her over with his words?

"Miss?" he now began. "I won't hurt you, I swear. But I need to ask you some questions."

She said naught in reply. She couldn't. His hand was still covering her mouth.

"I'm sorry for startling you. From what I glimpsed of your master's character, I saw the wisdom in saving my questions until after he had sought his bed."

He felt her shudder against him. He wasn't mistaken, then.

"I'm going to let you go. Please, miss, there's no need to scream. Can I have your word you won't?"

She nodded, and Dorian closed his eyes briefly. He had no choice but to trust her. She wasn't trembling in fear of him, at least. Maybe she would answer his questions honestly.

He opened his eyes and released her. She turned slowly to face him with her back to the door. Her lips parted, but no cry issued from them.

Brave. Or perhaps his gift was working on her.

Dorian held up his ungloved hands. "The merchant—Cutter—has a *mem* working for him. A woman. Do you know where she is?"

Her brown eyes sparkled with intelligence. "Aye, my lord."

"It's said she's the most powerful *mem* in Nulla."

The slightest of hesitations. "I believe she is, my lord."

"Has she already retired for the night?"

"Retired?" The laugh sounded odd coming from a servant, let alone a woman. "Oh, that she would have the luxury." She seemed to be fighting a smile. Was she so unafraid of him?

"She's a servant, then?"

The smile vanished. "Nay, a slave."

Dorian felt the faintest prick of pity. No doubt the merchant, Cutter, made a fortune from her gift. Though this wasn't the worst of Nulla's establishments—and as far as he could tell, not one of *those* places—the *mem*'s life was evidently not her own. Still, perhaps the situation would suit his purposes.

"Don't you know who I am?" The serving maid was watching him carefully, as if there was more than one question hidden in her words. She turned her head, and the lantern captured her features in an otherworldly combination of stark light and planed shadows. Dorian nearly slapped himself.

"*You* are the *alter*."

She seemed disappointed. "Aye, my lord."

How could he have missed it? Given her coloring, his first thought was that she was born of Lethe. It had never occurred to him that the *mem* would be an ordinary, otherwise unremarkable woman—almost a girl. Yet now that she stood in the light, he saw it. The hair . . .

He must have been too distracted to notice her in his mind. What secrets had he inadvertently revealed to her? He eyed his gloveless hands and her bare upper arms in turn. That must be why she had no fear of his intentions. She likely even knew why he had sought her help.

"I only ventured as far into your mind as I needed to put mine at ease," she said, as if she were indeed reading his mind. "I didn't even see your name."

"Dorian Ashwood," he replied instinctively, though as a slave or servant she could never address him as such. "That is, Lord Adamo."

"A thane, my lord?"

"Did you glean that from my mind or from my clothes?"

"Your clothes, my lord. But I will admit I glimpsed an image of your mountain city, Maera. It is very beautiful. Are you its ruling thane?"

"Not anymore." Lead weighted his stomach at the grim proclamation.

He would have to be more careful in the future. His gift worked more effectively through direct contact, but since it worked in other ways as well, he had never bothered to wear gloves. The *mem*'s gift evidently relied on skin-to-skin touch. One day, if things went well, she would have access to all his secrets, but until he trusted her implicitly, he would keep his distance.

"And your name, miss?"

"Sephone Winter, my lord." She dropped into a polite curtsey, and he seized the opportunity to study her.

She wore elbow-length, brown leather gloves. Thin, copper bands in the form of serpents coiled around her bare upper arms three or four times—like a genie of ancient myth—the head of each smooth-bellied beast finishing so close to its tail it seemed to be about to devour it. Her jaw-length hair was a striking, silvery white-blond, almost the same color as Jewel's fur. As she tilted her head, he saw the faintest hint of iridescence and mentally chastised himself.

He should have guessed what she was. A generous pinch of freckles was splashed across her nose, cheekbones, and even her forehead, though given the long absence of the sun from this part of Caldera, their presence was unexpected.

Miss Winter, indeed. The only warmth about her appearance was her eyes, a tawny brown like roe deer hide, stretched taut and yet curiously soft in her oval-shaped face. By the look in them, he guessed she was the kind of girl who not only wore her heart on her sleeve—absent as it was at present—but bled for everyone she met.

Might she assist him after hearing his tale? Hopefully, whatever she'd seen in his mind already made her a willing ally.

"Since these walls are thin, it's best I close the door." Miss Winter moved to do as she recommended. What woman willingly shut herself in with a stranger? She behaved almost as if she knew him personally. But that was impossible. He had never seen her in his life.

"I apologize again for intruding on you like this, Miss Winter. If there were another way to speak with you privately, I would have taken it."

"Sephone," was the only reply.

"I beg your pardon?"

"You can call me Sephone. I don't stand on formality, my lord."

And if I do?

"Sephone, then." She was a slave, after all. He glanced at the shelves behind him, an impressive display of liquid memories which would have few equals, even in Memosine. But he wasn't here to reminisce over the past. Quite the opposite.

"Since you likely already know why I'm here, I'll get straight to the point," Dorian said. "My wife and daughter—my only child—were brutally murdered some time ago."

He was right about her nature. Compassion overflowed from her eyes, furrowing her forehead. How did she bear the horrors of her profession? She was very young. Later, she would learn the advantages of a hardened heart.

"I am so sorry, my lord."

He knew she was. "Thank you. But it is not for sympathy that I detain you so late at night, and in such a manner." He swallowed. "You must know the worst of it. The extent of my . . . failure. You see, Miss Winter"—aye, formality was far more comfortable—"I was largely responsible for their deaths. A political deal I was negotiating on behalf of some of the other thanes soured, and my opponent—another lord of Memosine, you see—sought to exact his revenge. He had my family murdered before my eyes and . . . there were other evils committed as well."

His jaw tensed. "I relive it over and over in my mind. It is a torture far worse than any that could ever be inflicted on my physical body. I wish I could have endured it in their place, but . . ."

He trailed off. There was no need to share the rest of the wretched tale. Besides, if she agreed to help him, she would learn it soon enough. She would know everything about him.

He opened his eyes. The woman was gazing at him with such pity it touched him in a place he hadn't known existed. Aye, she was young, but maybe he had been wrong about her naïveté. Her eyes were a hundred years old at least. What had she seen? And what shadows flitted behind her lids when she slept?

Blindly, he swiped at the thoughts, scattering them like a flock of startled birds. He could not think of her grief. Not when he was so preoccupied with his own.

Finally, the *mem* nodded. "I can help you, my lord. But the mind-bleeding has certain . . . aftereffects. You may find that it sends you straight to sleep. Might you summon me to your temporary residence in the morning, or perhaps tomorrow afternoon?"

Dorian shook his head. How could he explain his plan, barely formed as it was? He had never been a reckless man, yet she would think him unhinged.

He settled on a gentle tone, drawing on the full power of his gift in the hope it would soften her to his cause. Perhaps it was unfair, and Lida would have scolded him for the unchecked use of his abilities, but he was desperate.

"You don't understand, Miss Winter. I don't just want the memory numbed. I have had the mind-bleeding performed twice, and the relief only lasts a few hours at most before I remember everything, and it is twice as horrible as it was before. Nay. From my vantage point, there is only one solution. I want to forget I was ever a husband or a father. I want to forget my wife and daughter ever existed."

He didn't remember me. Unconsciously, that day on the ice was
still there, lodged deep in his memories. He hadn't forgotten it in the
strictest sense of the word. But consciously, there was not even the
faintest twinge of recognition.

I ignored my disappointment. It was unsurprising, really, given the
brevity of our last meeting. If I hadn't touched his mind, I would never
have known him. He was a man now, though he had almost been of
age back then. His lanky, adolescent build had filled out, and he had
gained another head of height, now standing taller than most men I
knew. The lower half of his face was covered with a closely trimmed,
honey-colored beard, but his nose was the same, perfectly straight
and long enough to render his features more striking than handsome.
His skin was lightly tanned like the Marianthean stranger's. But how,
when Caldera never saw the sun?

Dorian Ashwood. Until now, I'd never known his name. Lord
Adamo to me, however. A thane of Maera, though no longer in
possession of power.

I want to forget my wife and daughter ever existed.

"It's impossible," I replied, though the horrors of his mind were
worse now I'd heard the tale to match. "Memories cannot be erased,
Lord Adamo, whether they are positive or negative. They can only be
numbed, and even then, the effects are only temporary, as you say.
Even the best memories are rarely extracted in their entirety. And, in
my limited experience, it is the best memories that make life bearable."

Even as I said it, I felt a spreading warmth in my stomach, like I'd imbibed some of Cutter's finest spirits. Liquid courage, Reg called it sometimes. It settled in your belly and made you do things you wouldn't normally countenance. Or so Reg said.

Lord Adamo stepped closer, a fierceness suddenly overtaking the terrible sadness, and if I hadn't already known his intentions, I might have recoiled from the intensity of his gaze. But heat bloomed in my chest, and my heart pounded as if I'd sprinted all the way from the canal. Was it compassion for his misery? Or the beginnings of another girlish fascination, like I'd once felt for Regis? Because this man, like Reg, had saved my life?

I stood erect. "I am sorry, my lord. It isn't my place to offer advice. You have lost more than I can comprehend."

His expression softened, but only slightly. "I would think that you of all people, Miss Winter, might be able to comprehend it."

The boy of fourteen was gazing at me again, with brown eyes even darker than my own. *Are you all right, little miss? For a while there, you weren't breathing. I thought for sure I'd lost you . . .*

I shook myself from the trance, noting he had reverted to *Miss Winter* again. "Aye, my lord. I believe I can."

Lord Adamo's anguish returned with the ease of a bird alighting on a branch. Likely it was never far away. "I hear you are the most powerful *mem* in Nulla, Miss Winter. Possibly in all of Caldera."

"So Cutter says, at least for advertising purposes."

He stepped closer. I registered the thick, pungent scent of pine, along with something far more familiar: woodsmoke and travel dust. "The memories you extract, Miss Winter, are of such quality that your master's shop is known all over Memosine. It is said you are able to preserve much of the feeling of the original memory, even once it is transferred."

I suppressed a nod, but not out of false humility. I, too, had thought as much, at least until meeting the veteran and his dog.

Have you ever tasted strawberries, young lady?

"I loved my wife," the lord continued, dropping his gaze, "and my daughter meant more to me than life itself. When I watched them die, a part of me died along with them." His fingers moved to a chain around his neck, groping the twin gold bands which hung from it—one larger than the other.

So, he had his own necklace. And his own string of regrets. That made two of us. A strange hardness settled over the warmth simmering in my stomach, like a thick crust over molten lava.

"I am sorry for your loss, my lord," I said at last. "But I am afraid I can do naught for you."

"Not on your own, perhaps," came the reply. "But there is a way, Miss Winter. Have you heard of the Reliquary?"

"The Reliquary?"

Gone was the man of sorrow, and the politician assumed his place, his gaze alight with purpose and sparkling with hope. The hardness in my belly cracked, and heat spilled out through the fissures, traveling along every vein and limb like a lit fuse, my fingertips twitching restlessly. Why was I reacting like this?

"It is a relic left over from the Old Times—before the world-that-was. Created by the gods for the kings of men, some say, back when men were graced with the *alters'* gifts. Its power would give me what I seek."

"The ability to forget what happened to your family?"

His gaze seemed to go straight through me, rather than settling where eyes normally would. "The ability, Miss Winter, to forget I ever knew them."

I hesitated. "You said you loved them, my lord. Forgive me for saying so, but why would you want to forget such a great love?"

There was anger there, but it was not directed at me. "Because, Miss Winter, the only goodness in my life has been destroyed by another man's evil. If I am to go on—and for a long time, I will admit, I was unsure I even wanted to—I must let go of what I had. I make no pretense of searching for happiness, or even contentment. Only a life devoted to the accomplishment of great and worthy goals awaits me now, and to pursue that, I must forget the life I had before."

"Then you mean to return to politics, my lord?" It was a surefire way to ensure a lifetime of unhappiness.

My question was impudent, and he raised his eyebrows. "My

enemies must not be allowed to succeed. With the Reliquary's help, I would alter only those memories that would distract me from my goal."

I felt a flicker of admiration. Young as Lord Adamo still was, he was the kind of man who might become the arch-lord of Memosine one day. Aye, the boy whose mind I had once touched was still there, though a lingering darkness hung over him now.

But the idea that this Reliquary could permanently delete memories . . . A shiver of excitement wormed its way through my unease. Might this artifact have the power to alter my own mind? To rid myself of the shadows which crawled over me, night and day?

Ludicrous. Impossible. However, Lord Adamo was a former thane, so I would humor him.

"Why do you need *me*, my lord?"

He shifted. "It is said that the Reliquary's memory-altering powers can only be accessed by a *mem*. You see, it would not only magnify your gift, but render its effects permanent. Since you are the strongest of your kind, Miss Winter, I have come to you."

I grimaced. *Of your kind*. As if I wasn't completely human. "And where is this Reliquary located?"

"Its location is yet unknown, though I believe it to be somewhere in Memosine."

"Why not find the artifact first, then return to me?"

He straightened. "I had hoped you might be able to assist me in its discovery."

I indicated the cuffs on my upper arms. "I am a slave, my lord. Why not first approach my master with your request?"

"It is your life, Miss Winter. And your choice. The quest to find the Reliquary may be fraught with danger. We do not know who or what guards the artifact or what protections were placed around it when it was brought here from the world-that-was. By all reports, it is a powerful piece of technology."

"I have no idea how things work in Memosine, Lord Adamo, but in this city, Cutter *owns* me. He will never let me leave."

"Not even for the right price?"

I bristled. Free choice failing, the lord thought to buy me? Or my services?

"With all you've heard about my gift, my lord, do you really believe Cutter will simply let me go?" His recent threat to sell me had been idle, nothing more. Without me, he had no means of earning income. His own extraction ability was inconsequential compared to mine.

"Nay," Lord Adamo replied, looking down at me, though his tone had gentled. "I didn't think he would agree to even a temporary loan. And I don't need to read your mind to know it was your master who gave you that bruise on your cheek."

I blushed, embarrassed he would notice. "It's the first time he's struck me."

"But I would guess, not the last."

True, perhaps, given Cutter no longer wielded Regis against me. And with his primary gift so strong of late, I would be hard-pressed to defend myself next time.

Lord Adamo extended a hand to touch my arm. Instinctively, I flinched and stepped back. His eyes flickered, but he said naught, and the hand returned to his side, the long fingers crimping slightly. "A trade, then, Miss Winter. Slaves escape from their masters all the time, you know. Help me find the Reliquary and utilize its power, and I will take you from here tonight. My every connection and resource will be at your disposal."

Blindsided by the offer, I briefly closed my eyes. "You may be powerful, Lord Adamo, but Cutter has eyes and ears everywhere. He'd come after me."

"Then I will instruct my own eyes and ears to watch for him. I have guards aplenty, Miss Winter. And influence enough that questions will not be asked. I can get you through the seam without any trouble."

I opened my eyes and met his gaze. "What about the papers?"

He smiled thinly. "Papers are altered far more easily than memories."

It was the one obstacle I had yet to overcome in all my planning. Nulla was surrounded by walls: flanked on one side by Memosine's border, encamped around the pocket of no-man's-land since it first contested the territory more than sixty years ago, and on the other by Lethe's border. The disagreement had never been resolved, and the pocket of no-man's-land remained. Several similar skirmishes taking place along the length of the seam had resulted in the formation of other neutral grounds and border towns, but none were so important—or so isolated—as Nulla.

Both Memosine and Lethe required travel documents to enter, and I did not know any forgers. Regis had known of one who still operated for a reasonable fee, but he had kept the name to himself, and now he was gone.

"It's impossible," I said again. It was the only reason Cutter let me travel so freely around Nulla. He knew as well as I did that there was no getting through the seam without his express permission, which had never once been given.

Lord Adamo studied me closely. "You cannot owe your master loyalty after everything he's done. Do you only hesitate because you do not trust me, Miss Winter?"

"Nay, my lord, I trust you"—his eyebrow lifted again, doubtfully this time—"but you must understand something. Something about me."

A wayward lock of hair tumbled across my eyes, and I tucked it behind my ear, ignoring the dismay that it would be gone tomorrow.

"I may be a slave, Lord Adamo, and an unwilling traverser of minds, but there is one kind of memory I will not touch."

"What kind, Miss Winter?"

"Love."

His face hardened.

"You must understand my reasons, Lord Adamo. The Reliquary aside, those who undergo the mind-bleeding are never the same afterward. There are . . . effects which last beyond the temporary. If I did what you ask, you would not be the same man."

"And who are you, Miss Winter, to decide this for me?"

I flinched at his arrogance—an air which I guessed was foreign to him, and suited him poorly. Confident, aye. Arrogant, nay. But the desperation had returned to his face. Didn't he see what he still had? My foray into his mind had been brief, but even so, I knew there were others who loved and respected him.

"I am no one, my lord, and well I know it. But I cannot take from you such a precious thing. Not when—" I choked off the sentence. He didn't need to know my reasons.

"Even if I offer it up willingly?"

"Even so."

Lord Adamo exhaled sharply, backing away. "And your master permits this?"

"He tolerates it." That was putting it generously. He had raged and threatened in the beginning. Still, it had always surprised me that Cutter eventually allowed other, weaker *mems* to handle the only memories I would not touch. In the early days, he had often performed the procedures himself.

"Was that why he marked you?"

"The agreement was made when I was six years old." After I had tried to run away . . . again. "I didn't quite understand then, but all I knew was I couldn't bear touching those kinds of memories, so Cutter agreed he would employ others to do so." When, in exchange, I'd agreed *not* to run away. "Even now, I never interfere with them." Or ever would. Especially since I'd discovered the truth about my parents' potion.

It was a difficult pledge to uphold, for most memories were tinged with love, or at least the craving of it. Lust was easy enough to manage. More a hunger than a feeling, it stained the minds of many who underwent the mind-bleeding, smeared across memories rather than being confined to them, like ink seeping through a piece of thin paper to imprint the pages beneath.

But love was elusive: altogether harder to define, and even more troublesome to grasp. When memories of love or loved ones were removed, they were always difficult to preserve, tending to congeal like cold porridge upon exposure to air. They were the only type of memory which did not last long outside a body, which made Cutter's bargain more stomachable, at least for him. It was easier and far more profitable to deal in fleeting pleasures, a fact Cutter knew well.

"I am sorry, my lord." Emboldened by his frank manner, I stepped into the space he'd vacated. "I would help you if I could."

"It is late, Miss Winter," was all he said. "And I've kept you from your bed."

I offered him a hesitant smile. "I wish you well on your quest, my lord. There are many who would help you find what you seek."

He carefully tucked the chain with its matching gold bands beneath his collar. His eyes were sad again, and for a moment I wanted to assist him any way I could. Inside my gloves, my hands tingled with warmth, and to stop myself from reaching out to him, I put them behind my back. Why did being near Lord Adamo make Cutter seem so insignificant? Even the memory of the fear Cutter had instilled faded in his presence.

Lord Adamo reached inside his cloak and extracted a pair of leather gloves, of the same color as his boots—and his eyes. "If you change your mind, Miss Winter, I'm staying a couple of days with Lord Guerin. I trust you know him?"

So Lord Adamo was the mysterious visitor. No doubt, he'd heard about me from Lord Guerin, or even Traemore.

I nodded. "Aye, I know him." I knew the lord of Nulla better than Lord Adamo ever could.

His eyes flashed in understanding. "I leave overmorrow. It's your choice whether or not you come with me. As I said, I will not force you, but the opportunity remains open."

Aye, I wanted to go. But it could never be—not even with him. I would not take from Lord Adamo the only thing I'd ever craved for myself. And if I fled Cutter, I wanted to be beholden to no one, not even the one man whose mind felt different from the rest. The one man, barring Regis, I thought I could trust.

As if he knew my answer, he only nodded. "Good night, Miss Winter."

He turned and reached for the door knob. I quenched a rising tide of despair, erecting a brave parting smile.

"Good night, my lord."

6

*Ice. Wet, slippery, cold, and—*sharp. *The brittle fragment beneath me lurched to one side, and I dropped to my stomach, spreading out to better distribute my weight. The ice groaned and hissed, bluer than a pair of naked lips in a blizzard. My fingers burned from where they clawed the edges of the thin disc, scraped raw and bright red. I couldn't feel my toes. Something crunched painfully, like a thigh bone breaking, and I felt the ice tilt to the side. I scrabbled for a better hold but, this time, encountered only air. I was sliding . . . falling. The ice stuck out of the water like a bony limb at an unnatural angle, more lethal than a dagger of broken glass.*

And then I was in the water, deathly cold, rushing over my head, sucking me down . . .

I jerked awake and sat up, breathing heavily. The tiny room was cold, but sweat streamed down my body. Sinuous plumes of white breath were visible by the faint light smudging the dusty window panes. *Dawn,* I had long ago learned to call it. Nulla was never gifted with anything so fine as a full sunrise. This was as good as it was going to get.

I shook off the nightmare, along with the last vestiges of sleep. *Just a dream. Just a dream.* Another of the many chants keeping me sane.

I swung my feet over the side of the bed, the springs groaning beneath my weight. Stared at the long gloves lying on the wooden crate covered with cloth that served as a bedside table, next to the pair of scissors and shard of mirror I'd gathered the night before. Lifted a hand to stroke the length of hair beside my ear. And reached for the gloves with the other.

One more day of dreaming, then I'll obey.

Cracking the thin layer of ice on the surface of the pitcher, I poured water into the basin and hurried through my ablutions, wishing I could scrub away the dream as easily. It was far easier to suppress somebody else's nightmares than your own.

I shivered. Long ago, I had learned to dress quickly, for even Nulla's summers were cool. Peeling off my nightgown, I donned brown leggings instead of the dress Cutter preferred, a fitted white shirt that covered my arms to their elbows, and a green, short-sleeved tunic over the top of both, belted at the waist and reaching to mid-thigh, where I kept my dagger strapped. The tunic was high-necked enough to conceal my resin necklace. Knee-high boots, a warm cap which covered my unshorn hair, and my rabbit-fur cloak completed the ensemble.

Cutter would not approve. But I would not freeze. So one of us, at least, would be happy.

Downstairs, Cutter was nowhere to be seen. I heaved a sigh of relief. A delivery of glass bottles had come first thing that morning, so I busied myself preparing them. It was a mundane sequence of tasks which included scrubbing them clean, filling them with the river water shipped in every week from Memosine, polishing the glass again, and affixing blank labels. It was one of the few tasks I didn't hate, though it was always better with Regis's company.

Regis. The familiar pang shot through my belly. The pain of losing my friend had dampened to a dull ache, but it could rear its ugly head at any time; a moment of unoccupied solitude was enough to tug the hasty stiches open, exposing the still-raw wound.

In the late afternoon, a message came from Lord Guerin's steward: the lord of Nulla awaited my arrival. I frowned. He had summoned me late in the day before, but I had resigned myself to a peaceful evening. There were rarely nightmares on the days I did not visit Lord Guerin— barring the recurring one of the ice.

"Get going," said Cutter after materializing from somewhere and plucking the paper from my hands. There was a distinct glint in his eye as he read the note. No doubt the lord of Nulla paid him well for my troubles. Enough to overlook the fact that I'd disobeyed his instructions once again.

"If you quit your dithering, girl, you'll be back here before dark."

Not exactly an incentive, considering the tirade that likely awaited me when I eventually removed my cap, but I dipped my head in what I hoped was a subservient nod of appropriately mindless proportions.

"Bah," Cutter muttered in disgust, turning away. "Useless girl."

Outside, the main street was oddly quiet; the flurry of activity around the canals had diminished to barely a hum. There was no sign of the old man and his arthritic hound. For that, at least, I was grateful, since the wind had devolved into a restless sprite which sucked rather than blew, finding all the hollow places inside my cloak and sliding icy fingers down my neck toward my throat, as if it might wrest away everything I owned.

Help me find the Reliquary and utilize its power, and I will take you from here tonight. My every connection and resource will be at your disposal . . .

Lord Adamo would leave tomorrow. How might things be different if I'd accepted his offer? Would he have whisked me away in the middle of the night, then and there, to Memosine? A grim smile formed as I imagined the look on Cutter's face when he discovered me missing.

I shook my head. Better that Lord Adamo understand from the beginning that he asked the impossible. One day, I would repay the debt he did not know I owed him . . . but in some other way.

At the manor house, Lord Guerin resembled more a skeleton than a man, his fine clothes hanging from his tall frame like a loose-limbed scarecrow. The look he gave me was cousin to a glare, but I had long since lost my fear of him. He had deteriorated shockingly in the few days since I'd seen him last.

Traemore hovered as usual, but Lord Adamo, at least, was nowhere in sight. *This is what you will become if you go through with this,* I would tell him if I saw him, pointing to the lord of Nulla. Youthfulness and innocence surrendered in the thirst for power and security, which, even once achieved, slowly gnawed away at contentment. Too late, the lust for youth and vigor again, by which time they would be long gone, the casualties of a war waged from the inside against an enemy infinitely more patient and far better-resourced than himself.

When the mind-bleeding was over, and Lord Guerin once more slumped in his chair, Traemore turned to me, his thin jaw quivering.

"Thank you, Miss Winter. Now, our lord will sleep more restfully. His manservant reported he was quite fitful last night."

I kept to the shadows as I once again wondered who did the real governing of Nulla: Lord Guerin, or Traemore, the advisor who evidently sought to replace him?

"Have you thought any more on my offer, Miss Winter?"

"Your offer, my lord? I beg your pardon, but I was not aware you had made one."

Traemore's eyes sparked at my audacious phrasing, but he kept his temper. "Of course, we did not speak of anything so particular as the details. I merely wondered if you had reflected on our conversation."

What had he said? I was rare. I had potential. I had a *future*. Yet so much had changed since I had stood before him last that I felt briefly lost. What kind of future could exist without a past? It was like wishing for a hand when you were not even in possession of an arm.

"Aye, my lord, I did. But I belong to Cutter." I winced at the admission. I belonged to no one. "No new arrangement can be determined without his knowledge."

"I see." Traemore's mouth twitched. "And what do *you* think, Miss Winter? Might he be willing to part with you?"

Merchant as he was, Cutter was not primarily motivated by money. His ambitions, I knew, plied a deeper vein. He imagined himself as a lord one day, perhaps even one like Traemore. And my abilities would serve him well in his ascendance to power. What better tool against potential opponents than a girl who knew the darkest secrets of half the city? And what better gift than the ability to instill fear in the heart of the bravest man?

"Nay," I said after a moment. "He will not part with me. My gift represents far more than money to him."

Something flickered in Traemore's eyes before he snuffed it out. Like Lord Adamo, he only nodded decisively. "Very well, then, Miss Winter. It is a great loss, but I understand. I bid you good night."

I saw no sign of the former thane of Maera as I left the house. Had he departed already, a day early? The trees, completely bare now, shivered in the breeze without their coats. Thankfully, the canal was only icy at the edges, the constant traffic wearing a narrow path through the fractured sheets. I steered the boat with practiced ease, as careful to avoid the brittle shards as I had the ones in Lord Guerin's mind.

The lord of Nulla would die any day. When he did, would the newly titled Lord Traemore succeed him? What use would the advisor have for me then? I had heard of murders committed over memories. Not necessarily pleasurable ones—though there were always those who craved elsewhere enough to kill for it—but memories that held secrets. Dark secrets. Innocent *mems* could die when caught in the crossfire of those power struggles, which was likely how Lord Adamo's family had been murdered. From all that intrigue, at least, Cutter had shielded me.

By the time I reached the halfway point along the canal, it was fully dark. There were few lamps in this part of the city, and the lantern stashed in the bottom of my boat wasn't lit. Thankfully, I knew the rest of the way by heart. The sounds of water splashing against a wooden hull came to me through the blackness, though no one emerged from the gloom.

When I reached the main thoroughfare, it was similarly empty. Fears of a skirmish between Lethe and Memosine sometimes kept the citizens of Nulla confined to their houses, but they rarely stopped the merchants. The wind, then? Or a delayed series of shipments that had sent everyone home?

I tethered the boat and reached for my satchel, sliding the strap over my shoulder. The fur of my cloak bristled against my ear as my boots found land again. I breathed a sigh, always glad to be clear of the ice. The temperature had plummeted since I'd set out, and the frigid air felt sharp and heavy on my lungs, biting and blistering my exposed cheeks. I pulled the rabbit fur around my face in an attempt to shield my skin from the most violent gusts. Tonight, the canal would likely freeze, a thick layer of ice wedging the moored boats in place. If it did, there would be no easy way to rescue Lord Guerin from his nightmares come morning, not unless I wanted to confront the worst of mine.

I had only gone a few paces when I saw a flash of brown in my periphery. I turned my head to the right, exposing my face to the worst of the chill.

Nothing.

Five paces further, I saw it again and stiffened. A shadow against the triangular shaft of light cast by a street lamp. A brown cloak, or maybe black. I blinked and stared into the gloom, but nothing materialized. I felt a prickle along my spine. I was being watched.

Or was I? *You're being paranoid. No one is following you.* I'd been stalked by nightmares so long they were bleeding into reality. I shook my head and quickened my pace. I had always carried a knife, like every woman living in Nulla, but I'd never thought I really needed to. My gift served me well enough.

I had nearly reached Cutter's tavern when I heard the soft footfalls behind me. I spun and saw a black-hooded figure, taller than me and stockier. It was no matter: he would be no match for my mind, whatever his size. But I'd barely removed the glove from my right hand when another pair of arms seized me from behind, a meaty palm smashing against my mouth. My captor dragged me backward into a nearby alley.

Never mind my knife—I reached for my gift. The man would rue the day he ever touched me. But my eyes watered, finally registering the pungent scent of his hand, or rather, the damp cloth he held against my mouth. Slightly sweet, but distinctly artificial. Feeling my gift fading— *impossible*—I clawed at the gloved hand, trying to tear away the fingers. I could do naught if I were unconscious. I had freed myself of four of the thick fingers and managed to draw a sharp breath before another set of hands grabbed my arms, twisting them behind my back.

No chance of getting at my knife now. A third man?

"Steady, Miss Winter," came a polished voice—hardly the tone of an opportunistic thug. "We will only hurt you if you resist us."

They knew my name. Then it wasn't an attack of the nature I'd anticipated. Was this Traemore's doing? Or worse—Lord Adamo's?

I will not force you. Was the boy from the ice even capable of kidnapping? He was undeniably desperate. Unlike Traemore, who had little to gain by my capture—at least for now—when I was already gainfully employed by his master.

My gift struggled against the lure of unconsciousness. I sank to my knees, two of the three men sinking with me. The second man held the cloth against my mouth and nose with a firm hand on the back of my head. My cap had fallen to the cobbles next to my satchel. The third man was binding my wrists behind my back with leather cord.

"Let me go!" I yelled, my cry muffled by the cloth.

The first man crouched in front of me. "She's taking an awfully long time to succumb to the drug."

"She's an *alter*, what do you expect?" muttered the third man, finishing with my wrists. "Give her another dose. We have to get her out of here, and soon."

"There's no one about. I made sure of it." But the first man extracted a flask from his coat pocket and a handkerchief from another—a handkerchief, I observed faintly, not a rag—and proceeded to douse the cloth with the pungent substance.

Seeing it, and sensing the first man's hooded smile, I began to struggle again.

"Now, Miss Winter, I thought we agreed you wouldn't fight us." The man behind me twisted one of my wrists, and pain knifed through the limb. I moaned through the cloth as a wiry arm curled around my waist. My back was pulled flush against a hard chest.

"Hold her," came the second man's gravelly voice, and the new cloth was shoved against my mouth. My eyes rolled back in my head as the lids shuttered and every limb became too heavy to lift. The man behind me was the only force holding me upright, though the potency of my gift continued to cling to wakefulness.

A faint chuckle. "That did the trick."

The cloth was pulled away. With the last of my strength, I pried open my eyes in time to see one of the men produce a large gunny sack, holding it open. The man who'd wrenched my wrist lifted me into it, grunting with the effort, not that my body offered any resistance. My lower half was almost completely inside when the man abruptly sagged, gazing with disbelief at something in the vicinity of his chest. I blinked rapidly to clear the grit in my eyes. It looked as if he clawed at a crossbow bolt sunk into his ribcage, but that was impossible.

I fell to the ground, my head landing atop my fallen satchel. Glass crunched from within. I winced, more from fear of Cutter's reaction to the broken vials than the jarring. The two men who remained standing—one of whom still held the handkerchief—were whirling around, shouting as they presented their backs to me. Their yells were sharp enough to pierce my aching skull. They would surely rouse every man or woman in hollering distance. Or did it only sound that way?

I looked past my captors and saw that three men had entered the alley, one bearing the crossbow that had felled my attacker and another carrying a lantern. They were all above average height, but the crossbow wielder was a giant, tall enough to reach the topmost shelf of Cutter's tavern-shop without a ladder. The next-tallest man was armed with a long staff, while the shortest fellow—still a large man by any measure—wielded only his fists, though he appeared to know how to use them. Shapes blurred into a hazy mass of shadows, and I rested my head against the satchel. Everything was muffled now, as if the whole world had been blanketed by a heavy fall of snow.

Finally, complete silence. A shadow crouched over me, rolling me onto my back, removing the sack that encased my lower half. I winced as the weight of my body pinned my throbbing wrist—the one without a glove. Cold cobblestone pressed against my skin.

"Miss Winter," came a familiar voice. "Can you hear me?" Strong hands rolled me gently onto my side and a knife sawed through the leather cords. Warm skin brushed against my bare arm as my wrists were freed. The world jerked back into focus.

I sat up, only belatedly realizing that the world had yet to right itself in full. Lord Adamo crouched beside me, clad in common clothes rather than the elegant attire he'd worn the night before. Two hulking shadows stood behind him, while three other shapes lay strewn about the alley. A wooden staff was casually propped against the stone wall. Lord Adamo's?

I pulled my arm back against my chest. "Did you kill them?"

Lord Adamo glanced at the giant before returning his gaze to me. "One is dead. The others are only unconscious."

"Then they aren't yours?"

"Mine?"

I gestured to the prone shapes with my uninjured arm. "The men who attacked me."

Surprise webbed the tanned skin at the corners of his eyes. "Of course not, Miss Winter."

I replayed the sequence of events: Lord Adamo and his two guards watching from a distance as I was attacked and dragged into an alley. Sprinting after me. Disabling my attackers. I flinched. How did I know all that?

I looked down. His hand still rested at my elbow. My *bare* elbow.

I jerked away from him. Instantly, the world lurched dizzily and I reeled, tasting bile.

Lord Adamo grabbed my shoulders to steady me. "Easy, Miss Winter. We mean you no harm." He glanced at the wrist I cradled against my chest. "We should splint that."

"Nay," I said, biting my tongue to keep from passing out. "Not unless you want me to know all your secrets."

"I keep forgetting. Your gift is powerful." He moved closer. "Why not use it to pry my secrets from me, as you say?"

The warmth was back in my belly, warring with the effects of whatever drug they'd used on me. "Who says I haven't already?" I scrunched my eyes as the space between us spun in a dizzying kaleidoscope. "My lord."

"I would know if you had."

Then he could feel me in his mind? Why had he never said? But he had not known I was a *mem* at first, even when I'd delved into some of his past. And just now, I'd witnessed the events of the last few minutes from his point of view. Perhaps his awareness of my presence was limited to only the deepest layers of his memory.

"I saw you coming after me," I said at last. "In your mind."

His expression didn't change. "That is hardly a secret."

"My lord," came a deep voice from behind Lord Adamo. "We must leave here now or else risk discovery."

"Cutter's tavern is not far." I tried to pull myself from the lord's grip, but he was strong, and the drug tugged at the corners of my awareness. It wouldn't be long until my gift gave out, and I succumbed to the drug's influence. "Take me back, please."

"You're injured, Miss Winter, and if you don't mind me saying so, it doesn't look as though you're able to walk. Let me take you somewhere safe where we can tend to you."

"Safe?" I heard myself echo.

The second guard—the shorter of the two—drew close with his lantern, and I saw it.

Lord Adamo's hair. No longer than the length of my shortest finger, though it curled slightly at the ends, I had thought it an ordinary golden-brown. And no doubt it was in normal light. But in lantern light, the thick streaks of molten gold were obvious, even turning to copper in places. What would they look like in strong sunlight?

I released the breath I kept captive. "You're an *alter.*"

Lord Adamo smiled. "Aye."

"What is your gift?"

"If you haven't already gleaned that from my mind, Miss Winter," he spoke around a grin, "then I would clutch my remaining secrets to my chest a little longer."

I frowned.

"Now you know what I am, do you trust me more or less?"

"The same," I replied, trying to conceal my surprise. Why had I not seen the truth of him before? Or seventeen years ago? Was that why I felt so drawn to him? Because he was like me?

Lord Adamo's eyes flitted over my face, and I realized he was still holding me upright. His face was barely inches from mine. "I can feel you fading, Miss Winter. Make your choice."

He was right: every second I grew groggier. My eyes had nearly closed of their own accord. "Fine, my lord. I'll come with you. But you should know it's hard to . . . to think around you."

Of course, I hadn't meant to say that part out loud.

"A surprisingly common occurrence, Miss Winter," he remarked, sliding one arm beneath my knees and another beneath my back.

"My satchel," I whispered as he lifted me. "I mustn't leave it behind."

We rose to his height. It made me even more dizzy. "Bear has it, along with my quarterstaff. And your cap, too."

Bear? What kind of name was Bear? But the rest of the world slipped away in that moment, leaving me with more questions than answers and a single, piercing image of a man with hair like molten gold.

7

DORIAN

Dorian paused with the woman in his arms.

He couldn't return to Lord Guerin. Not when he suspected Nulla's lordling was behind the kidnapping of the *mem*—or his weaselly faced advisor, Lord Traemore. Dorian had seen enough of politics to recognize the spark of ambition in the man's eyes. A good thing, then, that he had decided to leave the lord's company a day early, taking up residence in an inn instead of Guerin's manor house. The *mem* would be frightened when she awoke in a strange place, but it was for the best.

"Are you quite sure you should be touching her, my lord?" Bas shifted nervously, switching the lantern to his other hand as he glared at Miss Winter. Her glove trailed from one of his coat pockets like a snake skin.

"She's unconscious," Dorian replied, noticing that the *mem*'s lips were slowly turning blue. "Come. We must get her out of this wind."

They followed him out of the alley and down the street toward the respectable half of the city. Bear, never ruffled by anything more catastrophic than burned toast first thing in the morning, kept his crossbow loaded but hidden beneath his cloak, while Bas trotted along at a more sober pace. No one was about, thanks to the ghastly weather. Perfect conditions for a kidnapping, though without the drug her captors had used on her, Miss Winter would have been better positioned to defend herself.

The previous night, for one heady moment, he had thought his relief in sight. That she would come with him to find the Reliquary.

He'd seen the yearning in her eyes. She had wanted to—or at least, wanted to escape Nulla and her master. And for some reason, even before she'd known he was also an *alter*, she'd trusted him implicitly. Had she delved so far into his mind? What had she seen there while he'd been distracted? Not enough, it would seem, to discern the nature of his gift. Perhaps his walls were better fortified than he'd thought.

But she'd declined his offer. Perhaps there was a young man tethering her to Nulla, a sweetheart she couldn't leave behind. Or she truly feared the reach of her master. Dorian didn't believe the spiel she'd given him about love. She'd probably seen Lida and Emmy's bodies . . . Dorian himself bleeding out on the ground. He could never keep those images behind his mental walls. After viewing all that, how could she not want to rid him of his torturous recollections?

"Shall I carry her for you, my lord?" Bear asked, coming up beside him.

Dorian shook his head. "She isn't heavy. And besides, we're nearly there." Still, he took the opportunity to redistribute her weight, taking care not to jostle her injured arm. Her head fell limply against his shoulder, the blunted ends of her short hair tickling his bearded chin. As if by unspoken agreement, Bear moved ahead of him as they approached the inn, shielding them from passersby, while Bas produced a cloak and draped it over the lass. Best onlookers not know a former thane of Maera carried an unconscious and powerful *mem* to his rooms.

But if they wanted to speculate about her presence in his personal chambers, they could do so to their hearts' content. Rumors in the cities and towns of the no-man's-land tended to fester between the walls of the seam, but rarely spread to other places. Hence the appeal of this place for many visiting lords with a pressing desire for anonymity.

Thankfully, the innkeeper's wife was the only one who saw them enter the back stairs, and she made no comment about the young woman slumped in his arms. Dorian carried the *mem* up two flights of stairs and down the corridor to the door at the end. Bear opened it, and Dorian crossed over the threshold and placed her carefully on the bed. Jewel was nowhere in sight.

Dorian blew into his cold hands and glanced around. They'd obviously prepared this room for a lord of Memosine. There was a large fireplace to keep out the winter chill, lit some hours before, for the room was pleasantly warm. The heavy tapestries and thick rugs were spun from an earthy palette of browns, greens, oranges, and even muted purples, and in the center of the room stood the four-poster bed with curtains that could be pulled shut, topped with a covering of brown fur. There were few windows, since there was little light to be had anyway, and the only ones were no wider than a heavily squinted eye, deeply recessed, and crisscrossed with lead—no use losing precious heat to the elements. As it was, the room was probably too warm for Jewel's liking.

After depositing Miss Winter's satchel and cap on the table and leaning Dorian's quarterstaff against the wall, Bear stationed himself beside the locked door, still holding his loaded crossbow, while Bas moved to stand near the bed.

"How long will she sleep?"

Dorian removed his cloak and sat beside her. "Hopefully long enough for me to do this." He reached for her bare arm, the one she'd held gingerly to herself, and carefully felt along the length of the limb. She didn't stir.

"Nothing broken, thankfully. Possibly sprained, though." Remembering how she'd disliked him touching her, he took the glove Bas handed him and slipped it back on.

Bas flexed his bloodied fingers. "She's younger than I thought she'd be, based on her reputation."

"Aye, still a girl, in some respects. But she's a fair bit stronger than she looks. Plucky, too."

Her lips still had a bluish tinge to them, possibly because her cloak was damp from when she'd fallen. With Bas's help, he removed it, pausing when he saw the small knife strapped to her thigh over her leggings.

"My lord," Bear said from over his shoulder, having approached the bed, "best you divest her of that, too."

"Nay." Dorian ignored the concerned glance his guards exchanged, remembering how slight she'd felt in his hands. So long as she didn't touch him, or any of them, she was no different than an ordinary woman. "Let her keep the blade."

"You trust her?"

He looked down at the *mem*. Remembered the compassion in her eyes as they conversed in her master's tavern. The wistfulness in her voice. Barely out of her girlhood, she was only a tool wielded by powerful men. Unconscious, she looked . . . almost like Emmy.

Dorian shook his head to clear the thought, then glanced up. Seeing his men had taken the gesture as his answer, he quickly said, "Aye, I trust her well enough. But keep your wits about you."

She stirred, then, though her eyes remained shut.

"Miss Winter?"

"Sephone," she managed, then added, "Miss Winter sounds like some kind of wicked forest sprite." She opened her eyes, balking when she saw the three men standing beside the bed. She planted her hands beside her to sit up and winced at the silent protest of her sprained wrist. Drawing the hand to her chest, she eyed her discarded cloak.

"Easy," Dorian said, with the same tone he would use for a startled horse. "We mean you no harm. This is the safe place I spoke about."

"Lord Guerin's manor house?" Her wide eyes sampled the room. With her white-blond hair sticking out in every direction, she looked exactly as he imagined a winter sprite might.

"Nay, an inn. More neutral territory." Dorian gestured to the guards behind him, clearing his throat so they would step back a pace. They took the hint. "This is Bear and that's Bas. My two most trusted bodyguards. You have naught to fear from them."

Her eyes flickered, and he thought he could imagine what she was thinking. Were they recent acquisitions, or had they been hired before his family's murder? The familiar pain speared his heart. If only the brothers had been present that terrible day instead of away on a futile errand. Though it had been his own command which sent them away, Dorian knew they shared in his guilt.

"How did you know I was in trouble, my lord?"

Dorian leaned back. Something about this girl unstoppered the memories he'd so carefully repressed. "I was on my way to your master's tavern when I saw you. I followed you, hoping to talk to you again . . . to perhaps persuade you . . . but before I could reach you, you were attacked. My men and I came as quickly as we could."

He watched her eyes stray to Bear. As frightening as his beastly namesake in ordinary daylight, how must he appear to her now? Still, to her credit, she showed no fear of the tawny-haired giant.

"Why would Traemore want to steal you, Miss Winter?"

Brown eyes flicked back to him and narrowed.

"*Sephone.*"

"Sephone," he repeated. So long as she didn't ask to call him Dorian. If she agreed to help him, there would be familiarity enough between them.

She dampened her lips. "Why do you believe it was Traemore?"

"I recognized the men from Lord Guerin's household, which, as you are likely aware, is now run entirely by Traemore. And I am familiar with the ambitions of men of his ilk."

She nodded slowly. "He has spoken to me twice now about securing my . . . services. On a more permanent basis."

"And you declined?"

"Aye. Cutter would never part with me willingly."

"So, he thought to kidnap you." Dorian frowned. "Even a man of Traemore's station could not hide you forever. Not in this city. Perhaps he was going to take you elsewhere."

"Perhaps. But you said that not all his men were dead, my lord. He'll know you helped me."

Dorian shook his head. "It was dark. And my men and I were disguised. Even so, we will leave at dawn, just in case word reaches Traemore that we are still in the city."

Her eyes moved to the door. Was she homesick already? Perhaps this was another chance—his final chance.

"Bas." The man snapped to attention. "Go find Jewel, would you? Tell the lady I require her presence. Bear, would you please wait outside?"

Bas huffed, but both brothers obeyed his bidding. When he returned his gaze to the *mem*, she was rubbing her forehead. "My thoughts are so strange."

"Strange?"

She nodded, her eyes a little glazed. "What is your gift?"

"My gift? Perhaps it is the drug that affects you."

"Nay, it was the same last night. I feel . . . different around you, my lord. Not myself." She gave her head a shake. "I wouldn't have said that normally."

His mouth quirked. "You are not the first woman to stand in awe of the aristocracy."

She ignored his snark. "I have had more than enough to do with the aristocracy, I assure you. Yet for some reason, I can't help but speak my mind to you. Why, I wonder? I'm not normally so—"

"—courageous?" he finished for her.

"Bold." She met his grin with a frown.

"Perhaps it's because I'm a foreigner. The accent throws you off, makes you less concerned about manners."

"I have met lords aplenty from your country," she replied firmly, "and none of them made me feel like I was drunk."

"Drunk?" He straightened, surprised. Perhaps she was more affected by his gift than most. Because she was a *mem*? Seeing she was nearly overcome, and not wanting her to say something she later regretted, he retreated toward the hearth and bid the gift to keep out of his words. Even if he unconsciously failed to curtail his power, the effects of it would probably fade in time—it certainly had for Bas and Bear, who contradicted him as often as they obeyed—but in the meantime, he wanted her to think clearly. To decide her future for herself, out from under the influence of his gift.

The easing of her muscles was visible even from his new vantage point across the room. He guessed she was ordinarily a brave woman, for despite the withdrawal of his gift, she continued to speak her mind.

"If you won't tell me your primary gift, Lord Adamo, might you share your secondary one?"

Dorian planted a hand above the mantlepiece and leaned into it. "Would an honest answer compel you to share yours?"

"I don't have one."

"You don't have a secondary gift?"

"Nay." Her mouth tipped ruefully. "Perhaps that's why my primary gift is as strong as it is." He watched her as she rose to her feet and came toward the fire. She must have had some inkling that physical proximity was involved in his gift, for she was careful to keep her distance from him.

"That is . . . most unusual."

Instead of a reply, she bobbed a slight curtsey. "I thank you for your assistance, Lord Adamo, but I must be getting home."

"Home?"

"Back," she amended.

"At the risk of sounding like Traemore—and this is no kidnapping, I assure you—can I not convince you to stay?"

She hesitated. On an impulse, he held out his bare hand to her. Certainly not a romantic declaration—whatever the historical significance of the gesture—but something almost equally intimate, given her gift. Bas would yelp if he saw him.

"Look into my mind," he urged. "See the truth of it."

The *mem* remained where she was. "You and I have opposite problems, Lord Adamo. You wish to forget your past. I would do anything to know more about mine."

Was that his opening? Desperation surged through him more strongly than the River Memosine in full flood. Months of looking for a suitable *mem,* and he had never come across one as powerful as her. Or one so painfully honest. He had known, instinctively, that he could not trust the others, but he could trust her. He was certain of it.

"We can fell both problems with one blow, Miss Winter. Help me find the Reliquary, and you may use its power to look into your past. To see what the veil of human forgetfulness has hidden."

She stood so still, he feared she'd frozen solid within.

"I swear I'm telling the truth. Even so, look into my mind and see it for yourself, though I warn you not to venture deeper than you must. Shadows lurk in the dark places."

An unexpected tear hovered at the corner of her eye. He already knew she had too much pride to let it fall.

"The shadows stalk you too, do they not, Miss Win—*Sephone*?" He stepped closer, trying not to let his gift spill into his words. Clarity of mind aside, it might have the unintended effect of driving her away. "You know what it is to feel pain . . . terrible pain without any hope of a cure, without hope of anything beyond a temporary cessation of agony. For yourself, you might not see the value of forgetting a history. But perhaps you would see the value of setting aside the torments of those whose darkness you needlessly bear."

Her eyes flickered, and he knew he'd guessed correctly. She was not as serene as she looked.

"Look into my mind," Dorian repeated, extending his hand again. "Probe everything I know about the Reliquary. Witness the deaths of my wife and daughter—however much of it you can stomach. Know the truth of my intentions."

Still, she hesitated. "You can feel me in your mind, Lord Adamo."

"I built a wall deep within my memories long ago. I will know when you are about to breach it, Sephone. Do not fear, I will keep you out of the places you cannot go."

"It may hurt."

He didn't flinch. "It always hurts. But you can't do any more damage than has already been done."

One final weapon remained in his arsenal.

"You've never stepped out of Nulla, have you, Sephone? At the very least, do you not want to see a little bit of the world?"

Her indecision evaporated. Crossing the distance between them, she slipped the glove from her uninjured arm and curled her cold fingers around his.

8

I probed gently, only as deep as I had to, anxious not to invite the onslaught of carnage I'd encountered before—the horrific sight of mangled bodies I was sure never strayed far from Lord Adamo's conscious thought. Though he was still young, his memories were almost as bloody as Lord Guerin's. I guessed the most troubling ones were hidden behind the walls he'd spoken of previously—the battlements I could now see lurking beyond a thick curtain of mist.

As before, I encountered nothing nefarious in his mind. At least, none of the images I'd come to expect from those who frequented Cutter's tavern. I was in no danger from him. Even if I hadn't known for certain that he wasn't the womanizing sort, Lord Adamo thought me unremarkable, a fact which was clear from the dull luster surrounding his mental image of me and other women he'd known compared to the golden brilliance limning the memory of his beautiful wife. He had long loved her, not straying from the pursuit of the woman even after she became his wife.

He was still in love with her.

Of course, he would likely be unaware he shared such a confidence. Few knew that while *mems* couldn't read thoughts, thoughts were often easily deduced. Men were far slower than women to guard their secrets, even once they understood the delicate workings of my gift, and most lords saw me only as a slave.

But there was none of that within Lord Adamo. At one touch of his mind, I felt I knew him. He was a man of honor and chivalry, brought low by circumstance. A lord of uncommon loyalty who inspired the same quality in others, whether they were subject or peer. He would hold me at a distance, but he didn't see me as less. It was just as I remembered.

I saw, to my disappointment, no hint of his gift. Whatever he had been doing before to affect my emotions, he wasn't doing it now. It was under his conscious control, then. But likely invisible. And, like the Marianthean stranger's gift, it wasn't dependent on physical touch.

I moved on to the Reliquary. A cursory scan through Lord Adamo's memories confirmed he told the truth: the relic was rumored to be powerful, not only in regards to the deletion of memories, but the manipulation of them. If it was real, it would magnify my powers a hundred-fold, allowing me to erase and edit the past at will. I passed over the fruitful conversation the lord had had with a merchant from Erebus and moved west, to his home city of Maera. I savored lungfuls of the sweet mountain air like it was honey. And the sunlight—

Wasn't all of Caldera covered by the gray? But nay, Lord Adamo had apparently spent many days from boyhood to manhood in the sun. The actual sun, with a hint of a blue sky overhead, more expansive than I'd imagined. Lord Guerin's memories of sunlight were nearly sixty years old.

I saw a woman running through a sun-dappled garden. Lady Lida Ashwood—Lord Adamo's wife, the former thaness of Maera—with hair a lemony gold. She held the hand of a little girl, not older than four or five, with the same color hair and pale, creamy skin. As I watched, the woman dropped to her knees and rolled in the grass, hardly caring that the movement accumulated an array of twigs and leaves in the ruffles and folds of her dress. The little girl gave a delighted squeal and followed suit, plunking herself in the woman's lap as soon as she was upright again.

I felt Lord Adamo wince, and his hand tightened over mine. His skin was warm, making me acutely aware of how icy my fingers were in his.

"Go on," I heard him say, but at that moment the garden scene vanished, replaced by the grisly sight of his dead family, their bodies lying as broken and limp as masterless puppets. "Keep going."

"I could numb this memory for you, my lord."

He shook his head violently, though his skin became hot enough to scald me. Was I nearing the wall he'd spoken of? I let go of his hand.

We both stepped back. Veins throbbed in Lord Adamo's neck, and sweat trickled down his forehead and temples. He opened his eyes, and they were twin pools of murky, bottomless pain. Not even Lord Guerin had ever looked so tortured.

"I am sorry, my lord. I didn't mean to cause you pain. I tried to keep to the pleasant memories."

"There are no pleasant memories," he replied through gritted teeth. "Not anymore."

"Then you could see what I saw?"

"Aye, vaguely. Mostly when you were viewing memories of *them*."

How had he done it? Was it part of his gift? No other person—besides the old veteran—had ever been so conscious of my presence in their mind. I watched him indirectly. "The little girl was your daughter?"

"Aye." His voice was brimming with anguish. "That was our Emmeline."

"She's beautiful."

"She was." He sagged against the wall beside the hearth, planting his shoulder and forehead in the solid stone. "There's something you should know, Miss Winter. Rufus Karthick—Lord Draven, the man who arranged their deaths—is still hankering for my blood. If you help me, it is possible he may come after you too. In Caldera, men like Traemore and Guerin tend to be the rule rather than the exception."

I opened my mouth to answer just as a knock sounded on the door. I hurriedly pulled on my glove. Was this the lady Lord Adamo had mentioned before? I wondered if he had remarried, though I had only seen one woman of significance in his mind. But before Lord Adamo could admit the visitor, a figure shoved against the hard wood and burst over the threshold. I glanced up, surprised by Lady Jewel's unorthodox entrance. But instead of a woman, it was an animal that padded into the room. A wolf with fur almost the same color as my hair who immediately fixed startling, sapphire-blue eyes on me.

"Ah," said Lord Adamo, recovering some of his earlier composure and going to the wolf, dropping to his knees beside her. "The lady has deigned to return to us." He embraced the wolf in a bear hug and rubbed the magnificent animal's head, ears, and chest with an affection I'd only seen between man and animal once before—the homeless veteran and his dog. The wolf permitted the attention, surveying Lord Adamo with a look that could only be described as haughty. After a few seconds, she lowered her head and licked his hand. Her bushy tail did not beat against the floor, as a dog's might, but was tucked sedately around her body like a queen's mantle.

"This is Jewel," Lord Adamo said over his shoulder, watching for my reaction. The wolf returned her attention to my face, black lips curled in a supercilious expression that was neither grin nor scowl. Her ears flicked forward as I knelt next to Lord Adamo and extended my hand. The lady wolf sniffed it, then focused on me again, intelligent eyes drinking me in from head to toe.

"Jewel joined my family the night Emmy was born," the lord said. "She came into the city from the mountains one night and simply presented herself at our door. Over the course of several months, we tamed her—or she tamed us. Lida said it was a sign from the old gods that our daughter was well-protected." His voice thickened, and he turned slightly away.

His phrasing surprised me only a little. Even though Calderans had long since left their ancestors' gods behind—lying forgotten or dead along with the rest of the world-that-was—it was still common to invoke them or their protection. After all, one never knew which ones might still be listening, even here in the New World, or how obliging they might prove to be. For myself, I wondered what powerful deity would ever overlook such a slight to offer his services.

I looked into the sapphire eyes. Jewel studied me unflinchingly, no more condescension or wariness in her gaze. Remembering Felix, I inched the glove from my left hand and extended it to her again. Black tendrils danced on my fingertips, wreathing my knuckles in twisting, wriggling vines. Lord Adamo stared at them. Had he not seen them when I touched his hand?

Without a sound, Jewel moved forward and angled her body so my flattened palm fit against her graceful neck.

"Can you—" Lord Adamo began, a trace of wonder in his voice.

But the black tendrils didn't sink beneath the surface of the wolf's fur. Disappointed, I leaned back, the black threads evaporating. I would have liked to reassure the beautiful animal of my intentions, even if I could not peer into her mind.

There was a chuckle. "My gift doesn't work on her, either."

My attention remained focused on Jewel. The glittering blue of her eyes was deeper than any pool on a summer's day; deeper, even, than any example I'd seen of her namesake. I stroked her fur coat, my fingers tracing the jagged break in the wolf's fur before my mind comprehended what it was.

The scar stretched for at least eight inches across her chest, slanting diagonally downward toward her left leg. The skin there was knotted and devoid of fur, not that it diminished the wolf's beauty.

"That's from the day my family was murdered," Lord Adamo said. "Suffice it to say that Jewel has her own reasons for coming with me."

Then she was a companion in her own right, rather than a pet or a guard dog?

I looked to the guard, Bear, standing beside the door still holding the crossbow—a strange mechanical contraption I'd only ever seen at a distance. The shorter man, Bas, stood next to him, leaning against the wall with his arms folded, his face a careful mask. Lord Adamo's quarterstaff was propped against the wall in a similarly casual fashion, the ends of the innocuous-looking weapon tipped with iron.

Slowly, I turned my eyes back to Lord Adamo, who was still patting the wolf. Crouching half in shadow as he was, the metallic streaks in his hair had returned to their usual dull shade. If he was careful, he would appear ordinary, but direct lantern light or firelight would always betray him.

I wondered if his former subjects knew he was an *alter*.

"If I come with you to find this Reliquary"—as I spoke, Lord Adamo looked up and met my eyes, but he said naught, and Lady Jewel had not moved an inch—"I cannot take the memories of your family from you, Lord Adamo. Not now that I have seen your great love for them. Such a love is rare, my lord, rarer than you know. When I stumble upon it, I cannot touch it, for it is one of the great mysteries of life: a beautiful flower in a muddy, trampled field." I thought of the old veteran again and wondered why he intruded on my mind with increasing frequency.

Even this . . . is only a shadow of the real thing.

Was it love he'd been speaking of, or only strawberries?

I went on, "But the memories of your family's deaths, my lord, and any pain associated with them, I will erase for you in full—if I can. These are the conditions of my coming with you."

Now it was my turn to wait. The brown of the lord's gaze reminded me of the nightingale's wings. Was the veteran right? That the world I had seen so often in the minds of others was not the world as it truly was? And was that for better or for worse?

But for the first time, my path was clear. If I remained in Nulla, it could be months or even years before I could escape Cutter. In the meantime, Traemore might attempt to kidnap me again. No doubt, he would have unspeakable things in mind for me. Cutter was hardly the worst of masters.

I didn't want to be their pawn; I wanted to find Regis. I wanted to see the world and the sea and the sun. Maybe its sweet warmth would burn up all the horrors that churned inside of me. I'd had enough of the gray.

And perhaps I would find a love like Lord Adamo's, a love that surpassed even what I'd once felt for Regis.

Finally, the lord spoke. "You drive an impossible bargain, Miss Winter. You would condemn me to remember their lives but not the truth of their ends? It seems the worst kind of torture."

So, it was back to Miss Winter again.

"You will remember they are gone, my lord. I will not take that. But everything else . . ." I decided to bare a tiny corner of my own mind. "I would do anything to remember even the slightest part of my history, Lord Adamo. I cannot take from you even the smallest fragment of that which I crave for myself."

The brown wavered. Slowly, he nodded. "Then you have a deal." He clasped my gloved arm briefly, then got to his feet. His lips curved in the ghost of a smile. "To a productive and fruitful alliance, then, Miss Winter."

To anyone who did not know him well, or had never visited his mind, the expression on his face would resemble passive acceptance. But I knew. It was the look of a man who places his hope in the power of persuasion.

Somewhere along the way, Dorian Ashwood would try to change my mind.

Lord Adamo glanced at his guards. The one called Bas sent him a meaningful look which the lord promptly ignored as he turned back to me. "You will be safe with us, Miss Winter."

"And what of your safety?" I replied. I knew Bas's sort.

Distrustful. Guarded. Afraid.

As well he should be.

"Care to provide your own reassurances?" Lord Adamo followed my gaze to his bodyguard. "For those who require them, that is."

Bas scowled.

"Don't touch my bare skin and I can't scry your secrets." I wrapped my arms around my middle. "Unless someone means me harm, I won't enter their mind without their permission." I directed the last part at Bas, faintly aware that Bear was snickering behind his enormous hand.

Lord Adamo rubbed the ears of the lady wolf. "At the very least, Jewel trusts you."

"How can you tell?"

"If she hadn't, she would have growled or barked you out the door."

"Nay." I stared into the sapphire eyes. Somehow, I couldn't imagine the graceful wolf doing anything so savage. Then she opened her mouth, and I caught a flash of sharp teeth, whiter than a fresh fall of snow. I wondered what marks the lady wolf had left on the attackers of Lord Adamo's family. Not that I would ever pity them their injuries.

"Aye," said the lord, still watching me, "she did exactly that to the last four *mems* I interviewed. None of them came near enough to look at her, let alone touch her."

A hint of dry humor entered his voice.

"Whatever the nature of her test, Miss Winter, it would seem you passed."

I woke to a gloved hand on my shoulder and a deep voice in my ear. "We must leave now, Miss Winter, before first light."

Lord Adamo. Clearly, he had seen the wisdom in donning his gloves, or perhaps he was merely cold now the fire had burned low.

"First light?" I repeated, with a different emphasis. No telling smudges strained through the narrow windows.

"Well, lesser dark," he replied as he leaned back.

I wanted to ask him about the sunlight I'd seen in his mind, but he moved away, slipping through the door with surprising stealth for such a tall man. I shoved back the heavy fur bedspread and sat up, testing my right wrist and arm. It was greatly improved—only a minor strain. I wouldn't even bother with a splint.

I stared at the luxurious bed hangings. It felt wrong to sleep in such a fine bed fully dressed, especially when its intended occupant, a former thane, slumbered only yards away. But Lord Adamo had insisted on settling himself in one of the armchairs, and he and his guards had alternated watches throughout the remainder of the night. I had expected the wolf to sleep beside the fire, as a dog might, but instead she had claimed the armchair nearest Lord Adamo, her head resting almost daintily on her large paws.

Spying Bas watching me from beside the now closed door, I left the warm bed more quickly than I liked. Whatever they intended to do, I wouldn't slow them down. Bemoaning the loss of my mirror fragment, I did my best to smooth my hair and rumpled clothes. The contents of my satchel had not fared well. All the vials except two were broken, and they would be all but worthless to me: more essence of strawberry. I carefully removed the broken glass, my gloves proving useful for the delicate task. All of the liquid had dried, though the interior of the satchel still smelled faintly of strawberries. I grabbed my cap and cloak and was pulling on my boots when a large shadow fell over me.

"Miss Winter," Bear said with a tiny bow, "the carriage is waiting for you."

"The carriage?" I stared at him. I knew, of course, that lords and ladies occasionally traveled in such finery, but in Nulla? Lord Guerin had a fancy canal boat he used for special occasions, though I had never seen him astride a horse.

How far had Lord Adamo carried me last night? To the very edge of the city? Beyond?

"Aye, the carriage," the guard repeated with a slight smile. "A humble breakfast awaits you there."

Escaping Nulla could not be so easy. What was the lord thinking? Didn't he know Cutter would have allies everywhere? Likely, they already knew I'd spent the night in the lord's personal chambers.

Still, a carriage ride would be a pleasant memory to take back to Cutter. *At least you won't have sore feet when he catches up with you,* I told myself.

As if he had deduced my fears, Bear thrust a bundle of dark material into my arms. I took it hesitantly. It was a lined cloak of the same luxurious material as the lord's, minus the exquisite brooch.

"It is hooded, miss," the giant said, still watching me. "The lord's idea."

To cover my hair. My cloak already had a hood, though Lord Adamo had evidently not noticed, or perhaps the garment was too threadbare for his taste. Still, the new cloak would be another layer of warmth. After pulling on my old cloak, I arranged the new one overtop of it, noting that it fastened off-center, near the shoulder, and hung nearly to my ankles. It was lined with fur even softer than the bedspread. I stuffed the cap into my satchel.

"Bear, did you say your name was?"

A decisive nod.

"Is that your real name?"

"Nay, miss, something far more pompous."

"You won't say?"

"Nay. I dislike my given name as much as Bas dislikes his."

I glanced at the door, but the suspicious guard was gone. "And what's *his* real name?"

"Well now, I don't mind sharing his secrets. It's Sebastian."

"A pleasant-enough name."

Bear smirked. "For a dandy, perhaps."

"You seem like you've worked together for a while. Do you get on well?"

"We have to, miss. It's a matter of life and death, I would think."

"How do you mean?"

"Bas and I are brothers. We must cooperate or else find ourselves at the other's throat."

I looked at him in amusement. "Who is older of the two of you?"

Bear scrubbed his thatch of tawny hair, then shifted a large hand to scrape the stubble on his cheeks. If I had to guess, neither guard was much older than the lord. "Who do you think, miss?"

"Bas."

"Because he's the responsible one?"

"Because his worry lines are more pronounced."

The giant laughed—a full, belly laugh that shook his shoulders and chest. "I can worry with the best of them, don't you—well, I was going to say don't you worry. Now, miss, if you've finished your little interrogation regarding my family tree, that carriage is still waiting for us, and the lord with it."

I grinned, pulled the hood over my hair, and followed him down to the stables behind the inn, mindful to avoid staircase squeaks, though no one seemed to be about. In front of the stables stood a large black carriage tethered to four black horses. It appeared a ghostly apparition in the mist that had descended overnight, the large carriage lamps barely penetrating the gloom.

Even with the extra layers, I shivered as Lord Adamo approached. "Miss Winter, allow me to assist you." Without hesitation, he opened the door and handed me inside. My eyes took a moment to adjust to the darkened interior, but it was not the blackness which made me blink rapidly as I sank against the velvety seat.

Didn't Lord Adamo remember I was a slave? He showed me uncommon courtesy, even for a woman. I tried to remind myself that he wasn't anything like the men I'd known, but a cynical voice inside of me wondered if perhaps this was all part of his attempt to win me to his cause. Yet Bas, who was exchanging words with the driver and a handful of guards I hadn't known Lord Adamo commanded, ruined the intended effect with another suspicious glance in my direction.

Before I could return it with a glare of my own, Lord Adamo climbed inside, settling on the forward-facing seat opposite mine. Jewel bounded in after him, though her posture as she positioned herself on the seat was as dignified as any lady's.

Reins slapped against horseflesh, and the carriage jerked forward. I sank deeper into the seat, trying to look anywhere but at Lord Adamo and his strange companion. How had I come to be here, on the road to an unknown city with a perfect stranger and his pet wolf?

But he's not a stranger, came the swift reminder. *You know this man as well as you know Regis. Better, even.*

At least the sour-faced Bas was to ride outside the carriage, or perhaps beside it on a horse of his own. Everything else considered, I was grateful to be out from under his stare. He was not nearly as amicable as his brother.

I snuck a glance at Lord Adamo. He had evidently noticed my unease, for he leaned forward to rummage in a basket at our feet, his knees brushing against mine incidentally. I jerked away, moving closer to the other side of the carriage.

He passed me a wrapped package. I unwound the cheesecloth to find several pieces of bread, five slices of ham, and a wedge of cheese, along with two boiled eggs.

"Humble fare, Miss Winter, but it must do for now."

I stared at him, remembering that Bear had used the same word. But this was a feast, even by old-world standards. Most foods in Nulla were fermented or moldy, and not because they were intended to be consumed that way, or because age improved the taste. "What about you, my lord?"

"I've already eaten." Jewel tilted her head critically, and Lord Adamo gave a faint smile. "Though the lady always appreciates an extra snack."

Over the next half hour of bouncing and jerking that apparently constituted riding in a carriage, I savored the fare, feeding most of the ham to the lady wolf, who accepted the morsels with another condescending incline of her head, as if she were the one doing me the favor.

When I had eaten my fill, I plucked the crumbs from my lap one by one and carefully stowed them in the cheesecloth. Lord Adamo had barely moved a muscle, staring out the window at a landscape no more illuminated than it had been a half hour past as if the fierceness of his look alone could penetrate the darkness.

Finally, he glanced at me, and must have seen my consternation, for he leaned forward again.

"What is it, Miss Winter?"

"The carriage, my lord. I didn't expect—"

"Did you think I would smuggle you out of Nulla in a gunny sack?"

"It would have been far less conspicuous." I pointed outside at the lingering shadows, where the dawning day seemed determined to make a mockery of my words. "We're leaving before first light."

"It is not so unusual. The night cloaks many secrets. It will do nicely for the concealment of ours."

"My lord, regardless of the time, anyone could have seen us leave in this contraption. Cutter—"

"A more furtive departure would only arouse suspicion, Miss Winter. Besides, we will not have the carriage with us forever. It is only for appearances' sake. Once we pass through the seam and reach Iona, it will be horses and rough terrain, I'm afraid."

Maybe he did know what he was doing. "Do you have any idea where to start your search?"

"Aye, an idea. That is where you come in." He clasped his gloved hands between his knees and leaned closer still.

"Miss Winter, from now on, I must call you by a different name."

I raised an eyebrow. Perhaps he would finally call me by the name I preferred.

"I had travel papers prepared for you so we may pass through the seam into Memosine unquestioned. They lack only the name."

"You prepared papers for me before you knew I'd agree to come with you?"

He gave a brief nod. "When I met you the first time, I had a feeling about you."

I let the surprising revelation lie. "And what is my new identity?" It had to be better than being named after the most inhospitable season of the year.

"I thought to refer to you as my sister who has been living in Nulla, but is now returning to Maera with me to rejoin our parents."

"Your sister?" I repeated, eying his gold-brown locks and thinking of my own white-blond hair.

"Aye."

"We could never pass for siblings, my lord."

He regarded me more closely. "Perhaps not, but you're too young to pass as my wife."

I felt a twinge of something prickly, as if I'd taken a tumble in a patch of gorse. I had gleaned the lord's age from his mind: thirty-one years. Half as old as our gray world. But not so old that a false union between us was impossible. Certainly not a gap that warranted the almost fatherly look he was giving me now.

"Lady Nightingale, then," I said on an impulse, remembering the songbird I'd seen.

Lord Adamo frowned.

"My new name. We only met recently, as adults. I am your long-lost sister from a different mother."

"A Lethean lady, I would say, judging by your coloring."

I straightened my spine. Was that where Cutter had found me? Lethe, a land which shunned the past as fervently as Memosine sought to embrace it? Perhaps the mountains I remembered were not the Jackal Mountains, Lord Adamo's home, but the Grennor Mountains, which lay southeast of Nulla.

"Aye, a long-lost sister," Lord Adamo murmured to himself. "Perhaps an illegitimate child from my father."

"After having seen what goes on in Nulla, it is not so far-fetched, is it?"

"I saw only as much of your city as I had to."

"It isn't my city."

"Of course. I know that." He shook himself, one hand absently entwined in Jewel's fur.

I covered a yawn, wondering why, even with the cloak, the carriage seemed so cold. The spreading warmth I'd felt the night before was only a dim memory.

"Your wrist, Miss Wi—Lady Nightingale. Is it better?"

I nodded, lifting the limb and testing it for his benefit. "No damage."

"And the drug they used on you? Any lingering effects?"

Any thought of yawning vanished. I had rarely felt fearful walking the streets of Nulla, not since I'd discovered the extent of my power. But now . . . It had taken only three ordinary men to overpower me. Well, not the men themselves, but the drug they'd used on me. I shivered, remembering how easily the substance had suppressed my gift. Until now, the only man who'd been capable of such a feat was Cutter.

Lord Adamo's mouth twisted sympathetically. "They won't come near you again, I promise."

"It's not that." I tried to explain. "They shouldn't have been able to touch me like that."

He raised an eyebrow. "Three men against a defenseless woman?"

"I wasn't defenseless."

Both man and wolf stared at me without comprehension.

"One small knife is hardly a defense, Lady—" the lord began.

"Not the knife." I turned away. "It hardly matters now."

He settled deeper into his seat, the question he wanted to ask burning in his eyes. But the restraint I'd seen in his mind eventually won out.

"It will be an hour or two before we reach the seam. Should you wish, it would be a good time to seek some more rest."

Though I didn't know how I had managed to sleep in the bumpy carriage, I woke sometime later to find that the conveyance had paused. I was lying on the seat itself, my legs curled up beneath the cloak and my hood covering most of my face. Lifting my head, I touched my cheek and felt the imprint of the seat fabric.

Lord Adamo and the wolf were gone. I sat upright, my heart rate accelerating with the painful leap of dread. Was this the end of our hasty flight? Had Cutter caught up to us already? Worse, had the lord betrayed me?

The door opened and Lord Adamo climbed inside. He gave me a puzzled look.

"Are you all right, Miss Wint—Lady Nightingale?"

I swung my legs down. "Fine. Where are we?"

"We're about to pass through the seam. I stepped outside to hand over the required documents. I didn't think it necessary to wake you, since you were sleeping so deeply."

My heart stuttered even at his reassurances. I skidded over to the window, nearly plastering my face to the glass.

"There's naught to see, not in this gray," came the lord's voice from behind me.

How wrong he was. Nulla squatted in the center of a no-man's-land—a barren, pitted expanse that stretched for miles around the bulk of the city. Its muddy canals were a festering cesspool of misery, freezing in winter and bloating in summer. Apart from the stately specimens in Lord Guerin's manicured garden, not a single tree in or surrounding Nulla stood higher than a man, and nothing green flourished save the algae that bloomed when the water quality was particularly poor. The carriage had followed one of only two safe roads out of the city, and though it had been too dark to see our progress, I knew what surrounded us on all sides: a blistered and hellish landscape, a grim legacy of the war and sabotage that preceded Nulla's birth.

But this—this was different. Though the sun had yet to filter through the gloom in Caldera's version of dawn, there was enough light to see that the world outside was now gently undulating instead of pockmarked. A modest amount of green covered the hills, along with irregular clumps of shadows—*trees*, I realized—actual trees, sprinkled liberally over our surroundings, rather than planted deliberately by a lord's command.

I swung around to face Lord Adamo. "But I thought most of the world was . . . well, more like Nulla." I'd only ever caught glimpses, never enough to form a coherent image.

The lord smiled gently. There were only ten years between us, but his weary expression stretched them to thirty or more. "It *is* like Nulla, Miss Winter. More than you know." He stared out at the landscape. "Caldera labors and groans beneath the curse of the ancestors. No matter how green it becomes, you must never forget that."

"*Lady Nightingale.*"

He grinned, looking more like a young man. "Lady Nightingale. I am sorry."

"I don't know about this lady business, my lord. Would a former thane really refer to his sister by her title?"

He tilted his head, considering. "He might if he had never known her."

At that moment, Jewel climbed back into the carriage, and the lord reached past her and shut the door. The conveyance lurched forward. A lump formed in my throat as we approached the wall separating the neutral ground from Memosine, joining a stream of traffic that had materialized from nowhere. Lord Adamo appeared unruffled, despite possessing forged papers. What if the guards detained us or questioned us more extensively? No one would believe the lord and I were siblings, even half-siblings. Though I could declare honestly that I had known him since childhood.

I had expected the wall to be something like the mighty masterpieces of old, a work of art out of a storybook. The reality was something else entirely. Rather than being made of stones that fit neatly together, it appeared to have been constructed almost entirely from rubble. It wasn't terribly high, being only twice the height of a man in most places—and varying even on that measure. With so many footholds and handholds, Regis and I could have scaled it easily.

Even the gate was only a hacked-out hole in the structure, patrolled by a dozen or so guards from Memosine and a handful from Nulla—the latter distinguishable by their crimson armbands. All of them wore brown leather jerkins instead of armor, and the most heavily armed had crossbows or pikes. I frowned. Surely they couldn't patrol the entire wall—

"Don't let their numbers fool you." The lord had evidently guessed the direction of my thoughts. "The wall is well-protected on the Memosine side."

"Only on the Memosine side?"

"It's not getting into Nulla that's difficult," he replied. "It's getting out again."

So I had heard. I tensed as we approached the head of the column. To the east, I knew, was a river gate that traveled beneath the wall. Would it be guarded as well? No doubt the Memosine guards searched any incoming cargo thoroughly.

To my surprise, the carriage was waved through without delay. I shrank from the window as we passed beneath the wall, though none of the guards had even bothered to look our way. I glanced at Lord Adamo, who was idly patting Jewel. He smiled at my expression.

"I told you I would arrange everything."

"They barely even looked at us."

"They already inspected our papers. Everything was in order."

Was he so influential? I had thought him only a middling thane, but perhaps he was better connected than I'd realized. "Did you bribe them?"

"Of course not." He scratched behind Jewel's ears and muttered, "Not this time, anyway."

"Cutter is well known in these parts, my lord—I daresay, better known even than you. What will happen when he alerts the guards to his escaped slave?" I wrestled with a rising panic. "He could kill me."

The lord sobered, his eyebrows knotting. "You're under my protection now. Besides, once we reach Iona, Cutter will be in *my* territory."

The warm feeling had suddenly returned, heating my belly and traveling along the length of my arms, licking into my fingertips. My panic slowly subsided, yielding to a more welcome sensation—a simmering readiness, like a soldier might feel on his way to a war he has long since accepted he must fight. But the need to caution Lord Adamo remained.

"It will not take much to discover that a black carriage left Nulla before first light and traveled this way. You and Lady Jewel are memorable, my lord. And Cutter has money aplenty to loosen tongues."

I didn't mention Cutter's gift of instilling fear or that he had some ability as a *mem* himself. Even without his gifts, his instincts were sharper than a wolfhound's.

"For that, we have the second carriage," the lord said, fixing his dark eyes on me.

"The second carriage?"

"A diversion. One might say a decidedly southwestern diversion. It will slow him down, or at least halve his resources."

He grinned again, and I could not help smiling back.

"Never fear, Lady Nightingale. Once we reach Iona, I will arrange a disguise for you that will discourage any further questions. And by the time he arrives in Iona, I think your master will find our trail has not only gone cold, but vanished altogether."

9

DORIAN

His gift had calmed her, at least enough not to ask any more panicked questions in the hour or so it took to reach the outskirts of Iona. He had concluded that it must affect her more than the average person, for she seemed to almost come alive in his presence, even though he was hardly aware he'd released any of his power. Not for the first time, he wished he was not immune to its effects so he might better gauge its potency.

Though Miss Winter was clearly afraid of her master, she was not at all afraid of Dorian—not even after learning he wielded more influence than she'd first realized. Her posture appeared relaxed, though her eyes remained riveted to the window as the blackish-gray of the morning gave way to a dreary whitish-gray. If not for the fact that he'd been awake most of the night, and had thus been acutely aware of each passing hour, he would have thought it near dusk.

A raw flame ignited in his chest, searing his lungs. Oh, how he wanted to be back in Maera with Lida and Emmy. He quickly squelched the burst of longing. He had learned never to disturb those memories, not unless he wanted to be scalded by reality when he abruptly returned to the present.

Miss Winter continued her vigil as they approached Iona, soaking in every detail and development with childlike delight. Dorian sank back against the seat, having visited the city many times before. He supposed Iona was prettier than Nulla, in the same way that water is preferable to mud. Not walled like Maera, but nonetheless heavily patrolled, with an impossible crisscrossing of deep-rutted streets that would probably confound Miss Winter's mind after the fetid, lifeless grid that was her home city. But to him, it was just another place Lida would never again accompany him.

He had never seen Iona so busy. The streets were packed with throngs of people—more for the *mem* to take in. He watched her eyes widen. The carriage reached a gridlock as it entered the main street, becoming stuck behind a cluster of carts as people swarmed the street around them.

Miss Winter sat back from the window. "They're angry."

"Iona's thane is nearing the end of his term. There's probably some kind of protest up ahead. He isn't the best of lords."

The *mem* leaned forward again, searching the faces of those who pushed and shoved around them. A horse whinnied, and Dorian straightened. Jewel's ears pricked.

"Their cheeks are hollow," Miss Winter was murmuring. "I thought it was only Nulla that saw such hunger. And the children . . ."

There she was again, the heart-on-her-sleeve girl. Dorian followed her gaze. The people of Iona certainly seemed a thinner and more bedraggled lot than when he'd last visited. The hard, brittle place inside of him cracked slightly, a hairline fracture that ran the length of the vast space. He found himself watching the *mem* as she watched the townspeople.

If anyone could understand his loss, it would be her. Was that why he'd decided on her after only a few minutes in her company? Her compassion blew some of the dust from his long-dormant memories, his stowed-away heart. After Lida and Emmy's deaths, he had closed himself off to the pain of others, unable as he was to bear the portion assigned to him. Sephone Winter was a slave, and yet she turned her focus outward rather than retreating into herself. How did she manage that? And what would she do when she realized the rest of Caldera was more a cousin to Nulla than a stranger?

A man hollered something vulgar, and one of the horses shrieked, as if in reaction. The carriage jerked and shuddered as the horses shifted in their harnesses. Dorian recognized the raised voices of his guards.

"Stay here," he instructed Miss Winter, who flinched as a fist banged on the side of the carriage. He opened the door—a difficult feat with the crowd pressing so close—and squeezed out, leaving Jewel to guard the *mem*. His gift, of course, would be useless here.

"There's naught for it, my lord!" Bear called as he reined in his horse beside Dorian, looking like an enormous boulder lodged in the path of a swelling river. "The traffic only gets worse up ahead."

Dorian glanced up at Bas, perched on the coach seat next to the driver. "How far are we from the inn?"

"Not far, my lord," Bas replied. "You could leave the carriage here with me and the driver and continue with Bear on foot." He waved a hand to indicate the two mounted guards Dorian had hired in Erebus, now bringing up the rear of their procession. "They can follow at a distance. Best get the girl to safety."

The bodyguard's expression had turned skeptical. While Bas wouldn't slip up and refer to her as *Miss Winter*, they'd be hard-pressed in getting him to call her *Lady Nightingale*. Bas wouldn't be moved, as Dorian had been, by the relief that she had chosen a different name than his, for there could only ever be one Lady Adamo. And when he found out she would be masquerading as Dorian's sister . . .

Someone shoved against Dorian's back, and he caught himself, quickly regaining his balance. He called up to the driver. "Are you all right with that plan, Kade?"

The driver nodded and hastily returned his attention to calming the panicked horses. Dorian retreated to the carriage, the townspeople moving out of his path when they saw Bear on horseback behind him. Prying open the door, he glimpsed Miss Winter, her white hair ghostly around her pale face. He extended a gloved hand to her.

"A slight change in plans, Lady Nightingale. I'm afraid we'll have to walk the rest of the way."

She barely hesitated in taking his hand, but held it only as long as was required to reach the ground safely. He had noticed that about her, how she avoided human touch. She even ate with her gloves on. Was it because she was a *mem*, or because she was chary of him after all?

Jewel followed Miss Winter. They would have to retrieve their possessions later, including his quarterstaff, which he had neglected to fasten to his belt. Bear had dismounted and led his horse beside them, flanking Miss Winter on one side as Dorian did on the other, while Jewel trotted behind. Miss Winter had the sense to keep her hood up, concealing her uncommonly short hair. No point in any of the townspeople marking the fact that Lord Adamo had recently acquired a slave.

Dorian tried to shield the *mem* as they pushed through the crowd, heading in the opposite direction to the human tide. What had them so riled? Lord Faro was a pompous fool, but he had been that way for years. Besides, the people of Iona were normally a sluggish folk, much like the thane who ruled them. Very little stirred them to leave their beds, let alone their houses. Perhaps Faro had a challenger at last.

After some time, they reached the sidewalk, and at a nod from Dorian, Bear went ahead of them. Dorian took the *mem*'s arm as she peered into a shopfront cluttered with glass bottles.

"They're memories," she said in wonder, forgetting to flinch at his touch.

"The streets of Iona are full of such places," he replied, gently steering her away. "None have the reputation of your master's shop, though."

"You've visited them, then?"

"Aye." Little did she know that he had been inside every single one. Not one *mem* had been suitable for the mission he was planning; the quality of the memories they extracted was either dull or hazy, and their powers were weak, unfocused, or not yet in full bloom. A single sip of a memory purchased from Cutter's shop had revealed a startling potency that persuaded him to make the trip to Nulla directly. The youngest of the *mems* he'd interviewed, Sephone Winter had more talent than all the rest put together.

Now he just had to transform her into a woman who could pass as his sister.

The crowds dissipated as they traveled further from the city center. From the shouts of passersby—in both the common tongue and the language of Memosine—he learned that Faro indeed had a new challenger, a man even younger than Dorian. Each of the major cities of Memosine operated under their own system of election, though all were required to produce a thane who would rule over the city and answer to the arch-lord.

In Iona, the ruling thane was appointed by a private council, which, until now, had been almost completely in Faro's pocket. Dorian hoped his arrival would go unnoticed, for if Faro knew of his presence, he would parade Dorian's friendship in front of the council members as proof of his influence with other lords. And Dorian had no wish to see any of them. They were all remnants of a life better forgotten.

Reaching the inn where he had stayed when last in Iona, Dorian led the way up the servant's stairs to the rooms Bear had procured for them. There were two this time, joined by a common door. On seeing them, Dorian winced at the realization that he and Lida had once stayed in the very chamber where Miss Winter would become Lady Nightingale. It was an almost perfect replica of the room in Nulla, as luxurious and nondescript as any he'd temporarily inhabited from Calliope to Orphne.

Dorian watched as the *mem* ran her wondering gaze over every corner of the room. "Bear will guard your door tonight. We'll leave on the morrow, once all the arrangements are made."

"The arrangements, my lord?"

"Your disguise." He purposefully avoided looking at the bed, not wanting to think of Lida. "If you are to become Lady Nightingale, you must look the part."

A knock sounded at the door, and Bear entered, looking disgruntled. "Good news and bad news, my lord."

"Bad news first." Dorian braced himself.

"One of Lord Faro's minions saw you leave your carriage. He's invited you and your lady companion to dinner."

Dorian bit down on a curse. For a sluggish man, Faro moved quickly. "He knows she's my sister?" Coughing over the word for emphasis, he glanced at Miss Winter, whose back was to them as she peered out the window at the street below.

"Aye, though I put out the word, just in case."

"Thank you, Bear. And the good news you mentioned?"

His bodyguard nodded at Miss Winter. "There's no talk of an escaped slave."

At that, she turned around. "Cutter hasn't come for me?" Despite her casual tone, Dorian saw what she attempted to hide: her rigid posture, clenched fists, and corded throat.

"Yet." Dorian moved to the window. "We cannot linger here." *For your sake and mine.* He thought of the sleepless night that lay ahead of him. At least she wouldn't hear him tossing and turning in the other room, attempting to make his body comfortable while his mind floundered in agony.

At the steadiness in his tone, a calm settled over her, and she turned to face the window again. He'd been careful to keep the urgency of their escape from her, pretending nonchalance even while his gut churned with anxiety. He was well aware that by stealing her, he'd acquired a dangerous enemy. Cutter's reach extended well into Memosine. Only a fool would underestimate him.

But the former thane of Maera had his own resources. He would hide Miss Winter in plain sight, beneath the noses of the very lords most likely to recognize her. After leaving Iona, they would plunge into the wilderness, leaving behind the established roads. By the time they resurfaced again—hopefully with the Reliquary in their possession— Cutter would have given up on the chase.

Dorian hauled in a breath. Relief was in sight. And the *mem* would be well compensated for her troubles.

One step at a time.

He winced again, thinking of Lord Faro and the type of parties he liked to throw. It would be a big first step. As if she knew how many hours of work lay ahead of them, Jewel tossed her stately head and made for an armchair.

"A word, Bear," Dorian said to his bodyguard, with a tilt of his head that indicated it would be had outside.

"Now lift up your shoulders and breathe in," came the stern, matronly voice from behind the screen. Dorian heard Miss Winter's indrawn gasp of pain.

"It's too tight. It doesn't fit."

"It fits well enough, my lady. Now take another breath."

She must have obeyed, for the dressmaker clucked her tongue in approval. Dorian waited near the fireplace at a safe distance, Jewel draped gracefully across the couch opposite. She looked distinctly bored.

"I don't understand, my lord," Bas whispered, hovering at his shoulder. "If you need this girl for your quest for the Reliquary, why not leave her as she is? Why go to such lengths to pretend she is your sister?"

Dorian turned to face his bodyguard, whose features were rigid with tension. So, Bear had finally informed his brother of their plan. "Her former master will pursue her, Bas. And I am hardly out of the public eye. A disguise protects us both."

Bas's lower lip curled. He snagged it between his teeth and began to chew with startling ferocity. "You haven't known this girl longer than a day. You don't know her from a stranger."

"She could say the same of us, Bas."

"Well, she has the advantage on that front."

Dorian frowned as Bas continued to glare at the screen, behind which the dressmaker was transforming a slave into a lady.

"You can't trust her sort, my lord."

"*Alters*, Bas, or only *mems*?"

Bas's eyes went wide as he realized his error. "You're hardly one of *them*, my lord."

"I am absolutely 'one of them,' Bas, whoever 'them' is. Miss Winter had no more choice over the appearance of her gift than I did."

He wondered when hers had first manifested. He had only been seven when his parents, despairing of servant after servant who could not help but speak their minds, had finally seen the iridescence in their son's hair and realized the truth.

"Besides, Miss Winter ventured only as far into my mind as I allowed her to. You have no need to fear she will stumble upon our secrets."

By our secrets, of course, he meant the secrets of Bas, whose past was a mystery to everyone except Dorian and Bear. Dorian guessed he was anxious to keep it that way.

Bas's frown turned sullen as Miss Winter stepped out from behind the screen; the dressmaker was close behind, her hands glued together in satisfaction. Miss Winter was decidedly less pleased.

"My gloves," was the first thing she said to him.

"Thank you, Dela," Dorian said to the dressmaker as he climbed to his feet. "That will be all. Bas here will arrange for your payment."

A pointed look at the bodyguard was enough to compel Bas to accompany the dressmaker out into the corridor, leaving Dorian alone with Miss Winter.

He turned back to the *mem*, who was wringing her hands, and not at all in satisfaction. Yet Dela had done well. In contrast to her usual attire, Miss Winter wore a sleeveless emerald-green dress made of some shimmery fabric that fell in loose folds to her feet. Wearing the stays she had been protesting before, and with the wide, copper-colored belt at her waist, her figure could almost be called lissome, though her skin was too pale to be fashionable, and the face powder could not conceal all of her freckles.

But the real transformation was her hair—or rather, the wig covering her hair. The brown, curling locks had been twisted into a coif at the back of her head that appeared both simple and elegant. Her slightly darker eyebrows meant that the hair color looked almost natural.

Dela had not just done well, she had outdone herself. What good fortune that her unparalleled skills came with discretion to match. Dorian trusted her because she had once waited on Lida, and not for the first time, he mentally praised his wife's good judgment. She had always had a good sense of people.

Even at the end.

Miss Winter toyed with the cuffs encircling her bare upper arms. "I understand that you must attend Lord Faro's gathering, my lord, but I cannot leave here without gloves."

"They will only arouse suspicion." He smiled to put her at ease; though good humor had once been second nature for him, his cheek muscles now felt stiff and unyielding. "There are plenty of *alters* in

Iona, Miss Winter. Some of their gifts are quite remarkable. Not all hide away as you do."

"Not all have to."

Dorian thought of Bas and was silent.

"What if you said I was sick?" Miss Winter toed one of the elegant slippers, which had replaced her knee-length boots, submerging the bejeweled shoe in the thick fur carpet.

"Again, suspicion." He crossed the room to stand in front of her, nodding at the serpentine cuffs. "I'm afraid they'll have to go, too."

"Gladly." She tugged them from her arms, depositing them in the satchel that lay beside the bed. "What about you, my lord?" she asked, glancing at his hair.

"On occasions like these, I use a powder that conceals the iridescence. If your hair was as long as a free woman's, you could use it instead of wearing the wig. When it is long again, I will share it with you. You will be able to conceal your gift if you wish to."

A wistful look drifted over her features before she brushed it away. A longing to be more than the slave she was? Or mere feminine vanity? After all, she had probably never been allowed to grow her hair.

"Then your subjects don't know of your powers, my lord?"

"Of course they do. Or rather, they did. In Maera, there is no reason to hide who I am. But Lord Faro is something of a showman. I would rather not be put on display tonight." *Or any other night.*

"Why can you not decline the invitation altogether?"

"As I said—"

"Suspicion."

"Aye. We must keep up appearances. And if you were truly my sister—Lady Nightingale—it would be considered the height of rudeness to shun Faro's gathering, unless you were on your deathbed."

Ignoring her hopeful look, his attention snagged on the necklace she was still wearing.

"May I?"

She nodded, and he lifted the charm from her skin, studying the delicate white flowers trapped forever in their transparent resin prison. Simple, but exquisite, like the charm itself.

"This is yours?"

Another nod. "From my parents. The only thing I have from them." A sudden energy sparked in her eyes—hope, he thought. "Do you recognize the flowers, my lord?"

"Not really, but something about them tickles my memory. Like waking from a dream and having the faintest recollection of the details."

The light in her eyes didn't drain away, as he might have expected. "Perhaps you could try to remember."

"To be honest, Miss Winter, in most matters pertaining to the past, I do my best to forget."

"Lady Nightingale."

Again, she surprised him, staring into his eyes as an equal. It would seem that they had something else in common despite their disparate looks and pasts: a will that was not easily swayed or broken. Yet beneath her aristocratic confidence was a certain vulnerability that, like iridescence itself, sometimes eluded the eye.

At least the lessons he must give her in how to be a lady would be short. She already possessed the spirit. He had only to show her the steps, and only for this one night of pretending.

He extended his arm to her. "Lady Nightingale."

Without my gloves, I felt almost naked as I walked beside Lord Adamo, clutching his arm from the inside. But I did not need my powers to discern that with every step, a change came over the lord. By the time we reached the street where Lord Faro's manor house stood, my hand was practically pinned against his side.

At first glance, Iona had seemed as much like Nulla as summer was like winter. There were actual streets instead of filthy canals, though they were muddy from recent rains and scarred by the passage of many feet. Still, they were wide and largely free from refuse, lined on both sides by tall buildings, two or even three stories high. Some of them had more than a lick of paint in shades besides brown or black, and I had even seen flowers in some of the window boxes. I had to bite my tongue so I did not ask to stop at every shopfront, for it appeared that some inhabitants of Iona had more in mind than the immediate pursuit of past pleasures.

But by the time we stepped out of the inn after dark, heading for the manor house on the north side of the city, with Lord Adamo's guards trailing at a distance, a different city awaited. The passionate protestors had vanished, replaced by the same sorts who inhabited Nulla at night. Though it had appeared a respectable part of town, there were figures slumped against the walls of houses or shops; bottles of varying shapes, colors, and sizes clutched in their hands; their eyes so glazed it did not seem they even registered the wintry chill. Several figures walked along the street, huddled in blankets or ragged cloaks, gazing longingly into dusty shop windows that gleamed with warmth. There were at least half a dozen women, and even a few children, with their skin exposed to the elements—not by choice, and not unlike myself.

I gripped Lord Adamo's arm more tightly. "My lord, there are—"

"Do not look, Lady Nightingale," he replied through gritted teeth. "It is not your burden to bear. Not tonight, at least."

"Not tonight? When might be a suitable time?" Heat licked through my veins.

Lord Adamo halted in the middle of the street, forcing me to a stop beside him. The same glazed, indifferent look had settled over his eyes. "What would you do for them? The effects of your gift last but a few days at most."

My arm slipped from his. "What of food and other essentials?"

"Don't you see, Lady Nightingale? These people long for far more than food."

Without another word, he continued along the street.

I had always assumed it was only because of men like Lord Guerin and Traemore that most of Nulla's citizens lived in poverty. Memosine greatly surpassed Nulla in wealth. Was Lord Adamo right, that Nulla was not the exception in Caldera, but the rule?

You can't save the whole world, Seph, Regis had often told me.

At the thought of Regis, I hurried to catch up with Lord Adamo. Melancholy and wounded man or not, I had to play my part as his sister, or else Cutter would hear of my ineptitude. And even an entire city's worth of indifference would be nothing compared to his wrath.

Trying not to fidget with the uncomfortable weight of hair that was not my own and the painful intrusion of several dozen pins, I followed Lord Adamo up a flight of stone stairs and into the foyer of a manor house that made Lord Guerin's mansion look like a tree house. Though it had appeared inconspicuous from the street, on the inside it was a marvel of polished wood, white marble, crystal glass, and wallpaper so exquisite it might have been hand-painted.

A servant took Lord Adamo's dark blue mantle and my cloak. The lord extended his arm again, and I accepted it, careful to touch only his sleeve. He guided me to the right of the parlor as if he'd been in this house before. Sure enough, we passed through a magnificent set of gold-leaf double doors into a room five times the size of Cutter's tavern. We were quickly lost in a crowd of people and plants.

I blinked twice. *Plants?* Yet the room was no mere sitting room, but an indoor hothouse that boasted more greenery than I'd seen in a hundred forays through Lord Guerin's mind. Broad-leafed plants several feet taller than a man were stationed at various points around the room, presiding over animated clusters of chattering people, while curtains of fragrant, flowering vines had been draped extravagantly over wrought iron frames, creating natural arbors and alcoves where more private conversations might be had.

The ivy-like tendrils of one of the largest plants trailed along the mantelpiece of an enormous marble hearth at the opposite end of the room, while bunches of wildflowers were stashed in vases on almost every visible surface, along with hundreds of lanterns and naked candles held aloft on iron candelabra. The heady, spiced perfume of dozens of varieties of flowers drifted in the air, mingled with candle wax and the full spectrum of human scent.

In the center of the room, most ludicrously of all, was an enormous fountain, water spouting from the beaks of two entwined marble swans rousing themselves to flight. The fountain itself was made from what must have been thousands of tiny fragments of hand-painted pottery and cut glass, sparkling like jewels in the lantern light. Adding to the effect was a glittering chandelier about four feet at its longest point, dripping tear-shaped crystals from the highest point of the vaulted ceilings.

I had never seen anything so beautiful.

Lord Faro's guests were no less impressive. Though there were always flickers of the world-that-was in Lord Guerin's mind, naught could have prepared me for the exotic riot of color that was the upper class of Iona.

In my travels to a long-dead world, I had once seen a bird called a peafowl. The male of the species boasted an enormous train of feathers on which was suspended dozens of haunted eyes. Its plumage might have been the unspoken theme of the evening's fashion, a somewhat garish palate of iridescent blue and green, gold, bronze, and copper, proudly incorporated into dresses, jewelry, or even tiny crowns woven into hairstyles far more elaborate than mine. Even the men wore tunics in the same rich shades as the women. Most of the guests were standing and talking, though a few couples danced to the lively music emanating from a nearby instrument—invisible to my eye at present, but likely a pianoforte—or playing games at tables.

Amid such beauty, I knew better than to imagine tongues would wag on our entrance. Perhaps the busybodies of this upper crust could find something to gossip about Lord Adamo, who looked rather striking in his black breeches, scarlet tunic, embroidered shirtsleeves, and knee-length boots.

But they would hardly spare a glance for his sister. Even in the finery he'd selected for me, I was plain next to him. I'd observed as much in the mirror Dela had directed me to after fixing my hair. If naught else, a childhood in Nulla, at Cutter's knee, had taught me to see things for what they truly were.

Still, my one task for tonight was to blend in. I was meant to be illegitimate, after all. It was the sole responsibility of an illegitimate child to never attract any more attention than the circumstances of one's birth already had. Luckily, I had had a great deal of practice at that as a slave.

Lord Adamo, who seemed as unaffected by the sumptuous display before us as he had been by the street outside, leaned down to whisper in my ear. "Do you see the *alters*?"

I shook my head.

"Look." He pointed across the room at a young man with hair the color of liquid gold who was surrounded by a large group of onlookers. Holding a violin beneath his chin, he stroked the strings so lovingly it might have been his own wife he caressed. The faces of those around him were seized in an almost divine rapture, their eyes closed and their hands clawing at their breasts, as if the room had become unbearably hot.

"What is he doing to them?"

"He plays only a simple melody, but to them, it sounds like an orchestra, an audible form of ecstasy. He can make them feel any emotion he wishes."

My mouth fell open as Lord Adamo continued his tour, indicating a woman who was seated at a small table nearby with several others. Her violet skirts and glittering amethyst jewelry were unremarkable compared to her hair, which was as white as my own but so long it hung to her waist in lustrous, interwoven braids that looked softer than silk. As the woman spoke animatedly with her companions, a reddish jewel materialized in her left hand. A ruby, I realized, just as the gem caught the sideways glance of a lantern, scattering fractals of vivid crimson light around the room, splashing onto the faces of her admirers, who clapped with glee. Every person in the room swiveled to watch her.

Nay, there was no chance of them noticing me.

I turned back to Lord Adamo. "What just happened?"

"Lady Cilla has the ability to capture the essence of something—a thought, a feeling, an image, or even an idea—in a jewel like the one you see there. She then uses her power to project it outwards. It is not so strange. You do something similar with your memories, do you not?"

"My memories hardly flood an entire room with light."

Was the lord's gifting as remarkable as these? He had already revealed he had not one, but *two* gifts. Why would he not share the nature of either with me? I was sure one of them had something to do with the warmth I sometimes felt in his company.

"Adamo!"

The lord tensed as a man approached us at a jog, his arms flung open wide as if he welcomed a brother and not merely a friend. He was not much older than Lord Adamo and had a pleasant face, but his ridiculous ensemble ruined some of the effect. Dressed in a gleaming, gold tunic with silver breeches and polished copper boots, even the air around the newcomer seemed to shimmer, though no iridescence clung to the man himself. He wore his flaxen hair dangerously long for a free man, securing it at the nape of his neck in a ponytail with a gold-colored ribbon.

"Lord Faro," Lord Adamo returned with a short dip of his head just as the other man drew him into a bear hug. I felt Lord Adamo's cringe, though our host seemed not to notice.

Lord Faro released him and stared at me. Faint lines tugged at his mouth, whether in pleasure or disapproval, I could not say. "And who is this lovely lady, Adamo? You have remarried at last." He spoke in the common tongue, like most of Iona, though his pronunciation betrayed a distinct accent.

"It is only eighteen months since I lost Lida," Lord Adamo replied through lips so tightly pursed I wondered how they managed to emit any sound. "This is my half-sister, Lady Nightingale. We were only recently acquainted after the circumstances of her birth were brought to my attention."

I tried not to stare at Lord Adamo, pity pulsing through every vein. *Eighteen months*? No wonder he was so desperate for relief. He was still in deep mourning for his wife.

My musings were interrupted by Lord Faro, who had swooped on my hand with astonishing speed, raising it to his lips for a kiss. I tried not to cringe as the soft pressure of his mouth was followed by a half-second of vulgar images that might have belonged in the devil's own family album. His mind was altogether too much like Lord Guerin's.

I bowed and smiled at our host, hoping my disgust was invisible to him. "A pleasure to meet you, Lord Faro. Thank you for hosting us tonight."

He nodded and began a conversation with Lord Adamo, which appeared almost completely one-sided, punctuated by hearty slaps of the lord's shoulder and abrupt interjections of "ah, those were the days!" There was no mention of the man who'd apparently challenged him.

My attention wandered. The violinist's admirers had dissipated, and he was now deep in conversation with a raven-haired lady in a semi-private arbor that hid both their faces from view. Lady Cilla was still at her table, playing some sort of game with rounded stones marked with differently colored chalk. Whatever the rules, judging by the delight on her face, she seemed to be winning.

"Lady Nightingale."

I glanced up at Lord Adamo, who was watching me carefully. Lord Faro had disappeared.

"Might I introduce you to my acquaintances?"

Noting he did not say *friends*, I nodded and allowed him to lead me around the room. Not all present had titles, though there seemed to be several lords and even a few thanes visiting from neighboring towns and cities. They were only mildly curious about Lord Adamo's long-lost sister, seeming far more interested in whether or not he had yet avenged his murdered family. I saw his face tighten at every careless question or shameless probe, his lips a flattened line.

I was in no better shape.

"Excuse me, my lord," I whispered after the eighth man had kissed my hand. I twisted my trembling fingers together behind my back. "But I am a little thirsty. I might seek some refreshment, if you don't mind."

By the look on his face, Lord Adamo was clearly engaged elsewhere, and not pleasantly so, but he nodded. "Of course, Lady Nightingale."

I slipped away, heading for the table that offered liquid refreshments, catching a glimpse of Bas weaving between shifting bodies, dressed in humble servant's garb and offering trays of appetizers to the guests. From Lord Adamo's instructions, I knew Bear would sleep for a few hours before taking over guard duty when we returned to the inn.

If possible, the room had grown more crowded, and I soon lost sight of Lord Adamo. Someone trod on the hem of my dress, and I reached down to hitch it up, bemoaning the absence of my gloves as yet another person brushed against my arm, their mind exposed to my perusal.

Turning, I nearly collided with a man about Lord Adamo's height. He reached out and gripped my arms to steady me, concern flashing across his youthful features.

His hands might as well have been made of burning coals.

I gasped, peering into his mind as easily as I had gazed into Dela's mirror earlier. Bile rose in my throat. There was blood—so much blood, I could taste its coppery tang in my mouth. A woman screamed, her voice streaked with blind terror. A young girl's lip wobbled, fat tears dribbling from the glassy corners of cornflower-blue eyes. Blond hair slick with crimson-red, the same color as Lady Cilla's jewel—

It's not real. It's not real . . .

But it was real. It just wasn't happening right now.

I jerked back from his hold, trying to reconcile the nightmarish horrors I had witnessed with the amiable, handsome face before me . . . a face that somehow looked familiar. Thick, rust-colored locks drifted almost lazily about his ears. He had a pair of well-shaped eyebrows of a slightly darker hue than his hair, and blue eyes, a warmer blue than Jewel's.

Were they his memories? Or another's, consumed like one of Cutter's potions? For I had recognized the faces . . . that lemon-gold hair . . .

"Lady Nightingale, isn't it?" The man inclined his head, surveying me from wig to jeweled slippers, though his gaze would find little on which to linger, even with the help of the stays. "Lord Adamo's little sister." Lips that could only be described as sensuous curved in an appealing smile. "I must admit, I do not see the resemblance." He spoke in the common tongue, as if he instinctively knew I wasn't born of Memosine.

I scrabbled for composure, hoping he would attribute my nervousness to my near-fall. "Lord Adamo and I are only half-siblings, and my mother was Lethean-born. But I'm afraid I do not know you, my lord."

"Rufus Karthick," he replied. "Though you may call me Lord Draven."

The blood surging through my veins turned to ice. Lord *Draven*? The man who had ordered the murders of Lord Adamo's family—

"Would you like to dance, Lady Nightingale? I hear the music starting up again."

I stared at his proffered arm, my thoughts racing as I searched for a reason to politely reject him. He didn't know I was a *mem*. He didn't know that without gloves, every second I spent in proximity to him would be an eternity of torture. But what about Lord Adamo? What if I saw something in Lord Draven's mind which could bring the lord's family's killers to justice? Even if Lord Draven proved to be innocent, he might still know something.

"I don't really dance," I finally answered lamely, though it would be easy enough to discover the steps in his mind. I was a fast learner that way.

"I have been told I dance well enough for two."

A servant—not Bas—came past carrying a tray with an array of colorful glass vials arranged in a seashell pattern. Though Lord Adamo had said there would be a feast afterward, I knew many of the "dishes" would be liquid memories. In Nulla, most of the food the common folk grew or imported was plain and serviceable, meant only to keep us alive. Much of it was fermented for longevity. But the upper class of Nulla had long been in pursuit of finer fare, hardly caring that some of the dishes they "tasted" had been consumed more than sixty years ago.

As I watched, Lord Draven plucked a vial from the tray—the same emerald-green as my dress—unstoppered the cork, and tossed the drink down his throat. His eyes briefly lidded in pleasure.

"Ah, peppermint candy. Delicious."

He stepped closer and I smelled it on his breath—the unmistakable scent of peppermint. I remembered—as well as you could remember a memory that was not your own—how it tasted: like I'd sucked on a sharp breath of cold wind.

"You're not in mourning like your brother?"

"Nay," I quickly replied. "I learned of that terrible tragedy only recently. I hope my brother finds the killer soon. It is a dreadful loss."

His eyes flickered with faux sympathy. "A dreadful loss, indeed. Well, Lady Nightingale, it grows late. Shall we dance?"

Lord Draven extended his hand again. A violin had joined the pianoforte, and the tune had turned mournful. I had heard of these Memosinian parties, which reveled in the glories and triumphs of the ancient past until the early hours of the morning, telling stories and singing songs about the world-that-was, even sharing in their long-forgotten victories. A man like Lord Draven might consume hundreds of vials during the course of such an evening. Memosinians were always hungry for something new, which Cutter typically translated as a desire for something very old—something which felt novel only because it had been briefly lost to living memory.

Do it for Lord Adamo. I frowned at the small voice in my head, reminding me I still owed the lord for the debt I'd incurred as a young girl. Regardless of whether or not he knew what I owed him.

But the reminder was enough. With only the briefest of hesitations, I reached out and placed my hand in Lord Draven's.

I had been in contact with him only a second before I knew two things for certain. The first was that Lord Draven wasn't an *alter*, which I'd fleetingly feared.

The second was that he was indeed the man responsible for the murders of Lord Adamo's wife and daughter.

On learning the truth, I nearly wrenched my hand away. A tidal wave of nausea turned my stomach. It was one thing to see horrors in the mind of another person, but it was something else entirely to know that the man with whom you were dancing was responsible for them. And not just because he'd ordered it done.

Because he'd accomplished the grisly task himself.

I saw Lord Adamo—or Dorian, as Lord Draven thought of him— lying semi-conscious and bleeding on the ground, barely six feet from the mutilated bodies of his wife and daughter. He hadn't known Lord Draven was present that day, only discovering afterward that his rival had ordered the attack. But I knew the name of the man in the brown hood with the scarf concealing the lower half of his face. I saw what the shadows had refused to reveal that night, the night Dorian Ashwood's world had shattered forever.

Trapped in Lord Draven's embrace, I followed his lead in the dance, heedless of the song a tenor was singing nearby, his words no more comprehensible than smudges of ink. The lord's hold was firm, one hand clamped at my waist while the other gripped my hand. He did not twirl me as the other partners did, preferring to keep me close, within the realm of his peppermint-scented breath.

I bid the black tendrils of my gift to remain unnoticed. Most casual brushes with another person's skin were not enough to summon them, but they usually appeared with a more deliberate incursion into a mind. Hopefully Lord Draven was too occupied with his dancing to notice the delicate vines sinking into his palm.

"You seem distracted, Lady Nightingale," he said after maybe a minute had passed, or possibly a hundred years. I was sifting through the vile horrors of his inner world, searching for anything that might aid Lord Adamo in bringing the man to justice.

I dragged my eyes up to his, deciding on a sliver of the truth. "I'm sorry, my lord. I grew up in Nulla, you see. Unlike Dorian—I mean, Lord Adamo—I'm not used to fine dresses or fancy parties. It's all a bit . . . overwhelming."

There. Even Lord Adamo would be pleased with that explanation; the seemingly careless slip betraying my familiarity with my supposed brother and the honesty that hinted at a lack of ladylike decorum. To emphasize the point, I deliberately missed a step, catching the corner of Lord Draven's boot.

Would that I could stomp on the whole foot.

Lord Draven proffered a patient smile. "You will learn our ways in time, my lady."

Little did he know that I knew more of his ways than I could possibly stomach. The small lunch I had eaten earlier curdled in my belly, and I knew I wouldn't consume anything else tonight.

"You know, Lady Nightingale, I heard that Lord Adamo had a sister. But he says so little about his family, I consider it a joy to finally meet one of their number."

"He never knew I existed," I replied, clamping down my fury. "Not until recently."

"An illicit love affair?" Lord Draven's eyes lit with curiosity. "Adamo's father and your mother?"

It seemed unfair to besmirch the reputation of a man I did not even know, a man who was quite possibly happily married. But Lord Adamo had agreed to this deception as our cover story.

"Aye. She was a servant, a Lethean woman. He didn't know she had had a child until several months ago when she finally sent word. Dorian came to find me on his father's behalf."

"No doubt he was overjoyed to discover he had family members he didn't know he had left." The blue eyes glinted at his private joke.

I forced myself to shrug. "We are very different, but we are learning to get along."

Lord Draven gave a rich, effortlessly elegant chuckle. Were it not for my gift, I would never have known him to be the hideous monster he was.

His fingers curled around my lower back, securing me closer to him. The peppermint wafting from his mouth might as well have been sulfur vapors. He gripped my hand more tightly. "Adamo can be brooding and difficult at times. But you can always call upon my assistance, Lady Nightingale, should you ever require it."

I'd sooner summon the devil for a mind-bleeding. With every ounce of courage I had, I dredged up a smile I hoped looked both sweet and naïve.

"Why thank you, Lord Draven. You're too kind." A vague and insipid comment, which a normal girl of my age might make when flattered by an older man.

"One can never be too kind, Lady Nightingale, but you make me want to try."

I realized then, belatedly, that he'd drawn us away from the other dancers and into one of the little alcoves, one of the towering, leafy plants shielding us from onlookers. I'd allowed myself to be distracted by his memories and his conversation. A quiver of uncertainty went through me. Might he know who I really was? But he couldn't—Dela had been sworn to secrecy, and I'd already seen that Lord Adamo's bodyguards were devoted to him.

"You know, my lady, there's something different about you." His hand slid from my fingers to my wrist. I felt his raw, masculine strength. My usual concrete self-assurance that I could easily defend myself using my powers already bore a tiny fracture in the wake of the drugging and kidnapping attempt. Somewhere out there was a substance which counteracted my gift. And this man had already proved he was capable of murdering women and children. His ascension to power had left a long trail of corpses in its wake, including that of his own brother. If he discovered I was a *mem—*

"I cannot quite put my finger on it." He stroked the rapid pulse at my wrist, gazing down into my eyes. Again, I was startled by a flicker of familiarity—the feeling that I'd met him before. But I'd never known anyone by the name of Rufus Karthick, at least not until Lord Adamo had called him Lord Draven.

"Thank you for the dance, my lord. But I must return to my brother now."

"Of course."

He didn't let me go. Could he see my true hair color beneath the wig?

"Will you be long in Iona, Lady Nightingale? A pretty name, by the way."

"Thank you. And nay, we leave tomorrow." I clenched my teeth so hard a muscle spasmed in my jaw.

"I will be sad to see you go so soon. You can't be persuaded to stay a little longer?"

Did he think I was fooled by his faux charm and handsome face? "I believe my brother's mind is made up."

"Perhaps Lord Adamo will allow me to call on you in Maera."

"I don't know. He can be quite protective, my lord."

With shocking familiarity, he leaned forward and cradled my chin in a pincer grip of thumb and forefinger, angling my head up to his. Peppermint-scented breath drifted across my forehead. "I highly doubt it, my lady. Dorian Ashwood is rather poor at guarding what is his."

Jerking myself from his hold, I stumbled back, nearly tripping over the hem of my dress. He laughed.

My heart raced. He knew. Had he been baiting me this whole time? What else did he know about me?

"Who are you really, Lady Nightingale? You are no more Adamo's sister than I am." His eyes narrowed. "His new wife, perhaps?"

"I must go."

He reached out and grabbed my arm, tightly enough to bruise, and this time, I reacted. Black vines encased his wrist in a writhing, tangled mass. Lord Draven watched them in horror as I plunged deep into his mind, reaching for the full force of my gift. The aching cold to which I was always somehow immune followed in my wake as I stumbled through his memories, icing every recollection of the past hour, including when he'd first sighted me beside Lord Adamo.

When it was done, I came to myself and tugged from his grip, gasping with relief when I easily came free. Lord Draven resembled a man in shock, his mouth partly open and his eyes wide and staring, no trace of the derisive laughter that had been on his lips before. How long would the effects of the mind-bleeding last? Hours, days? I had never unleashed my gift with such potency before. If Lord Draven was permanently affected—

Leaving him still standing there, I spun away and plunged into the crowd, none of whom apparently noticed me emerging from the alcove. My vision curled and blackened at the edges like paper held against a flame, and I glanced down. My hands were shaking violently, the palms pale and clammy. Finding a space clear of other guests, I sank to my knees, dimly aware of something cold pressing against the left side of my body.

I blinked. The mosaic fountain. The trickling of the water should have been a balm to my troubled soul, but instead it grated: a puny, ineffectual sound compared to the roaring in my head.

A hand closed over my shoulder, and I jumped, my gift sparking to life again. It couldn't be Lord Draven already—

"Mi—my sister, are you all right?"

I turned to find Lord Adamo crouching beside me, his forehead creased in obvious concern. Had he seen Lord Draven, or my dance with that foul beast?

When I didn't answer, he reached into the fountain and wet his bare hand, then pressed the cold moisture gently against my forehead. It was like a soft caress after a succession of heavy blows. I relaxed beneath his touch, my eyes closing, remembering the day on the ice. The first mind I had touched—the only, besides Regis and the veteran—that was honest and kind and courageous.

I gradually opened my eyes. "I can't stay here any longer, Dorian."

His own eyes flickered. If he objected to my use of his given name, he didn't show it. Instead, he nodded and glanced briefly around. "You and me both, Miss Winter. I will give our regrets to Lord Faro that we cannot attend his feast after all."

By the time he returned, I had regained some of my senses. A servant brought my cloak and Lord Adamo's mantle, and Lord Adamo escorted me from the room. Very few glances followed us, since most of the guests were moving toward the chamber to the left of the entrance parlor, their expressions eager and excited as they speculated about what new dishes would be featured.

Outside, the brisk wind revived me a little. I clutched Lord Adamo's arm in the pitch dark. "There's something I have to tell you—"

"Not here, Miss Winter," he murmured. "Back at the inn."

I was nearly frantic by the time we arrived at my room, glad to see Bear was unharmed as he wordlessly exchanged places with Bas, who had returned with us. Jewel slept on my bed, barely stirring as Lord Adamo dismissed his guards. He faced me.

"What happened, Sephone? You look as if you've seen a ghost."

I had. At least, the ghosts of his butchered family. And I had just relived every single blow which had robbed them of their lives.

Warmth swirled through my body, banishing the filth of Rufus Karthick's mind. We might have been standing next to the fire for all that I abruptly thawed, my foggy mind pierced with sudden clarity.

And then I remembered why Lord Draven seemed so familiar. The recollection pulled me beneath the waves of panic again, and I was not immune from those frigid waters, in the same way I had been unable to save myself that day on the ice.

"He killed them," I blurted. "He killed them *himself*."

He frowned. "Who?"

"Lord Draven. Rufus Karthick. He's in Iona. I iced his memories temporarily so I could get away, but—"

"Slow down, Sephone. You're not making any sense. You did what to his memories?"

I tried to calm myself, remembering my encounter with Lord Draven. "There's more, my lord."

"More?" He was still struggling to comprehend the information I'd already given him.

"This Rufus Karthick. I've met him before."

11

DORIAN

Once his gift had calmed her enough to speak, she started at the beginning. By the end of the telling, every cell in Dorian's body was brimming with rage. It took every ounce of self-control he possessed not to leave Miss Winter with his men and return to Faro's manor house to murder Lord Draven himself.

But by now, Draven would be long gone. And besides, Dorian knew better than to assume the man was unprotected. His own bodyguards would almost certainly be among the guests. It was astonishing Draven had allowed Miss Winter to get so close—but then, he had likely assumed she was an ordinary woman.

Not after tonight.

"I am sorry," Dorian said when she finished. He realized, too late, that he couldn't have made her any more vulnerable than if he'd asked her to attend the party unclothed. She looked utterly despondent, sitting in an armchair beside the crackling fire with her hands clasped tightly. "I lost sight of you. I had no knowledge Draven was there, let alone that you were with him."

"I thought I could uncover something useful—"

Dorian glanced at her sharply. "Wait . . . you knew who he was from the start?"

"Aye, at least just after he grabbed me, when he introduced himself. I thought I could help you—perhaps find out the truth."

And so she had. Eighteen months ago, on the night of the ambush, the assailants had all been hooded, so Dorian hadn't known for sure of Draven's involvement. The *mem* had been reticent on the details, but he saw her desolate expression. She knew now how his wife and child had died. The achingly familiar loss swept through him, and he battled to keep his mind on the present—with no more success than a man who couldn't swim floundering in an angry sea.

But some of Miss Winter's plight filtered through his pain. She could have gotten herself killed.

"It was foolish to engage him, Miss Winter. He is a dangerous man."

"I can protect myself."

Dorian held her gaze in gentle reminder that not all enemies were so easily vanquished. After tonight, Draven would hunt her down alongside him. Impressive as her gift was, he would soon know she was not invincible.

"I'm sorry," she said, her shoulders slumping. She had abandoned the wig and looked more like her normal self. "By using my gift, I have given us away completely. But when I saw what he did to your family—the extent of his jealousy and hate—I just couldn't control—"

Dorian sidestepped her reminder of his loss. "I won't ever advise you to exercise restraint where Draven is concerned, Miss Winter. But do not shoulder guilt unnecessarily. You said Draven already knew that I wasn't your brother."

"Aye. But once he regains his senses, he will know what I am. Only one type of *alter* can do what I've done."

"Yet, if you hadn't done it, he would not have let you go."

It was a mercy she had been able to defend herself. He knew Draven would never have let her leave Lord Faro's house alive. How could Dorian have borne finding her lifeless body in an alley somewhere, knowing it was his association with her that had caused her death?

There was one further mercy, though he doubted it would be any consolation to her. Now that he knew what she was, Draven wouldn't kill her. Miss Winter was valuable to a man like Draven. He would want her alive. And, if captured, she would be better off dead. "You said you've met him before," he reminded her urgently. "When?"

An emotion he couldn't quite identify settled over her features. Disgust? Revulsion? "Aye, but he went by a different name back then." Seeing the distinctly greenish tint that colored her cheeks, he rummaged around in his bag. He passed her a small vial which she eyed uncertainly.

"Is it—"

"Just ordinary liquor," he assured her. "With a little extra something for the nausea."

"You have such a thing close at hand?"

"There are many things in this world which make a man sick to his stomach, Miss Winter. It is always wise to be prepared."

He spoke, of course, of far more than a nausea repellent. By the look of her, she understood. She uncorked the vial, sniffed, then cautiously sipped at the amber liquid. The greenish tinge slowly disappeared, leaving her features pale and drawn.

"I was very young when I first saw him," she said, "only six or seven. Cutter called him something else—I don't recall the name—but I remember the red hair and the blue eyes." She swallowed. "Even Cutter didn't like him, which is saying something. He said the man's mind was one of the darkest he'd ever entered."

"Cutter is a *mem*?"

She nodded. "Aye, though it's only his secondary gift. His primary gift is . . ." She paused. "Cutter has the ability to transmit fear. Fear so potent and all-consuming you can hardly think—or even breathe."

He remembered the bruise on her face. "So that's how he controlled you."

"Nay, he was always too afraid of my own gift. Instead, he controlled me by punishing my friend, Regis. But when I defied him the last time, he used the fear gift on me. I don't know how, but it has grown in power over the years. Though I think it cost him as much to wield it as it cost me to endure it."

"Where is your friend now?"

"Reg? Cutter sold him." Her voice caught. "But one day I'll find him again."

There it was again—the heart on her sleeve. How had she borne the vileness of Lord Draven's mind?

"Cutter was right about Draven," he acknowledged. "He is a different class of evil. Did you touch his mind that time as a child?"

"Nay, I only saw him at a distance. He came to the tavern one day and told Cutter he wanted to buy me. At first, I thought he was my father, come to rescue me at last. At that time, you see, I believed my parents were still alive. He was so tall and strong and handsome, and the way he looked at me . . ."

She trailed off, as if collecting her thoughts from some terrible place where they had strayed.

"Cutter never tells anyone he has some ability as a *mem*, and usually people pass his intuition off as mere good business sense. That night, he caught a glimpse of Lord Draven's mind, and though his money was good, he refused to sell me. When I asked him why, Cutter said only that no child belonged in that man's care."

She paused again, then continued, "I was upset for days. It seems very foolish now, but the stranger seemed so good and kind, and Cutter was always a harsh master. But tonight, I saw the worst of Lord Draven's mind. And though I don't know what despicable purpose he had for me and my gift, I finally understood why Cutter refused him. It would seem even Cutter has a conscience, however deeply he buries it. I never thought I would be grateful to him for anything."

"I am"–*sickened*–"not surprised." He took the armchair beside hers. "I will bring Draven down, I swear. Even if it costs me my life."

"Are you going to kill him?" Fear flashed across her face. Was she afraid for him?

She'd underestimated him. "Nay, I won't kill him—though I admit I have considered it many times. Lord Draven is the thane of Argus, a powerful seat and contender for the arch-lord of Memosine. His connections are better than mine, and he wields more influence with the other lords. For now, at least, I cannot challenge him openly. If I were to try and assassinate him, it would only cause hardship for my family—and for Maera—for the arch-lord's soldiers would almost certainly arrest me.

"But I swore on my wife and daughter's graves that I would destroy every last inch of Draven's life, as he destroyed every part of mine. He will be brought before the Council of Eight in time. And he will answer for his crimes and die a criminal's death."

"Why not work toward that end now, my lord? Why seek the Reliquary first?"

"Because I cannot—" *Sleep. Think clearly. Eat. Breathe without pain.* "For eighteen months now, I have not been able to think of anything but them. I am not myself, Miss Winter. If I am to destroy Draven, as calmly and methodically as this situation demands, I must first be ruler of my own head."

He stood. "Even so, that was my secondary purpose in securing your services. As we search for the Reliquary, I will need your help to gather the necessary proof to convince the Council of Eight to arrest Lord Draven."

"But his involvement in your family's murders—"

"Speculation, according to the Eight. Lord Draven covered his tracks well. Since there was so little evidence, they could do naught."

"And if I was to testify to what I saw in his mind?"

"You know better than anyone how easily memories may be influenced. For that reason, the courts of Memosine do not allow *mems* to give evidence under any circumstance. Lethe and Marianthe are the same."

She continued doggedly, "But if you use the Reliquary to forget about your family, won't you forget what Lord Draven did to them? How can you testify about an event you don't remember?"

He hesitated. Clearly, he had underestimated *her.* Her keen intelligence continued to surprise him. "I am a lord, Miss Winter. But unlike Lord Draven, I am no longer a thane. If I am to make him answer for his crimes before the Eight, I must do so clearly and dispassionately. Otherwise, I will be dismissed as merely a grieving husband and father."

He saw she understood.

"Your gift allows you to remove the pain of memories—if only temporarily. When we find the Reliquary, it is my hope that you will be able to take away my pain permanently. I will still have everything I need to face the Council. After Lord Draven is dead, I will ask you to remove the memory in its entirety."

Compassion radiated from her. "I could help you forget now, my lord. For a little while, at least. The mind-bleeding—"

"Nay." He turned abruptly to the fire, now burning low. "Twice was enough for me. Pain deferred is only pain doubled, you see. I won't put my hope in temporary treatments. Not if there is a cure."

He glanced at her to find she was gazing at his hair. He'd brushed the powder from it, and the iridescence would be obvious by firelight. Should he share the truth of his gift? But she trusted him; that much was obvious. She would find out everything else in due course. Enough secrets had been shared tonight.

She averted her eyes and stared into the fire. "You're assuming I will change my mind about helping you to forget your family."

"It's a contradiction, is it not? You offer to numb my memories, and yet you refuse to remove them in their entirety."

She stood to face him. "What else is there to warm us in this frozen world besides love, Lord Adamo?"

"There is justice. There is duty."

"You could be happy again."

"Nay, Miss Winter. Every man has one chance at happiness, and I have had mine." He stroked the wedding bands at his throat. If he couldn't have Lida and Emmy, he could spend his life working toward a better world.

A world where they might have lived.

But that was enough reminiscing for one night. Miss Winter could see inside his mind, but she had no business knowing his heart. She was still a stranger.

"I had hoped to leave in the morning, but Draven will be on our trail as soon as he regains his senses. I fear we must leave tonight."

She glanced at her green dress. "I will be glad to leave this behind."

"Dela brought some supplies for you, Miss Winter, including suitable clothes. I think you will find she has thought of everything."

He hoped she could ride a horse. Although, he didn't think she was the complaining type. She had slept in the carriage, at least.

"You're calling me Miss Winter again, my lord. Is this the end of Lady Nightingale?"

"Draven knows we are not related. He will likely spread the truth to others—and Cutter may hear of it. I believe we may abandon the ruse."

"Then perhaps you could just call me Sephone."

Dorian did not respond.

"You referred to me as Sephone tonight," she prompted, "twice."
So he had. "After you called me Dorian."

Irritation filtered through him. He felt Jewel brush against his leg, her wet nose pressed into his hand—whether seeking or offering comfort, he did not know. It always surprised him how soundlessly she moved about a room. It had been Jewel who had kept him from the worst despair after Lida and Emmy died, forcing him to get out of bed each morning to feed her and take her for walks, since she had never allowed any of the servants, or even Lida, to accompany her. He had thought her self-centered, only to later realize that, though he had been the one to do everything for her, it was she who had saved *him*.

Sephone Winter's solicitude was a far more dangerous offering. Even without her gift, he sensed she could see straight through him. *Lord Adamo* was a flimsy covering for the broken man who lay beneath, a man who tarnished every good thing he touched. Even his association with Lord Draven had nearly gotten her killed tonight.

Aye, she must know, from the outset, that he could never be her friend.

"Miss Winter, if you please. At least for now."

Without waiting for her reaction, he bid her goodnight and headed to his room for a night of sleepless self-examination, Jewel trotting behind him.

"Can you ride, Miss Winter?" Lord Adamo asked me as he fastened the shortened version of his quarterstaff to his saddle. The weapon was more intricate than I had first realized, not only tipped with iron but able to be compressed to a fraction of its usual size. Was it even made of wood? Tightening a strap and adjusting a stirrup, he came around his horse and looked down at me.

"Not really," I replied, "though I'm sure your men will make quick work of teaching me how not to fall."

Bear, standing beside me in the darkened stable, smiled warmly at my quip. Bas looked like he'd swallowed a cupful of vinegar instead of the tea he was expecting. I didn't need to visit either man's mind to know who I preferred as a teacher.

Extending one enormous palm, Bear patted the sorrel mare the lord had selected for me.

"Ivy's a good deal steadier than Marmalade," Bear mused with a glance at Lord Adamo's smoky black roan, who was snorting and pounding the ground with his hoof. "You shouldn't have any trouble with her."

"Marmalade?" I repeated.

Bear grinned. "Cause he's so pretty you think he's going to be sweet, but he has a bit of a nasty bite."

"Have you ever tasted marmalade?" When Bear nodded, I directed the question at Lord Adamo.

"Of course," he replied, his amusement no less than Bear's.

"For real?"

"Aye, for real, Miss Winter. How else?"

I stared at the gelding. Its coat couldn't be further from the color of the spread I'd seen once in a mind—though never tasted myself. I'd never even eaten an orange, though I knew the rind was bitter and the inside was sweet, in the same way one knows a stove is hot without having to touch it. Marmalade's neck jerked to one side, his teeth snapping together around some unfortunate airborne prey. He settled down, then, looking as smug as Jewel after devouring an entire plate of cured ham.

Hopefully he wouldn't hurl the lord to his death.

I pressed closer to Ivy, who nickered softly. The wiry strands of her mane were oddly reassuring, even through my gloves. Lord Adamo came to my side. "The first step is learning to mount. Shall I help you?"

For some reason, his simple question felt surreal. It was the middle of the night, and a former thane was offering to help me mount a horse named after a plant I'd never seen before today, while the devil himself possessed a horse named after an ancient breakfast spread I'd never tasted.

I glanced at Lord Adamo. He was nearly unrecognizable in the same common clothes he'd worn when he'd rescued me in Nulla—a plain brown tunic over a loose brown shirt, with black breeches stuffed into tall leather boots. The dark blue mantle with its black fur collar and brass brooch was gone, exchanged for an ordinary-looking brown cloak with a humble clasp. Bear and Bas were similarly dressed, though Bear's size was difficult to downplay, even in faded clothing. I wondered where Lord Adamo would keep the carriage and the black horses that had drawn it.

Thankfully, the lord had allowed me to abandon both wig and dress, and I enjoyed the relative freedom of clothes and boots which matched the men's. They'd even permitted me to keep my knife. But best of all, I had been overjoyed to leave the serpentine arm bracelets in my satchel. In a few months' time, my hair would grow even longer, and no one would ever take me for a slave again.

So long as Cutter didn't find me first.

Lord Adamo's expression had gone from expectant to questioning in light of my silence, and I quickly nodded to accept his help. But he had no sooner reached for the stirrup than the coach driver, Kade, burst into the stable, panic on his face.

"You must hurry, my lord. Lord Draven's men are searching the inn."

The men leaped into action. Lord Adamo grasped me around the waist and lifted me onto the saddle, all but shoving my boots into the stirrups. They were too short for me, but there was no time to make the necessary adjustments.

"Hold on." Grabbing my reins, he tossed them to Bear while he mounted Marmalade, then reached for them again. I was dimly aware of the two brothers taking charge of their own mounts—Bear's bay stallion and Bas's liver chestnut mare—and then Lord Adamo was wheeling Ivy around. Before he could whistle for Jewel, she sprang from the shadows, the blue of her eyes flashing in the gloom. I remembered the lord's instruction and seized the front of the saddle as a single thought pierced my awareness.

If ever there was a moment to turn back, this is it.

I thought of my parents, who had given me up to a mere stranger. The idea of the memory potion which had sustained me for so many years. If not for the passing *lumen* with his gift of truth-revealing, I might still be in Cutter's household, yearning for something I would never have. Not even my gift could have kept me from despair, for while I could see inside the minds of others, my own memories had always been wreathed in shadows. I remembered very little before the day on the ice.

Lord Adamo was right. The Reliquary was my only chance to discover the truth. And the lord was my best chance of uncovering my past. There was no turning back now.

And so I held on as Lord Adamo led Ivy out of the stable and into a world I'd always wondered about—a world finally within my reach. A world in which—one day—I might even find the love that haunted my dreams.

I expected Lord Adamo to relax our frenetic pace as we cleared Iona, but if anything, our speed only increased. I'd hung on to Ivy for dear life as we rode through the darkened streets, hardly anyone about to watch us flee. Only Bear and Bas accompanied us, the other guards presumably dismissed or ordered to remain behind. Jewel loped along beside Marmalade, matching whatever pace the roan set.

After an hour or so of heavy riding, Lord Adamo finally slowed. My knees ached from the too-short stirrups. My muscles were cramping and my backside was unspeakably sore. How would I feel after a full day of riding?

I looked around as the first rays of grayish light filtered through the trees. On leaving Iona, we had plunged almost immediately into thick pine forest, Lord Adamo following a narrow trail beneath trees that leaned so close, one needed to be constantly alert for stray branches that could smack you from your horse. He had handed me my reins as soon as we left the outskirts of Iona, and thankfully Ivy had no need of further instructions, being content to follow Marmalade.

A stream gurgled nearby, the steady rhythm punctuated by the popping call of a bird I didn't recognize. The scent of pine filled my lungs to bursting, as heady as any memory potion, but somehow far richer. Once again, I was struck by all the green. I'd expected the rest of Caldera to be barren and lifeless like Nulla, but this forest was old, dating back to the world-that-was.

Still, even at dawn, the sky remained overcast, the fog-smoke that had concealed the sky for as long as I could remember lingering above our heads, making it impossible to see more than a few yards ahead. At least Lord Draven would have a fine time tracking us.

Lord Adamo drew Marmalade to a halt. As he and the others dismounted, I tried to follow suit, only to discover that it was still a very long way to the ground. I dangled in midair for a few seconds before I felt hands around my waist, bringing me safely to earth. Expecting Bear, I was surprised to see Lord Adamo instead.

"You're a fast learner for a novice rider," he said.

One of the advantages of carrying several centuries' worth of life experience in my head, though since Bas stood nearby scowling, I thought better of mentioning it.

"Ivy deserves most of the credit."

Lord Adamo laughed. He seemed different, driven by fresh energy. Was this the man he'd been before the massacre of his family?

I am not myself, Miss Winter. If I am to destroy Draven . . . I must first be ruler of my own head.

Warmth swirled through my chest, far more potent than Cutter's liquid courage, and I wondered if the lord knew how he affected his listeners. Or perhaps that was just me.

I steeled myself against the bubbling sensations, stepping back so far I bumped into Ivy's flank. Lord Adamo's hands around my waist had been gentle, and he was the kindest man I'd encountered, but I knew better than to melt at the knees.

I was only a servant to him. He had reminded me of that last night when he'd refused to call me Sephone.

Bas still wore a scowl like he was afraid the pendulum of fashion would swing the other way, rendering the expression outdated. I focused on his dislike—anything else besides Lord Adamo.

"Where are we going, my lord?" Bear asked.

Lord Adamo beckoned us to gather near him. Extracting a rolled parchment from his saddlebags, he unfurled it to reveal a map of Caldera, more detailed than any I'd seen, and so yellowed I wondered if it had been made in the years following the war. The borders had changed little since then.

Lord Adamo knelt and pinned the map open with several large pinecones. Even Jewel followed his finger. "We're here, just outside Iona. My contacts believe our best chance of finding the Reliquary is starting with the library in Calliope. If we keep traveling west to northwest, we'll eventually stumble across the moors, and from there it's a week's hard riding to reach the capital."

I nodded along with the others.

"Providing Miss Winter's former employer doesn't pick up our trail, there's a good chance we can lose our pursuers on the moors."

I winced inwardly at the lord's choice of the word *employer* over the far more accurate *slave master,* but tapped my own finger against the city lying south of Calliope. "Didn't you say Lord Draven is thane of Argus? Won't we be dangerously close to his dominion?"

Lord Adamo shook his head. "You forget I was once thane of Maera, which is almost as close to Calliope as Argus, and on far better terms. Fortunately, I have friends in the capital who will assist us, though they may choose to do so anonymously."

Friends, he said, rather than the acquaintances he'd detested in Iona. I hoped he was correct in his assessment. I didn't want to run forever.

"And after Calliope?"

"With your help, Miss Winter, I believe we will uncover one or several good leads to follow that will direct our future course."

Bas was once again wearing an unpleasant expression. "And if any one of our many enemies catches up to us? We are only three men . . . my lord."

His brother shot him a withering look. "Courage, Bas. You make us sound like ordinary men. Don't forget, we have two *alters* with us." He tilted his head at Jewel. "And a lady wolf."

Ignoring Bear, Bas appealed to Lord Adamo directly. "Once again, I would recommend you retain several more men-at-arms, my lord."

"As I said before, Bas, this quest is a delicate matter, not the sort I could easily entrust to strangers."

Bas's eyes swung pointedly in my direction. I could almost hear his accusation.

What about the stranger you picked up in Nulla?

"Enough, Bas. I have always encouraged you to speak your mind to me, but I still expect you to obey orders. I have made my decision, and it is final."

The bodyguard huffed and turned away to tend to his horse. Lord Adamo rolled up the map and turned to me. "We have a long ride ahead of us, I'm afraid. We can't afford to stop again until nightfall. Can you manage it?"

"Of course."

Proving he was not so mired in his thoughts as I'd first believed, he moved to Ivy and proceeded to adjust my too-short stirrups.

Just like the boy from the ice, I could not help musing. He might turn away from the suffering of his people, but the youth of fourteen was still there, feeling the pain of others as deeply and profoundly as I did. Even his grief could not mask who he really was. Surely, he could yet be reached—

What are you thinking? I instantly chided myself. *It isn't for you to save him from his sorrow.*

But the desire remained, stubbornly resisting my efforts to smother it. It gathered momentum as the lord helped me mount again—though Bear might have done as well. By the time we were on our way again, I'd nearly forgotten Cutter and Lord Draven in my mental wandering.

Once upon a time, Lord Adamo had given me back my life.

If only I could give him back his.

That night, I was so sore it was all I could do to tumble off Ivy's back and try to remain standing. This time, Bear was there to steady me, guiding me to a small overhang of rocks while Lord Adamo tended to the horses and Bas collected firewood. Even Jewel assisted, carrying large sticks between her teeth to the fireplace Bear was building with several heavy stones. When I tried to help, he raised a massive hand.

"Not tonight, Lady Nightingale. Maybe tomorrow, but not tonight. Wait until you can stand without falling over."

I smiled, liking this well-mannered giant who looked at my face, not my gloves. "It's only Miss Winter now."

"Nay, Lady Nightingale suits you better. Two well-bred ladies"—he glanced at Jewel, who'd rejoined us and was lying down with her paws folded primly in front of her—"is much easier to remember."

Bear proved himself a good cook, though he insisted the meat and vegetable stew was *humble fare*, as Lord Adamo had the breakfast in the carriage. Bas ate faster than any man I'd seen, then shoved aside his bowl and declared he would fill the waterskins at the stream. By Bear's raised eyebrow, I guessed it was some kind of silent protest. Lord Adamo merely shrugged, retrieving a bedroll from Ivy's saddle once dinner was over and bringing it to me.

"Rough lodgings, I'm afraid, Miss Winter." As he spread the blankets on the ground, he nodded at Jewel. "I've asked her to stay close to you, though I guess she would have done so anyway, for she seems to have taken to you."

The lady wolf's favor likely had more to do with the amount of meat I'd sent her way during dinner than any innate preference for my company, but I said nothing to the lord, not wanting Bear to overhear. We had never had much meat in Nulla, and the rich fare the others considered plain sat heavily on my stomach.

"Shall I take the first watch?"

Lord Adamo shook his head. "There's no need."

"But our pursuers—"

"The lady will alert us if anyone draws too close."

"You set watches back in Nulla."

"Aye, only because there were so many people around. It makes it more difficult for her to sense danger."

I understood, then, why he was so relaxed—at least, relaxed enough to dismiss his extra guards. "Jewel's gifted, too, isn't she?"

He nodded. "It took me a long time to realize it was more than just a wolf's protective instincts. After"—he drew in a breath— "after the attack, I learned to trust her nose for danger. She will sense an approaching enemy long before an ordinary wolf could see or smell them."

"Then she's from the line of the animals affected by . . . the war. After, I mean."

"Aye."

No one knew what had happened during the war to bring about the various gifts, for they had only manifested after the terrible conflict, along with the gray . . . though ancient legends told of gifts that had also existed in the Old Times, given by the gods to a choice selection of mortals. Nonetheless, something had happened to bring about the return of the gifts, and the gray seemed as good a candidate as any other.

Many believed the fog-smoke was magical, and that if an expectant mother breathed deeply of the vapors, her child would be born an *alter*—a seeming blessing, though not everyone welcomed the reawakening of the old powers. Others said that since we Calderans saw so little of the sun, the *alters* were nature's way of reasserting its light. All *alters* had some form of iridescence, whether in their hair or their eyes or their skin, in varying shades and degrees of brilliance. My own hair was only faintly iridescent, though without a mirror, and with little light, I'd rarely caught a glimpse of it.

I had never met an animal who was gifted. If only Jewel had been at my side the day I'd encountered Lord Draven.

"Regardless of her gift, wolves are pack animals," Lord Adamo continued. "Jewel considers you part of her pack now. She'll protect you to her death."

Only faintly reassured, I returned my attention to the lady wolf. Though her eyes were closed, her ears were pricked. They twitched once as Bas returned from the stream with the waterskins, but she didn't open her eyes.

The men retrieved their own bedrolls, Bas setting his up on the other side of the fire, as far away from me as possible. Lord Adamo had unrolled mine between the rocky overhang and the fire, giving me both warmth and protection. He lay down on the other side, Jewel lounging gracefully between us. I expected the wolf to leave me for the lord as the temperature dropped and I snuggled into my blankets, but she only moved closer—so close, I could feel her body heat.

Lord Adamo's face lit with amusement. "I knew she approved of you."

"I hope she doesn't mind sharing my dreams."

The amusement vanished, like the snuffing out of a candle. Darkness once again cobwebbed his features.

Bear called out, "You have a bear and a wolf to protect you, Lady Nightingale. I assure you that you'll come to no harm tonight."

"When you're as large as my brother, there's no need to be afraid." Bas's tone was faintly sarcastic.

"Hush, Bas. You could persuade a child the sun was blue."

"I'm not the one gifted in the art of—"

"Bear's right," Lord Adamo interjected. "Quiet now. We all need our rest."

The brothers fell silent. Lady Jewel lay as if carved from stone, though when I stretched out my hand to touch her, her side rose and fell in the cadence of regular breathing. Besides Ivy, she was the first living being I had touched without fear of awakening the past. On the other side of the wolf, I knew Lord Adamo was still awake, for though he hadn't moved, his breaths were shallow and irregular. With his back to the fire, only his hair was visible, gleaming in the firelight like oxygen-rich coals. Then he shifted onto his back, and I saw the profile of his bearded face, his long nose and strong chin.

My gift could help him sleep, but the lord had declined the offer most emphatically. Remembering Lord Guerin, and the ghost of the man he'd become after so many mind-bleedings, I understood his reticence. Too often, my gift extracted the man along with the memory. Still, something inside of me ached to know he suffered so acutely. What being didn't hunger for temporary relief?

Perhaps it wasn't attaining the state of sleep that was difficult, but that he feared his dreams as much as I feared mine. Perhaps he knew that when he slipped into the dreamworld, he would be vulnerable, unable to repel the attacks he could more easily withstand during the day.

Once again, I thought of the boy from the ice. Nothing had troubled Dorian Ashwood then.

How far the once-thane of Maera had fallen. How much his life now resembled mine, except for the fact that he suffered not only in his grief, but in the knowledge that he'd—just for a moment—had everything he wanted. It was a small mercy I'd never known peace or beauty or comfort, for then the rude expulsion of it from my life would have been unbearable. Far better to be impoverished from birth than to know plenty and suffer the sudden exile of it. No wonder he thought himself beyond any chance of happiness.

But I could change that. I would show him the world I still believed in—even if it existed in fragments and flickers, even if much of it had faded or been traded away. There was still good aplenty. There was still much to hope for.

I would show Lord Adamo the things he could no longer see.

The water was so cold it was like being pierced with a thousand glass splinters at once. I sucked in a breath as my head went under, but instead of air, I inhaled more water. It punctured my throat all the way down to my

lungs, and I panicked, my aching limbs flailing madly. I was weightless, but at the same time sinking down, down, toward the murky depths of the canal. I couldn't swim. No one would brave the fractured sheets of ice to come to my aid, not for a runt of a slave girl who had been foolish enough to run away.

Black spots appeared in my vision as I continued to thrash. My last breath evaporated in a burst of bubbles, gleefully heading for the surface while I was condemned to sink below. In a final, futile gesture, I thrust my hand upward, high above my head, encountering nothing more than the slick edge of the ice and more freezing water.

And then a strong hand caught mine—

I jerked awake. Jewel was gone, and Lord Adamo's face hovered above me, his hand on my shoulder. When he withdrew it, I found myself regretting the loss of his warmth.

"Another day awaits, Miss Winter. Are you well?"

The day he spoke of appeared as fatigued as he was, though I guessed it was barely past first light. I blinked. "Just a dream."

"We will pass through a town today. Best to keep your hair covered."

I went through the mechanical motions of eating breakfast, helping the men to eliminate all traces of our camp, and mounting again, barely registering my aching muscles and the restricted range of motion in my left shoulder, which I'd foolishly lain on for half the night. I was still so preoccupied with thoughts of ice fragments and lanky rescuers that I failed to avoid a very visible tree branch, resulting in a long scratch across my cheek.

By midday, we were nearing the town Lord Adamo had spoken of, and I was feeling like myself again. Marmalade set an impressive pace for a horse named after a jam, and Ivy trailed dutifully after him, with the brothers bringing up the rear. Last night's animosity had given way to an easy camaraderie as they ribbed each other. Lord Adamo cast an occasional amused look over his shoulder at their banter.

"Do they always bicker so?"

"Always, Miss Winter. Their mother believes it first began in her womb."

"They're twins?"

Bear rode up beside us. "You asked which of us was older, my lady. You never specified by how much."

"Aye, it started in the womb," Bas called from behind with uncharacteristic good humor. "Look at the man! Can you imagine how much space he took up? It's no wonder I was desperate to escape."

At that moment, the town suddenly rose up from the forest, no more than two dozen buildings looming out of the gray. Made from wood rather than stone, many of them were ramshackle and neglected, and they looked hastily constructed, as if someone had intended them to be a temporary substitute for a proper and permanent building which never eventuated.

Following Lord Adamo's example, we dismounted to lead the horses through the main thoroughfare. "Don't make eye contact, and they'll be unlikely to remember us," he instructed, pulling his hood over his hair.

But he had no cause for concern, for there was some kind of commotion up ahead which had the villagers crowded around a raised platform, jostling each other to get a better view. As we neared the scene, Lord Adamo's hand closed around my gloved forearm. The length of Marmalade's body blocked the platform from sight.

"Best not to look, Miss Winter," he said, voice low. "It's an execution."

I carefully extracted my arm from his grip. "You needn't shield me."

"Nay, I expect you've seen much worse. But since there are at least a dozen Memosinian soldiers present, I'd advise you to keep a low profile."

He moved away, making a show of craning his neck to stare at the unfortunate prisoner, as any curious passing traveler might. His bodyguards followed suit, and Marmalade's flank continued to act as a barrier between me and the crowd, as the lord had no doubt intended.

Gripping Ivy's reins, I watched the few faces I could see from my limited vantage point. Most were eager, some angry, others disgusted. A middle-aged woman wept bitterly, her head resting on a younger man's shoulder, while another villager wove through the crowd away from the platform, his face covered with a dark hood. He appeared to be moving with some haste, and when he caught sight of me, he changed course and headed in our direction.

It was then that I saw the soldiers, their eyes raking the crowd as if they were searching for someone.

"Lord Adamo—" I started as the stranger approached me, but the lord was on the other side of Marmalade. Where was Jewel? Wouldn't she sense if there was danger? After casting a quick backward glance at the soldiers, the stranger peered into my face. His eyes sparked with recognition.

One of the soldiers shouted, but in that moment, the crowd erupted into a mixture of applause and cries of dismay. The unfortunate prisoner must have lost his head. The stranger darted forward, trapping me between Ivy and Marmalade, hiding us from his pursuers.

"Help me," he muttered, then grabbed me around the waist and pulled me in for a passionate kiss.

I would have unleashed my gift on him if I'd not immediately known who he was by the images floating at the forefront of his consciousness. He was an *alter*. The soldiers were hunting him. He had sought sanctuary in this village, only to discover that they hated *alters*. The person now being executed was not a man but a female, hardly more than fifteen years old. She was an *alter* herself, born with faintly iridescent skin.

And there was one other thing.

The stranger's hood slid back a little as he lifted his head, revealing black hair with hints of purple and green, and eyes that might have belonged to a peafowl for their blue-green iridescence. Smooth lips curved in a languid smile as he studied my face.

"First kiss?" he asked with a raised eyebrow.

I controlled my voice. "Of course not."

Black threads darted in and out of an invisible loom between us, and he winked. "Lucky you, then."

It was the *lumen* from Cutter's tavern. The man who'd uncovered Cutter's deception, inadvertently setting me free. Another shout came from behind him, and he reached for me again.

For a second time, I didn't respond. I had no choice but to allow it. If I pulled away or raised the alarm, the soldiers would spot him, and

I didn't want to watch another innocent person die. Despite his charm and bravado, I registered the desperation an ordinary woman would have failed to notice, in the wild beating of his heart.

He was terrified. How long had he been running?

The troop of soldiers passed by without detaining either of us, and I quickly extricated myself from his grasp.

"Right," I said, reaching for Ivy's reins, which I'd dropped when he grabbed me. "Now you can tell me why you're running away."

"Don't say you didn't enjoy that."

Cheeks flaming, I slapped him across the face. Of all the insolent—

He didn't flinch. "Afraid to know your own mind, miss?" He stepped closer. "I seem to recall that—"

His body went slack, his eyes rolling back in his head as he crumpled. Behind him stood Lord Adamo, his face a mask of fury. He seized the *alter* beneath the armpits, still gripping his quarterstaff in his hand.

The man who'd assaulted Miss Winter went limp in Dorian's grip. Bas stepped up to heft some of the man's weight while Dorian quickly turned to the *mem.*

"Are you all right?"

She looked ashen. "It wasn't pleasant, but he wouldn't truly have harmed me, my lord. I know him."

"You know him?"

"Aye . . . well, nay. Not really. I've met him once before."

The execution having concluded, the crowd was dispersing around them, and Dorian had no desire to make a scene.

"Your assistance, Bear," Dorian grunted, and the bodyguard bounded forward to take his half of the stranger's weight. Jewel stood nearby, leaving him to wonder why she hadn't alerted him to the attacker. Was it the crowd? Or was Miss Winter correct in her assumption that she wasn't in danger?

And yet he'd seen it. Over Marmalade's back, he'd witnessed the forceful kiss—which she'd surprisingly allowed—the brief verbal exchange, and the slap. Dorian only lamented that it had taken that long to reach his quarterstaff in the closely pressing crowd.

Then he spied the stranger's iridescent hair. "Away. We must get. away from here."

Supporting the man between them, as if he had merely collapsed from grief, the brothers dragged him from the crowd, leading their horses with their free hands. Forgetting Miss Winter didn't like to be touched, Dorian placed a hand on her back, steering her from the scene. He didn't stop until they'd cleared the village and found the forest trail once again.

Bas lowered the unconscious man to the ground while Bear retrieved his crossbow. Dorian turned to the young woman, who had regained some of her color.

"Who is he?"

"I don't know his name. Like I said, I only met him once, in Cutter's tavern. He was the one who uncovered Cutter's deception about my parents' memory potion."

Dorian blinked. "Your what?" As she recounted the story, his eyes strayed to the resin pendant around her neck.

She pointed at the stranger. "It was that man who revealed that Cutter was lying to me."

"You mean he's a—"

"Aye, a *lumen*. And he's running from those soldiers we saw." She shivered, and Dorian wondered what else she'd seen. "It's good we left that village as quickly as we did. They despise *alters*."

That explained the girl. A pity they'd arrived too late to intervene on her behalf—although intervening in an execution would make their presence unforgettable.

Miss Winter was still eyeing the stranger. "I don't think he can control his gift."

"I can't," muttered a voice blurred with pain, and the stranger cracked open his eyes, probing the back of his skull with cautious, black-gloved fingers. "What did you hit me with? A brick?"

Dorian stood over him. "A staff. Why did you attack Miss Winter?"

"That's a fine description of a kiss. I didn't attack her. We were merely creating a distraction."

Judging by the accent, he was Marianthean. But his grasp of the common tongue was excellent, almost refined. Not a member of the aristocracy, but well-educated, though his weatherworn skin proved he'd seen some hardships.

"He's speaking the truth, my lord," the *mem* assured Dorian.

"I thought that was *my* gift." The stranger raised himself into a sitting position and shoved back his hood, revealing feathery hair even the

finest rooster would covet. He looked between Dorian and Miss Winter.
"It would seem I've landed myself in a veritable nest of *alters*."

"Speaking the truth is your gift?"

"Not exactly," the stranger replied. "I can lie through my teeth if I
want to, and nobody will be any the wiser." He staggered to his feet,
grinning like a cat through the occasional grimace of pain. "Allow me
to demonstrate."

Dorian tensed as the man approached Miss Winter, ready to reach
for the quarterstaff now strapped to his belt. Bear raised his crossbow.
But the stranger only quirked a smile.

"You're grateful for what I did for you in Nulla, aren't you?"

"Nay, I—" Black vapors of light wove between them like snakes,
causing Bas to hiss and step back.

"And you think I'm handsome." He stepped closer and brushed her
arm with his.

Miss Winter raised her hand to slap him again, and he neatly spun
away, addressing Dorian this time. "In my presence, the spoken word
reveals itself as truth or lie. That is the essence of my gift."

"Who are you?"

He gave a low, sweeping bow, more mocking than deferential.
"Cassius Vera at your service. Or simply Cass."

Another *alter* who insisted on informality. "Very well then, Cass, I
think you owe Miss Winter an explanation. Why are you running?"

"Miss Winter?" Cassius Vera bent his head toward her, extending his
hand. "A pleasure, then and now."

She didn't take it. "Please answer the question, Mister Vera."

"Cass." He winked. "I hail from Marianthe. And I'm an *alter*. Isn't
that reason enough for a Memosinian soldier to take a disliking to me?"
He swept a casual finger between Dorian and Miss Winter. "And what
relation are you?"

"She's my sister." Dorian realized his error just as black, snakelike coils
no thicker than the circumference of his thumb rippled through the air.

Cassius Vera grinned. "I thought not."

Dorian frowned. He had heard of *lumens*, but never met one. Clearly,
they were dangerous company. They would have to watch every word
they spoke.

"Where are you headed, Cass?"

"To Calliope, I think. I'm seeking new employment."

His black hair had been recently cut, and roughly. Another escaped slave?

"Lord Adamo, a word," Bas said through gritted teeth.

"If you'll excuse us a moment."

"A few yards should do it," the *lumen* replied. "My gift won't work beyond that range."

"Much obliged," Dorian said curtly, and strode away twice that distance, Miss Winter, Jewel, and his bodyguards joining him. The *lumen* remained where he was, intently studying the dirt beneath his fingernails with a faint smile.

"A man like that could be useful," Dorian said before his bodyguards could speak, recognizing the bristling look on Bas's face.

"Or unspeakably dangerous," Bas countered. "Didn't you hear what he said, my lord? His gift affects everyone except himself. He can lie without consequence. A man like that—no wonder he's on the run. He can't be trusted."

"Aye, we'd have to watch him closely. But think on it, Bas. Such a gift would make enemies of many men without even trying. And remember, there are those who use *lumens* in their interrogations. Cocky or nay, he may be right to fear for his life."

Dorian glanced down at Jewel beside him. She looked serene—no hackles, no bared teeth, no stiffened body. She had no issue with this man. And Dorian had learned to trust her judgment.

"We will follow where you lead, my lord," Bear said slowly, his crossbow still pointed in the stranger's direction. "But I would remind you that, *alter* or nay, he assaulted the lady. I would not entrust him with the real nature of our quest until you are certain he is trustworthy."

Nodding, Dorian turned to the *mem*. "Miss Winter?" So far, she hadn't spoken. Her gaze was fixed on the man, evidently deep in thought. Indeed. She had been inside his mind. "What did you see?"

When she looked at Dorian, her eyes were still unfocused. "He has a past, aye. But he *is* right to fear for his life. If they find him, they will . . ." She wrapped her arms around her middle, not finishing the sentence.

Dorian nodded in acknowledgement just as thunder rumbled overhead.

He instinctively stiffened, his bodyguards doing the same. A protest on Bas's lips died as he glanced nervously at the sky. Jewel growled, her blue eyes sparking.

"What is it?" Miss Winter said, her eyes darting between them. "It's just a storm."

"That is no ordinary storm, my lady," Bear informed her. "Not in this part of the world."

Dorian ran back to the stranger, who had gone pale as well, his arrogant posture dissolving as he paced back and forth. "There's no time, Cassius Vera. We are headed to Calliope. Before I invite you to travel with us, I must know if I can trust you."

The *alter* didn't hesitate. "I mean you no harm. Have your *mem* look inside my head if you wish it. You can trust me." Though no light coiled between them, the expression in his eyes was unmistakably sincere. He shoved his gloved hand toward Dorian, who took it, gripping it firmly.

"Well, then. Do you know of any shelter nearby?"

"There's an abandoned building left over from the world-that-was. It's ten minutes hard riding in that direction," he said as he pointed. "I had to flee with only the clothes on my back, so unfortunately I have no horse."

Dorian glanced at the sky. Every minute counted. Miss Winter was the lightest, so Cassius would have to ride double with her. Judging by the look on her face, she had arrived at the same conclusion.

"I expect you to be a gentleman to her," Dorian warned before heading for Marmalade.

The cocky stranger from before resurfaced. "I'm always a gentleman. My lord."

They rode as fast as they could through the trees, as quickly as they could manage without breaking one of the horses' legs. Cassius Vera proved himself to be a competent rider, and Dorian was thankful for the horsemanship in light of a pace that might have unseated the less-skilled

Miss Winter. Cassius seemed to have sensed her inexperience, for he had put her before him instead of behind him, and though Dorian knew she hated it, it would keep her from falling.

The forest had sprung to life ahead of the storm. As the gray thickened and the temperature dropped, jagged spears of multi-colored light flashed overhead. Roe deer flitted soundlessly through the trees, while foxes, weasels, brown hares, rabbits, and mice retreated into their respective burrows. Red and brown squirrels scurried to their homes in tree holes, along with tawny owls and other birds. Winter was always an unpredictable season in Memosine—the season of extremes—but here, on the edge of the moorland, the magic of the gray was especially potent. It was no wonder the village was so violently opposed to *alters*, for their close proximity to the moors had likely spawned many of them.

The abandoned building was where Cassius had said it would be, leaving Dorian to wonder if he'd sheltered there before. By the time they reached it, the gray was so thick it was becoming difficult to breathe, and even Jewel appeared winded. Miss Winter's breathing was strident as Bear helped her down.

"Is it poisonous?" she gasped, covering her mouth with a gloved hand.

"Nay," Bear said between coughs. "But if it gets thick enough, you can pass out."

Thunder cracked overhead, and Bear's stallion shrieked and reared. In the space of an eyewink, rain began falling in sheets.

"Bring the horses," Dorian ordered. "Move as quickly as you can."

Grabbing Ivy's reins, Cassius led the way to a cluster of enormous stones covered in moss. After he squeezed through a gap only large enough to admit one horse at a time, Dorian led Marmalade after him, keeping one hand on his quarterstaff in case it was a possible ambush.

But the earth only yielded to a paved path, cracked and overgrown with moss and bracken. Crumbling columns in various stages of decay lined the path, which had likely once been a colonnade, leading to an enormous stone archway covered with ivy and infested with weeds.

Cassius handed Ivy's reins to Miss Winter and stepped beneath the archway, pressing his shoulder against a solid oak door, which had somehow escaped decay.

"I'll need your help with this, Thane. It's a little stuck."

Ignoring the reference to his former title—evidently Cassius paid
close attention—Dorian gave his reins to Bear, who had managed to calm
his horse, and joined Cassius at the door. It finally shifted between their
combined efforts, shuddering before creaking inward on old hinges. A
musty odor drifted from within, stale and redolent with memory.

"What is this place?" he heard Miss Winter ask as they passed
beneath the archway into an enormous hall, dripping water all over
the stone floor. Weeds had claimed much of the space, but he could
discern two wooden staircases curving upward on either side to meet
a second story, which overlooked the main hall, and at least a dozen
slitted windows that would let in whatever light there was to be had.
The vaulted ceilings were crawling with ivy but looked solid, unlike the
broken columns outside.

He knew better than to entrust himself to the rotted wood of
the staircases. Leaving Bear and Bas to tend to the horses, Dorian
accompanied Cassius deeper into the chamber, which was more
greenhouse than entrance hall. It had once been a mansion, he thought,
or some kind of temple or monument, since there were traces of broken
furniture that might have been tables or chairs, and the occasional
worm-eaten tapestry or artwork. Several marble sculptures grouped in
a small alcove were crusted with moss, bearing witness to a lingering
damp, but the roof was holding its own without any leaks. He hoped it
would bear up a little longer.

They passed beneath another stone archway into a room that
resembled a library, tall shelves made of some dark wood leaning against
every vertical surface. The volumes they had borne had long since rotted
away. But at least this room seemed waterproof and had escaped the
assault of greenery, which had overtaken the hall. Though the room was
devoid of furniture, a large fireplace stood at the end of the chamber
beneath a carved stone mantelpiece three times larger than Lord Faro's.
A tidy pile of wood sat beside the hearth.

Ah. There was the furniture.

"A remnant of the *praeteritum*?" Dorian asked the *lumen*, whose
roving gaze about the room seemed to indicate he had not been here
before. "The past?"

"Aye, I heard talk of it in the village. They won't come near this place. They think it's cursed."

"Perhaps they're right." Miss Winter was dripping wet and shivering, her white-blond hair limp around her ears. Beside her, Jewel looked little better, thumping her tail against the wooden floor in disapproval, forming a small puddle.

Cassius Vera turned in a slow circle to face them. "So, my lord, it seems you finally resolved to trust me. What made you change your mind?"

"Who says I'm a lord?"

"Your men, apparently. Not that they were thinking to disguise it at the time, in their zeal to evict me from your presence. Lord Adamo, is it?"

Dorian would have to be more careful. He couldn't lie around this man, not that he considered himself to be in the habit of telling untruths. "You called me thane before. I no longer possess that title." Green ribbons drifted unhelpfully across the chamber toward him.

Cassius shrugged, but his shoulders were stiff. "Once a thane, always a thane."

"And you were a slave, weren't you?"

The stranger's eyes sharpened. "Clever, Thane. How'd you guess that?"

When Dorian didn't reply, Cassius looked at Miss Winter. "The last time I saw you, you were a slave, too."

"My fortunes have changed since then." Even her voice sounded cold, and not because of the *alter*. They were all soaking wet. If they didn't get a fire going soon, they would have more to worry about than an enigmatic stranger or a magic-ridden thunderstorm.

With a quiet command to Jewel to stay with the *mem*, Dorian left the chamber. He had not gone far before he heard Cassius Vera's taunting voice echoing through the space.

"Miss Winter, is it? Is there a first name to go with that frigid title?"

Quickly returning to the doorway, Dorian hesitated, then flattened himself against the wall outside, listening. Perhaps the stranger would be more truthful out of Dorian's earshot. After all, Miss Winter had already visited his mind.

"Sephone," she replied, her tone still cool.

"A lovely name for a most unusual woman. And how did you come to be in this part of the world, Sephone?"

"I am in the service of Lord Adamo."

"He didn't kidnap you, then?"

"Of course he didn't kidnap me." She sounded riled. "He offered me an opportunity for employment, and I took it." There was a brief pause, then, "You should tell the lord your past and what pursues you. He will be sympathetic to your cause."

"As you are?"

"I'm a *mem*, remember? I saw what happened to you when you touched my arm."

"Ah, your gift." Cassius Vera's cockiness had receded, revealing a hint of vulnerability. "I wasn't always a slave, you know. I was born free—the same as you. When I was young, I joined Marianthe's navy, believing I would be among the first to discover brave new worlds beyond our shores." He laughed, an abrasive sound that possessed more bitterness than mirth. "You saw the good captain in my mind? His cruelty to those men he considered beneath his notice and guardianship?"

"I saw." Her voice was barely audible.

"Then you know that when he discovered my gift, he was so afraid I'd spill all his secrets that he had me arrested . . . despite my years of faithful service. And you know how I was used by Marianthe's most benevolent authorities to interrogate their enemies against their will . . . and mine."

"I know."

"Then you won't share any of this with your new master."

"He isn't my master."

"*Mems* are used in interrogations too, you know. In Marianthe. Probably here in Memosine too. Their evidence might not be admissible in a court, but evidence isn't the only thing that's valuable. You could have been enslaved along with me, Sephone. Lucky for both of us, we escaped."

No wonder this *lumen* hated titled folk. His government had used his gift in the worst possible way. Dorian carefully shifted his weight, hoping Jewel wouldn't give away his presence.

"You have naught to fear from Lord Adamo. He won't betray either of us."

"Oh? *Lumens* are rare in Caldera, Sephone, as rare as *mems*. You don't know the aristocracy like I do."

This time, her voice was strained. "I think I *do* know the aristocracy, Mister Vera."

"Cass."

"Cass. I promise you we aren't in any danger. Lord Adamo is an *alter* himself."

"Oh?" Cassius said again. "Even I have heard of Lord Adamo. Once a serious contender for the arch-lordship of Memosine, or so I heard after spending only five minutes in this country. Thane or nay, he's wealthier and more powerful than you know, Sephone. What's to prevent him from turning me in to curry favor with the Marianthean lords?"

"Honor. I know him. He detests the very idea of slavery."

How could she claim to know him so well? Aye, he valued honor, but what good was that when he'd failed his family in the very hour they needed him the most? And whatever she said, he *had* stolen her from Cutter, rather than taking the necessary steps to try and free her. She risked her very life by coming with him.

"And what is the lord's gift, Sephone?"

"I . . ." Her voice faltered. "I don't know."

"You don't know? If he trusted you half as much as you seem to trust him, don't you think he'd have told you by now?"

"He'll tell me when he's ready."

Cassius laughed again. "Foolish girl. At least Adamo has the sense to keep his cards close to his chest."

There was the sound of quickening footsteps, and Miss Winter flew through the archway past Dorian, Jewel close behind. She faltered when she saw him, her brown eyes sobering as she realized he'd overheard their conversation.

"Miss Winter—"

But she was gone. At Dorian's nod, Jewel went with her. When he turned around, he saw the *lumen* watching him.

"So you were eavesdropping, Thane?"

It was useless to deny it. "I expected you had something to hide. You proved me right."

Cassius studied the retreating figure of Miss Winter. "You didn't meet her master, did you, Thane?"

"I did." More green ribbons. The man's gift was unnerving, to say the least.

"Then you know he will punish you both if he catches you. The same way he punished your Miss Winter for disobedience the day I first met her."

Dorian recalled the bruise on her cheek. Apparently, Cassius Vera had been there the day Cutter delivered it. But the agreement between them was none of Cassius's business.

"Miss Winter knew what she risked to come with me. As for you . . ." Dorian folded his arms and leaned his shoulder against the stone archway. "Both Miss Winter and the lady wolf appear to trust you, Cassius Vera, so I'll do one better than not turning you in to your former masters. I can offer you paid employment over the coming months." Trusting his instincts, Dorian briefly outlined his quest for the Reliquary, giving only the barest explanation of his reasons for pursuing the ancient artifact.

Surprisingly, Cassius's mouth twisted in sympathy at the brief mention of Dorian's loss. "This Reliquary. Can it do other things besides permanently altering memories?"

"Like what?"

"Enable one to control their abilities, perhaps."

Ah, his truth-revealing gift. No doubt it troubled the *lumen* more than he let on. What person would ever feel comfortable in the presence of green and black ribbons swirling in the air? Sometimes lying acted in the service of self-preservation. And if Cassius had a weakness for the fairer sex, as Dorian suspected—

"It is rumored to be a relic of considerable power. It may have many functions we do not understand."

Cassius digested this, nodding slowly. "I'll do it." His grin turned sly. "But you should probably purchase another horse for the journey. Your Miss Winter doesn't like to be touched."

"Get all that from the slap, did you?"

The man continued smiling as Dorian turned to leave.

"One more thing, Thane."

Dorian swiveled, waiting.

"She hates it when you call her that. Miss Winter, I mean."

"You can read minds too?"

"I don't need to be a *mem* to read that girl. She has devoted puppy dog written all over her." Cassius paused. "It's a touch formal, don't you think? And I don't think she's fond of the season itself."

"It's her name."

"She's been inside both our minds. Probably knows all our deepest, darkest secrets. Daft to keep calling her *miss*, I think." He grinned. "Dorian Ashwood, isn't it?"

"Lord Adamo."

"Touchy fellow, aren't you? Afraid to be on equal terms with a slave?"

Dorian sent him a withering look. His gift would be wasted on a man like Cassius Vera. He had boldness enough for ten men.

"You wouldn't believe the truth if your own gift declared it to your face." And he spun on his heel and left the room without waiting to see if the ribbons were green or black.

The storm continued into the late hours of the evening. Lord Adamo had ventured outside and returned coated in white, announcing it was now blizzarding.

"What about Draven?" Bear asked. "He can't be far behind us."

"He'll be as marooned by this storm as we are. But the turn in the weather is to our benefit. The snow is thick enough to cover our tracks."

"What's one more enemy?" Bas asked with a glare that also encompassed both Cassius and me. "The list grows longer every day. I'm enjoying contemplating all the new potential ways of dying."

Lord Adamo returned the glare. "If you must do so, Bas, then do so quietly."

We had retreated into the old library, leaving the horses hobbled in the great hall, as Lord Adamo called it. Cassius had got a fire going, and with the door to the library closed, it filled the space with a pleasant warmth, banishing the chill from outside. I was thankful Lord Adamo had kept my old cloak in one of the saddlebags, for my new one was soaked. I edged as close to the fire as I dared, Jewel sprawling beside me.

"What makes that storm so dangerous?" I asked Lord Adamo as he lowered himself to the ground on the other side of Jewel. I had discovered that the wolf liked to be scratched around her ears and on her belly—but not near the scar. "We never had such happenings in Nulla. And I saw—well, I thought I saw rainbow-colored lightning—"

"You saw correctly." He brushed the snow from his hair, removed his gloves, and extended his hands toward the fire. "It is not ordinary lightning. The bolts seek the flesh of humans—especially *alters*. They are drawn to the magic that courses through our veins. To remain exposed in such a storm is to tempt death."

No wonder he and the others had been in such a hurry to reach shelter.

The lord continued, "I have seen very little of Lethe, so I cannot speak for that country, but many parts of Memosine were touched by the same magical forces that created the *alters*. There are animals capable of extraordinary things, like Jewel. Trees that do not grow in the same way as ordinary plants. Every year on the moors, near the beginning of spring, the wildfires come, engulfing the heather in an inferno that can burn for days. And in the ancient places, where people from the Old Times or the world-that-was lived before us . . ."

He rubbed his beard thoughtfully. "Suffice it to say, Memosine boasts as much beauty as it does barrenness. And as much mutability as permanence, for a man can frequently return to something he thought he knew with vivid clarity, only to find it altered beyond all recognition."

I felt an odd sensation like a heated beverage—tea, perhaps, or even coffee—gliding down my throat. It wasn't just the fire warming me. It was something about Lord Adamo himself. I remembered Cassius's challenge.

If he trusted you half as much as you seem to trust him, don't you think he'd have told you by now?

I swallowed and asked the next question foremost on my mind.

"Is the rest of Memosine like this?" When Lord Adamo looked at me, I tried to explain. "Everything is so green and full of life—"

He nodded, understanding. "It wasn't always, Sephone, at least not after the war, and then Memosine was ravaged by wildfires and storms. But when the gray came, the landscape began to change . . . to return to what it had been. Our forefathers called it the Greening. It has been thirty or so years since the world came back to life, though the wildfires and storms have continued to plague us from time to time."

I only stared at him.

"What is it?"

"You called me Sephone, my lord."

He actually sighed. "Aye, forgive an old, stubborn fool. There's no need for the *my lord*, either. Just Dorian."

As if that small speech had cost him greatly, he leaned back on his hands, staring into the fire. A tiny growl from Jewel reminded me that I had paused in my patting duties. I obediently resumed them.

Dorian.

Name or no name, Dorian didn't remember our association. I could resurrect his memory for him using my gift, but it wouldn't be the same. I wanted him to remember me of his own accord. Even though I'd changed.

"You're not old," I said, smiling.

"You're mistaken." His returning smile was wistful. "I'm a hundred years old, and twice as weary."

Footfalls sounded behind us, and Cass plopped down on my other side, closer than I preferred. "So, Thane," he said, shooting a glance at Dorian as he mimicked his casual posture. "What's the nature of this gift of yours?"

Across the room, Bas was practicing his prize-winning scowl. I wondered if he'd ever considered entering it in a competition, for he could give Cutter a run for his money. Some might even go so far as to call it a gift.

"Forbearance." Surprisingly, Dorian grinned at me. "Long-suffering."

Cass laughed as black ribbons drifted from him to the lord. "Don't they say patience is a virtue? Why not a gift?" He reached out and patted my glove. "These are soaked, Sephone. Why haven't you taken them off to dry in front of the fire?"

I'd sooner attempt a snow angel in the main street of Nulla.

"I prefer to keep out the world." Surreptitiously, I edged closer to Jewel. At least the green ribbons now spiraling around my arms declared me truthful.

Having already removed his cloak and gloves, Cass rolled up his damp shirtsleeves, exposing intricate tattoos covering the entirety of his forearms. Despite my reservations, I leaned closer to study them. They depicted colorful scenes from both Marianthe and the world-that-was—a tall ship with billowing white sails, a compass and captain's spyglass, a jeweled sword like the knights of old might have carried, and a broken hourglass with the sand spilling out. There was a mechanical contraption

I'd once learned was called a steam train, and even a patch of ripe strawberries. Spying the curvaceous outline of a woman near his right wrist, I hastily withdrew my gaze.

Cass smirked at my spreading blush. "You like to keep out the world, Seph? Well, I like to keep it in."

No one had ever called me Seph except for Regis. I might have been flattered, but for the fact that I'd peered into his mind. I wouldn't hesitate to trust Cassius Vera with my life—he'd once taken a beating for a fellow sailor he barely knew—but I'd never entrust him with my heart. Even if he was the most handsome man I'd ever seen.

I stood, stretched, and faked a yawn, something which was never so difficult once the idea was conceived. "I'm tired. I'll see you both in the morning."

"Skittish little thing, isn't she?" I heard Cass say to Dorian as I made for my bedroll, not even bothering to keep his voice low.

Blessedly, Dorian didn't reply.

When we stepped outside the next morning, the snow was so thick that Jewel immediately sank to her throat. The ruined colonnade had disappeared beneath a glittering layer of white, obscuring the façade of the abandoned mansion. It would have been impossible to find once the snow began falling. The green forest surrounding us had been transformed into a fairy land of mystery and wonder. Unlike the dirty slush lining Nulla's streets, this snow looked clean and fresh.

"As much as I'd like to stay inside another day," Dorian said with a grim look, "it's best we move on. Draven won't be hampered by this."

Cass agreed. Apparently, Dorian had brought him up to speed last night, and not just about the Reliquary, but the adversaries hunting us.

So began a long and miserable day. I thought I had been cold before, especially that day on the ice, but that had lasted only minutes before I was plucked from the water and enfolded in a pair of strong, warm arms. Even Cass's high spirits dimmed after hours of trudging through several feet of clinging wetness, for in many parts it was impossible to ride the horses. Mercifully, my boots were waterproof, having been carefully repaired in Iona while I was forced to wear the slippers.

By late afternoon—the thick gray and additional snowfall made it impossible to tell the time with any accuracy—Bear called to Dorian at the head of the column. "There's another small town ahead, my lord. Shall we stop and rest a while? The ladies are looking mighty chilled."

I blessed the man's heart and choice of words, for Jewel had mastered the terrain early on, as only a wolf could, and showed no signs of feeling the cold. It was only me who had nearly frozen solid.

Dorian turned, barely recognizable in his snow-covered mantle. "Of course. If there's room, and *alters* are welcome, we'll stay the night."

It was quite an *if*. But my spirits buoyed as the town came into sight, and Ivy lifted her head and whinnied, Marmalade answering a moment later. The town—or at least the inn—proved to be friendly, even after the proprietors saw Cass's hair, and the brothers accompanied the innkeeper's nephew to the stables with the horses. Perhaps the coin Dorian had briefly flashed was enough to quell any suspicions about three *alters* traveling together with two ordinary folk—one of whom was a giant—not to mention the white wolf. Or was it because he had made the request in his native language? I had rarely heard him speak it before.

I followed Dorian and Cass into the tavern, which sold both memory potions and normal liquor. Surprisingly, Cass preferred the ordinary stuff, downing half a mug of mulled wine before Dorian had procured rooms upstairs.

"Have a drink with me," Cass said to me with a warm smile, patting a seat next to his, close to the roaring fire. Once again in good spirits, he didn't seem bothered by the snow melting from his clothes.

Dorian eyed him. "I think she'd prefer not to freeze to death."

Cass grinned, leaning back in his chair. "That's what the fire is for. And the liquor."

Rolling my eyes, I shook my head at him and followed Dorian up the stairs. The lord unlocked two adjacent rooms, indicating one was for me and the other for the men.

"The lock on the door is solid, Sephone. But if you need anything, you have only to call for me or Bear."

I noticed the omission of his other bodyguard's name. If I were being murdered, no doubt Bas would applaud my attacker.

"Thank you, my—uh, Dorian," I amended as I noticed Jewel, who'd come with us, was limping slightly. "I think something's wrong with the lady."

He glanced down as his forehead knitted with concern. He guided Jewel into my room, where the fire had been recently lit. Crouching beside her, heedless of the puddle forming around him, he bent and inspected the injured paw—her front left.

"I can't see anything."

I knelt beside him and peeled off my gloves. The wolf watched me with glittering sapphire eyes as I took her paw from Dorian and studied the pad. Keeping my gaze on the magnificent animal, I gently touched sections of the foot, watching for her reaction. There, near the leftmost toe, or was it called a claw?—a distinct flickering of the eyes and flattening of the ears, what might have passed for a wince of pain in a human. Inspecting the foot more closely, I found it: a wooden splinter no longer than my smallest fingernail, but embedded deeply into the pad. Left any longer, it might have done serious damage.

I looked up at Dorian. "Can you hold her still while I remove it?"

"I will, but you needn't worry. She knows it must come out."

Nodding, I bent to my task. Dorian wrapped his arms around the wolf's back and chest, more embracing than restraining her. But Jewel remained rigidly still while I worked on the splinter, glad my own nails had grown a little of late, for none of us carried surgical tools. A minute later, the splinter came free. Only the tiniest of growls emanated from Jewel's chest as I tossed the bloodied shard into the fire. When Dorian released her, she bent her head and licked my hand.

"I think she is saying thank you," Dorian said, rubbing the wolf's ears.

I smiled at Jewel. "I'll try and find a bandage."

"She'll only tear it off."

"Some ointment, then. In case of infection."

"Aye," the lord said. "Thank you, Sephone."

His face was still partially submerged in the wolf's fur. I willed him to look up and recognize me. But he only patted the lady wolf and stood.

"A woman is bringing some dry clothes for you. I'll leave you to change." And then he was gone, leaving me with Jewel and a puddle of foolish thoughts.

There was little merriment that night. By the time the woman had found me some dry clothes and I had adequately defrosted, only Dorian and his men were still downstairs. Cass had retired early, apparently so tired he could barely hold his head up. I tried to ignore the glare of Bas as Dorian spoke quietly with Bear, his finger tracing a path on the map he'd brought.

"You heard the woman in Iona. There's talk that the forests down south are home to strange things. The Reliquary could well be—"

"Then what about Lethe, my lord? They have forests aplenty too."

"I won't cross the border into Lethe unless I have to, Bear. The gray is thicker there, as well you know. It's said to interfere with the powers of *alters*."

Dorian glanced around the room. "But for now, I think it is time for dinner."

There was more of what he considered humble fare—likely the best the innkeeper could produce at short notice—but all three men declined the selection of memory potions offered to them. When the brothers yawned in unison, Dorian ordered them to bed. They went without protest.

Dorian looked exhausted, but he made no immediate move toward his own bed. I considered offering again to help him sleep, but he looked so unlike his usual self that I thought better of it. If his nightmares truly worsened following a mind-bleeding, I didn't want to cause him further pain.

Finally, I stood. "Good night, Dorian."

"I'll see you to your room."

I blinked.

Where's your father, little one? I'll take you to him if you can point me in the right direction.

I followed him upstairs. Drifting in old memories, I nearly bumped into him in the corridor, belatedly realizing he'd come to a standstill. I came around him to see what had captured his attention in time to hear a giggle. Cass came around the corner, his hair unmistakably ruffled.

I felt Dorian stiffen beside me.

Apparently, there were different classes of fatigue.

Cass jumped as he saw us, then relaxed, flashing me a wide smile as he gently closed the door behind him and held a finger to his lips.

"Lost, are we?" Dorian asked sarcastically, ignoring the silent admonition to lower his voice.

"I know exactly where I am." The words were faintly slurred.

"You're drunk."

"And you're nosey. *My lord.*"

"Do I need to enquire after the welfare of the lady?"

Another smile. "Not a lady. But she was willing. They always are."

The pretty woman, younger even than myself, who'd brought me the dry clothes? Was that why she had appeared so distracted . . . and pleasantly so?

I'd seen enough of Cassius Vera's past to know two things: that such happenings were habitual for him, and that he spoke the truth about the willingness of his lovers. But it didn't stop him from winking at me.

"If you've jeopardized our quest in any way, Vera—"

"Of course I haven't," Cass smirked. "I can lie through my teeth, remember? My own secrets are always safe. It's everyone else who has to watch themselves."

Dorian glared at him. "You're a wretch and a scoundrel. We leave here tomorrow, and what will she say when she finds out?"

"She knew I couldn't stay."

"And what about her father, man? You insult the generosity of our host—"

Not wanting to hear any more, I slipped past Dorian and made for my room, Jewel trailing behind as if she shared my disgust. I'd met too many men like Cassius Vera. My wariness toward him had been justified.

It was only after I'd lain down to sleep that I realized what had eluded me before: during the entire exchange between Dorian and Cass, there had been no green or black ribbons.

15

SEPHONE

The journey that should have lasted no longer than a week now threatened to stretch into two.

As cold fronts swept in from the sea, the weather could deteriorate quickly, and it was difficult to make any headway when the trails and roads were choked with snow. For the most part, we followed a small tributary of the River Memosine, and I gaped at the sight of frozen waterfalls and icy pools both alluring and treacherous. There was little sign of life, but Dorian said the rivers were well-stocked with trout, salmon, and other fish, their numbers controlled by otters, stoats, and in the spring, golden eagles and osprey. Once, I thought I saw a beaver surface through a hole in the ice, no doubt protecting its underwater lodge.

By the time we reached the moors, the snow had begun to melt, though the gray lingered. I tried to picture it in summer, as I'd once seen in a mind: rolling foothills covered in blooming purple heather, with patches of cotton grass, moss, bracken, and crowberry spreading in every direction. The occasional cluster of wildflowers guarded by zealous honeybees, and the sun flitting in and out of clouds. What would it be like to watch the moorland burn?

Whatever its colors in other seasons, now it was only a vast expanse of white, tufts of grass poking up through the thinnest patches. There were remnants of the world-that-was everywhere I looked: a section of old stone wall, crumbling into ruin; a pair of parallel iron tracks, crusted with moss and choked with gorse; even the occasional set of stepping stones across a river. And plenty of things I didn't recognize or understand, even with the glimpses of the old world I'd seen in the veteran's mind.

"Wait until you see Calliope," Dorian remarked when he caught me studying yet another pile of ruins. "I've never seen a more colorful city."

"Even compared to Maera?"

"Aye, even compared to Maera."

How had I seen so much and yet so little? But the minds of those I'd visited for the mind-bleedings rarely traveled beyond the walls of the seam, content to profit from those who came to Nulla seeking novelty. I had sometimes thought that perhaps the rest of Caldera must be dull and barren for them to envy us in our squalor.

How wrong I had been. Even in winter, the moorland had a loveliness to it that was difficult to put to words. Still, I found myself longing for the high places, for the mountain cities and the sky-high lakes only a few souls had ever visited.

For the sun, fickle as it was.

At last, we reached the far side of the moorland, and the gray shifted long enough to reveal even larger foothills to the north. We entered a small village on the edge of the forest at what might have been sunset. Several children came out of their houses to watch us as we passed, some accompanied by young mothers.

Seeing Cass grin at several of the prettiest, I bit my lip to avoid sounding a warning to the women of the village to take their belongings and run. If the past few villages were any indication, they'd find him irresistible.

"Aren't they put off by your gift?" I asked him. "They need only to speak and—"

"All the more reason not to talk," Cass replied with a grin.

I shook my head, repulsed by his shallowness. "And the liquor?"

"Call me old-fashioned. I enjoy the same pleasures as any man, but I prefer the old vices. These fancy liquid memories aren't the same."

"You mean, they don't numb your past so well as the traditional methods."

Something flitted across his face, gone before I could identify it. "Who says I'm numbing my past, Sephone?" He looked just like Jewel after she'd been given a plate of food. Guarded, like she didn't want to share her treasures, but hyper-observant, as if she was still more than capable of coveting the treasures of others.

"If you can't speak the truth to others, at least admit it to yourself." I spurred Ivy into a trot and moved past him. Thankfully, Dorian had bought Cass his own horse at the first village we'd sheltered in. Though I doubted Cass would see me as a potential conquest, I had no wish to be in close proximity to him.

A better horseman than I, he caught up to me as we entered the town. "I'll admit I have a penchant for some things this world no longer produces. Strawberries, for one. I'm certain you remember that preference. But as for the old-fashioned things—"

"Quiet," Dorian suddenly ordered, holding up a hand. He murmured something to his bodyguards in their native language, and Bear nodded. Dorian spurred Marmalade to come between us. "I don't like the feel of this place. We'll move on and find shelter elsewhere."

"But Thane—" Cass began in protest.

"You'll find plenty of hearts to break in Calliope."

"Dorian," I said. "I don't know about the other horses, but Ivy's exhausted, and I think she might have a stone in her shoe. Do you know of any shelters ahead?"

Dorian glanced around. "I haven't been this way before," he admitted. "I usually stick to the main roads."

"Can we not stay, and remain on our guard?"

"I'm not the one you should be worrying about, Sephone."

We both looked at Cass.

"What?" he exclaimed, throwing his hands up. "I'll be on my best behavior."

"That's hardly a strong endorsement." Dorian returned his attention to me. "Very well, we'll stay the night. But keep your eyes open. We're not far from Argus now."

And Lord Draven. I tried not to shudder, remembering everything I'd seen in that man's mind. Though Dorian believed it had snowed enough to mask our trail, Lord Draven might be able to track us in other ways . . . including following the trail of broken hearts left in Cass's wake. And then there was Cutter . . .

The inn's proprietors were cautious but polite. Cass remained at Dorian's side until, like a wolfhound, he caught scent of the free-flowing liquor, and then he was gone to flirt with a raven-haired woman on the other side of the tavern. Her hair was so black it shone purple-blue in the light. An *alter*? She and Cass certainly made a handsome couple. Only a few yards away, Bas was trading insults with Bear, while Jewel had stayed beside the fireplace in my room. Was it normal, in a crowd of people, to feel so alone?

"Are you all right, Sephone?"

Glancing up and finding Dorian's eyes on me, I realized I'd been staring into my mug of mulled wine for several minutes. My half-finished plate was still in front of me, proving that even if one diligently pushes food across the entire surface area and back again, it doesn't reduce in size.

"Aye, of course I'm fine. Why do you ask?"

"You seemed . . . I don't know. Sad."

Could I tell him why? The boy from the ice would want to know. But why burden this man, who had endured more than his fair share of troubles?

"Oh, nothing really." I fiddled with the food on my plate. "I'm twenty-one today."

"It's your birthday? Why didn't you say so?"

I shrugged. "It's just another day."

He studied me a moment. "You're thinking about your parents, aren't you? The memory potion you hoped to have from them?"

Oh, but he was perceptive. "I thought today would be the beginning of the rest of my life. I was just thinking I'm not used to living without the hope of something . . . well, *more*."

"You are more hopeful than anyone I've ever met, Sephone," Dorian said. "You see beauty in everything—including the places where no one else has thought to look. Perhaps you're merely learning to hope in other things. Maybe even better things." He leaned forward. "When we find the Reliquary, you'll be able to discover more about them. Your parents, that is."

"If we find it."

"Well, I'm hoping, too." He reached inside his mantle and withdrew a tiny glass bottle stoppered with cork. Briefly taking my gloved hand, he placed the bottle in my palm. "I thought about the flowers from your necklace the night we attended Lord Faro's party. When I described them to one of the servants, he went to Faro's cellar and returned with this. I don't know if it's the right one—the man didn't even know what it was called—but Faro's collection rivals that of most lords."

I examined the bottle. Small enough to fit in my palm, the surface of the glass was rippled, but so thin it was almost translucent. The faded label bore a tiny sketch of a flower almost identical to the ones trapped inside my resin necklace. I thought of the old veteran and his strawberries. Was it the same flower? And if it was, would the fragrance be the same as the real thing?

Dorian cleared his throat. "Since you said you were nearly twenty-one, I decided then to give it to you on your birthday. I didn't know it was today." He gave the vial a rueful look. "It's not the same as a memory from your parents, not in the slightest. But I hoped it might help you remember them."

"It's beautiful." I met his gaze, hoping he wouldn't notice the tears shimmering in my eyes. "Thank you, my lord."

"I thought it was Dorian now." He was smiling faintly.

"It is. Sorry."

"Will you drink it tonight, or save it for later?"

"I think I'll save it. Maybe it can help me find the real thing."

"See, Sephone? There's your hope back again."

"And what about you? What are your hopes for the future?"

I nearly slapped myself. It was entirely the wrong thing to say. The carefree youth vanished, quickly replaced by a man who looked like he'd pawned his soul. "A star can only fall to earth once, Sephone. Like I said before, I had my chance at living."

"Stars fall every day." Was he talking about his wife? "You might fall in love with someone else."

"I will never remarry, Sephone, not even for subterfuge's sake. It simply wouldn't be fair on the woman." I didn't need Cass's green ribbons to understand the sincerity in his eyes.

I opened my mouth to answer, but something behind me had caught Dorian's eye, and I turned to follow his gaze. The raven-haired woman—who had disappeared with Cass not long before—had returned and was speaking to a man with pale hair who had come down the stairs after her. Donning their hoods, they quickly departed the tavern.

"Didn't she—"

Dorian clambered to his feet. "Aye, I think it's time we check on our *lumen.*"

I stashed the bottle in the pocket inside my cloak and hurried after him. The brothers abandoned their ongoing argument, made a show of yawning and stretching, and followed at a slower pace. But they caught up to me on the stairs.

I had barely reached the top of the staircase when I heard the groans. Dorian was kneeling beside a disheveled figure slumped against the external frame of a closed door.

Dorian glanced up. "Bas, keep a lookout on the stairs. Bear, see if you can find any trace of the black-haired woman or the blond man who was downstairs before. Sephone, if you wouldn't mind—" He gestured to the other side of Cass as his bodyguards hurried to obey his orders.

I sank to my knees. Cass's face was almost as colorful as his eyes, with smudges of purple amidst the blue and green. One eye was swelling shut, while a cut near his ear had bloodied the side of his face.

"I think . . . I've been . . ." Cass gasped, clutching his ribs. " . . . robbed."

"Of your looks, aye," was Dorian's reply. "Don't worry, you'll get them back eventually." He slid an arm beneath the *lumen*'s upper back and carefully lifted him. I took Cass's other arm and allowed him to lean on my shoulder as we steered him into the room adjacent to mine. Bas remained at the top of the stairs, face tight as he scanned our surroundings. *This is why we don't pick up strays,* I imagined him saying to himself.

When we reached the closest bed, Dorian eased Cass onto the mattress, immediately bloodying the sheets. I dug out bandages from Bear's saddlebags and carried over the pitcher of water and basin from the sideboard.

"Where's Jewel?" Dorian asked me, and I heard his unspoken query. Why hadn't the lady wolf warned him of danger?

"She's sleeping in my room," I told him, then added with a slight smile, "Perhaps she doesn't consider Cass part of her pack."

Dorian's lips twitched as he took the bandages from me. "I'll do it," he said, with an explanatory nod at my gloves.

"S-Sleph's not in any danger from me," Cass slurred, his eyes closed. "My gift won't work on either of y-you right now."

"It isn't your gift I was thinking of," Dorian replied, beginning to clean him up.

I was curious. "Why won't your gift work on us?" It was odd to see Cass without the green and black ribbons of light. I'd almost gotten used to them.

"Because I'm d-drunk. Liquor neutralizes my gift. W-women can say what they like around me. Can't even detect the truth when I touch 'em. It's sweet oblivion. B-bl-blessed relief."

So that was it. Was that why he drank so much, to numb his troublesome gift? Or simply because it aided him in his womanizing?

Cass's eyes flickered open, and despite Dorian's quip, I knew that no beating would ever rob the man of his beauty. His irises were as iridescent as dragon scales, his hair so smooth it might have been made of oil.

Dorian began to bandage the *lumen*'s head. "What happened to you?"

"I was attacked. The woman had a friend hiding in her room, and when he'd f-finished beating me, they robbed me and left me for dead."

"You ought to be more cautious."

Cass winced. "Pick another time for your slermonizing, Thane. My head aches."

"Could it be Lord Draven?" I asked Dorian. "One of his men?"

He washed his hands and wiped them on a towel. "Draven wouldn't pick one of us off and then leave. Nay, I'd say young Cass just needs to watch whom he befriends. Even so, I'll set another watch tonight. And I'll alert the innkeeper to potential trouble, if Bear hasn't already done so."

I arrived downstairs just as Bear returned to the tavern, grumpy and wind-bitten. "No sign of them," he said when he saw me. "No doubt they're spending their reward someplace else." Beside him,

Jewel shook herself, flinging snow in every direction. She moved so silently, I hadn't even realized she'd left my room.

The rest of the night passed with nothing more eventful than Cass emptying the contents of his insides several times. I could hear Dorian's voice through the thin walls. The words were inaudible, but the tone was distinctly compassionate. Kind, like the boy from the ice.

Early the next morning, I mounted Ivy and watched as Bear and Dorian helped a near-whimpering Cass into his saddle. Only superficial injuries, but they would make riding uncomfortable.

"Lot of use he's going to be in Calliope," Bas muttered. Within seconds, green and black ribbons mingled together in the frigid air between the two men. Apparently, even Cass's gift couldn't decide if the statement was true or false. Or perhaps that was merely the lingering effects of his intoxication.

As Bear hid a smile, I glanced over at Dorian, only to catch a glimpse of a shadow behind him. A man stood on the porch of the inn, watching our party. His hood hung low over his eyes, concealing most of his face. I opened my mouth to call to Dorian, but when I looked again, the man was gone.

I mentally shook my head. The hooded man was nothing more than a figment of my imagination—a memory splinter, most likely. For the past few days I'd had nightmares, my subconscious borrowing the troubles of the hundreds of minds I'd visited as soon as I closed my eyes. Only when Jewel lay beside me did they become tolerable.

For seventeen years now, I had been living in shadows.

It was time to wake up.

"Will I be glad to get out of this saddle," Cass declared with a grimace, one gloved hand cradling his ribs while the other clutched the reins. "I could use a good bed too."

"I thought Mariantheans preferred hammocks," I tossed back.

"Mariantheans with bruised ribs have wildly different preferences to Mariantheans without bruised ribs, Seph." Apparently, the attack had failed to cure him of his compulsive need to charm the opposite sex, for he turned in the saddle and winked at me. I rolled my eyes at him.

We were only a day from Calliope, according to Dorian's calculations, and nearing another ruin where he planned to stay the night. Thankfully, we'd seen no sign of any enemy to date, whether vengeful slave master or jealous lover.

Our night's shelter had long ago been reclaimed by the surrounding forest, but, like the mansion outside Iona, its shingled roof was still intact. It was far less impressive a structure, smaller than Cutter's tavern but with the same vaulted ceilings of the mansion's main hall. Several windows permitted light into the space, most of them badly broken, though there were still shards remaining on the edges, enough to discern that they had been made of stained glass fused together with lead.

The men picked a campsite away from the drafts, near the front of the building. Any furniture had long since been used as firewood, but Bas had collected our own firewood along the way at Dorian's command. The bodyguard allowed me to start the fire beneath his strict supervision, giving me a grudging nod when I was successful.

After the others retired, I lay on my bedroll and closed my eyes.

For once, Jewel slept next to Dorian, while I'd picked a spot further away, tucked against a curved stone wall that gave me almost complete privacy from the men. If this was some kind of temple, as I suspected, the alcove might once have been a sanctuary, though what they had worshipped here was anyone's guess. There were no gods remaining in Caldera, Cutter had always said, just as there were no longer any kings. All we had left of them were memories.

I recalled the dusty bottles of inky-black liquid on Cutter's shelves—bottles even Cutter never touched. Apparently, they weren't good ones. Had the gods perished along with the rest of the world-that-was? Or had they merely forgotten about us? Though Cutter never spoke fondly about them, the world they had left behind was still beautiful. Beautiful enough to suggest, if one listened intently, a certain underlying benevolence.

I slipped into the dreamworld. I was back on the ice again, but this time I was viewing the memory as an observer. I watched as a tall youth with curly brown hair knelt on the edge of the ice-crusted canal, lowered himself to his belly, then carefully inched his way across to the gaping hole. A dozen or so men and women clustered around, all sharp whispers and puffs of white breath. None of them moved to help him, though one had a coil of rope hoisted over his shoulder.

The boy reached the hole and peered over the side of the ice sheet before plunging his bare hand into the frigid water, again and again. Seconds passed before he gave a shout. I watched my four-year-old self surface, barely conscious, my white-blond hair streaming water. The boy gripped me with both hands and pulled me from the canal, careful to distribute our combined weight with every movement. Around us, the ice groaned and shifted, warning of the strain.

My four-year-old eyes were closed now. Someone had thrown the end of a rope, and the boy swiftly tied it around my body in a makeshift harness. I was dragged to the side of the canal, still bleeding water, while another rope was tossed to the boy lying flattened beside the ice hole.

Then he was beside me, crouching over me. I was on solid ground now, but my eyes were still closed. "Little miss!" he called, holding me in his arms, gently slapping my cheeks. "Little miss!"

"She isn't breathing, lad."

The boy laid me on my back and knitted his long fingers together over my chest.

I jerked awake, imagining I was vomiting icy water all over myself, only to realize I was still in the stained glass building, tears striping my cheeks. A man crouched over me, his hands on my shoulders.

"Dorian?"

"Cass, actually." The words weren't slurred, but the breath that puffed against my forehead was tinged with liquor. I instinctively stiffened, sliding a hand toward the knife strapped to my thigh.

"I'm awake."

"I know. I came in from outside and saw you gripped in a nightmare. I thought you'd appreciate being woken up."

Well, I didn't, and it wasn't a nightmare. I wanted to see the boy's face as I regained consciousness, his look of heartfelt relief when he realized I lived. Not the shadow looming over me now with unknown intentions.

"Thanks. You can let me go now."

"Wait, there's something else I can do to help."

I doubted there was anything he could help me with at this hour, and I opened my mouth to tell him so, but before I could speak, he'd moved his hands to the bare skin where my loose shirt met my gloves.

Ribbons of light poured from his palms, as blue as Jewel's eyes, even in the darkness. Shocked into stillness, I stared as the liquid strands sank beneath my skin. A spark traveled along the length of my arm toward my heart, and for a few seconds I felt weightless, as if he had picked me up and tossed me into the air like a child. Some of the aching heaviness in my chest shifted. Then the spark died, and the light returned to Cass's palms, this time as red as blood.

I bolted upright, flattening my spine against the stone wall, and he let me go. I felt lighter, somehow, and the ice was very far away. Every shadow that stalked me was far away. "What did you do?"

His smile was barely visible by the light of the dying fire, but I knew it was more genuine than any I'd seen him wear to date. "Most Calderans have trouble sleeping, Seph. Thank goodness we *alters* have some tricks up our sleeves, eh?"

"That was part of your gift?" But the ribbons had been red and blue, not green and black.

"Aye, my secondary gift."

"You can . . ." I trailed off and repeated my question. "What did you do to me?"

"Strictly speaking, I shared in your troubles for a moment. Shouldered the sorrow alongside you, if you will. A burden shared is a burden halved, and all that."

I stared at him. Entranced by his primary gift, I'd failed to look for his secondary one in his mind. It was eerily similar to my own ability, but different, too. "You can control this gift, then?"

"Aye. Thank goodness, else I'd be one sorry fellow." He seated himself cross-legged beside me. "I can not only absorb sorrow, I can transmit it, too. My own, or sorrow funneled from others. But I rarely use it for that purpose. It's difficult to get anything out of a blubbering mess."

"Then you don't use it to seduce women?" I chided. "Share their sorrows, perhaps?"

"Nay, Seph. I'm far too selfish."

"And what do you do with this sorrow?" How would he manage mine?

"Oh, the usual things. I run very fast. Climb very tall trees." He sobered a little. "Pain cannot be created or destroyed, you know. It can only be transferred."

I nodded slowly. *Don't I know it.*

He leaned back on his hands, apparently content to talk the night away. "What's your secondary gift?"

"I don't have one."

He tossed his head disbelievingly. "Every *alter* has one. Gifts always come in pairs. Sometimes, even in threes."

"Not for me."

"Odd." Frowning, he reached up and brushed a tear from my cheek. "You were crying."

I batted his hand away. "How long were you watching me?"

"A minute at most. What were you dreaming about?"

"What everyone dreams about. The past."

"Oh?" Shifting slightly, he settled against the wall beside me, his shoulder brushing mine as he made himself comfortable. "Tell me about it."

I moved, putting distance between us. "I hardly know you."

He laughed. "We've been riding together for days. You've been inside my mind. And I've taken on some of your sorrow. I would think that makes us friends, at least."

I shot him a withering look I knew he couldn't fully appreciate in the semi-darkness. "There's not much to tell."

We were far enough from the brothers that they couldn't hear our quiet conversation, but Dorian slept close by. If he was having another sleepless night, he would be privy to everything I shared.

"You were a slave," Cass began helpfully. "How did that come to pass?"

I sighed. Perhaps if I quelled his curiosity, he would leave me alone. "My parents died when I was four, just after my powers appeared. One of the sicknesses from the old world, Cutter said. Apparently, my parents appointed Cutter to be my guardian, but had only just enough time to sign the papers and make me a final memory potion before they died."

"Why 'apparently'?"

"Thanks to you, I discovered Cutter was lying about the potion. Perhaps he was lying about everything else. Maybe my parents are still alive somewhere."

"Then he made you a slave, instead of adopting you?"

"Aye, that's the heart of it. On discovering my gift—if he didn't already know about it—he forced me to wear gloves. He took me from my home and brought me to Nulla. Soon after, I began working as a *mem*."

Cass actually shuddered. "Terrible thing to do to a child."

After a long silence stretched between us, Cass wet his lips.

"I was a slave, too."

"I guessed as much back in Nulla."

"Oh?"

"The hacked-off hair. No barber could be that incompetent."

He chuckled and reached inside his cloak, bringing out a braided length of hair, the ends banded to keep it from unravelling. "I've kept this for weeks. For some reason, it was hard to part with. Time to get rid of it, I think."

Getting up, he walked gingerly over to the fire and tossed the braid into the coals. It flared briefly, then the flames devoured it as if it had never been.

Cass tilted his head and sniffed. "Smells terrible," he commented, then returned to my side.

"What did you do with your wrist cuffs?"

He grinned. "Melted them down in a blacksmith's forge. The sum they fetched me paid for my journey here." He sobered, as if remembering he'd been robbed of even that meager sum. After a moment, he eyed me carefully. "You make no attempt to hide your status. Why?"

"Easier for a male slave to claim a new life than a female one." I indicated my short hair. "How could I hide *this*?" I had hated wearing the wig, even for a few hours.

"Perhaps the thanc will free you once he finds his treasure."

Dorian would have to possess the official papers for that—or perhaps he could forge those as easily as he'd forged the travel documents. "You shouldn't call him that."

"Call him what?"

"Thane. You don't know what he's been through."

"Lord Adamo hardly holds the monopoly on suffering, Seph." A melancholy was settling over him, weighting his darkly lashed eyes and flattening his mouth. "You should know that better than anyone."

"Get some sleep, Cass." I tried for a lighter tone. "Though I'll admit it's easier to talk with you without your . . . your . . ."

Despite his sour mood, he grinned. "Now you know why I drink."

"There has to be another way to control it."

"There isn't. Hence why I'm helping the thane find this Reliquary." He stood, brushing dust from his breeches. "Sleep well, Seph."

Surprisingly, I found myself softening toward him. "Thank you . . . for what you did."

The smile remained in his voice as he wandered back to his bedroll, the aroma of burnt hair still lingering in the air. "You're most welcome."

17

DORIAN

Another night passed without satisfactory sleep, but not for the usual reasons. It was Jewel who had first alerted Dorian to potential danger, raising her shaggy head and peering toward the alcove where the *mem* had made her bed. By the light of the dying fire, Dorian had seen Cass's silhouette bending over Sephone's sleeping form and stiffened, only for Jewel to lie down again with the faintest of growls, a gentle reassurance that the man did not wish Sephone ill.

Still, Dorian watched her as she awoke, ready to come to her aid. When the red and blue ribbons appeared, he nearly bounded to his feet. But then they vanished. He lay in the darkness and listened to their quiet exchange. The old gods forgive him, he had listened to it all, feeling an odd sense of kinship with Sephone Winter for her losses. Now, after all was quiet, he lay awake, contemplating the *lumen*'s statement.

Pain cannot be created or destroyed, you know. It can only be transferred.

One of the unspoken rules of the world. But once he possessed the Reliquary, the natural order of things would be rewritten. He had loved Lida and Emmy, and he hated to forget them, but it was impossible to live without them. It was better for him and his people this way.

Perhaps Sephone Winter would benefit from the same intervention. Even if she didn't remember her parents, she suffered keenly from their absence, like the pain felt by an amputee for a limb he no longer possesses. Perhaps he could help her forget, too.

In the morning, Dorian sought her out as she was returning from attending to personal needs in the forest. Her hood was pushed back to reveal snow-white hair that gleamed faintly in the dawn light. She was happier than he had ever seen her, and childlike delight suffused her plain features, rendering them luminous.

"I came across a red fox with a litter of kits," she said when he approached. "You should have seen them, Dorian. They were so—" She caught his expression and stopped. "What is it?"

"I overheard you talking with Cassius last night. I wanted to make sure you were all right."

"You were awake?"

He nodded.

"The whole time?"

"Aye."

A faint blush bloomed in her cheeks. "I'll admit, I thought the worst of him. But he only wanted to help."

And a strange secondary gift he had, too—sharing sorrow. "Still, if you feel uncomfortable in his presence, I'll send him away."

"I knew the shape of him when I looked into his mind, Dorian. Cass has never harmed a woman—not like that. But even if he had tried anything, I can protect myself."

He raised an eyebrow. "As you did with Draven."

"I've rarely had to use my gift for that purpose," she insisted. "Usually, if I get a sense that a person wishes me harm, I can divert their attention to something else or avoid them altogether. It's rare that someone can take me by complete surprise."

"Like in Nulla."

"That was a first." She crossed her arms. "It won't happen again."

Whatever her reassurances, she was more vulnerable than she realized. He thought again of the attempted kidnapping. What if her former master discovered there was something that neutralized her gift? Dorian had never doubted Cutter would come after them. And three *alters* traveling together was a sight not easily forgotten, especially with Cassius in tow.

"I want you to be careful in Calliope. We'll stay only as long as we need to glean information, but I don't want you going anywhere without Bear or Bas. I hate to restrict your freedom in this, but I think it best—"

"Of course," she agreed. "Though I'll admit a preference for Bear's company over Bas's."

"Bas is a good sort," Dorian said. "We all have pasts, Sephone. Bas just guards his secrets more fiercely than some."

"What's all this about secrets?" Exiting the ruin, Cass came up to them, eyes dancing. "What did I miss?"

"And some don't bother to guard their secrets at all," Dorian added wryly.

Sephone shot Cass an exasperated look and moved past the *lumen*, heading back inside. When Cass extended his arm to touch her shoulder, she neatly sidestepped him and continued on her way.

He stared after her a moment before returning his attention to Dorian. "It's not just me, is it? She doesn't let you touch her either, right?"

"You shouldn't be touching her *at all*, Cassius. Last night or now."

The *lumen* didn't appear to have heard him. "Do you think she could read my mind if I touched her while she was asleep?"

"If you so much as—" Dorian began in a warning voice.

"What, kiss her again? You fancy the girl for yourself?"

Something prickly jabbed at his insides. "She's like a little sister to me." Shards of green light speared the air between them, proving the statement truthful.

"Little sister, Thane? Not the feeling I get from her." He grinned at Dorian's scowl. "Still, she doesn't let you close, either. She doesn't let anyone close except the wolf."

"Her name is Jewel."

"And yet, I can see she craves affection and companionship."

Dorian straightened, capitalizing on every inch of height he possessed over the other man. "A craving you will not take advantage of, Cassius."

"Is that a request or an order?"

"Whichever of the two will make you heed it more."

The *lumen* suddenly grinned. "She's only a friend, Thane. Nothing to fear."

Dorian forced himself to relax. Whatever Sephone had seen to put her mind at ease, he had met plenty of men like Cassius Vera. And Sephone was young, newly twenty-one—a winsome blend of innocence and worldly experience who would be unused to male attention. To a woman like her, Cass would appear handsome and charismatic, all dazzling charm and smooth manners. Dorian didn't want to see her become another broken heart abandoned in the *alter*'s wake. Or worse, for Cassius Vera's philandering to attract attention and get Sephone—or any of them—captured or killed.

"When we're in Calliope," Dorian's voice held a grim warning, "I'd advise you to be more discreet in your nocturnal activities, lest you put your new friend in danger."

To his surprise, Cass's expression turned serious. "The lady *mem* won't come to any harm on my watch, Thane. Now how about we go find this Reliquary?"

His duty having been discharged satisfactorily, Dorian nodded.

Dorian might have been cross with Cass earlier, but he could not deny that whatever the *lumen* had done the night before had altered Sephone. Or perhaps he had not changed her at all, only revealed a side of her Dorian had never seen before, for the face that had formerly guarded all of its expressions was now open and carefree, taking in the world as Emmy might have . . . once upon a time.

He shook away his thoughts.

As they approached Memosine's capital late in the afternoon, Dorian tried to view the city as if he were seeing it for the first time. Calliope was situated on a river island, the castle perched on the highest peak one of the original features, built many hundreds of years ago by a people long dead. When the first refugees from the world-that-was had arrived in this part of Caldera and discovered the crumbling keep, they had seen the advantages of a fortified residence that would offer continued protection from the north, and so they focused their efforts on restoring the fortress to its former glory.

Of course, one might say that everything Memosinians did was in the name of former glory. Dorian, like all children born to Memosine, had been raised on tales of valor from the world-that-was, legends of the mighty heroes of old battling and defeating fearsome creatures and rescuing fair maidens from the lairs of their enemies.

The forest melted away as the vast River Memosine came into view, the gray having cleared enough to reveal the imposing sight. Dorian heard Sephone gasp from astride her horse as she stared at the medieval battlements of the arch-lord's castle. The city was arrayed around it like a king's robe, the stiff white collar beginning at the base of the stone walls protecting the bulk of the keep, and the train pooling far below, where the waters of the mighty river lapped at yet another vast wall circling the island.

An enormous stone bridge with at least six distinct archways connected Calliope to the mainland. At the end of winter, when the snow from the mountains melted, the river would swell, covering the bridge and cutting off the capital from the rest of Memosine, but the floods never lasted for long, and the bridge always held firm. It had been constructed by the first Memosinians, including Dorian's own grandfather, and was an impressive feat; though Dorian reminded himself that before its demise, the world-that-was had been technologically advanced in many ways, having foregone the power of the horse for the strength of the iron wheel. Like the old keep, much of their knowledge had crumbled away when they were forced to flee their homeland, but Memosinians liked to imagine they were as entrepreneurial as their ancestors.

"Arch-Lord Lio is this year's ruling thane," Dorian said to Sephone as the others rode up behind them. "He has long been a friend of Maera, and of my father. He was the thane of Idaea before he was elected to rule over all of Memosine."

"Any chance he'd take your side against Draven?" Cass ventured.

"Arch-Lord Lio will not take any side, Cassius. He is friendly to Maera and to my family, but his oath prohibits him from supporting one lord against another. Under better circumstances, I would seek his hospitality in the castle, but I think it wise we make our own arrangements." Green ribbons threaded through every word, a reminder that Cass was present . . . and sober.

"Better circumstances, Thane? As in, something besides keeping company with a *mem* and a *lumen*?" Cass flashed a grin. "And whatever gift you possess, of course."

A growl rumbled from Bas's chest—or maybe that was Jewel. Ignoring Cass, Dorian turned to Sephone to find her still staring at Calliope.

"It's beautiful."

"Aye, beautiful—and potentially deadly. Once we cross the bridge, there's only one way out, and that's the way we came in. Keep your wits about you and your hair covered." Dorian glanced back at Cass. "Both of you."

Sephone nodded, the first to follow as he guided Marmalade away from the riverbank and toward the bridge, where a cluster of soldiers armed with crossbows stood looking bored—and cold. When Bear produced their papers, the guards waved them on, not even bothering to look at any of the riders, most of their curiosity reserved for Jewel. Very few noticed the hair of an *alter* in the presence of the wolf.

They traveled beneath the ancient portcullis and into the crowded heart of the city. The main road, made of paved stone, wound around the island and upward, leading toward another gate that would admit them into the main castle. Once upon a time, Dorian would have escorted Lida and Emmy there and found the castle welcoming, but Arch-Lord Lio knew nothing of his quest, and he intended to keep it that way.

With space at a premium, the houses and shops of Calliope were crammed into close proximity, some buildings with dubious structural integrity of their own held upright by a sturdier neighbor. The streets were impossibly narrow, in some places so close together that a six-foot ladder might have been laid between the second-story windows of opposite buildings. As it was, endless strings of washing hung across the space, the colorful yet tattered garments fluttering in the gentle breeze high above their heads like flags.

Dorian was forced to dismount. The others followed suit, and he motioned for Sephone to walk ahead of him.

A shout caused her to halt abruptly. A crush of people and carts were blocking the street, and the paved stones ahead of them were strewn with broken glass. She stepped back. He reached out to steady her, instinctively drawing on his gift.

With his hand on her, he knew the moment she relaxed. But she only turned and looked up at him, frowning. "Don't do that."

"What?"

"Whatever you're doing." She wasn't angry with him, however; he only sensed curiosity.

He let her go, though little did she know his gift would work almost as well without touching her. The street cleared, a man and woman arguing over something off to their right, another man sweeping away the glass with a stiff broom, while a pair of women continued haggling as if they'd never been interrupted. He caught Cassius eyeing several of the more dubious establishments beyond the marketplace, evidently drawn like a bee to nectar.

Taking the lead, Dorian chose a quieter road where they could walk more freely. Jewel trotted along beside him, avoiding the muddy slush that remained from the recent snowfall.

"What's that?" Sephone asked, pointing at a building with a white-columned façade rising majestically from the street. She wouldn't be able to see it from their vantage point, but the structure she'd noticed had a square pyramidal roof with four large triangular glass panels—not made of ordinary glass, either, but thousands of colored fragments fused together with lead. When the sun came out, as it often did in spring and summer, it bathed the tiled floor below with liquid light. He'd seen little in Caldera that could compete with its beauty.

"Ah, that's one of Calliope's gardens."

"A garden? In winter?"

"Haven't you heard of Calliope's famous garden-museums?"

She shook her head.

Ah. He gave a small smile. She would have to discover them for herself.

Dorian led the way down a side street to a narrow, two-story house tucked between two larger shopfronts. The shop to the right was now a butcher, judging by the lingering odor of raw meat wafting from within. The last time he'd visited this street, it had housed odd relics from the world-that-was. Handing his reins to Bas, he rapped three times on the red-painted door and stepped back to wait.

There was the sound of running footsteps, and a female voice called out, "Coming!" A few seconds later, the door was flung open.

"My lord!"

Dorian was instantly enfolded in Toria's plump, motherly embrace. He was then held at arm's length to be inspected through heavily squinted green eyes.

"I'm not wearing my glasses," she said, shoving at her fringe of graying hair as if that might help her see better. "But you look thinner, Lord Adamo." She looked into his face. "Though far better than when I saw you last."

He was a little puzzled. That had been only at a distance, on the day she left for Calliope. A soul-crushing combination of life-threatening injuries and despair had kept him from attending the funerals, though he had visited Lida's and Emmy's graves as soon as he could stand on his own.

"I came to see you while you slept," she said in answer to his unspoken question. "The physician said you slept so little, I didn't have the heart to wake you. I just wanted to make sure you were still whole."

Except that he would never be whole—not until the day he forgot his heartache in its entirety. But Toria understood his pain, for she had loved Lida and Emmy fiercely, in her own way.

He smiled at her briefly and then turned to the others. "Bas, Bear, and Jewel, you already know. Toria, this is Sephone Winter and Cassius Vera. They recently entered my employ. Sephone and Cassius, this is Toria Vanaran. She was my daughter's nursemaid and remains one of my family's greatest friends."

Cass pushed back his hood. "A pleasure, Lady Vanaran."

"Just Mistress Vanaran, or Toria, if you please." She blinked as green strands appeared from nowhere. "What in the name of all that is—"

"If we could prevail upon your hospitality, Toria, I will explain everything," Dorian hastened to reassure her. He had many friends in Calliope, but Toria was one of the few he trusted with his life. She deserved to know the danger she would be inviting into her home by sheltering them.

"Of course, Lord Adamo." She turned away from Cass. "Though the horses, I'm afraid, won't do well in my sitting room. As I recall, they don't appreciate tea and biscuits. Perhaps the Mardell brothers wouldn't mind escorting them to the livery down the street?"

At a nod from Dorian, Bear collected two more sets of reins and went on his way. Bas lingered a moment.

"Go ahead, Bas. Come back as soon as you can."

Bas grabbed Marmalade's reins and set off. When he looked to Toria again, she was studying Sephone, who had yet to remove her hood.

Toria glanced at him. "You finally found one suitable, then, my lord?"

"Aye, more than suitable."

"Then you mean to go through with it?"

"As I said in my letter. It is the only way."

She pursed her lips, but said nothing. "Come inside, then, all of you, before you catch a chill. And I'll see about that tea."

18

Toria deposited them in the sitting room while she bustled into the kitchen, Jewel following on the promise of a treat. Cass flopped into a recently re-upholstered armchair, heedless of his dusty clothes, while Sephone wandered around the room, studying the faded paintings with more intensity than an art critic.

"Fascinating." She stopped before a rendering of a woman sitting on a stretch of sun-soaked beach, the wind whipping her long auburn hair into a tangled mess behind her, her bare toes peeking out from beneath her floral-patterned dress. A gull soared in the currents above her head, the sun glancing off one white wing. Sephone lifted a gloved hand toward it.

"I would think you've seen more vivid images in minds, Seph," Cass remarked, leaning his head against the back of the armchair. His face was still a colorful tapestry of bruises.

"Sometimes," she replied, withdrawing her hand and turning to face him. "But memories of the world-that-was are impossibly old, and they can be shadowy or fragmented. Handling them is like handling old parchment. Viewing them is like being in a dream where you get an impression of something without seeing the details. Unless it's a nightmare, in which case—"

"In which case it can be as clear as crystal," Cass finished for her, and she nodded. She'd definitely seen more horror than beauty.

"I'll need your help tonight," Dorian said. "Both of you. Besides visiting the library under cover of darkness, there are several sources to question. Bear has been chasing some preliminary leads, but he's gone as far as he can go."

Cass heaved an exaggerated sigh. "It can't wait till the morning?"

"Nay, unfortunately not. This task requires both your gifts. Therefore, Cassius, I'll need you sober. Can you manage that?"

"Of course." Dark eyebrows drew low over flashing green-blue eyes. "My lord."

"Sephone?"

She was staring at the woman on the beach again, her gloved fingers clutching the shorn tips of her hair. He wondered, briefly, what she would look like as a free woman, hair grown down to her waist.

"Sephone?" he repeated.

She jumped and spun around. "Aye? Oh, of course."

She looked tired. But he reminded himself that the longer they stayed in Calliope, the more danger they would attract. It was best to get on with what they'd come for.

"Then dress warm. It will snow again tonight."

Dorian ground his teeth in frustration as the hour approached midnight. Cassius Vera might be a useful addition to any interrogation, but for all other tasks, he was unhelpful. The young woman who worked in the great library as a shelver of books and memories—Abbia, a friend of Toria's—had allowed them entry after dark, but after spying Cass, she was about as comprehensible as a fish under water. If only Jewel had come with them instead of staying to guard Toria, the young woman might not have been so enraptured.

Sephone was little better after viewing the library for the first time. Though it was difficult to see anything in clarity by lantern light, she was obviously awed when they walked through the delicate wrought iron gates and down the shadowed halls, which glowed slightly blue from the illuminated stained glass windows in tiny alcoves to either side where, during the day, scholars would sacrifice their backs over dusty tomes.

She even trod lightly, trying to quiet every squeak of her boots on the waxed floorboards, though it was night, and the place was deserted.

They reached the main hall, three stories high and lined from floor to ceiling with books, memories, and other relics from the world-that-was. The ascent of the dozen wrought iron staircases gracefully wound upward to the second and third mezzanine levels, with lightly frosted glass panels at the far end of the hall, which overlooked Calliope. Lanterns illuminated the vast space with a soft glow.

"I've never seen anything like it," Sephone breathed.

"It's far more beautiful by day," Dorian told her and turned to Toria's young friend, who was giggling at Cass. "Would you be so kind as to direct us to the section on the Reliquary, Abbia?"

The woman blushed. "Of course, my lord." She gave a quick curtsey and led the way to a small chamber abutting the main hall with an unusually low doorway. A musty odor greeted them as they entered, dust motes swirling in the light thrown by Abbia's lantern.

Sephone looked around. "What is this place?" Carved wooden cabinets with fitted glass panels housed hundreds of relics, many of them bottles of every shape, color, and size. Some were impossibly delicate: a tiny bottle made of a purple-blue flower; another shaped like a bird captured in flight; a third that might have been fashioned like a pair of wings, curled protectively around a golden orb. One slim vial was the precise color of Cassius's hair. In the middle of the room sat several chairs bordering a solid wooden table, scarred by age and use.

"This room houses the rarest and most precious things from the world-that-was," Abbia answered in a hushed tone. "Books of which we only have a single copy—or even a single fragment—and memories from the earliest years of the old world. Even jewelry and hair pieces. The cabinets are kept locked, and I don't have access to the key, but the books mentioning the ancient relics are on that shelf over there." She pointed to a narrow bookcase which bore a thick film of dust. Five tomes leaned heavily against each other—as fatigued as Dorian felt—two as thick as his longest finger, the rest only marginally smaller.

He bit down on a sigh. They had a long night ahead of them, and he'd hoped to spend some of it in the taverns—questioning sources, absorbing local gossip, and utilizing Cassius's and Sephone's gifts before Draven's spies caught wind of their arrival. At least they were out of the cold—though Bas, standing guard outside the library with the night watch, would not be so lucky.

Dorian turned to Abbia. "Would you please let my bodyguard know to come inside the library a way? We will be here for some hours yet."

She nodded, stealing another glance at Cass. "Of course, my lord." Leaving behind her lantern, she departed.

Cass groaned and flopped into one of the chairs. "Hours, Thane? I thought you wanted us for interrogations. My skills are wasted on book learning." He cast a longing look through the open doorway in the direction of Abbia's retreating form.

Sephone had already retrieved the five volumes from the shelf and set them on the table. She flicked through the first few pages of one and glanced at Dorian. "It's in the common tongue."

"Aye, the trade language of the world-that-was." Coming to stand beside her, he checked the other books. "Though this one's in Memosinian." He set the large, dark red book to one side. "And this is in Marianthean." He dropped the largest volume in front of Cass. "There you go. You *can* read, can't you?"

"Of course I can read." Cass scowled.

"What are we looking for?" Sephone asked, her eyes bright. Apparently, the thought of hours of possibly fruitless research invigorated her as much as it fatigued Cass.

"Any mention of the Reliquary, or any ancient relic. Even a passing one."

"Isn't all of this ancient?" Cass grumbled.

"The Reliquary predates the world-that-was." Dorian took the chair beside Sephone and opposite Cass. "Even to them, it was considered ancient."

"What makes you think it's in Caldera?" Sephone asked. "It could have been destroyed or buried with the rest of the old world. Or claimed by others."

He knew what others she was referring to. Caldera was not the only land mass to survive the apocalypse. Several places in Atlassea—the forbidden name of the world-that-was—had sheltered the last remnants of humanity. Starving and ill, Dorian's ancestors had been driven from their homes in search of better land. On arriving in Caldera—one of the few places still able to support life—they'd built Memosine to memorialize the world-that-was, while the Letheans claimed their homeland with the singular purpose of forgetting it. Marianthe had been formed shortly afterward, when a group of men and women defected from the fledgling nation, wanting to find the sea.

But every Calderan knew that the world their ancestors had left behind still posed many dangers. In Memosine, every child was raised to fear the north, a place from which marauders could descend at any time, attempting to steal what they had worked so hard to build. Dorian could still remember the stories his grandfather had told him, of twisted men who behaved like wild animals.

He shook his head. "Nay, the first Calderans brought it here with them. Some say it was the Reliquary which kept them alive when so many fleeing the devastation died on the way to safety."

He turned to Sephone. "I assumed you could read from your earlier reaction. Please forgive me if I am mistaken."

"I can read," she assured him. "Regis taught me."

Her friend. Or her sweetheart. He must have been a young man of fine quality, for she seemed immune to Cass's charm.

She bent over her tome—the second-largest—as Dorian began to look through his. Grousing to himself, Cass grudgingly began flicking through the book Dorian had given him. He would remind the *lumen* later that he was now in paid employ.

The hours sped by as Dorian searched through his volume, then reached for another. There was plenty of information about the world-that-was—most of it impossible to understand perfectly—but barely a handful of references to ancient relics. Only one of those referred to the Reliquary, and even then, it was only a general history of the relic containing information he already knew. There was nothing about what it looked like or where it had come from:

The Reliquary is one of the famous treasures of the ancient world. Once lost to us, its finding was one of the greatest discoveries of the century and an inspiration to millions, though the curse that is believed to surround this ancient relic dissuaded some from seeking it out . . .

Dorian closed the book with a snap and a cloud of dust. "Any luck?" he asked the others.

Cass rocked back on the hind legs of his chair, balancing his tome on his lap. "Nothing, Thane. At least, nothing about your Reliquary. There's a fascinating origin myth about how the sun god—"

Dorian rolled his eyes. "Sephone?"

"Nothing so far, I'm afraid." She set down a second book, keeping it open. "However, I've got a little way to go yet."

Despite the spark of hope in her voice, she looked exhausted. What time was it? Four in the morning? None of them had slept yet—but it couldn't be helped. It was best not to be seen in public, and therefore foolhardy to approach the library during the day.

"We have to come back tomorrow night then." There was no choice.

"Just a little longer," Sephone insisted. "I'm almost done."

"All right," he agreed and glanced at Cass, only to realize his chair was empty. The tome had been returned to its place on the shelf. "I'll be back in a moment."

The *mem* barely looked up as Dorian left the room.

It was easy to track Cass, since whispering echoed eerily through the hall, the vast space muffling the specific words but failing to disguise the tone. He followed the sounds to a small alcove where the *lumen* stood close to Toria's young friend, his hand on her shoulder, his tone placating. Abbia's pretty features were contorted in a scowl.

"You're one of them, aren't you?" Disgust tarred her voice. "A *lumen*."

"Abbia, I—"

Dorian felt her slap as if she'd struck him and not Cass. Cass flinched, holding his cheek.

"Abbia, you should know—"

But she was gone.

Dorian folded his arms. "She found out about your gift?"

"Reminds me why I never attempt these conversations sober," Cass muttered, scowling.

"I thought you weren't much interested in conversation."

"Snooped on that chat, too, did you, Thane?" He leaned his

shoulder against the wall and pressed his flaming cheek into the cold stone. "How very noble of you."

"Your gift won't matter to the right woman."

"Speaking about your wife, Thane?" Cass failed to notice Dorian's sudden tension. "I don't know what kind of *alter* you are, but I'm a *lumen*, remember? Not exactly a party gift. Few are interested in knowing the truth—if anyone is—and no one likes to be proved a liar, least of all by themselves."

"Whatever your gift, Cassius, perhaps you'd do better to make something of yourself instead of wasting your time with women whose names you never remember."

Cass smirked. "I never waste time, Thane. Abbia and I were having a deeply fruitful conversation."

"Until she slapped you."

He sighed. "That's why I don't reveal my gift to women."

"And yet you shared it with Sephone."

"She's a *mem*. She would have found out anyway." His grin was sly. "Like she'll discover your gift, eventually."

At the thought of Sephone, Dorian realized he had left her alone too long. But when he returned to the chamber, she was still there, though now fast asleep, her hand on the table, one finger still on the final page of the volume. He moved it and returned the book and its dusty companions to the shelf.

He laid a gentle hand on her shoulder. "Sephone?" She jolted awake. "It's time to go."

She nodded sleepily and scrubbed at her eyes. When she rose, he got the sense she was sleepwalking. In the great hall, Dorian thanked Abbia, who was still shooting glowering looks at Cass. Upon entering the blue-tinged corridor, they were greeted by Bas, who appeared undeniably grateful they were on their way at last, even forgetting to scowl at Sephone and Cass.

Sephone made it inside Toria's house before she slumped against the wall, looking like she might collapse on the floor at any moment. Seeing Cass moving in her direction, Dorian brushed past him and scooped her up. She was too tired to protest, and he carried her up the stairs to the loft room Toria had prepared for her earlier. Emmy's

former nurse had insisted they trespass upon her hospitality for at least a few days. With east-facing windows, a sloping roof, and hand-painted walls, Sephone would be thrilled when she woke in the morning.

He bent and laid her on the narrow bed, unable to help releasing the smallest part of his gift. If she'd been awake, it would have made her more alert, but for those so close to sleep, it had the opposite effect, and gave them the courage to endure their dreams.

And from what he knew of the world—at least, the world Sephone had been exposed to from a young age—she could use a little courage when she faced reality again in the dreamworld.

He removed her boots, but the rest of her undressing would wait for Toria's arrival. She curled beneath the blanket he draped over her and murmured, "You make me feel so brave, Dorian."

"Aye, bravery's one word for it," he replied before he realized Cass stood behind them. Green coils of light sprang into being, drifting from the vicinity of the *lumen*'s chest and illuminating the tiny room. Sephone's lids fluttered closed.

"So that's it," Cass's eyes gleamed. "You're a *calor*."

There was no point in denying it, not with Cass's gift on hand to so effortlessly prove him a liar. For once, he wished the *lumen* was not sober.

"Aye, among other things." Though an *alter* was always named after their primary gift, not their secondary one. He must be more tired than he thought to make such a mistake. Hopefully Sephone wouldn't remember their conversation—or his slip-up—in the morning.

Cass was still gazing at the *mem* on the bed. "Now I know why you kept it from her."

"I didn't keep it from her. I simply haven't shared it with her."

"Call it what you like, Thane, but she won't be pleased when she wakes in the morning."

If she remembered.

Warmth.

That was what the boy from the ice had given me, all those years ago. When he grabbed my hand, I had felt the heat of his skin even through the frigidity of the half-frozen canal. Adrenaline had licked through my fading body, rousing me to clench his outstretched hand with all my strength. And afterward, when I'd come to beside the canal, seeing a brown-eyed lad kneeling beside me—

My eyes flew open as I sat up in bed. Words from the night before flashed in my mind.

You make me feel so brave, Dorian.

Aye, bravery's one word for it.

Green light, then Cass's almost jubilant accusation. *So that's it. You're a* calor.

I hadn't heard the rest of their exchange. I only dimly remembered light streaming in in the morning, and a woman—Toria—drawing the curtains, then helping me into a nightgown. Sleep had quickly claimed me once more.

I looked around. The room was dark again, proving I had slept the entire day. There had been no nightmares to wake me, so I hadn't stirred. A single lantern sat on a bedside table, limning the room with a pleasant glow. I swung my legs over the side of the bed, wincing at the aching muscles of my thighs, hips, and backside. I doubted I would become accustomed to horseback riding anytime soon. My stomach growled, reminding me I hadn't eaten in many hours.

Seeing a dark blue dressing gown draped over the back of a chair,

I put it on, tying the cord securely around my waist. The faintest hint of citrus lifted from the fabric, along with something else—cinnamon, perhaps. Another thing I'd only scented in a mind.

Grabbing the lantern, I stepped into the hallway. Toria's house was small, but there were at least two other rooms on this level—both with closed doors. I picked my way down the hallway and carved staircase, careful to avoid creaking timbers. No sooner had I reached the bottom than the main door was flung open, a gust of wind smacking it against the opposing wall. I startled, bracing myself, but it was only Bear who strode through the doorway. Dorian, directly behind him, supported a semi-conscious Cass. His other hand gripped his quarterstaff, extended to its full length. He seemed relieved when he sighted me.

I rushed forward. "What happened?"

Setting aside the staff, Dorian shook his head. "Shh, I don't want to wake Toria." Cass was now fully unconscious. Dorian adjusted his hold and, with Bear's help, carried the *lumen* into the sitting room.

Bas entered through the main door, followed by Jewel. He darted a thin-lipped glance at me as he closed and locked the door.

"Bas," Dorian called from the sitting room, "go check on Toria, would you?"

"As I told you outside, my lord, the house is secure. Jewel and I have been watching the door for hours. No one could have come in, and the girl is obviously unharmed—"

"Humor me, Bas."

Grumbling beneath his breath, the bodyguard pushed past me and continued up the stairs. Jewel accompanied me into the sitting room, where Dorian and Bear had laid Cass on a long couch. The wolf took up residence on a padded armchair as I hesitantly approached the couch.

"Is he—"

"Drunk again, aye." Dorian raked a hand through disheveled hair. "But that's not the reason he's unconscious."

"What happened to him?" Cass bore no visible injuries, besides the beating he'd already endured.

Dorian and Bear exchanged a look, and Bear left the room. Still kneeling on the floor, Dorian glanced up at me. "He snuck out a few hours ago, when Toria went to bed. With Draven so close on our heels, I didn't trust him on his own, so Bear and I followed him, lying low. He'd only been at the tavern for an hour when somebody recognized him. One of the men hunting him, I think. Cassius escaped, but the man chased after him. Luckily, Bear and I arrived before the bounty hunter could do much damage to our *lumen*. Still, he has a nasty bump on his head. I imagine he'll have a fierce headache come morning."

He turned to me abruptly. "Sephone, I need you to do something for me. I can't allow Cassius to come with us if there's something he isn't telling us."

"What do you want from me, Dorian?"

"I need you to look inside his mind again, determine what's hunting him. If there's any secrets he's hiding."

It was only then that I realized I wasn't wearing my gloves. Toria must have removed them. "I've never used my gift on anyone without their express permission, except in self-defense." My eyes went pointedly to the unconscious Cass. "This isn't self-defense."

"If he were conscious, he might not let you see the truth."

I crossed my arms. "As in, he might have hidden his secrets behind some kind of mental wall? Or perhaps he has a hidden gift he hasn't shared with us?"

Dorian blew out a heavy breath. "You know."

"Aye, I know. At least, I heard." I reached for the nearest chair and sank into it, my legs oddly shaky. "I know you have the ability to persuade others to do your will. To influence them according to your desires. A perfect gift for a politician, don't you think?" My voice went deathly quiet. "You drugged me in your own way."

"It's not like that." He crossed the room to me and took the adjacent chair. "At first, I didn't realize how susceptible you were to my gift. Once I did, I was careful not to influence your decision to accompany me. But it isn't what you think, Sephone. My gift is a force for good. It's—"

"A force for good, Dorian? You made me no better than Cass. You manipulated me into accepting your offer—"

"I told you, Sephone, it's nothing like that."

I fell silent, but was somewhat stricken by his pleading look. I reluctantly decided to humor him. "What is it, then? Who are you really?"

He leaned forward, face earnest. "There isn't really a name for what I am. Some use the word *calor*, but it doesn't explain how the gift works. The best way would be to show you." He extended his hand.

I jerked away. "You've shown me enough. Tell me instead."

His dark brows knotted together and his broad shoulders were undeniably taut, but he met my gaze directly. "You said that your master transmits fear, correct?"

"Correct."

"And Cassius can transmit sorrow. My gift works in much the same way, except what I transmit—what I impart to others around me—is courage."

I stared at him.

"Courage, bravery, boldness, whatever you want to call it. My gift works invisibly, filtering through my every word and gesture, emanating from my person with no more effort than a thought. It is independent of direct touch, though physical proximity and contact improves the potency of the gift. And I can control it, except when I'm sick or injured."

I recalled the day on the ice again. How his touch had stirred me to fight for my life instead of succumbing to the canal. How he'd resuscitated me against all odds, despite the water clogging my lungs. I suddenly knew why I'd felt so impossibly warm in his arms when I should have perished from exposure. Even when Cutter had arrived calling my name, and the boy had unwittingly carried me to him, thinking him my father, I had been able to address my master without my knees knocking.

Unknowingly, Dorian Ashwood had given me the courage to face my fate. I'd been so focused on the goodness and kindness I saw in his mind that I'd failed to notice his invisible gift.

Then there was the day I'd nearly been captured. I recalled how his touch had held the effects of the drug at bay until I'd let him go. In his company, I had barely thought of Cutter, even though I knew what he could do to me if he found me. I replayed all the times since our first meeting that Dorian's gift had emboldened me and calmed me, every scene now bearing new meaning. I owed him far more than either of us realized.

Still . . . I could not help feeling betrayed. I crossed my arms over my chest, one hand toying with my resin necklace. "You deliberately hid your gift from me."

"Nay, I didn't. I was surprised you didn't discover it when you first entered my mind, though perhaps it is invisible there, too. But as I told you from the first, there is a wall inside my mind, Sephone. Another *alter* taught me how to put it there, how to fortify it until it was impossible to breach."

"And what lies behind it? More secrets?"

"Nay, Sephone. Behind it is the worst of what happened to my family. You saw them dead. Their"—he nearly choked— "their bodies. But you didn't see how Draven did it. And what came before. I kept you from seeing the worst of it."

He was wrong.

"I saw it, Dorian," I said softly. "Not in your mind, but in Lord Draven's. I saw it all."

It was too unspeakable to put into words, and not even a murmured "I'm sorry" would suffice after what I'd witnessed. I reached out for his arm, careful to avoid his skin, but he grasped my hand, his eyes staring into space, sudden unshed tears in the corners. With our hands joined, I felt his anguish as if it were my own, the horrific deaths of his family as if I'd been the one to call Emmy daughter. Unbeknownst to him, what I'd seen in Lord Draven's mind had lodged memory splinters so deep I knew I'd never be able to remove them.

As if discerning his mood, Jewel came to sit at her master's feet. He numbly reached down to pat her with his free hand, and she whimpered like a puppy.

"Then you know the truth." His voice caught. "How I failed to protect them."

I squeezed his fingers, careful to keep to the periphery of his mind. "I saw you bravely defending your family until your attackers proved too numerous. I saw you lying on the ground, bleeding out from a near-mortal wound. I saw no signs of failure, Dorian."

"Then you didn't look long enough." He pulled his hand from

mine, breaking the link between us. "My gift will wear off eventually, you know. Prolonged exposure to my company tends to do that. It did for Bas and Bear. And for my wife, Lida."

"And your daughter?"

He grimaced. "Like you, she was more affected by my gift than most. I thought for a long time that it was because she was of my blood. But considering your reaction, it cannot be that on its own. Emmy could be courageous—or perhaps bold—to the point of recklessness. At the age of five, she would go off where she wanted, whenever the thought came to mind."

"On the day she died, I was busy working, since I was the thane of Maera at the time. Emmy came to find me, and Lida discovered her missing and went after her. They were both with me when Draven and his men attacked. They should never have been there. If not for my gift, I would have been alone, and it would have been only me who was killed."

Then Dorian blamed himself twice over.

"You were badly wounded," I objected.

"Aye, I was." He dropped his head into his hands. "By the time Draven's men departed, Lida and Emmy were already dead. But Draven—though I didn't realize it was him at the time—didn't finish me off, believing I was only moments from death myself. He wanted me to take my final breaths in full view of what he'd done to my family. After he left, my soldiers arrived. The man who came to my aid would have let me die, but he, too, was affected by my gift, which emboldened him to try and preserve my life long after others might have given up."

"He saved you."

"Nay, he cursed me, Sephone. If only he had let me die, I might have had some peace. But he prevented me from losing any more blood, and they rushed me to a gifted *healer*, who repaired most of the internal damage. I came close to death several times, but each time, something dragged me back. When I woke, I had this." He briefly raised his shirt, exposing a jagged gash across the length of his abdomen, only recently healed. I knew enough about abdominal wounds to know a person rarely survived them, *alter* or nay.

Jewel laid her head on Dorian's knee, and he plunged his fingers into her white fur, stroking it absently. "The lady has her own injuries from the attack. We match, you see. For Jewel knows what it is to live with scars."

It was against my nature—or rather, the upbringing that had shaped my nature—to desire contact with anyone. Though I'd felt pity for Lord Guerin and any of the hundreds of minds I'd entered over the years, until now it had been a mechanical emotion, an animal instinct, no more voluntary than a knee-jerk reaction. But I wanted to reach out to Dorian, to comfort him in his grief. He was the only person besides Regis and Cass—and the veteran—who didn't seem to fear my gift.

Perhaps I could repay such kindness by refusing to fear his.

Several feet away, Cass stirred and groaned.

"I won't trespass in any mind without permission," I said, getting to my feet and returning to tend to Cass. "But Cass will not betray you, Dorian. I'm sure of it."

Of course, that meant taking my word for it. Did he trust me as much as I trusted him?

"What if Cassius has a wall inside his mind, too?"

"I saw your wall, Dorian. Cass has nothing like it."

Unfortunately for me.

"All right," Dorian assented and got to his feet. "Let's get the *lumen* to his bed."

To Dorian's frustration, Cass slept the entire night and most of the following day. I accompanied the lord and Jewel to the marketplace to question contacts, as he'd apparently done with Cass the day before. But my reluctance to use my gift on anyone without their express permission rendered me not nearly so useful as Cass, whose gift of truth-revealing worked without qualms, and more often than not, I ended up standing outside a room waiting for Dorian.

"You're looking tired, Seph," said a voice from beside me. Cass. "The thane still persisting with his interrogations, huh?"

Dorian was quietly conversing with the shopkeeper, Jewel at his heels. Cass surveyed the contents of the shop with a languid eye, from the relics on the table between us to the shelves of liquid memories behind the counter.

"I'm sure you could do better, Sephy."

My gloved hand in my pocket, I fingered the memory potion Dorian had given me. "Don't call me that."

He only gave me an indolent smile. "Has the thane found any solid leads yet?"

"No," I said crisply. Not for lack of trying. Dorian pursued the Reliquary with a single-minded determination that was admirable. But only rumors lingered in Calliope, and some of those accounts, sworn to be as reliable as a grandmother's trusted recipe, had the feel of memories that were second- or third-hand and thus warped by time. The Reliquary was variously located in Memosine, not a day's ride from Calliope, or deep in the heart of Lethe, or even buried on a beach in Marianthe. None of us would live long enough to trace all of the rumors to their dubious sources.

"The thane and I overheard some talk," Cass said into my ear, standing much too close, "about a man who reportedly knows the location of the Reliquary. Silvertongue, his name is. Silas Silvertongue. But there's only one problem."

"What's that?" I asked, stepping back a pace.

"Nobody knows where he lives." He filled the gap I'd vacated, leaning his hip against a table inches from me. "You'd think a man in possession of such priceless information would leave a forwarding address."

"So, Cassius, you finally decided to join us."

We both turned to see Dorian, Jewel at his side. The lord was glaring at Cass.

Cass folded his arms across his chest. "So, Thane. You want to read my mind?"

A growl loosed from Dorian's chest—or possibly Jewel's. "How long were you listening?"

"Whoa, Thane." Cass raised his palms defensively. "Much too

fierce a reaction for a man who's eavesdropped on me not once, or even twice, but three times."

"We should leave," I intervened, seeing that the elderly shopkeeper was still watching us closely.

But as I turned to grasp the doorknob, Jewel growled, and Dorian grabbed my forearm.

"Wait."

Seeing Cass tense as he looked past me, I likewise looked out the shop windows to where a crowd had gathered in the narrow street. They seemed to be focused on a procession coming from the direction of the castle, parting before it but closing ranks tightly in its wake.

"Soldiers," hissed Cass as the door opened and Bas burst in, followed by Bear. Fear tinted both their expressions.

"Soldiers, my lord," Bear unknowingly echoed Cass. "Belonging to Arch-Lord Lio."

"Lio?" Dorian visibly relaxed.

Bas drew closer. "Lord Draven must have arrived last night. He went directly to the arch-lord and convinced him you were a traitor plotting Lio's demise. You are now a wanted man, Lord Adamo. Every soldier in the city is after you."

Dorian shook his head. "Lio knows my family," he said, letting go of my arm and heading for the door. "He knows me. I must go to him directly and explain—"

"Nay, my lord." Bear reached out and planted a hand in Dorian's chest—the only man in the room capable of physically overpowering the lord. "Even if you could get to the arch-lord, Lord Draven's men are everywhere. They will capture you before you reach the castle, and they will have their own warped version of justice to enact."

I remained at the window, only half-watching the crush of people outside. A man with a familiar build strode past, his shaven head standing out amongst the crowd. He didn't turn, didn't even pause in his stride, but I uttered a sharp cry and dropped to the ground, pulling my hood lower over my face as Cass looked out the window in confusion.

"Sephone?" Dorian started for me. "What's wrong?"

"Cutter," I choked past the bile rising to my throat. "He's here." I was suddenly drowning in the memory of the bands of fear encircling my ribs, constricting like a python, cutting off my air.

Though Dorian made no attempt to touch me, I felt the caress of his gift as if I'd stolen a gulp of one of Cutter's finest spirits. The warmth glided down my throat like honey, neutralizing the bile and melting away my fear, even while the direness of our situation remained uppermost in my awareness. Dorian's gift might nullify fear, but not the will to act.

I sent him a grateful look. But the courage he'd lent me drained away as I remembered Cutter's gift again. "What if my master has joined forces with Lord Draven? He's an *alter*. He can—"

"Forgive me—I could not help overhearing your predicament," came a timid voice, and we looked over to see the shopkeeper, wringing his liver-spotted hands. His eyes were the color of cloudy apple cider.

"It's no matter," remarked Cass wryly. "We're all serial eavesdroppers here."

Dorian helped me to my feet, steering me away from the window. "I'm sorry to bring you trouble, Mister Keon. We'll be on our way shortly."

"Not just from here, my lord. You must leave Calliope entirely. And quickly. You can prove your innocence another time, when it is safe to return." The shopkeeper addressed Dorian with the affection of a father. Another of those he considered more friend than servant? "I know a way."

I glanced at Dorian. "I thought you said there was only one way out."

"There is." Dorian studied the shopkeeper.

"Nay, my lord. There's another means of leaving Calliope, but you won't be able to take your horses. You'll have to outrun your pursuers on foot."

No Ivy? No Marmalade? How far could we make it before Lord Draven or Cutter caught up with us?

Dorian exchanged a look with his bodyguards. "We have no alternative," he finally said. Determination settled across his features, and I caught a glimpse of the thane, who was not easily cowed. "Please, Mister Keon. If you would be so kind as to show us the way."

20

By the time they reached the bank of the River Memosine, it was once again dark, but with the descent of the gray, the night was so pitch-black Dorian could barely see three hand lengths in front of his face. Once they were well on their way, they could light the lanterns Keon had given them, but for now, it was better to embrace the cover of darkness. He might even grow to be thankful for its concealment if it kept them alive until morning.

He jumped from the longboat into the icy shallows, guiding the vessel to a thin, pebbled stretch of beach where several boats were strewn hull side up. Bear followed suit on the other side of the boat, resisting the pull of the current downstream, while Bas handled the oars. Not waiting to disembark conventionally, Jewel jumped into the river and began swimming for the beach, reaching it the same time as Dorian. She shook herself dry as he and Bear dragged the boat onto the shore.

Dorian had been surprised at Keon's loyalty, for in helping them to escape Calliope via the trade docks beyond the lower walls, Keon risked incurring the displeasure or wrath of both the arch-lord and his vassal. If they ever discovered his actions. But no one had seen them slip from the back entrance of Keon's shop, or steal down the adjacent alley. No one had come after them as they found the trader's door in the lower wall, the soldiers not having yet reached that part of the city, and they'd blended easily into the crowd in the busyness of dusk. As his bodyguards readied Keon's rowboat, Dorian lingered to thank the man who'd so faithfully served his father.

A thin covering of snow lining the riverbank and a brisk wind testified that a cold night lay ahead of them. Keon had stuffed what provisions he could into packs for them, including several warm blankets, but they would have to wait until the next village to acquire bedrolls, horses, and the necessary tack. Dorian hoped Toria would have the sense to hide the few belongings they'd left behind, including Sephone's satchel, which contained her arm cuffs, the proof of her slavery. The hastily scribbled note Keon promised to deliver to Toria would have to do, though Dorian knew she'd worry for his welfare.

Still, it was fortunate they'd all been together when the soldiers arrived. Bear had apparently chased after Cass when the *alter* departed Toria's house earlier, and Bas had already been outside the shop, standing guard.

While Bear steadied the boat, Dorian extended his hand to help the others down. Cass jumped lightly over the side without his assistance, casting no shadow of doubt over his Marianthean heritage. Sephone came more slowly, staring at the surface of the lake as if she feared a monster would appear to devour her. When she hesitated to take his hand, he gripped her waist instead, registering the faintest hint of citrus before depositing her safely on the shore.

The brothers emptied the boat of their packs before dragging the vessel fully onto the pebbles and turning it upside down. Keon or his son would come for it when it was safe and the gates of Calliope were open once again.

Dorian hefted his pack. "Come on."

He intended to head south, avoiding the lake town of Argus and making for Idaea, where the elusive Silvertongue was frequently sighted, according to Keon. Possibly a *calor* like Dorian himself, judging by the name and the ubiquity of his reputation.

They plunged immediately into snow-laced forest. They would need to cross the river again at some stage, to put distance between themselves and Argus, but for the time being, Dorian permitted it to meander companionably beside them. They'd been walking for only an hour when Jewel's ears pricked and she drew up short, the fur on the back of her neck bristling. Her black lips curled as a steady growl emanated from between her sharp teeth.

A high-pitched howl pierced the night. Audible even above the rushing of the river, it ascended several discordant notes before trailing off in a long screech, like a claw scratching a jagged line across a pane of glass.

Every muscle in Jewel's body went rigid.

"Wolves," Cass ventured. "We can manage wolves."

Bear readied his crossbow while Dorian watched Jewel, dread settling heavy upon him. "Nay, they aren't ordinary wolves. Some foul weapon of Draven's, no doubt." He glanced at Sephone. Her expression was impossible to make out in the darkness. "Can you run?"

He could see her nod.

"Then run. Now!" he commanded them all.

Their urgent progress was hampered by their packs, the almost complete darkness, and the icy ground. Several times, a member of their party slipped and nearly fell, just barely catching themselves before hurtling on. Sephone kept up easily, running beside Jewel, while Cass lagged behind, clutching his ribs. Meanwhile, the howls grew louder, proving their pursuers were gaining on them.

Finally, when Cass looked ready to collapse, Dorian called a halt.

"They have our scent," Bas said between pants, bent over with hands on his thighs. "We'll never outrun them, my lord. We should stop while we still have the strength to face them."

Dorian glanced around. It was impossible to see anything in the gloom. "Light the lanterns," he instructed, and Bear hurried to remove his pack, his body tremoring as he searched for his flint. None of them, barring Cass, had had much sleep, but Bear would be exhausted. Even a giant required rest.

A lamp flickered to life, followed by another. Bas nervously scanned the small clearing as the howls increased in frequency. Dorian retrieved his quarterstaff and snapped it to full length with a flick of his wrist, while Sephone drew her knife. Surprisingly, Cass reached into his boots and withdrew two jagged blades, each one the length of his forearm.

"You didn't think to use those last night?"

"I didn't have the chance with that bounty hunter sitting on my spine," Cass shot back. "And then I was knocked out, if you recall."

Bear set his lantern on the ground and reached for his crossbow. "I can only reload so quickly, my lord. They will reach us before I can kill them all."

Dorian nodded, motioning for Sephone to get behind him and Cass as the howling became a baying, at least a dozen wolves joining in the unholy chorus. Shapes appeared between the trees; hazy at first, then becoming better defined as they approached the circle of light. Beside Dorian, Jewel made a sound midway between a growl and a bark.

"Courage, my friends," he said, voice level, as the first wolf emerged from the shadows, its shaggy coat an inky-black so dense, all they could see was a pair of iridescent golden eyes. Dorian reached for the full potency of his gift, letting it envelop their small party. He had never been able to feel it for himself, but he observed the effects on his companions: a sharpened gaze, a pair of fists raised in a defensive stance, a set of steeled shoulders. Behind him, Sephone shoved back her hood.

Dorian had barely registered the *twang* of Bear's crossbow before the lead wolf slumped to the ground, a bolt through its throat.

The other wolves were quick to avenge their leader. With unnatural speed and agility, they lunged forward. Dorian sprang to meet them, jabbing one in the chest with the iron-tipped point of his quarterstaff before ramming the other end into a wolf's unprotected ribcage. The animal faltered while the first wolf bolted past him, heading for Jewel and the others. With everything he had in him, Dorian brought the staff down on the second wolf's back and heard a loud *crack*. The wolf yelped and crumpled, allowing Dorian to deliver a fatal blow.

At least they bled and died like ordinary animals.

Something snapped at his heels, and he whirled around to meet a new assailant, just dodging the animal's lunge at his throat. Snarling, Jewel dived into the fray, the fur around her maw already wet with blood, her deadly claws extended.

He heard the *twang* of Bear's bow behind him again, and another shadow slumped to the ground.

There were no more than thirteen wolves—uncommonly fast, but smaller than Jewel. So long as they could keep their feet, and their hold on their weapons, they might prevail. But as he spun around to engage another wolf, he saw that Bear had dropped his crossbow and was fending off a wolf with his bare hands, blood dripping from his upper arm. Having drawn his knife, his brother slashed at the beast, attempting to drive it back. A trio of wolves surrounded Sephone and Cass, snarling as they advanced with black saliva dripping from their fangs.

Dorian's heart stopped. Not saliva.

Poison.

The beasts were venomous.

Jewel launched herself at the trio, Dorian close behind. In the corner of his eye, he saw that the brothers had killed their lupine assailant.

"Get to the trees!" he ordered his bodyguards. "We'll try and pick them off from above!"

Venomous or nay, the first wolf was no match for Jewel. Her teeth gleamed ruby red as she turned from tearing out the throat of her opponent and lunged for the second. Dorian brought his staff down on the head of the third, narrowly avoiding a bite at his thigh. Poison from the beast's bared maw dripped black onto the slushy white ground. Muscles tensed, Dorian circled the wolf—or perhaps the wolf circled him—waiting for the animal to strike.

In politics, many an enemy triumphed because a man was too hasty, making his move without thinking it through. Wolves were no different.

Fatigue blurred his vision, but he dodged the wolf's next lunge, stepping to one side as he drove the point of his staff into the animal's side, then rapping it over its hindquarters. The beast was relentless, coming at him again and again, its reflexes honed by both instinct and magic, and if not for Dorian's years of training with Jewel, he would have almost certainly succumbed. He was dimly aware that Cass and Sephone were fleeing toward the nearest tree, and that the brothers were staggering toward each other. Bas got to Bear and supported his bleeding brother, who was once again clutching his crossbow.

But nay—Cass stumbled, his boot catching on something, sending him careening into the snow. Dropping his twin blades, he moaned and clutched at his ribs. Sephone, who had nearly reached the tree, turned and saw him. Despite Cass's holler to leave him and start climbing, she ran back to his side, sheathed her blade in the holster around her thigh, levered herself beneath his arm, and helped him to his feet.

Jewel had joined Dorian's fight, and together, they finished off the third wolf. He straightened, gripping his staff with sweat-slickened fingers. Sephone and Cass had now reached the tree, and she was helping him up, shouting instructions; though, like any sea-faring Marianthean, Cass had probably been climbing since before he could walk. He found the lowest branch and deftly reached for the next highest. With more agility than Dorian had thought a woman of her stature could possess, Sephone swung herself onto the first branch, still calling out to Cass above her. Perhaps she had some Marianthean in her as well.

Dorian had breathed an inward sigh of relief that they were finally safe when the shadow came out of nowhere. It lunged at Sephone's dangling foot, enormous jaws closing around her ankle.

He felt rather than heard her scream. She lost her grip on the branch as the wolf dragged her downward, only releasing its hold when she crumpled to the forest floor, landing half on her side, half on her back. As the beast circled, Dorian sprinted for her, Jewel darting ahead of him. The black wolf sprang forward, howling as Sephone twisted and sank her knife into its side. It snapped at her wrist so fast it was a miracle she was able to jerk away. The beast recovered quickly and launched itself at Sephone's chest.

In a split second, just when the wolf was practically on top of her, Jewel hurled into its uninjured side, her teeth closing around the beast's exposed flank. The wolf's whimper was cut short as Jewel bit into its throat.

The remaining beasts scattered, melting into the darkness.

Dorian threw down his staff and sank to his knees beside Sephone, who was writhing with pain. Cass, who'd started back down the tree when Sephone was attacked, dropped to the ground and crouched on her other side. His face was ashen.

"Sephone!" Dorian gripped her gloved hand. "Sephone, lie as still as you can. I have to check your wound for poison." He moved to her ankle as Jewel circled the dead wolf's prone body and returned to his side. She was covered in blood, but none of it appeared to be hers.

"What happened?" Bas breathed, coming up behind them. Bear followed at a slower pace, a handkerchief pressed against his bleeding bicep. Judging by the amount of blood, the wound was painfully deep.

Cass was still staring at Sephone, though he made no move to touch her. "She saved my life," he said, the words sounding oddly hollow. Then his gaze abruptly sharpened, and he turned to Dorian. "What do you mean, *poison?*"

"Those weren't ordinary wolves." Dorian bent over Sephone's ankle. "Their bites carry poison."

"Poison," Cass mouthed soundlessly as Dorian began to ease Sephone's boot from her foot. The wolf's fangs had punctured the leather, making it difficult to remove. Sitting up, she screamed again, and this time Cass moved behind her, letting her head rest against his chest as he held gently but firmly onto her shoulders. "What kind of poison?"

"Those wolves are nicknamed Nightmares," Dorian replied as Sephone's face contorted. He carefully eased the boot from her foot and peeled away her blood-stained stocking. Using his gift on her with abandon, he noted the precise moment when the tears ceased falling and her teeth gritted instead. "The poison isn't deadly, but it can cause hideous hallucinations and painful convulsions that last several hours."

He inspected the ankle. It was a bad injury in itself, with at least six deep puncture wounds in the shape of lupine teeth, and several more superficial marks that would become nasty bruises. If she could walk, he doubted she would be able to for long, judging by the amount of black poison dribbling from the punctures alongside the blood.

"It's several hours to the next village," Bear said, his forehead creased with worry, paying no heed to his own arm. "And they may not have a healer, gifted or otherwise."

"We can't return to Calliope," his brother replied. "They would—"

"Hush, both of you, and let me concentrate. Bas, get me some bandages, would you? Cassius, find some clean snow to put on Sephone's wounds. And Bear's," he added before the giant could join in.

Both men moved to do his bidding, Cass carefully lowering Sephone to the ground before stumbling away.

When they returned, Dorian covered her ankle with a thick coat of snow, directing Bas to do the same for his brother. Besides the puncture wounds in Bear's arm, none of the men bore more than superficial marks and grazes. It would seem the wolves only injected poison into the deepest bites. Dorian watched as the snow slowly turned black, then replaced it with a fresh coat. The other men stood guard, watching nervously in case the Nightmares returned.

After half an hour, the snow absorbed no more poison, but Sephone's ankle was blue with cold. He carefully bandaged the wound, cleaned the remaining poison from her boot, and though it was painful for her, helped her to slide it back on. Better to suffer momentary discomfort than to lose her limb to frostbite.

"I can walk," she whispered, looking paler than the freshest batch of snow Cass had found, even with the warmth of the lantern splashing across her face.

"I doubt it," Dorian replied, compacting his quarterstaff and strapping it to his belt. "There was too much blood to tell, but I think your ankle may be broken."

"Then leave me here." She set her chin. "I'll be okay."

"In a few hours' time, you'll be convulsing or hallucinating or both, Sephone. I'm not leaving you anywhere."

She must have heard the resolution in his voice, for she didn't argue the matter further. He wasn't sure how long he could carry her, exhausted as he was, but between Bas and himself, they would manage. And if they could find shelter—

"I'll take her." Cass suddenly stood beside him, his usual carefree manner nowhere in sight.

"You're injured, too," Dorian objected. "Bas and I will make do."

"My lord, if Bas could take my pack, I could—" Bear began. He was sweating, a clear sign the poison had already entered his blood.

"The same goes for you, Bear. Now, we must be off before any manner of other horrors catches up with us."

Snow began falling softly, and despite his bravado, Dorian suppressed a shudder. The *altered* wolves were an old Memosinian legend. Before today, he'd never seen one, let alone an entire pack. He knew who had summoned them, but it was pointless to be afraid. Whatever Draven attempted to do to him next couldn't be any worse than what he'd already done.

By the time they halted later that night, the snow was falling thickly enough to cover their tracks—hopefully enough to mask their scent too. They found shelter in an abandoned two-room cottage, its shingled roof intact and the interior covered with a thin film of dust. As if its owner had only recently vacated the place, the remains of a moldy meal sat atop the small table.

Dorian carried Sephone inside the bedroom and laid her on a straw mattress. She had long since lost consciousness, and though her vitals were steady, her skin was sheened with sweat, her body trembling and spasming on the large bed. Cass shook the snow from his hair and set about starting a fire in the hearth. The mysteriously absent owner of the cottage had even stacked firewood in a tidy pile, as if anticipating their need.

Jewel jumped up on the bed and lay down at Sephone's feet, exhausted. Dorian would have to clean the blood from her fur come morning.

"My lord." Bas stood in the doorway. "I'll be tending Bear in the other room if you need me."

Dorian nodded. "And I'll be here if you need me. Is he still conscious?"

"Aye, but barely. He says he has insects crawling beneath his eyelids, and he won't stop shaking, even though he's practically sitting on top of the fire." Bas cast an oddly sympathetic look toward the *mem* writhing on the mattress, then disappeared.

Wind howled down the chimney as the snowstorm picked up outside—blessedly only an ordinary storm. The shutters rattled but held fast; the cottage had been well-constructed.

Sephone moaned and rolled onto her side. "So cold," she mumbled, her lids fused shut but her eyes roving restlessly beneath the thin layer of skin. "Get them off me . . ."

Removing his heavy mantle, Dorian sat beside her and looked pointedly at the *lumen* tending the fire. "I want you to promise me you won't tell her about this."

"Tell her about what?"

After carefully sliding off Sephone's boots—mindful of her injured ankle—Dorian removed her gloves, cloak, and sheathed dagger, then bundled her into his arms and began rubbing her back and shoulders to warm them. It certainly would have been awkward if she were conscious, but he was not about to let Cass, a serial womanizer, do what he could accomplish himself. Sephone had begun to convulse, her body knotting then relaxing the next moment. Exclamations from the next room proved Bear was doing the same.

Perhaps if she were warm, she would suffer less. Shivers wracked her trembling frame, and she fought him, clawing at his chest as she cried out, uttering nonsense about poisonous mushrooms and birds with needle-sharp teeth. In her delirium, she was surprisingly strong. He wrapped his arms around her, trapping her own arms to her sides, grateful there was no need to guard his mind with her unconscious.

He heard the scrape of Cass's boots on the floorboards and glanced up. The *lumen* had finished with the fire and was standing beside the bed. "Why wouldn't you want her to know about this?"

"Because she's proud."

Cass's gift pronounced the statement true, but a thin vein of black curled through the largest green ribbon.

The *lumen* raised an eyebrow. "Anything else, Thane?"

Sephone had gone limp in his arms. Dorian decided to be honest. "Because I made it clear from the very beginning that I could not be her friend." Green light swirled in the wake of his words.

"Once a master, always a master, eh?"

"Nay, it's not like that," Dorian retorted. "I'm not that kind of man. And I've never owned slaves."

"So Sephone said. Whatever happened to 'Courage, my friends'?

Or do you only claim the friendship of others when you believe you're about to die?"

Guilt wormed through him. Was that how it looked on the outside? His friendships with Toria, Keon, the Mardell brothers, and others like them, attended to only when he needed something?

"I know you think I'm a souse and a carouser, Thane, but I'm no stranger to the tragedy of being born an *alter*. Like you, I've wished away my gifts a thousand times or more. They are of far greater use to others than they ever were to me." He narrowed his eyes. "You gave us courage to face the wolves—and I was grateful for it—but I can't help wondering: what good is a gift of courage when you're drowning in fear yourself?"

"I'm not drowning in fear, Cassius."

"Maybe not of wolves, but a man can slaughter a dragon and jump to high heaven on encountering a harmless spider. What about your fear of the future?" He glanced pointedly at Sephone in Dorian's arms, once again convulsing. "What about your fear of friendship?"

"I may be guilty of trusting too few of my friends, Cassius, but there is also the mistake of trusting too many."

Cass snorted again.

"And besides, I doubt our definition of *friendship* is the same." When Sephone finally relaxed, Dorian shifted so her head fell against his shoulder. "I have never broken a woman's heart just so I could observe how the pieces fell."

Green ribbons declared him truthful, and the *lumen* scowled. "I doubt we'll ever be friends, Thane, so consider this the advice of an acquaintance. Sephone Winter isn't the kind of lass you can easily lie to, even without a truth-revealing gift present in the room." His expression turned wry. "Take it from me."

21

SEPHONE

The wolf's poison licked through my veins, stirring up seventeen years of nightmares. My body jerked and spasmed uncontrollably. A deep voice spoke comforting words near my ear.

"Fight it, Sephone! You will get through this, I promise. I have you; you have only to fight it . . ."

The boy from the ice. I was cold—so cold, but he gave me the heat from his body, keeping me alive. Or perhaps that was his gift, and he merely loaned me the courage to confront my shadows. I felt his fingers in my hair, caressing the short strands, supporting my head when the poison briefly paralyzed me. Once, I thought I felt the brush of his lips against my forehead. They were warm and comforting, just like him.

My fever broke—did he leave, or did he stay? The morning brought clarity, but not a welcome kind. Memories assaulted me . . . memories belonging to long ago.

Memories of the end of the world.

Very few people get to watch the world end twice. But I had seen it hundreds of times, in splinters and fragments and shards, through the lens of a dozen different minds. It never got any easier to watch.

I recalled it as if I'd witnessed it myself. How fierce storms and other disasters decimated the greatest achievements of the world-that-was—architectural, economic, and technological—the ensuing hunger, forcing those who lived in cities to relocate to the comparatively untainted countryside. The diseases they'd brought with them, which killed indiscriminately and rendered many of the survivors unable to bear children. The spirit of greed which prompted many to horde resources, and the specter of violence which possessed others to commandeer them.

Worse than the memories were the emotions staining them. I felt a dozen different versions of regret, of wishing there had been more time, of bemoaning the years wasted, though at the time they had seemed to be well-spent. A man's sight is never so sharply focused as when he is gazing behind him; it is only when he turns to survey his future that everything grows myopic and dim.

I felt the fear and surprise and despair and apathy and hatred. Those who had survived the succession of disasters and the resulting starvation and disease were among the few. Fewer still had made the journey to the isolated land we now called Caldera—one of the last parts of the world relatively unaffected by the catastrophes that had befallen everywhere else—and they comprised only a fraction of the world's population and cultures. And those few, like Lord Guerin, had done unspeakable things to survive, even before the war that was fought in the dawn of Caldera's creation.

I closed my eyes against those memories . . . never more than a single thought away. Beauty—I needed to think about beauty. The exquisite perfection of an untouched snowdrift. The particular shade of the heather blooming with such abandon on the moors. The scent of strawberries, sweet and woodsy.

But so much of the beauty in the world came from my memories, and many of those memories were not mine. They were but shadows of the things I'd seen in the minds of others, mere echoes and duplicates of the real. How could a borrowed dream counteract the poison of a waking nightmare?

I was hovering near wakefulness when another image—this one surprisingly vivid—slid before my consciousness. It was a city—a beautiful city—set in the middle of a lush, green valley surrounded by vast cliffs. Dozens of waterfalls tumbled from those cliffs to froth and lather below, and it was then that I realized the city was situated on an island in the middle of a lake. It must have been somewhere high in the mountains, for the city's highest towers were wreathed with snowy clouds . . .

My eyes gradually opened. I was alone. And yet, still warm—I sat up and Dorian's heavy blue mantle slid from my shoulders. My bandaged ankle throbbed, and the events of the night before came flooding back. How long had I been dreaming?

The vision of the city lingered in my mind. Was it the wolf's poison? A product of mere hallucination? I had never seen it before. But it had felt so real.

I gingerly moved my legs over the side of the bed and winced at the barest pressure of my injured foot on the ground.

"Wouldn't do that if I was you." Cass stepped from the shadows, his sleeves rolled up to expose colorfully tattooed forearms.

"Why not?" Seeing my gloves laid out beside me on the bed, I dragged them on. They were warm and dry, thanks to the fire, which still burned hot in the hearth.

He observed my grimace as I once again tested if the foot would bear my weight. "I would think you've already discovered *why not*, Sephy."

"I told you not to call me that."

"Seph, then."

"Is Bear okay?"

"You get bitten by venomous wolves and that's the second question you ask?" His eyebrows rose in amusement. "Aye, he's well. It seems he received far less poison than you did, for he woke a few hours ago."

Or the poison had not realized it contended with a giant. "Where's Dorian?"

As I spoke, a door opened in the next room on a rush of icy wind. The fire wavered in the cross draft but held steady.

Cass turned. "Speak of the—"

Dorian appeared in the bedroom doorway, trailed by Jewel, whose coat was its usual shade of glossy white. Behind them came a slight young woman, barely older than myself, with braided silver hair and rounded, pretty features. She glanced around the room, her gaze coming to rest on Cass, by far the most striking of our otherworldly trio. Her light brown eyes widened, but she said nothing.

"This is Ilissa," Dorian said, beckoning her forward. "She's a gifted *healer*."

Cass retreated to the other side of the tiny room, his eyes fixed on Dorian and not on the girl. "You made it to the village, then?"

"Aye," was the only reply, but even that was enough to strike me dumb. It was still early morning, but Dorian and Jewel were wind-bitten and covered with snow, which meant they'd hiked the however many hours to the nearest village, and back again. All in pursuit of a *healer* for Bear and me.

The young woman, Ilissa, came forward and instructed me to extend my leg across the mattress. With deft but gentle hands, she unwrapped Dorian's bandage and inspected my ankle closely. I winced at the swollen limb, purple-black with bruises and still seeping crimson from the puncture wounds. I half-closed my eyes at the memory of the wolf's jaws clamping around my ankle, dragging me down—

"There are several bad breaks," Ilissa concluded in an oddly bright tone. She glanced at Dorian. "It's good you didn't let her walk on it, or she might have done irreversible damage."

Then the lord of Maera had carried me once again. How far this time?

I tried not to shudder as she laid her bare palm against my lower calf. I was so busy keeping out of her mind that I barely noticed the working of her gift: an itchy, pricking sensation like tiny, invisible hands were stitching me back together from the inside out. I wondered if the use of her gift affected her as much as my gift affected me. She did seem fatigued as she wiped her forehead and leaned closer, studying the puncture marks again. But then, Dorian had likely roused her from her bed.

Ilissa grasped my ankle again, this time closing her eyes. "I'm better with bones than muscles, but I'll do what I can for the rest."

I felt the pricking sensation again, a pleasant warmth enveloping my ankle in its wake. She finally raised her head and smiled wearily. "There, I think that should do it."

I stared in amazement at my ankle. The puncture wounds had nearly disappeared, leaving behind only the faintest of scars. Even the bruises were mostly gone. My skin bore a faint yellowish tinge, but that was all.

She helped me to my feet, smiling at me beneath brows and lashes as silver as her hair. Even without venturing into her mind, I knew that if things had been different—if I had not been a slave, or in Lord Adamo's employ—we might have been good friends.

"Thank you," I said sincerely when no daggers of pain shot through my formerly injured limb. "I don't know how to repay you."

"I will take care of payment—" Dorian began.

"Nay," the *healer* said firmly. "It's a gift. But I must be on my way now."

Pretty as she was, I expected Cass to follow her as she left the room with Dorian and Jewel, but he barely looked at her. Instead, he approached me. Hesitantly, I thought.

"You should have asked her about your ribs," I said, pointing to them.

"They'll heal on their own terms," Cass replied with a dismissive wave of his hand. His blue-green eyes were intent on mine. "You saved my life last night, Seph."

"The wolf's bite wasn't fatal."

"You didn't know that when you came back for me. You risked your life."

"What are friends for?" It was something people from the world-that-was used to say when they weren't entirely comfortable accepting a compliment.

He extended his hand, palm up. "Friends, then. Only for real, this time."

I hesitated. But Cassius Vera's gratitude was genuine, as was his offer of friendship. Besides Regis, I had never had a true friend. Dorian made it clear he regarded me as a little sister, or even a daughter. And Jewel, lady or nay, was only a wolf.

I reached out and grasped his hand, the same way I'd once gripped Dorian's, but this time, I was an equal.

"Friends." As coils of green light tangled with the unfamiliar word, Cass's lips curved into a true smile.

Outside the cottage, five saddled horses were making a mess of the freshly fallen snow, to Jewel's disdain. Cass explained that Dorian, Bas, and the lady wolf had left early in the morning for the village, leaving him to guard the invalids—not that he used that word. Bas had procured the mounts and more provisions for our journey south while Dorian tracked down a *healer*. Ilissa's village was not hostile to *alters*, and she came with them willingly, returning to her home on her own horse after firmly refusing Dorian's offer of an escort.

Bear looked weary and spent, but he mounted without assistance, the easy use of his injured arm suggesting Ilissa had healed him also. When Bas glanced at me, his expression carried none of its usual simmering heat. Instead, something like respect flickered in his grizzled visage. Perhaps in my attempt to help Cass, I'd finally proven myself to the suspicious bodyguard.

Once again on horseback, we made good time, my still-aching body adjusting to the rocking gait it instinctively remembered. My new mare was more high-spirited than Ivy, but she seemed content to follow the others.

When the trail permitted, I rode up beside Dorian. I had already returned his mantle to him, but I had yet to deliver my thanks in full. When I did, he only nodded, lost in his reverie.

"Does it snow in Maera?"

He lifted his head and gazed around at the white as if he'd forgotten it was there. As if he'd forgotten *I* was there. "Aye, it does."

"Like this?"

This time, he looked at me. "Nay, far thicker than this." He smiled a little, his brown eyes coming alight. "Emmy loved to play in the snow. But most of all, she loved the snow ponies."

"Snow ponies?"

"Shaggy wild horses that roam the lower reaches of the Jackal Mountains. They're a pest and a nuisance, but Emmy found them lovely."

I thought of the story behind Marmalade's name. "Why are they called the Jackal Mountains?" I asked.

"That's easy. Because they're small and numerous, and at night they howl in the wind. And because when viewed from a high angle, they appear like rows of sharp teeth."

I shivered, remembering the *altered* wolves.

"Sorry," he said quickly. "I shouldn't remind you."

I shrugged. "For you to remind me, I would have to first forget it, wouldn't I?"

"I only wish I could have reached you sooner." He chewed on his lip, evidently contemplating something besides the wolf attack. "Is it so bad for you? The mind-bleedings, I mean."

My mind wandered. How much of the truth would I share with him before he remembered me? Then I thought of Cutter and answered, "In the beginning, it was terrible. I was only a child, and I cried constantly. But with time, I learned to see through the cracks of the awful things to the good beyond."

"And what about when there wasn't any good?"

"There's always good, Dorian. For us to recognize beauty, we have to have known ugliness. The comprehension of goodness requires some familiarity with evil. For light to truly shine, we must first be surrounded by darkness. It's the way of the world, is it not? Death and devastation, followed by the Greening and life."

I could see it now—now that I was outside Nulla. If the gods were indeed the forces behind the world, they had written that truth into the fabric of everything they'd made.

But Dorian's features had tightened. "Except that every woodsman or traveler worth his salt knows light attracts danger. Bandits, soldiers . . . even wolves. Everything good is eventually smothered by evil. You'll understand that when you're older, Sephone."

I had no idea what to say in return. Beauty, like iridescence, depended on where you were standing. Persuading Dorian Ashwood that goodness remained in the world after everything he'd lost was like attempting to convince a man the sky is blue when he has only ever known it to be gray.

I fingered the necklace at my throat. "There's always hope, isn't there?"

"For a fresh start, perhaps." He shook himself and looked at me. "Was that why you never ran away? Because you hoped things with Cutter would improve?"

"I did run away, Dorian. With you."

"Not then . . . before."

I stopped short of reminding him that I had run away before. I was so little, so different . . . how could he remember me? He had been the one who'd returned me to Cutter. Even if he hadn't known the merchant wasn't my father.

At last, I said, "If I'd run away on my own, I wouldn't have gotten far. I would never have even made it through the seam without your help."

"Then perhaps fate put us together, Sephone." He inclined his head. "You're very much like her, you know."

"Your wife?" My heart began to pound a strange rhythm. Something unwelcome fluttered in my stomach.

"My daughter." He leaned over the pommel of his saddle to duck beneath a tree branch laden with snow. "Emmy was a lot like you. Curious about the world, eager to carry the burdens of others. Lida had been told she could not bear children, so Emmy's arrival was a wonderful surprise for us. My daughter always believed the best of everyone, hoping for the sun even on the cloudiest of days. No dose of bitter reality could ever shatter her illusions. Not even at the end."

I heard what he did not say. He mistook my youth for naïveté, my sheltered life for ignorance. But it was not years that divided us. Nay, it was the wall of suffering he'd built around himself. Such a wall would prevent anyone—even a *mem*—from venturing close.

Dorian's voice dropped. "Emmy was a gift I never thought I would possess. But the gift was reclaimed by the giver."

He was grim and silent for the rest of the day, until we finally dismounted. As he helped me down from the mare, I laid my trembling, gloved fingers in his, remembering the golden glow I'd seen in his mind surrounding the well-worn image of Lida Ashwood. My stomach had no right to flutter like a lady's fan in his presence. Not only because he was a lord, but because he was still in love with his wife.

But the ache in my chest was even more tender than the brief affection I'd once felt for Regis. If I could read my own mind, no doubt there'd be a gentle glow surrounding my mental image of him. The boy who'd saved me. The man from Cutter's tavern.

Luckily, he didn't seem to notice my reaction as he leaned down to my ear. "I am sorry for my disheartening words, Sephone. Hope is a gift. Hold onto it as long as you can." He let go of my hand, and I blushed as I saw Cass standing beside his horse, watching us.

Hope is a gift.

In that moment, I knew, without knowing how I knew it.

Dorian's daughter had been an *alter*.

"You look weary, Thane," Cass declared, looking at Dorian's figure slumped over his horse's neck ahead of us. "Your bodyguard says there's some kind of settlement ahead, and it's dark. We should stop for the night."

Despite his mocking tone, Cass was right. Dorian had pushed us hard for three days, anxious to put as much distance between us and Calliope as was humanly possible. We were all acutely aware that Lord Draven could send more wolves to track us, or something far worse.

I shuddered. Were there *altered* bears and *altered* mountain lions in existence, too? *Altered* jackals? But nothing was worse than Lord Draven himself . . . or Cutter. With his gift of inducing fear, my master would be a better tracker than any magically enhanced wolfhound.

Dorian answered without turning. "We will rest." He must have been more fatigued than we guessed, for his gift danced through my veins in the wake of his words, enlivening every aching limb.

I can control it, except when I'm sick or injured . . .

The dense forest began to slope steeply upward. Pine and birch trees dwindled and finally vanished altogether as we crested a small hill. Dorian ordered a halt at the flattened top, and I pressed my lips together against the sharpness of the cold on my teeth.

I looked up and a breath caught in my throat. "Is that . . . moonlight?"

The gray had thinned until it resembled a tonsure crowning the hill, leaving the highest point of the slope bared to the night sky. Crystalline moonlight trickled through the gap, along with the light from a handful of stars, purer and more brilliant than I could have imagined, like diamonds displayed on a piece of black velvet. I shoved back my hood and drank it in like sunlight.

I turned to the others, only to find they were staring at me. "What's wrong?"

Cass was the first to speak. "Your hair, Seph . . ." He shook his head. "Never mind."

"There." Dorian pointed beyond the hill as the gray shifted again, splintered by shards of moonlight. "A bridge over the river. See it? It's not far."

I was reluctant to abandon my stargazing, but the men were exhausted. Even Jewel trotted along at a sober pace as we descended the other side of the hill and made for the river. We were almost immediately enveloped by the gray again.

The western bank was no more than fifty feet across, but a thin layer of ice had formed over the surface of the river. Too cold to swim and much too fragile to traverse. As the brothers raised their lanterns, I saw what Dorian had observed from the hill. It wasn't a conventional bridge, but an enclosed cabin which straddled the narrowest part of the river, rectangular in shape and barely ten feet wide. The end points of the structure rested firmly on foundations of tightly packed earth, while the wind whistled through at least a dozen openings on either side. Windows, I realized. Or at least, they had been. Just as the structure had once been part of an old-world vehicle called a train.

Cass dismounted, and the rest of us followed suit. His eyes were wide as he took in the large-scale relic, and I remembered it formed one of the tattoos on his arms.

"Is it safe?" Bas asked nervously.

"It seems sturdy enough," Dorian replied, kneeling and inspecting the foundation on our side. "To be sure, we should cross one at a time."

"Can't we find another bridge downstream?"

"We don't know how long that will take, Bas, and the settlement we seek is on the other side of the river. This is as good a place as any to cross. I'll go first."

He barely hesitated as he took Bear's lantern and led his horse into the cavity, treading carefully. The stallion's hooves struck loudly against what sounded like wooden floorboards.

"I'm through!" he called from the other side, and Bas exhaled heavily in the frigid night. "I can see the lights from the settlement. Come quickly now, but be careful. Some of the boards are almost completely rotten."

Jewel followed without delay, though her ears flicked to either side as she walked, evidently not liking the sound of the wind sheeting through the gaps.

"You next," Cass said to the Mardell twins, lighting his own lantern. "Then Sephone, and I'll bring up the rear."

The brothers were too tired to argue. Cass stood beside me, his shoulder brushing mine as they inched across the short traverse far more slowly than Dorian had done.

"Don't be afraid," Cass said, glancing at me. His hair gleamed in the light of the lantern. "Worse comes to worst, it's just a little cold water."

"I'm not afraid."

Tiny, inky black ribbons snaked around the lantern.

"Funny," I murmured. "I didn't even know I was lying."

He smiled. "You're hardly the first, Seph."

Bas had reached the other side of the carriage-bridge and Bear was a quarter of the way across when shouts knifed the darkness behind us. I twisted sharply, catching only the barest glimpse of a small party on horseback atop the hill before the gray snatched it away again.

"There!" a man yelled. "Down by the bridge!"

All but dragging his shrieking horse, Bear sprinted the remaining distance across the carriage-bridge, the timbers creaking and groaning beneath the combined weight of the giant and his mount. Cass jolted into action, shoving the lantern into my hands, then grabbing the reins of my horse. Leading both beasts to the carriage-bridge's opening, he slapped their rumps, his shouted "*yah!*" urging them to find their own way across. Dorian and his bodyguards would have to catch them on the other side.

"Come on," Cass said, grabbing my arm as more hooves pounded behind us. Clutching the lantern, I stumbled beside him as we plunged into the hollow structure. The carriage had been stripped bare, the timber floor flimsy and sagging in places. Spying a gaping hole directly ahead, I yelled a warning to Cass.

"Watch out!"

He faltered, his boot going straight through the rotted floorboards. I grabbed his arm and we both went down, dropping the lantern in the process. I heard the cracking of glass, then a faint spluttering as the flame nearly went out. Seconds later, an orange-blue tongue began licking at the broken fragments, searching for fuel. After a faint *whoosh*, the wood surrounding the lantern flared to life.

Half leaning on me, Cass extracted his boot from the timber, and we struggled to our feet. I started to stamp out the flames, but he grabbed my hand. "No, Seph! Let it burn. It'll slow them down."

He was right. We were halfway across already. If the timbers caught alight quickly enough—and the roof was intact, which meant the wood would be dry—then we might be able to escape our attackers. But in the meantime, we had to hurry. The structure couldn't support itself for long with an inferno in its midst.

We hurried onward, picking our way across the timbers, bruised and weakened by the flights of the horses. Dorian met us at the far opening with his lantern. When I glanced behind us, the fire was well ablaze. A few more seconds, and the flames would block off the carriage-bridge completely. A few more minutes, and it would collapse into the river.

A man appeared at the other end of the carriage-bridge and pointed a mechanical contraption in our direction.

"Duck!" Cass yelled, knocking me to the ground as something whizzed across the space and embedded itself in the wooden lintel above the exit. Dorian, crouching beside us, hollered for Bear.

"Idiot!" shrieked a voice. "You might have struck her!" A man shoved past the first figure, stopping when he saw the wall of flame— now unbreachable. Timbers shuddered beneath us as the structure sagged. The newcomer coughed and covered his mouth, his bald head gleaming in the firelight.

I rose shakily to my feet and he saw me. The skin around his gray eyes cracked.

"Sephone!" Cutter shouted across the fiery divide, somehow managing to sound as deadly as the flames crackling between us. "You've caused me a great deal of trouble of late. But you can make good on it. Come home to me. I promise I'll be merciful."

"Like you were merciful to Regis?" I shouted back. "I'm never coming back."

I felt a hand on my shoulder. "Come on, Sephone." Dorian's voice was soft but urgent.

Cutter laughed harshly. "So that's your plan, girl? Throwing in your lot with wanted men? Regis's rejection too much for you to handle all those years ago? If I don't find you, someone else will, and believe me: they will not be so kind to you as I was."

"Let's get out of here," Cass muttered, "before that crossbow wielder remembers there's two other targets he's free to aim at."

But Dorian had gone suddenly still at a movement beyond Cutter. Lord Draven had entered the carriage, his rust-colored hair nearly the same hue as the flames now leaping toward the ceiling. Beside Dorian, Jewel's chest emitted the lupine version of thunder.

Lord Draven gave Dorian only a cursory glance before gazing at me. "I like the new hairstyle, Lady Nightingale," he drawled. "Or is it an old one?"

The timbers groaned and trembled, and I felt the carriage-bridge give way a little. It was shifting on its foundations.

"We have to leave," Cass repeated. "Unless we're all craving a dip in the river. Thane, what's gotten into you?"

I glanced at Dorian. Was he paralyzed by a hunger for vengeance? Tension emanated from him. His face was a maelstrom of fear, fury, and disgust. I seized his arm, and Cass gripped the other, but the lord was rooted to the floor.

"Dorian, please." I tugged on his arm. "Cass is right. We must go now." Jewel whined and pushed against his thigh.

But he didn't move. While Cutter swore under his breath, Lord Draven turned and called for his men. Were they going to try and leap across the inferno? Or simply pick us off where we stood?

I snatched off my glove and reached up to Dorian's neck. "You leave me no choice." Cass watched, half-horrified, half-entranced, as black vines leaped from my fingertips and sank into the lord's throat.

When I closed my eyes, Dorian's mind was an inferno all on its own. Struggling to find my footing on the shuddering floor of his inner world, I ducked as a cloaked figure hurled a memory at me in the shape of a dinner plate, followed quickly by another. Both shattered against the wall behind my head and slid down to join a pool of broken fragments. There were too many pieces to make out what they'd once been.

Across a vast, shadowy space that secreted heat and noxious fumes, the lord's mind was under attack. Grotesque shapes besieged his walls with the fury of a thousand rioters, thrusting their ladders against the weakest places, and slinking over the battlements with the stealth of wolves. I could sense Dorian shrinking beyond the stone.

Gentle redirection wouldn't work against such foes, nor would the smoke-and-mirrors techniques that sometimes enabled people to focus on things besides their pain. But I had never dealt with so many different memories, rarely at this distance, and never all at once. Only one thing could bring Dorian back to himself. I had no choice. It was this, or death for all of us.

"Sephone!" I heard Cass shout. "Leave him!"

I clung to Dorian, resisting Cass's attempts to pull me away. In the lord's mind, I stretched out my hands. An icy gust tore from my fingertips as the cracked ground beneath my boots cooled and hardened. I felt it spread from where I stood toward the walls where the lord's mind lay besieged. Shadows shrieked as they were frozen solid, the unbearable heat trapped beneath a thick sheet of ice. Twisted figures tumbled from the battlements and were enveloped by the frosty onslaught.

Dorian stirred, and I felt him come back to himself just as crushing exhaustion swept through every bone, tendon, and ligament in my body. I slowly opened my eyes to a train carriage almost entirely aflame, the heat thick and intense as smoke spilled out through the open windows. Cutter and Lord Draven were gone, but there was another crossbow bolt embedded in the wall near Dorian's head.

Cass seized my wrist. "Come on."

Choking on smoke, I staggered after Cass, Dorian and Jewel just behind us. Bear stood in the doorway holding his crossbow. When he saw us coming, he turned and began to run. Dorian and Jewel barely jumped off onto solid ground when the carriage was dragged backward by invisible hands. The six of us watched in horror as the makeshift bridge snapped in half and crashed into the river below with a mighty *whoosh*. I flinched at the sound of the ice sheets fracturing beneath its formidable weight—a sound I would never forget in a hundred years.

"Don't stop," Cass panted, grabbing me and half-throwing, half-shoving me into my mare's saddle. "Don't stop until they're out of firing range." He slapped the mare's rump and ran for his own mount while I clutched the reins and tried to hold on.

Though it quickly became apparent that our assailants could not traverse the river, and we had long since outrun the reach of their weapons, it was a lengthy twenty minutes before we halted outside the tiny cluster of glowing houses Dorian had seen earlier. I was almost as breathless as my horse.

My thoughts ran a race against my heartbeat. Cutter had joined forces with Lord Draven. He despised the lord, but he was more than happy to utilize his connections and resources. Together, they would hunt me down. Lord Draven would torture and kill Dorian and Cass. And the Mardell brothers. Maybe even Cutter himself, once he was no longer useful.

And when I was his prisoner—

I slid down the mare's side and tumbled to my knees, struggling to take one breath after another. Remembering what I'd seen in Dorian's mind, my stomach revolted, and I emptied my insides in the snow. Dorian, I dimly observed, was on his feet, but he moved like a man in a trance. His face was calm, his eyes oddly vacant. I'd seen that expression before.

"Well, Thane," Cass said with a smile in his voice, "if our willful destruction of an ancient bridge doesn't incur the arch-lord's wrath, I don't know what—" He caught sight of us both and abruptly stopped.

In a swift moment, Cass was kneeling in front of me, gently holding me upright. "What did you do to Dorian, Seph? Scrap that, what did you do to yourself?" My eyes began to lid as the surplus oxygen reached my brain and the overexertion of my gift took effect. Cass's eyes—far more beautiful than they had any right to be—brimmed with concern.

The answer to his question should have been easy, but my lips refused to produce the words. I'd performed a mind-bleeding—a soul-letting—on Lord Adamo. Against his will. When he realized what I'd done—

"Please don't let him hate me," I mumbled. The song of the nightingale played twice in my mind, painfully loud and piercing. And then I was asleep.

"Has she come to yet?"

Dorian's voice. I stirred, but my body felt as if I'd been drained of all my blood. Cass answered for me.

"Nay, she's still out. Not surprising, after the energy she expended on you and your demons."

"I didn't ask her to do it." The words were as taut as a rawhide stretched over a drum. Was Dorian angry with me?

"She saved your life, Thane. Mine, too. If she hadn't—"

"Enough."

Boots scraped across the floor. "I thought she was the one who wouldn't let anyone close, but it's you. No wonder she had such trouble bringing you back from wherever you went in your head."

There was a long silence, but no movement.

"Sephone can numb pain. I can share sorrow. If you asked it of us, Thane, we would both employ our gifts for your benefit. After all, didn't you sleep the whole night through?"

"What good is an untroubled sleep if you wake to a nightmare, Cassius? Even ice melts eventually." The anger had gone, leaving Dorian's reply hollow. I felt the ache in his chest as if it were my own. "I woke this morning expecting to find my wife beside me, only to remember that she is dead. Can your gift solve that?"

Without waiting for an answer, I heard him turn and leave the room, the door slamming in his wake.

"Mulish fool," swore Cass, close by me once again. "Thinks he's the only one who's loved and lost."

As feeling returned to my body, I managed to pry my eyes open. Cass was sitting in a chair beside my bed. Or rather, he was balancing precariously in the chair, which was reared on its hind legs as he leaned back against the wall.

The front legs slammed against the floor boards. "Seph, you're awake." He leaned toward me. "That was some feat you performed back there. As soon as we reached safety, the thane collapsed on a bedroll and slept like the dead."

"Are we in the settlement beside the river?" I looked around the room. It was clean but spartan, hosting only two beds and several more bedrolls arranged in a semi-circle around a fire. My chest tightened, thinking of the war party so close behind us.

Cass shook his head. "It was too risky to stop for the night—besides, we didn't want them to know what we did to their carriage-bridge—so we decided to press on. I think the thane napped in his saddle for half of it, but we made it through the night and most of the next day."

"I've been asleep that whole time?" I sat up, immediately aware of the stiffness in my shoulders. A bath certainly wouldn't go astray. My stomach growled, and I amended the list of priorities. Food first.

Cass grinned. "I've never met a woman who slept as deeply as you." He laughed as I flushed. "Don't worry, Seph. You didn't do anything embarrassing. Except when you told me you adored me."

"I did not."

His eyes sparkled. "You're as easily baited as the thane. Nay, you didn't, and you don't drool in your sleep. So that's pleasant."

"Where is everyone?"

"The thane's minions have gone to buy more provisions. The sullen one's horse threw a shoe, so they'll be a while. The thane, as you might have overheard, went somewhere to lick his emotional wounds."

I drew up my legs and wrapped my arms around my knees. At least they hadn't removed my gloves. Or any of my clothes. "Is he very angry with me?"

Something filtered into his expression, silvering his eyes. "I don't know exactly what you did to the thane, but I wouldn't have been able to move him on my own. And from what I saw the night before last, he was ready to go to his death. You didn't have a choice, Seph."

"You haven't answered my question."

He leaned closer, and I smelled on his breath proof that he'd been drinking—I had already noticed the absence of his gift. "I offered to share his sorrow, you know. But he said nay. Can you believe it? What man with a badly broken leg, when offered a sedative, chooses to stay alert in agony? The thane only wants to wallow in his past, with all the enthusiasm of a pig in mud. He can stay there for all I care." His keen gaze tracked my every reaction as he placed his gloved hand over mine. "But you care—don't you?"

"Don't do that," I snapped, withdrawing my fingers.

"I don't need my gift to tell me what is glaringly obvious to everyone except the two parties involved."

"You don't know me, Cass. And you certainly don't know Dorian."

"I know enough to recognize he's wild with grief. Few things are as terrifying as a man who has seen so much of his life that he cares little what he does with the remainder. Mark my words, Seph: Ashwood tends to recklessness."

"A fine statement coming from you, Cass. Dorian is far from reckless." I had never met a more responsible man.

"You say his name with great feeling." He moved to sit beside me, the mattress sagging beneath his weight. "You're in love with him, aren't you?"

My heart stuttered, my head throbbing. Was Cass still in possession of a portion of his gift and hoping to trick me into giving away my true feelings? I didn't answer the charge at hand, twisting away from him.

Yet that was answer enough.

"I see," said Cass, his tone laced with unmistakable pity. "And you believe you can save him from himself. Meanwhile, the tragically noble Dorian Ashwood believes he can save the world from men like Draven, even though he couldn't prevent his own family from dying."

I opened my mouth to protest his bluntness, but his hand squeezed mine.

"You should know, Seph. Those who are confident they can save the world seldom have any need of outside help."

Was that . . . envy in his voice? I turned to look at him and found the proof I sought in his eyes. Why would a man like Cass be envious of Dorian? Cass's appearance and presence made him dazzling to behold. No woman would look twice at Dorian with the *lumen* in the room.

Not unless they'd first been inside Dorian's mind. Not unless they'd been the one he dragged from the ice and resuscitated with the breath from his own lungs. Not unless they'd witnessed his loyalty, his kindness—

"I won't tell him, if that's what you're worried about," Cass continued offhandedly, the envy dissipating. He gestured at a gnarled oak outside the window. "But you'd have better luck getting that tree to embrace you than him."

He left me alone. I almost wished he would come back, for then I wouldn't have to confront the truth he'd discerned so easily, even without the aid of his gift.

I loved Dorian. I had loved him since childhood, since the day he pulled me from the water and held me in his arms. Even if he'd been ugly, I would have been entranced by the beauty of his mind. It was more than the courage I felt in his company. I was drawn to him like the other half of my soul.

But in his heart, he belonged to another. What I wanted could never come to pass, because he'd told me himself. He would never remarry.

Not unless you help him forget.

The thought, so small at first, quickly gained momentum in my mind like a snowball careening down a hill. What if I agreed to his initial request? There could be no place in his heart for me . . . unless he first made room. I recalled the sound of Emmy Ashwood's laughter, the brightness of Lida Ashwood's smile, and jealousy punctured my chest like half a dozen lupine claws.

I fingered the tiny memory potion Dorian had given me for my birthday. How could I erase such beautiful memories when they were exactly what I sought for myself? It went against everything I stood for. True love didn't privilege its own welfare over the welfare of others. Love never plundered another's joy in order to birth pleasure of its own. Love persisted in spite of pain, persevered in the presence of sorrow.

What Dorian didn't understand was that joy mixed with sadness rendered good memories all the more beautiful, like the presence of salt in a cake brings out its sweetness. But what he didn't know, I could show him.

I got to my feet, ignoring the trembling in my hands.

Falling in love, they called it. Because once you were falling it was impossible to catch yourself, and your fate depended entirely on the degree to which the ground you landed on would be forgiving.

Having come so close to death or capture, none of Dorian's companions complained when he pushed them onward to Idaea. On finally pausing in a tiny village, he had intended to have only a brief rest, but thanks to Sephone's intervention, he had slept the entire night through. With his dreams devoid of nightmares, he felt oddly rested . . . until he remembered.

The ancient powers preserve him, he remembered everything.

In the days following Lida's and Emmy's deaths, Dorian might have been grateful for Sephone's actions, the way a man is grateful to the bottle for the temporary oblivion he craves. But he had quickly learned that the respite never lasted, and that it was far better to meet the pain head-on.

He had barely spoken to her when he returned to the inn. But she sought him out anyway, her eyes soft and apologetic.

"Dorian, I—"

"There's no need, Sephone. Thank you for what you did." He gentled his voice as he met her gaze directly. "But please don't ever do that to me again."

Tears trembled at the corners of her eyes, and he might have explained himself, but at that moment, his bodyguards returned.

"There's no sign of Draven's party yet, my lord," Bear reported, unconsciously rubbing his formerly injured arm while Bas paced the tiny room. "But we should leave while we have the advantage."

"No complaints from me there," Cass added from the window. "But won't this Lord Draven know we're headed for Idaea?"

"He may believe we're fleeing to Marianthe. We'll lay a false trail over the next few days, asking questions in every village we pass about the road to the sea." There was little Dorian could do once they reached Idaea, with few connections in that part of Memosine, let alone allies. The closer they drew to the border between Lethe and Marianthe, the harder it would be to evade Lord Draven's reach.

But he didn't have a choice. Idaea was their best chance of finding the elusive Silas Silvertongue. And Silvertongue was their best chance of finding the Reliquary.

As they departed, Cass gave an exaggerated sigh. "What lengths a man will go to in order to get a decent night's rest."

Dorian ignored him. The *lumen* was excessively chatty as they set out, but Sephone barely responded, offering only monosyllabic replies or frowns in answer to his questions. Cass, for his part, appeared unfazed by her reserve.

That evening, they made camp in a nest of hills that encircled an old ruin. It appeared to be some kind of ancient outpost, with five crumbling outer towers—a sixth almost completely claimed by erosion—and an inner courtyard that might once have housed a kitchen and dining room. There was a second floor above, now exposed to the elements and choked with bracken and gorse.

Most of the snow had melted, and the gray had shifted to allow the smallest glimpse of failing sunlight through the fog—a rarity in this part of the world. Sephone watched it like a person entranced. When night fell, she lay on her back, some distance from the others, and continued to stare up at the full moon, shunning the warmth of the fire and even the bowl of stew Bear brought. An uncharacteristically solemn Jewel took up residence beside her.

Cass scampered down from exploring the ruin and collapsed in a heap beside Dorian. Crossing his long legs at his ankles, he held his palms to the flames. "The entire world for one of your thoughts, Thane." His tone was faintly sarcastic.

Dorian glanced at Sephone. Perhaps he'd been too harsh on her. After all, she'd only been trying to help him. Still, the memory of her in his mind, freezing his nightmares . . . the coldness of her skin . . .

"One would think she's never seen the moon before," Dorian found himself saying.

"She's from Nulla, remember?" Cass replied lazily. "She probably hasn't. Or the sun, though there is sun aplenty in my country." Then, as he looked over Dorian's shoulder, he straightened, staring. "Do you think she realizes?"

"Realizes what?" Dorian followed the *lumen*'s gaze. Sephone had pushed back her hood and, for a second time, her hair was bathed in soft, white light. Unremarkable during the day, he could not deny that she was *made* for moonlight. The celestial glow transformed her, limning her face in an iridescent halo that shimmered when she moved. As in Cass's hair, there were the barest hints of green, purple, blue, and even pink. If her hair were longer, she would outshine even the *lumen*. Beside her, Jewel's fur also glowed, but without any lingering iridescence.

"Enchanting," mused Cass. "But she doesn't know, I suspect. She's probably never stood in full moonlight before."

Dorian said nothing, though he had to agree it was a captivating sight. But Sephone's *altered* hair wasn't the source of her hidden beauty. Beauty was in a kind word which was uttered after a long day of wading through snow; in a selfless offer to tend to the horses while Bas snatched a few minutes of rest; in a gleeful exchange of childish verses with the travel-weary Bear. Beauty resided in the way she guided him to the memories of his family he'd forgotten—even without the help of her gift.

In many ways, she was ordinary, still bearing the slightest limp from the wolf attack. But even her ordinariness drew a person's eye.

One day, when Dorian had freed her, Sephone Winter would make some man a fine wife. Perhaps the Regis she'd spoken about with such obvious affection, her friend from childhood. Certainly not a trickster and philanderer like Cassius Vera. He grimaced at the thought.

Meanwhile, the *lumen*, clearly tiring of Dorian's reticence, stood and strolled over to Sephone. In contrast to her earlier manner, she sat up and greeted him—warmly, he thought. As Dorian lay down on his bedroll, their conversation drifted over to him, sans green or black ribbons.

"Can't sleep, Seph?"

"I don't want to miss a second of moonlight. But it's almost gone now. The moon is passing behind the clouds."

She was right—her hair had returned to its usual shade of white-blond.

"If you take my hand, Seph, I can show you the sun." Despite the intimacy of the invitation, Cass's words were devoid of their usual flirtatious tone.

"Then you've seen it often?" she asked incredulously.

"Most days," he replied. "How else do you think I got this tan?"

She laughed lightly. "I wish I could see it. Nay, I wish I could *feel* it."

"My tan, or the sun?"

She gave a light snort. "The sun, of course."

"The novelty wears off, after a while. The shine of everything in this world eventually fades away. Even the *alters'* gifts are not so remarkable in time."

"Aye, Dorian said much the same once. But I think even our ancestors would marvel at the gifts."

"You've seen it, haven't you?" Something deeper than curiosity threaded through Cass's voice. "The world-that-was? How it ended?"

"Aye, I've seen it."

"But you wish you hadn't."

She looked askance at him. "Why do you always do that?"

"Do what?"

"Try and trap people into telling the truth."

"Sorry. Habit, I suppose. We're much alike, Seph, you and me. Reading minds and revealing truth are not so dissimilar—"

"I don't read minds, Cass—"

"—and neither are numbing pain and sharing sorrow."

Dorian turned his head and watched from where he lay.

Firelight slanted across Cass's lips, but there was no smile. "Sorrow is just another form of pain, as my mother used to say."

"And you're better acquainted with it than you make out. Aren't you?"

A long pause trailed after her question.

"Aye," Cass eventually replied. "But you saw all that in my mind, surely."

"As I've said before, I never look more deeply than I have to . . . or than I'm invited to."

He sighed. "One day, I'll tell you the story. But tonight is far too fine a night to spoil with talk of the past."

But Sephone was determined. "This sorrow of yours, Cass. Can it be shared with another person?"

"Aye, it can. But I've never tried it."

Sephone sat up and slowly peeled off her glove. Hesitantly, she offered her hand to Cass. Something shifted in Dorian's chest. He knew what it cost her to do so. And he could guess what she would see in his mind.

Cass moved and sat cross-legged opposite her, but shook his head. "You can't, Seph."

"You did it for me, remember? I promise I won't go near your memories."

"That isn't my concern."

"I know." Her face was shadowed, but her voice was quiet. "Friends for real, you said. Doesn't the sharing of burdens go both ways?"

"Aye, so it does. But you're the first person to offer . . . well, to offer to share mine."

Another long silence stretched between them.

Then Cass straightened. "Very well, then. You share my sorrow, Seph, and I'll share yours."

Dorian watched Cass take her hand in his. They made a striking pair there, by the light of the dying fire.

"The effects will only last for a few hours or so," Cass said as blue ribbons wreathed their arms. "But sometimes a few hours is all you need to feel like yourself again."

As cerulean blue ribbons turned to scarlet around their entwined hands, illuminating their patch of darkness, the something within Dorian that had previously shifted gave way altogether.

For the first time, Dorian allowed himself to remember.

Four days later, they came in sight of Idaea. The southernmost city of Memosine squatted beside a broad curve of the River Memosine and boasted a much warmer climate than the rest of the cities Dorian had visited over the years. It was renowned for its unfettered trade with Marianthe—thanks to a thane who was more open-minded than most lords—and its hot springs, which some declared had magical properties.

Several ancient ruins on the outskirts of the city bore testament to the old world's legacy, one of them a mass grave. Dorian dismounted as they neared it, as did the others.

Sephone surveyed the lumpy field littered with hundreds of broken stones, the inscriptions mostly illegible. More than sixty years before, Memosine's army had engaged Lethe's not far from this place, and what remained of the world-that-was had been almost entirely destroyed by the forces of Lethe, who saw no reason to treasure the past.

"So many dead," she said, her tone hushed.

"What a grim place," said Cass, dismounting to stand beside her.

The two of them had grown close over the past few days. The *lumen* spoke of his years in Marianthe's navy, and Sephone told of the memories she'd handled while a slave to Cutter—and all the glimpses she'd seen of the world-that-was. The stories she told were strange and fantastical, sounding far-fetched even to Dorian, who had heard about the marvels of the old world his entire life.

He had gritted his teeth several times to prevent himself from trespassing on their conversation. As Cass had observed, he and Sephone were very much alike. They had both been enslaved because of their gifts. They had both been mistreated. By comparison, Dorian's childhood had been easy. His parents had kept his gift a secret until his late boyhood, by which time it was completely under his control.

But Sephone's parents had died, leaving her at the mercy of a greedy merchant, and something must have happened to Cass's family to drive him from his home. Dorian recalled the *lumen*'s words to Sephone the night she sheltered in the alcove.

Lord Adamo hardly holds the monopoly on suffering, Seph. You should know that better than anyone.

Cass turned suddenly and caught Dorian watching Sephone. His full lips curved in the faintest of smiles.

"I don't think I need to remind you, Cassius," Dorian remarked, fixing the *lumen* in his gaze, "that discretion is the better part of valor. Idaea contains a hundred different types of trouble. I'd suggest you avoid all of them."

"Watch your back, Thane, and I'll watch mine," Cass returned coolly.

As Sephone remounted, Cass reached up to help her into the saddle. It was entirely unnecessary, for she was progressing well in her horsemanship, and besides, she needed to learn how to mount without assistance. To Sephone's credit, she swatted his hands away.

Oddly irritated, Dorian swung his leg over his horse. A *lumen* was an exceedingly valuable tool in his hunt for the Reliquary, but as far as he was concerned, the end of Cassius Vera's employment could not come soon enough.

"**H**i there!"

I stiffened at the shout that came from further down the street. The pair of black-surcoated guards approached an old woman whose hair was covered with a dark blue shawl. They struck up an animated conversation—friendly—and I exhaled. They knew each other.

Beside me, Dorian gripped his compacted quarterstaff, the reins of his stallion in the other hand. "We mustn't move too hastily, or we'll attract suspicion."

"This is an enormous city," said Cass from my other side. "It will surely be impossible for anyone to find us here."

"You forget the arch-lord is the former thane of Idaea," Dorian replied. "He knows his city well, and Draven will be relying on that."

"Can't you seek a private meeting with the arch-lord?" I asked. "You said he was on good terms with your family."

"Aye, he is. And Lio is a good man, a fair lord. But Draven is now working with Cutter. I have no doubt that Draven has availed himself of your former master's gifts, perhaps even used them on the arch-lord or his men. It's certainly not like Lio to react impulsively."

"The arch-lord may not realize that Cutter's an *alter.*" Dread hugged the lining of my stomach. "Cutter has always shaved his head to hide his gift."

Poor Dorian. Everything he'd once cherished was slowly being taken away from him. He couldn't lose his beloved city, too.

I swept my eyes from side to side while keeping my hood lowered. Idaea was different than I'd imagined. This close to Memosine's border with both Lethe and Marianthe, the streets were a jumble of accents and skin tones, the tanned Mariantheans generally shorter than the Memosinians, but lanky and agile, like Cass. They liked to wear bright colors such as red and yellow, though their garments had been bleached and tattered by the sea, and they sang as they worked, unloading cargo from the river boats and poling large rafts downstream.

Though we were still a fair distance inland, I detected a briny scent in the air, and once I thought I heard the shrieking of a gull overhead. But very little else could be heard above the choruses of the river workers.

It was easy to be caught up in the clever rhymes and entrancing rhythm. Memosinians liked to sing legends about the heroes of old—lengthy songs with dozens of verses about things foreign to most Calderans, and they rarely used the common tongue. But Mariantheans sang about the pleasures that awaited at the end of the day, or at the end of a working week—or perhaps that was just the habit of the river workers. Since I could understand every word, many of the verses made my ears burn, something Cass noted with a grin.

"Shall I teach this one to you?" He began to hum a tune. "It starts off like this—"

"Nay," I replied, too quickly. "Thank you."

In every other respect, Idaea was the opposite of Calliope. Where Calliope's streets were narrow and crowded, Idaea's were broad and mostly clean. In many ways, Calliope was a monument to the world-that-was, with its castle and grand library, and the garden-museums I had yet to see, and tiny shops cluttered with relics. But Idaea's buildings were square-shaped, plain and serviceable, their exteriors rendered completely white, with very few embellishments or even signs of habitation—not even the occasional string of washing, or colorful flags declaring the ruling thane's allegiance to the arch-lord. The only contrast to the white came from black-shingled roofs built on the slightest of slopes.

"They are different on the inside," was all Dorian would say when I asked him. "You'll see."

We reached the end of the street, and a man came out of a whitewashed house as if he'd been watching us through a hidden window—for there weren't any windows visible, at least on this side of the dwelling. After an inaudible exchange with Dorian, he yelled something in his native language and a young boy came running through the doorway, pausing when he saw Bear, his deep-set eyes widening further as he glimpsed Jewel. The man shouted again, and the boy darted forward to take Cass's reins, then mine. He glanced up at me shyly, as if asking silent permission. Perhaps he didn't yet know the common tongue.

"Let him," Dorian instructed. "Bear, accompany the boy to the stables, would you? Bas, come with us."

The man led the way into the house. The doorway was also whitewashed and nondescript, but it opened into an enormous atrium with the largest skylight I'd ever seen, as if the builders of the house had envisaged sunlight for days on end. Today, it was overcast, but the space beneath the open, square-shaped roof nonetheless boasted a tiered water fountain of several large rocks delicately balanced atop each other, and around the gleaming pool were clusters of exotic flowers. Cass knelt and dipped a hand into the water.

"It's warm!" he exclaimed.

At a pointed look from Dorian, Cass reluctantly regained his feet, and we followed the man. I was soon dizzy from the array of colors on every visible wall and surface, a rich palette of terracotta orange, forest green, warm yellow, and deepest blue. As we passed what appeared to be a gallery, I glimpsed several paintings of the world-that-was, and even a few frescoes, though the color in them was faded and wan against such vivid surroundings. Deliberately frayed rugs covered the beige tiles, and I guessed that despite the brazen optimism of the house's furnishings, winters here were still harsh.

The dwelling that had seemed so small from the street proved to be enormous on the inside. It was more a compound than a house, a rectangular structure that enclosed a vast inner courtyard three or four times larger than Lord Faro's vaulted hall. We left the main chamber and glided soundlessly into a narrow corridor. Along our left stood doors to several rooms, all luxuriously furnished, while the wall to our right seemed almost entirely constructed from panes of colored glass. I looked through a yellow-tinted panel and was stunned to see not a courtyard as I'd expected, but a sheltered garden. Leafless weeping willows stirred gently in the breeze, surrounding a series of pools that glowed blue in the descending dusk.

"The pools of memory," announced our guide. He was middle-aged, with an eager smile but guarded eyes. "They are said to have healing properties."

He led the way to the end of the corridor, opening several doors as he went. The last, he indicated, was for me. Jewel preceded me into the room, which was small but fit for a thaness, with a large fresco of a rose garden on the opposite wall, a carved fireplace with an embroidered chair beside it, and a four-poster bed with a soft down cover and green silken curtains. Jewel immediately curled up on the bed.

When I returned to the corridor, Dorian was in conversation with the man. After their brief exchange, the man bowed and left us.

"Well, Thane," remarked Cass, peering out through the glass. "I'll admit working for you is a terrible trial at times."

Dorian's reply was serious. "I've stayed here before. Despite how open it appears, the house is well-protected, and Jewel will alert us to any danger."

"You certainly have friends in high places, Thane," mused Cass, turning and folding his arms. "But what if our host decides to tell someone about his new guests?" He indicated our surroundings. "This is hardly my idea of inconspicuous."

"Sometimes to blend in, you have to stand out," came the response, and I remembered the luxurious black carriage in which we'd escaped to Nulla. "But our hosts are used to discretion. A lesson you'd do well to learn, Cassius."

Cass regarded him sardonically. "And are we to ready ourselves for another nocturnal adventure? Perhaps this Silvertongue enjoys cards." His *altered* eyes glinted. "Or memories."

"Nay, we all need some sleep," Dorian said, an answering challenge in his own eyes. "Sleep, food, and rest. We will revisit our quest in the morning."

I saw little of my companions that evening. A middle-aged woman with silver beads braided into her hair brought me a veritable feast that I was apparently to consume all by myself—though Jewel, graciously, was willing to assist. When I had finished eating, I gazed longingly at the bed, and my eyes strayed to a sleeveless white dress draped over the back of the armchair, the hem embroidered with gold thread. It looked a little large for me—it would probably fall to below my ankles—but there was a braided gold belt next to it, which would gather any extra material at the waist.

I studied my grubby fingernails with distaste. I was filthy after weeks of traveling, my hair an impossible mix of greasy and dry. My ankle throbbed after days of pushing it well beyond its limits. I had more aches, pains, and blisters than an old woman.

I recalled the pools our guide had mentioned. Might they be as warm as the one in the atrium? Idaea was famous for its hot springs, and I thought I'd seen steam rising from the surface of the water earlier. Some of the smaller pools were relatively secluded, shielded from sight by trees that had retained their coverings. If I removed my outer layers but kept my shirt and leggings on, I could attain a state of relative cleanliness while preserving my modesty in case I was discovered. Then I would hightail it back to the fire and the clean dress and the soft bed.

I looked at the wolf lying on the bed. "Jewel? Want to accompany me on a quest for a bath?"

She cocked her head at me, as if slightly affronted by the suggestion she might require a dunking herself, then stood and stretched. With one graceful bound, she was on the floor.

"I'll take that as a yes." She was a lady, after all.

The wolf padded silently beside me as I ventured into the corridor. Dorian and Cass were sharing a room, the brothers another, but both doors were closed, Bear's snoring emanating from the twins' room. It was nearly midnight, and the lanterns in the corridor had been doused, leaving only stray beams of moonlight to illuminate the way. I dodged the pools of yellow, green, and red swelling on the floor and darted from shadow to shadow instead, feeling for the door to the garden. The knob was well-oiled and opened with the slightest of clicks. Jewel slipped out after me.

I shivered as I ran across the grass toward the willows. Wind blew through the hollows, but the ancient trees stood firm, their aged fingertips trailing the edges of the largest pool. The springs themselves appeared to be a mixture of man-made and natural, the borders of each one tiled with mosaics in different shades of blue and green, with flecks of gold and silver that mirrored the moonlight. The effect gave the water a distinctly bluish tinge, as if the entire reservoir were one enormous memory potion. Water cascaded from the largest spring to several smaller pools, each one frosted with ferns and other plants I didn't recognize.

I shivered again, but this time, it wasn't from cold. *The pools of memory*, the man had called them. My gifting was memories. Could the waters affect me or my powers?

"Any advice?" I asked Jewel. She glanced at me, reflected gold and silver glittering in her blue irises.

"I guess not." I ventured further in until I found a pool that gleamed more green than blue. Steam drifted from the surface in lazy spirals. I dragged off my boots, stockings, cloak, gloves, and tunic as warm vapors teased the edge of my loose linen shirt. After testing the temperature against my palm, I sat on the edge of the pool and eased my legs beneath the water.

I closed my eyes and sighed. It was heavenly. More than heavenly. I couldn't swim well, but the pool didn't look deep, and it was daft to pair warm legs with a frozen torso. I slid my entire body into the pool, gratified when my feet touched earth. After a few minutes, I submerged my head. The faintest hint of minerals greeted my nostrils when I resurfaced.

"Aren't you coming in?" I called to Jewel, who was sitting on the edge of the pool, sniffing the water. At my challenge, she jumped in, but apparently bathing for a wolf was more a matter of business than pleasure. She lasted only a minute before she was out again, shaking herself dry and proceeding to carefully groom her magnificent coat.

"Scaredy-cat." The pool remained the temperature of bath water, and I lingered, careful to keep as much skin as I could beneath the surface where it was warm. I eyed my abandoned clothes. It was as good a time as any to do laundry. As Jewel settled down beside the pool, I scrubbed at my garments, including the ones I was wearing. Expecting the water to turn as filthy as regular bath water, I was surprised when it retained its normal shade of mysterious blue-green. Was it similar to the water Cutter used in our memory potions? That water, too, was supposed to have magical properties, taken from the purest of sources deep in the Jackal Mountains.

Or so Cutter had said.

Spying my resin necklace, I lifted it from my chest, studying the way the otherwise drab flowers captured the light. Perhaps while we lingered in Idaea, I could conduct a quest of my own. Someone would know what these flowers were ca—

My breath seized in my throat, and I dropped the necklace. I waded as quickly as I could to the side of the pool and heaved myself up on the edge. Moving the necklace to one side, my fingers shook as I partially unbuttoned my shirt and looked down. I bit my lip to keep from crying out.

In the center of my chest, directly over my heart, was a faint, web-like pattern no longer than my thumb. Circular in shape, the mark looked as if a dragonfly's wing had lightly impressed itself against my skin. But I knew what it was.

The black tendrils of my gift.

I pulled myself fully from the pool and huddled on the edge, shivering. Was it the water? The pool of memory?

But I didn't feel any different. In fact, I felt better than I had in a long time. My gift was stronger than it had ever been. I was hundreds of miles from Lord Guerin and his nightmares. I no longer had a master, but an employer. I even had a friend. Two, if I counted animals. Three, if I counted bodyguards.

I hastily scrambled to my feet. I had no idea what to do. But one thing was clear: I could say nothing to Dorian or Cass about the webbing. They wouldn't understand.

I looked to the lady wolf, whose sapphire eyes on me were piercing in the filtered moonlight. My thoughts raced, and my head whirled. Then it came to me, as if she'd given me the idea.

An *altered healer*. A *healer* like Ilissa would know what was wrong with me. There would be plenty of *alters* in a city as large as this one. When our quest allowed, I would slip away and track one down. I just had to make sure Dorian and the others weren't aware I was gone. Perhaps I could convince Bear to cover for me, citing womanly troubles. That would stymie further questions.

"It'll be all right," I imagined Regis saying. *"You're worrying for naught, Seph."*

But even as I repeated it to myself, a drop of moisture glided down my cheek that had no prior association with the spring.

25

DORIAN

Dorian jerked awake as he was torn from yet another nightmare. He sat up, sweat trickling down his face and into his beard. Finally, he glanced at the opposite side of the room. Tension straightened his spine. The covers on Cass's bed were drawn back, but he was not there.

He growled and dragged on a shirt. The *lumen* was more trouble than he was worth.

The corridor was empty, bathed in tinted moonlight. Had Cass ventured into the city? Dorian's feet found the garden of their own volition, the grass cold against his skin. And then he saw the *lumen*, leaning nonchalantly against the solid trunk of a beech tree.

He barely looked up as Dorian approached, his gaze fixed on something through the trees as he spoke. "I thought you said your guard dog senses danger. Are we in danger, Thane?"

Dorian halted two yards from him. "She's a wolf, not a guard dog, and there's no danger, unless you're intent on working mischief."

"No mischief, Thane." He grinned, flashing white teeth. "At least, not tonight."

Dorian followed Cass's gaze to where soft moonlight had fractured the naked crowns of the trees, illuminating the cluster of pools where they'd bathed earlier. A woman knelt on the edge of the pool, fully clothed but having evidently just emerged from the spring by the way the damp fabric hugged her body. *Sephone.* Dorian caught a glimpse of gentle curves and moonlit skin before he shifted his eyes away.

Cass continued to stare.

"Show her some respect, man," Dorian said, irritated. "She won't be aware of your gaze, and she deserves her privacy."

"It isn't rude to look at something I find lovely."

"Look? You're ogling her." Reaching over, he clipped the *lumen* on the side of his head. "You dishonor her. She's our sister and our friend, not one of your loose women. Though I would object to your callous treatment of them as well."

Cass raised an eyebrow. "Well, she's not *my* sister. She's a woman. Even if you don't have eyes in your head to see it."

Dorian shifted his feet uncomfortably. He couldn't deny that she was no longer the unremarkable waif he'd first met in Nulla. The extra weight on her bones—the longer hair—looked good on her. But she was his employee. His ward, even. Without a father, brother, or friend to protect her, it was Dorian's responsibility to guard her from men like Cassius Vera.

When he glanced at the pool again, she was gone. Somehow, she'd slipped past without him realizing.

"Now I know how you remained devoted to only one woman for so long," Cass said with a mocking twist of his lips, "and why you'll be faithful to her memory until you die. So noble, Thane. So honorable. So readily and effortlessly esteemed by everyone you meet. Have you never once broken the rules?"

Dorian bristled. It took every last reserve of strength to hold himself back from hitting Cass in the jaw. Coming from any other person, such a summary of his character would have been a compliment. But from the *alter*, it sounded like an accusation. "Lida deserved nothing less than my complete allegiance. And if you knew women half as well as you think you do, you'd know that Sephone is worthy of the same."

He spun around and left without waiting for Cass's reply. Pausing outside Sephone's closed door, he wrestled with the urge to check on her. But she had proven she could look after herself. And besides, Jewel was with her. The lady wolf would keep her safe from harm. Reluctantly, he retracted his hand and returned to his bed.

Dorian kept an eye on Sephone the next morning, though Cass had remained in his bed the entire night. Something was amiss. She barely looked at any of them over breakfast, fiddling with her gloves and her necklace and taking every opportunity to pat Jewel, which meant hiding her face beneath the table. He guessed the wolf also helpfully disposed of most of Sephone's meal.

Cass and Sephone both accompanied him into the center of Idaea, along with Jewel. Bas remained at a distance, watching for trouble, and Dorian had sent Bear to follow other leads, should Silvertongue prove impossible to find.

But his sources in Calliope had been clear: Silvertongue was one of the few who knew the whereabouts of the Reliquary. He regularly came through Idaea on business, though what his business involved had been difficult to determine. Some type of merchant, perhaps, given the frequency of his travel.

By late afternoon, all they had were rumors, most of them contradictory. Silvertongue had been in Calliope a month ago. Silvertongue had relocated permanently to Marianthe for a sea change. Silvertongue was dead and buried outside of Orphne, having made the mistake of crossing a Lethean lord. Cass's gift, most helpfully, proved most of the rumors false, but where the speaker did not know if what he said was truth or fiction, even the truth-revealing gift refused to shed further light on the situation—literally.

"Well, Thane," said Cass, leaning against the grimy wall of a narrow alley abutting the marketplace, "I would say we've reached a dead end."

Dorian turned to Sephone. "That tavern owner who allowed you to read his mind, you saw naught of Silvertongue's whereabouts in his memories?"

She shuddered, but shook her head. "Nay. I'm sorry, Dorian."

And the tavern keeper was one of only a handful who agreed to let a *mem* touch his mind. But those who held secrets would never agree to such a thing, and Sephone was adamant in her refusal to gain information without consent.

Dorian tamped down his growing frustration. "Silvertongue was here a fortnight ago. That is true, at least." A barmaid familiar with the merchant had sighted the man.

"He could be halfway across Caldera by now," Cass replied. "He could even be in Lethe."

"By all reports, he's Lethean himself," Dorian acknowledged. "Perhaps we should go to Lethe."

Sephone took a breath. "My lord, if you wouldn't mind my brief absence, we passed a shop in the marketplace I'd like to visit." She touched her resin necklace by way of explanation, and he recalled the white flowers.

"Of course." He didn't see anything amiss in the request. "But take Jewel with you, and be careful."

Dorian's eyes tracked her down the alley until both she and the lady wolf were out of sight. But he was uneasy. As he'd said to Cass the night before, she deserved her privacy. For weeks now, she'd been traveling as the only woman in a company of men. But what if she were in some kind of trouble? She'd called him *my lord*, not Dorian. She didn't seem herself.

"Stay here," he said to Cass and Bas. "I'll return shortly."

He stepped out of the alley into the busy street. He found Sephone's dark hood easily, her familiar form weaving through the clusters of market stalls selling memories, relics, and other items of value. But she didn't pause to question the memory-sellers, or to enter several shops on either side whose signs indicated they also dealt in the lucrative business of the praeteritum. Instead, she headed directly to a tiny shop with a faded awning and a smudged glass windowfront that bore a single word in the common tongue.

Healer.

His brow furrowed. She was ill? Or had the ankle from the wolf attack not healed?

There was only one way to find out. Dorian strode to the door of the shop, twisted the handle, and stepped inside.

It took several minutes for his eyes to adjust to the dim light. A single lamp illuminated an array of dusty shelves, stacks of parchment, and dozens upon dozens of vials, jars, and bottles. A ginger cat curled possessively around the lamp, glaring at Jewel, whose ears had pricked up at his entrance. She sat on her haunches on the floor, her shaggy tail thumping the boards in an irritated rhythm.

Dorian reached down and scratched the wolf's ears. "Easy, girl. Your bite is far worse than his." The room was otherwise empty, but he saw a curtain to the back left of the shop, only half-drawn across the opening, and he discerned the soft murmur of voices beyond.

He reached for the compacted quarterstaff at his belt, keeping it ready in his hand as he approached the back room. He glanced down at Jewel. She did nothing besides return the cat's slitted glare.

"Sephone?" he called before sweeping the remainder of the curtain aside and stepping through the opening. "Sephone!"

Why hadn't Jewel warned him? With a flick of his wrist, he snapped the staff to its full length. Sephone was reclining on a low bed, her cloak and outer tunic in a haphazard pile beside her. A man perched on the side of the bed, fumbling with the buttons on her shirt.

"Dorian!" she exclaimed when she saw him. "What are you doing here?"

The man turned slowly, raising one eyebrow in a distinctly unhurried look. "Your husband, miss?" He didn't move from the bed.

Dorian stepped forward, brandishing the staff. "She's my ward. I'd advise you to step away from her."

At this, the man stood, mild surprise morphing to open outrage. Sephone gasped and bolted upright, pulling her cloak around her. "Dorian, it's not what you think. This man is an *altered healer.* I came to see him." She clutched the material around her chest.

Now that Dorian's fury had diminished, he could see what had escaped him before. The *healer*'s hair was a peculiar shade of iridescent green, like the shell of a beetle he'd once seen near Maera—impossible to disguise, but easy to miss by the light of the single lantern. His eyes and mouth were deeply recessed and creased in a dark scowl, but there was no ill intent in his expression.

Easy, Dorian had said to Jewel. He'd do well to offer the same advice to himself.

"I apologize," Dorian said, addressing the *healer.* "Would you give us a moment alone?"

The man muttered under his breath but left the room. Sephone watched, wide-eyed, as Dorian compacted the staff, returned it to his belt, and sat beside her.

"I followed you," he said without preamble. "I feared you were in trouble."

"Jewel would have alerted me if there was danger."

"She didn't tell me you were sick." He glanced at her covered chest. "I have no right to ask this, Sephone. But might you tell me what's wrong? Perhaps I could help you."

"I doubt it." She was so pale, he feared she'd pass out. He reached out to her with his gift, knowing she would recognize it now. Hopefully, it wouldn't push her away. But when she looked at him again, her brown eyes were clear and steady.

"I discovered it last night." With painful slowness, she released her grip on her shirt and began to unfasten the top few buttons. The gloves made her clumsy, and her hands were shaking. She pulled back the fabric to expose the section of skin directly over her heart.

He reached out to touch the webbing, certain it was some kind of insect or parasite, but the smooth pattern might have been tattooed on her skin. Her chest rose and fell sharply as her eyes almost pleadingly fixed on his. "Do you know what it is, Dorian?"

"Nay." The *healer* had returned, intent on Sephone. He was evidently not one to be ordered about for long, and Dorian gave up his place to the old man, who proceed to poke and prod at his patient.

"You say you discovered it yesterday?" the old man inquired.

"Aye."

"And has it changed in any way since then?"

Sephone nodded. "It had grown a little bigger when I checked it this morning. And I'm certain it was fainter last night."

"Are you in any pain?"

She shook her head.

"Any other symptoms?"

"Nay, none."

The *healer* leaned back and stared thoughtfully at the webbing, his hair gleaming a mossy green.

"She was bitten by a Nightmare wolf a week ago," Dorian offered. "Could it have—"

The *healer* cut him off with a brief shake of his head. "Nay, a Nightmare's poison is only short-acting. It lasts for one day at most, maybe two. This is something else entirely. Something is poisoning her from within. Slowly, but surely."

"Poison?" Dorian and Sephone asked in unison.

He nodded.

"Can you heal it?" asked Dorian.

The *healer*'s shoulders sagged. "Nay, mister. I am skilled in the removal of many toxins, but this is an unusual poison. Not dangerous to those nearby, but nonetheless impossible to treat. This is beyond my skill, *alter* or nay." The man lifted his head. "But she has time, yet. It's a very slow-acting poison. And she is gifted, so her abilities may shield her from some of the effects. It will probably take a long time to spread to the rest of her body."

"How long?"

"Months, at least. Most likely, years. But you shouldn't dally long. Right now, the poison is only skin-deep. When it enters her bloodstream—her heart—she will have but a matter of hours."

Sephone still hadn't spoken. But now she opened her mouth, closed it, then opened it again. "You mean to say . . . I'm dying?" The last word was a whisper.

"Aye," the *healer* said simply. "I am sorry."

"Isn't there any potential cure? There must be a remedy," Dorian pressed.

"I can give her something to slow the spread, but for this ailment, there is no known remedy. The webbing—I have seen it before. It comes from a poison for which we do not have a name, nor do we know where it originates." He hesitated. "However, I have heard rumors of a certain *healer*—an *alter*—who can mend the impossible. He may be able to help her."

"Do you know where this man lives?"

Again, the healer shook his head. "Like the poison itself, I don't even know his name, mister. But I once knew a woman who'd been poisoned, and she was very close to death. After a passing encounter with this man, she was restored. To this day, she lives a street away from my house. But the *healer* comes and goes. There has not been talk of him for many years now."

A nameless poison. A nameless *healer*. And yet another man, like the elusive Silvertongue, who apparently did not want to be found.

"Thank you for your time," Dorian said when it became apparent that the *healer* knew nothing more. "Would you be so kind as to give us another moment?"

The *healer* nodded and departed once again. Dorian took a seat beside Sephone and slid his arm around her shoulders. Rather than pulling away, she leaned into him. The smooth skin of her cheek brushed against his neck, but she didn't flinch. No doubt she was too stunned to consider entering his mind. At such close proximity, he could feel her shock, her fear . . . her powerlessness.

"I told you once that my wife couldn't have children," he began.

She glanced at him, bewildered. It must seem odd that he would share his own tale of woe in the wake of the *healer*'s devastating declaration.

"She had been very ill when she was younger," he hastily continued, "and the attending physician told her she would never bear a child. She was utterly devastated, though when she told me—after I proposed—I said it didn't matter to me. But Lida always felt there was something missing in her heart, in our family. After we married, I told her I would do everything in my power to find her a cure. And so, for two years, while my father ruled as thane, I brought every *altered healer* I could find to Maera. Eventually, Lida fell pregnant with our daughter, Emmy." He looked down at her. "And you know the rest."

Understanding was dawning in her face.

"I told you once before that the Reliquary has many powers, Sephone. One of those powers is the ability to heal. I'm certain it can help you. And I swear I won't rest until I've found it."

Her mouth twitched, though her eyes still held distress. "Because if I die, you won't be cured, either, Lord Adamo?"

His arm loosed around her shoulders, but he could tell she instantly regretted her words.

"I'm sorry. I didn't mean that. I just—I don't . . ." Tears dripped down her cheeks, and he felt the insufficiency of his comfort. He thought of when she was unconscious after the wolf attack, when he had kissed her forehead. Now, a squeeze of her shoulder would have to suffice.

"I'll do everything in my power to find you a cure, Sephone, just as I once did for Lida. Reliquary or nay." He rose. "The others will be getting worried." He looked at her with concern. "Shall I come back for you later?"

She shook her head, swiping at her cheeks. "Nay, I can manage."

Dorian left the room so she could get dressed. He passed several gold coins to the *healer*, who pushed a brown paper bag into his hand along with several whispered instructions. The *healer* glanced nervously at Jewel, who was still watching the cat in a bristling, currently stalemated triad of suspicion. Sephone soon appeared in the doorway, her hood drawn over her hair.

Dorian turned to the *healer* as something else occurred to him. "One last thing, sir, if you please. Do you know of any substance which is capable of suppressing an *alter*'s gift? Particularly a *mem*'s?"

Sephone's head came up, and he knew she was remembering the drugging attempt back in Nulla.

"Helmswort," the *healer* replied without hesitation. "The flower produces a pollen which, if correctly harvested, affects the powers of *alters.* Even my own gift. I have to be careful whenever I handle it. I don't like to lose my edge."

"Do people buy it, then? This helmswort?"

"Aye, of course. All the time."

"How much would it take to knock an *alter* unconscious?"

The *healer*'s eyes widened, and Dorian hoped he could count on the man's discretion. Surely he didn't consider Dorian was planning on drugging anyone. "An enormous amount, to be sure. Few could afford such a thing."

Dorian knew of one or two who could.

"Then you've never sold such a quantity?"

"Nay. Never. It is only ever used by those who wish to suppress their own gifts."

Cass would be interested to learn of such a substance, though he'd already discovered his own temporary cure. Dorian passed the *healer* another coin and reached for Sephone. Her voice as she thanked the *healer* was barely audible, but she spared a moment to pat the cat—to Jewel's obvious disdain.

Only when they were out in the street again did Dorian allow himself to consider the events of the last half hour, and the shattering truths he could no longer ignore.

Dorian lay in his bed watching shadows dance across the ceiling, unable to sleep. Not for the first time, he wished Cassius Vera away so he could toss and turn without consequence, but the *lumen* had surprised him by staying put. He'd not visited a tavern or a woman since they'd arrived in Idaea three days ago. Nor had he expressed a wish to leave the compound. He'd even appeared concerned when Dorian and Sephone returned to the alley, Sephone looking distinctly pale. But she'd been quick to push him away.

Friend or nay, it was clear she wasn't going to tell him anything. If not for Dorian's following her to the *healer*, would she have told *him*?

He stiffened as he heard a sound on the other side of the wall, like something heavy falling against the floor, muffled vaguely by carpet. Across the room, Cass slept on peacefully. Dorian reminded himself that Jewel was with Sephone. But what if the danger she faced was from herself? The wolf might not be able to sense such things.

A second *thump* bolstered his fears. He put on a robe, the entwined gold bands hanging from the chain around his neck jingling as he tied the cord. He went and knocked lightly on Sephone's door. It was only when he did so that he realized he'd forgotten his staff.

"Sephone?" he whispered. "Are you well?"

"Dorian?" came her oddly echoey reply. "Is that you?"

The door was slightly ajar, so he let himself in, closing it behind him. She was bent over the basin in the corner, and she sounded like she was choking.

Nay—not choking. Vomiting. A memory pierced him, but it was bittersweet rather than painful—the memory of Lida doing the same in the first few months of her pregnancy. Even while green with nausea, she'd rejoiced in the fact that, at last, she would have a child.

The memory dissolved, and along with it, the foreign feeling of jubilation. Lida was dead. And Sephone was dying.

He quickly went to her, bracing himself for the unpleasant odors as he reached for her hair, to pull it back from her face. She was dry-retching, not vomiting, and before he could do anything, she wrenched herself away and stumbled in the direction of the bed where Jewel lay, almost tripping over a fallen armchair. Was that the *thump* he'd heard?

She sank to her knees before it, as if she'd lost the ability to surmount it. He came and sat beside her. Jewel was lying on the bed, her head on her paws. Her normally sapphire-blue eyes were dull and lifeless. Maybe she didn't know what to do either.

"You know, Sephone," he began, trying for a lighter tone, "I might have expected to find Cass in such a state, but never you."

Her eyes fixed on his, and his attempt at humor fell flat at their expression. It was raw pain that crippled her, not drink or liquid memories. "You mustn't tell him about any of this. My—my vulnerability. My weakness."

"I won't. But there's no shame in it. You know very well what I think of Cass, but so far he's proven himself to be a trustworthy confidant where you're concerned. You needn't be afraid what he'll think. What any of us will think." He leaned toward her. "And you're wrong. Vulnerability isn't the same as weakness."

"What does a *calor*—or a lord—know about such things?"

"*Calor* or nay, lord or nay, I am no more courageous than the next man. But that's beside the point. Vulnerability and courage are brothers, Sephone. And they do not share a brotherhood of enmity, but of mutual dependence, the elder preceding the younger. Vulnerability comes first, emptying the ground of any obstacles"—he gestured at the chair which had tumbled over—"and in his wake, Courage comes. You cannot have one brother without the other."

She eyed him. "You're using your gift on me right now."

"Nay, I'm not."

"But I feel—" She broke off and placed a hand over her heart. "I can *feel* . . ."

"Perhaps it's my words which affect you, Sephone, and not my gift." He looked at her steadily. "You don't need to be an *alter* to share sorrow. Nor does one require a *calor* to impart courage. Sometimes words are enough."

"Or kindness."

"What did you say?"

"Kindness can be transferred as easily as sorrow." There were tears on her cheeks. "And you have always been kind to me, Dorian."

Always? He'd only known her for a matter of weeks. But perhaps as a *mem*, and with everything they'd endured, she felt she'd known him longer. He tamped down the warning in his mind and continued. If she could be vulnerable, so could he.

"I told you before that my gift affected Emmy more than most, just as it affects you. I didn't tell you why."

She watched him, waiting.

"My daughter was a *mem*, too. She was only five when I lost her, but I'm guessing she would have been powerful if she'd survived to adulthood. Possibly even as powerful as you. With a mere touch, she could flick through minds like girls of her age flicked through picture books. Somehow, she knew things, even without touching someone. She was connected to me, and to Lida, despite the fact that my wife wasn't an *alter*. Lida would call for her from the house, and she'd come running in from the garden, knowing exactly what her mother wanted. And at the end . . ."

When he broke off, Sephone slowly reached out and took his hand. He let her, knowing she would see the memory hovering at the edge of his mind. Still, he felt the need to put it into words.

"Emmy knew, at the end, that I couldn't save her or her mother. I saw it in her face. I . . . somehow, I felt it. She knew she was going to die. It—it tortures me that she knew I would fail her."

"You didn't fail her, Dorian," Sephone said quietly. "And if she was as perceptive as she sounds, she would have known you'd done everything you could to save her."

"Maybe so." He gripped her slender fingers. "But I won't let you die, Sephone. Not if there's a cure. I swear it."

"Always the politician," she smiled gently, "making promises you cannot keep."

For some unfathomable reason, he found himself compelled to show her all the times he had succeeded in keeping his promises, even if he'd failed at the very thing that mattered the most. He opened his mind to her perusal, parading a sequence of memories before her. How he'd strengthened the relationship between Maera and Calliope, and between Maera and the other major cities—excluding Argus. How Lio's predecessor had sent him as an ambassador to Lethe amidst swirling rumors of another war. How he'd been instrumental in restoring peace between Memosine and Lethe—even if it was hard-won and tenuous. Even if it had required considerable doses of his gift.

He wouldn't fail in this. Perhaps these memories could help her see that.

He opened his eyes and realized how close they were sitting. He was holding both of her hands. She was wearing a nightgown, and him only a robe. It was after midnight, and he was alone with a young woman in her room. He would have clouted Cass over the head for far less intimacy.

What are you doing, Ashwood? he chided himself. *You can't afford to let her in close.*

His words about vulnerability and courage rose to haunt him. He didn't need to dig down far to unearth a deeper fear. If he never found the Reliquary, he would fail doubly: not only because it would mean the end of all his hopes, but because it would be a death sentence for Sephone.

But if they succeeded in finding the relic, should he continue to ask Sephone to venture deeper into his mind—past the wall? She already carried the burden of everything she'd seen over the past seventeen years of her young life. What if, even with the Reliquary's help, he only caused her more suffering . . . or worse, hastened her death?

What if he was wrong, and it healed him but could do naught for her? He would be like Cassius Vera, faced with the choice of absorbing or imparting sorrow. Once again, the *lumen*'s words rose in his mind, a ghastly specter of truth that would not be suppressed.

Pain cannot be created or destroyed . . . it can only be transferred.

He didn't have to deliberate long. If they could only have one life between them, he would give it to her. But on that matter, his inner voice once again objected. If one of them had to die, neither of them could afford to be friends.

It was sound logic. But the man he'd once been—the man who'd once loved with all his heart—won out, and he couldn't stop himself from kissing her forehead before he released her hands and rose.

"Goodnight, Sephone."

He was nearly to the door when she finally replied.

"Goodnight, Dorian."

26

I tried not to replay it over and over. The golden iridescence of Dorian's hair in the lamplight. The warm regard of his brown eyes, so different from the anger that had kindled there earlier, when he'd believed me in danger. The strength of his hands—softer than Cass's, but rougher than a lord's hands should have been. The tanned vee of muscular chest between the lapels of his robe that made me blush even remembering it. And finally, the warm pressure of his lips against my skin, along with the soft brush of his trimmed beard.

Pull yourself together. I had bigger things to focus on.

But I couldn't forget. I would cling to the memory of the lord's comforting touch as fiercely as I had to the memory of the boy from the ice. Never mind that Dorian Ashwood had been married and widowed in the seventeen years I'd dreamed about him, or that Cass had been the one to steal my first kiss. Although only on the forehead, Dorian's kiss was the first kiss in truth. Whether or not Dorian thought of me as a sister.

I barely glanced at the webbing on my chest as I dressed. If Cass saw it, maybe he would think it was a tattoo.

After breakfast, when Dorian announced he wanted to return to a tavern near the marketplace, I nodded almost dreamily. Cass sent me a strange look.

"My lord," Bear said as they readied themselves. "Bas is feeling poorly this morning. He is insisting on coming, but—"

"Nay, Bear. Tell him to stay here. I suspect Jewel had too much to eat last night, for she's feeling poorly too this morning. She can keep him company." Dorian snuck a glance at me, and I smiled, remembering how many overly rich meals I'd fed to the wolf.

Well, a lady should know when to decline more food.

Bear nodded and we set off, the giant trailing at a distance. Rain fell like an army of frozen javelins as we walked, the street turning to muddy rivulets that soon became miniature rivers. Cass hummed a bawdy tune under his breath, his arms swinging beneath his cloak. Dorian set a brisk pace, as if Lord Draven himself rode behind us.

A bird flitted beneath the eaves of a passing house, and I paused to stare. Brown, buff, and white flashed at me almost cheekily before the bird darted to the next house.

A nightingale, here in Idaea? But then, if they'd visited Nulla, they would have almost certainly spread to other places. I briefly recalled its lovely song and the way the simple trills, whistles, and gurgles had touched the deep places inside of me.

And then I remembered the poison lurking beneath my skin, and an unfamiliar wave of emotion swept over me. I recognized it belatedly as bitterness. The songbirds were merely a relic of a bygone era, like the veteran and Felix. Captivating, but no more enduring than a memory.

As I turned away from watching it, I glimpsed a hooded figure trailing us, not a hundred yards behind, diving in and out of alleys, much like the nightingale itself. A knot formed in my throat, and I ran to catch up with Dorian and Cass.

"What is it, Seph?" Cass asked, visibly concerned at my expression.

"There's a man tailing us."

Expecting Dorian to react, I was startled when he only shrugged. "Aye, that's Bear."

"Nay, it can't be." I turned, but the street behind us was empty. Rain dripped beneath my hood and slid down my neck. "Bear is a giant. This man was tall but thin. And Bear's not wearing a hood today, only his usual gray cloak. This man's cloak was hooded, and his cloak was black, not gray."

Dorian looked about, then, as he beckoned us both into a side street.

"I've seen him before, Dorian. The morning after Cass was beaten, as we were leaving the inn. At the time, I thought I was dreaming. But he's here. In Idaea. And he's following us."

"She's right, Thane," Cass interjected. "I've seen him, too. Not today, but before."

"The morning after you were beaten?" Dorian swiveled to study him, raising an eyebrow. "I'm surprised you could see anything with your face as swollen as it was."

"I saw a man following me in Calliope," Cass retorted. "I managed to lose him before I reached Mistress Toria's house. Same description. Tall, thin, black cloak and hood."

Dorian's face grew taut, and he stepped close to Cass. "And you didn't think to tell me you had been followed?"

"I assumed you'd eavesdrop on me sooner or later, Thane, and then you'd discover it for yourself," Cass shot back, his fists curling.

I jumped between them, pushing them apart. "This won't solve anything."

"Nay," remarked Dorian wryly. "Besides, haven't you seen enough tavern brawls recently, Vera?"

Cass glowered, but remained where he was.

"We will continue on for now, so this man doesn't get suspicious." Dorian glared at Cass. "But keep your wits about you. As hard as that may be for some."

I followed them to the tavern, wishing Bear were closer. I always felt safer in his company. Or the lady wolf's. But then I remembered Dorian on the night of the wolf attack, moving almost as fast as Jewel as he expertly twirled his quarterstaff, which had the elegance of a sword and the brute force of a club. Cass had his long knives and I had my gift.

We were hardly unprotected.

The tavern might have belonged to Cutter for all it resembled the place where I'd grown up. Had it sold only liquor, it would have been almost empty at this time of day, but as it was, several tables and booths were filled with customers. While Dorian and Cass headed to the bar—its shelves stacked with memories—to flag down the bartender, I wandered through the tavern, keeping my eyes down and my hair covered. A month ago, I'd been planning to run away with Regis and the butcher's daughter, and now I was in Idaea, a city I'd never thought I'd reach. That, at least, was progress.

"Bring me another of these, if you please, miss?" A gravelly voice from a nearby table dragged me from my reverie. The voice belonged to a large man with reddened jowls, who promptly raised a blue-colored bottle in my direction.

"I'm sorry, sir, but I don't work here."

Not anymore.

"I don't care if you work here, miss. Just get me another of these, okay?" The words took on a faintly threatening tone.

"Leave her alone, Merl," came an indignant voice from behind me, "and use your legs for their intended purpose."

I turned to see a man with silvered hair framing a smooth-skinned face. Despite the shade of his hair, it was impossible to guess his age—he might have been forty or seventy—but he moved stiffly, as if his joints were painfully swollen. As Merl begrudgingly retreated to his table, the stranger winced and leaned on a cane I hadn't seen at first glance. Remembering the veteran, I went to him and took his arm to assist him to the corner booth he indicated, far from the others.

"Well, miss, you show an old man an uncommon kindness," he said as he settled himself, keeping his cane propped against his thigh, where it could be easily reached.

I lowered myself into the seat opposite him. "You were the one who intervened on my behalf, sir."

"Ah, that was nothing. I hate to see a woman bothered." He tilted his head, and despite the shadows clustered in this corner of the tavern, I discerned sharp eyes and an aquiline nose. "Are you new to these parts, Miss—"

"Sephone," I replied before I thought better of it. "And aye, I'm searching for someone."

"Oh? Well, I know most everyone around here. Perhaps I've heard of the fellow. Or the lady."

Could he help us? "They call him Silvertongue. Silas is his first name." I probed the old man's eyes for a flicker of recognition, but the yellow-tinted brown irises remained inscrutable.

"And what do you want from old Silas?"

"You know him?" Excitement built in my chest. Days of searching, and I had finally uncovered a lead—

"Aye, I know Silas. Pardon my caution, Miss Sephone, but around here, not everyone who comes looking for someone is after a cup of sugar. Might I enquire as to your purpose in seeking him?"

I hesitated. Dorian readily asked after the whereabouts of Silvertongue—a question anyone might pose, since the man was a well-known merchant—but he only disclosed the quest for the Reliquary to those he trusted. The old man in front of me looked kind, and he'd shown concern for my welfare. Could I trust him?

"I'm the soul of discretion, miss," said the stranger, giving me one of the winsome smiles of which only the very old and the very young are truly capable. "My lips are sealed."

There was nothing for it. We had no other leads, time was running out, and this man knew Silvertongue personally. I had to take the risk. "My friends and I are searching for an ancient artifact. It's rumored Mister Silvertongue might know where it is hidden."

The man's eyes sparked. "Ah, might you be speaking of the Reliquary?"

"Aye, that's the one."

"I've heard Silas speak of it a time or two. It dates back to even before the world-that-was. Very powerful. And very cursed."

"Cursed?" I repeated.

He nodded sagely. "It's said that the artifact's power can only be harnessed at great cost. A cost some men"—he inclined his head toward me—"and some women are not willing to pay."

I frowned. Dorian had said naught about such a price. Perhaps he didn't know.

The old man leaned forward on his elbows, silvered hair falling over his smooth brow in a gesture that was both boyish and conspiratorial. "I can take you to him, Miss Sephone."

"Mister Silvertongue is here in Idaea?"

"Aye, he's here." He reached for his cane and extended his hand to me. "I'll take you to him right now. But you must come alone."

I glanced behind me, looking for Dorian and Cass, but they were still at the bar. I twisted to face the old man again. "I have to tell my friends where I'm going."

"They'll understand," the man replied in a voice as soft as caramel.

"If we don't go *now*, we'll miss him. And only Silas knows where the Reliquary is kept."

I lifted my gloved hand, inching it toward his. Trying to order my thoughts beneath the old man's watchful gaze was like attempting to gain a secure foothold in a giant vat of butter. Why did my head ache all of a sudden? And why was my vision slightly blurred?

"That's it, Miss Sephone. Come with me—"

"Seph?"

A hand clamped my shoulder, and I jumped violently, twisting to face my assailant.

"Seph?" Cass repeated, a puzzled look on his features beneath his hood. "Who were you—"

I spun back around, but the seat opposite me was empty. How had the old man moved so fast hobbling on a cane? And why had he fled? I realized I hadn't even asked his name.

I turned and approached the closest table, where a grim-faced man nursed an amber-colored memory. A sour realization was dawning in my stomach.

"Please, sir, do you know who that man was? The silver-haired man I was speaking to before?"

"Would think you knew who you was talkin' to," he replied perfunctorily.

"Please," I begged. "Don't you know—"

"Of course I know 'im," growled the man. "Everyone knows old Silas. Slippery Silas, they call 'im. As good a name as any. He's harder to hook than an eel."

Acid was rising in my throat. "Do you know his last name?"

The man looked at me like I had asked him why grass was green. "Would think you knew that too after speakin' with him for so long, miss. Silvertongue is as Silvertongue does."

I raked my eyes over the room. There was only one exit, and that was the way we'd entered. I raced over to Dorian, who had just finished his conversation with the bartender.

"He was here," I said breathlessly. "I was speaking with him."

Dorian took my forearm. "Silvertongue?"

"Aye." I hastily relayed the entire encounter to him and Cass, who'd come up behind me.

Barely a half hour later, I was ready to pull out every strand of my hair. There was no trace of the old man, and only a few customers had witnessed my conversation with him. Not even the eagle-eyed bartender remembered him entering, and no one in the surrounding streets had seen him leave. Silvertongue had evaporated like a puddle on a hot day.

We went out of the tavern and into an empty side street.

"I should have known it was him," I moaned, leaning against the cold stone of a building. It offered more grime than reassurance. "But there was naught—no sign of iridescence, no sign of his gift." Then again, there had been barely any light.

"Silvertongue may not be a *calor*." Dorian frowned. "You said he tried to persuade you to come with him alone?"

"Aye."

"And you almost did?"

I glanced at Cass, who was kicking at a stone jutting out from the dirt. "It was like I couldn't help myself. I wasn't thinking. Until Cass touched my shoulder, and then I could reason clearly again. When I turned around, Silvertongue was gone."

Dorian's frown deepened. "I don't think this man is a *calor* at all. I think our friend Silvertongue is named for his gift."

"Persuasion," said Cass.

"Aye. And there's something else."

I held my breath.

"Silvertongue knows we're looking for him. And for whatever reason, he doesn't want to be found."

That evening, Dorian announced his intention to leave Idaea the following morning. It was too risky to remain in the city any longer, and besides, Silvertongue had likely already departed. None of us had seen the hooded man again, but if he was working for Lord Draven, it was only a matter of time before he found us.

A shadow had come over Dorian as we returned to the compound, and at dinner, the lord resembled the melancholy shell I'd first encountered in Nulla. Even Cass was uncharacteristically quiet.

After the meal, I found Dorian in my room, sitting on my bed. My heart executed an aerial somersault, quickly brought back to earth when I realized he was leaning over Jewel.

"Is she any better?" I said, sitting on the other side of the wolf, who was curled atop my covers, her head resting on Dorian's lap.

He rubbed her flank. "She's still feeling poorly, I think."

"I'm sorry, Dorian. For everything."

I'd failed him. Our one lead to find the Reliquary, and I'd muffed it.

"None of this is your fault," he replied, meeting my eyes directly. "Not Silvertongue nor Draven nor the fact that the lady wolf's eyes are bigger than her stomach."

"We'll find the relic," I promised, burying my gloved fingers in Jewel's fur. "Even if it takes my dying breath."

He looked as if he wanted to reassure me but wasn't certain my declaration wouldn't become a reality. "I've been puzzling over what Silvertongue wanted with you. By all reports, he's an ordinary merchant."

"Perhaps he's a merchant with ambition, like Cutter."

He nodded slowly.

"Did you know about the curse, Dorian?"

His hand paused mid-stroke. "Are you speaking about the Reliquary?"

I released a pent-up breath. "Then you did know."

"It's a fairy tale, Sephone. All ancient relics are supposed to have curses attached to dissuade people from seeking them out."

"But what if it's true?"

"You mustn't believe every story you hear."

Seeing that he was in a difficult mood, I left him with Jewel and retreated into the garden, finding a path that wound beyond the springs into a grove of orange trees. Healthy as they were, I wondered if they were fruit-bearing, for I'd always wanted to taste an orange. Slivers of moonlight had wormed their way through thickening clouds to pierce the brooding shadows. The distant trickle of the water traveling from pool to pool was oddly soothing, along with the scent of minerals drifting on the breeze. The garden was so much bigger than it had seemed from the house.

Catching the aroma of citrus, I peered into the closest tree. There—I could see a sphere gleaming in the moonlight. I pushed up on my toes, wondering if the fruit would cheer Dorian, if Maera had orange trees aplenty. But I'd no sooner closed my fingers around its smooth skin than a hand came around my mouth, another arm banding my middle. I was dragged backward like I had been by the wolf.

Instinctively, I bit down as hard as I could on the thinly gloved palm covering my lips, satisfied when I heard a grunt of pain. If only I'd had my knife with me, I could have done more damage. I raised my knee and kicked behind me, but missed, my foot snagging in the heavy folds of my cloak.

But my backward momentum had knocked my assailant off-center, and I felt myself falling. I landed on top of him and quickly rolled to one side, landing in a patch of wet grass. Not even bothering to cry for help, I wrenched off my right glove as the man lunged for me again. Now to find a patch of bare skin and make him rue the day he was born—

Instead, I stilled, as helpless as a leaf snap-frozen in a sheet of ice. The veins in my throat corded and throbbed. A bloodcurdling scream bubbled up from my stomach and seized in my throat. Only the tiniest of gasps escaped my chilled lips.

How could I have been so easily disabled? The man straddled me, but his grip on my neck was hardly firm. Then I caught the gleam of a shaven head in the moonlight and I understood.

"*Sephone.*" Cutter's familiar voice shredded my remaining defenses. "How good it is to be reunited at last."

27

DORIAN

One more minute and then he must move. But when the minute passed, followed by another, and Dorian still hadn't shifted, what remained of his ailing motivation threatened to evaporate altogether.

Jewel suddenly lifted her head from his lap. She whined and pushed at his arm, and he begrudgingly stirred.

"What is it, lady?" He stroked her noble face. "Shall I take you to a physician after all?"

This time, she released a faint growl. Her sapphire eyes flashed, and she tried to get up, only to sag against the covers again. Was he going to lose her, too?

"Rest," he said in what he hoped was a soothing voice. "Sephone will return soon."

Another growl, followed by a pointed look at the door. Dorian's eyes widened in understanding. "Danger?"

A third growl confirmed it. He leaped from the bed, remembering that Sephone had said something about visiting the garden. "Stay here," he called behind him, dimly aware Jewel was now limping toward the door.

Blessedly, his sorry self had had the presence of mind to remain armed. He pulled his staff from his belt and snapped it to its full length, then sprinted into the garden. Where would Sephone have gone? He ran toward the springs, but they were unoccupied. He began down one path, halting when he heard a voice, low and menacing. It was coming from the other direction. He returned to the glowing springs, and this time, he glimpsed another set of flagstones leading away from the pools, slightly downhill.

He moved swiftly down the path, his ears open to the smallest sound or movement, but there was naught but the whistle of the wind through the trees. An owl hooted overhead, and he instinctively tightened his grip on his staff. Sephone was close—he was sure of it. Something deep within him was suddenly attuned to her presence.

The path opened into a tiny orange orchard of no more than ten trees. The faint scent of citrus danced on the breeze, reminding him of Maera.

And then he saw her. She was lying on her back in the grass, her hands—one bare, one gloved—clawing at another set of hands around her throat, which were clad in fingerless gloves. Her attacker was strangling her. Her eyes were wide and panicked, while the remainder of her body convulsed. Something was preventing her from using her gift.

Cutter has the ability to transmit fear. Fear so potent and all-consuming you can hardly think—or even breathe.

Dorian's heart seized, and he had no need of thought. The staff fell from his hands, and he dived forward, lunging for her assailant. His body hit the stranger's with a *thump* and, together, they rolled away from Sephone. He sucked in a breath, partially winded. The man was shorter than him, but powerful in the shoulders, like a wolf. Snarling at Dorian, he pulled himself upright into a half-crouch.

"Lord Adamo! You'll be sorry you challenged me."

"*Cutter.*"

Before he could reach for his staff, the man jumped on top of him, thick fingers grabbing for Dorian's neck. He was heavier than expected, and difficult to dislodge. Dorian got in several punches to the man's chest before a returned blow to his face rendered him momentarily blind. He felt Cutter's hand close around his throat. Expecting the merchant to attempt to strangle him as he had Sephone, he was surprised to discover the man's grip was weak and ineffectual. Had he winded the older man more than he'd realized?

"Dorian!" Sephone called weakly to him from several yards away, still clutching her own neck. "Don't underestimate him. His gift—"

Cutter frowned and ripped his glove from his hand, pressing his fingers against Dorian's neck as if he felt for a pulse.

"I don't understand." The man stared at Dorian. "You should be paralyzed."

His sight having returned, Dorian struck out at the merchant, his fist catching him somewhere near his nose. Blood spurted from Cutter's nostrils as Dorian shoved the man to the side. The merchant recovered quickly, drawing a knife from his boot and coming at Dorian again. He twisted away, only dimly registering that Sephone had thrown herself at her former master's back and was trying to dislodge the blade from his hand, both of hers now fully gloved.

"Get off me, girl!" he yelled. Blindly, he lashed out at her with the hand clutching the knife, and she gasped and fell back, clutching her face, blood dripping from between her fingers. He turned on her, brandishing the blade as she scrambled away from him. "Which do you prefer, girl? Paralyzing fear or a new scar?"

Her diversion had given Dorian the chance to reach his staff and stagger to his feet. With a resounding *thwack*, he brought the staff down on the man's shoulders with force enough to dislodge the discs in his spine. The man dropped his knife and slumped to the grass, his features contorted in agony as he released a silent scream, exposing the stumps of several yellowed teeth. As he rolled onto his back, Dorian kicked the knife away and pointed the iron tip of the staff at his chest.

"One sudden move, and you'll have several broken ribs to contend with in addition to an injured spine."

"I don't understand," Cutter said again, wild-eyed. "You should be—"

"Your gift doesn't work on me, merchant. I'm a *calor.*"

Out of the corner of his eye, he could see Sephone staring at him. Her bloody glove still concealed half of her face. Had she been marked permanently?

Voices swelled nearby as Dorian tightened his grip on his staff. Only when Bear ran into the clearing, followed closely by Cass, did he relinquish his position to the giant, who had thankfully brought his crossbow.

Dorian knelt in front of Sephone, whose hands were pressed against her face. "Let me see it."

"It's worse than it looks," she protested.

"You haven't even seen it yet." He gently pulled her hands away, hissing when he saw the long gash above her right ear, running almost parallel to her hairline. It was deep enough that she would need stitches, or a healer, whichever they could procure first. The arc of the knife had even severed several lengths of white-blond hair. He pulled a clean handkerchief from his pocket and pressed it against the wound, despising the sight of the blood that had already sheeted across her eyebrow and cheek.

It was his fault.

"Allow me, Thane." Cass knelt beside him and took up the handkerchief. "You see to our prisoner."

Nodding, Dorian stood and turned to Cutter. He held tight to his staff as he circled the fallen merchant. Once again, he was struck by the sense of familiarity that had pierced him at their first encounter.

"Have we met before?" he demanded.

"Before?"

"Before I saw you in Nulla."

"I hardly know, Lord Adamo," Cutter managed to sneer. "I do business with many of your kind."

A timely reminder that Draven might be close at hand. "Were you acting alone tonight, or does Draven know you're here?"

"Why do you ask? Are you afraid of him?"

Dorian jabbed the end of his staff into the man's ribs. "I suggest you answer my questions truthfully."

He coughed. "Threatening torture, my lord?"

Dorian glanced at the *lumen*. "Cass?"

"At your service, Thane." There was no mockery in Cass's voice as he handed the bloodied handkerchief to Sephone, extracted a long knife from his boot, and took up residence beside Dorian. He glowered at Cutter. "Answer the lord's question. Does this Lord Draven you've recently cozied up to know you're here?"

"Of course." Cutter realized his mistake too late, clamping his lips together as black coils snaked between him and Cass. His gaze sharpened as he surveyed the other man. *"You*! You're the *lumen* who trespassed on my property."

"Aye, the one and the same."

"You're all fools," Cutter spat, now glaring at Dorian. "You've no chance against Lord Draven. He wants your scalp nailed to his front door, and he won't rest until the deed is done."

"Draven underestimates me, just as you did."

Cutter's insect-like eyes swiveled to Sephone, who had ventured closer. "And you, idiot girl. Do you honestly believe you'll be safe with this man when Draven comes for him? I managed to persuade the illustrious Lord Draven of your value—in an attempt to keep you alive—but unfortunately for you, I rather oversold your abilities. I'll be hard-pressed to save your skin now that Draven wants you for himself."

"Especially since you're now intensely preoccupied with how to save your own skin." Cass rotated the sharp edge of his knife blade as if deciding how best to insert it into Cutter's flesh.

"So you thought to come for Sephone yourself," accused Dorian. "To kidnap her from under Draven's nose."

Wisely, Cutter sealed his mouth shut.

Cass knelt and briefly grasped the merchant's fingers. "Aye, that was it," he said with a wry glance up at Dorian. He chuckled at his surprise. "Didn't I tell you, Thane? There's more than one way to discern the truth."

Cutter had gone deathly pale. "Get away from me, *lumen*."

Shrugging, Cass stayed where he was. He looked at Sephone. "Anything else you want to know from this wretch?"

Something lit in her expression and her fear melted away. "My parents." She fixed her eyes on her former master. "Tell me the truth about my parents."

Cutter scowled, then coughed again. "Your parents are dead."

Black ribbons swirled in the lantern light. Dorian pressed the tip of his staff against the merchant's throat. "You're lying."

"You won't hurt me, Lord Adamo," he smirked. "You're far too noble to strike out in cold blood."

"*He* is." Cass's hand shot out. "Luckily, I'm not."

This time, crimson red ribbons poured from Cass's palm as he seized the merchant's gloveless hand in his. Cutter's face crumpled, and he screamed, his body contorting. Tears ran down his face in dirty rivulets as he began to sob uncontrollably.

"Please," he begged. "Please stop. Enough—"

"What are you doing?" Sephone demanded, dropping the handkerchief and darting forward, but Dorian caught her, holding her back against his chest. She didn't resist him, though he felt her tremble.

Cass hardly blinked. "I'm merely giving him a taste of the sorrow he caused you."

Dorian watched the weeping, sniveling, groveling mess with growing pity. Whatever Cutter had done, he was a human being. A grown man who now flailed like a child in a tantrum. "That's enough."

The *lumen* ignored him. "He needs a dose of his own medicine."

"Cassius," Dorian said, setting Sephone aside and stepping forward. "I said that's *enough*."

Light poured back into Cass's hands, this time glowing blue. He released the merchant and rocked back on his heels, looking calm, almost serene. Sephone's face was pale beneath the blood. Dorian's hands were drawn into tight fists at his sides.

Cutter squirmed, whimpering in a fetal position. His bloodshot eyes roved over them sightlessly.

"There," the *lumen* said with satisfaction. "I think he'll be truthful now." He looked at Cutter. "Speak, man."

Cutter stared up at Sephone. "Your parents are alive."

Color rushed back into her cheeks, hope dawning in her eyes.

"A-a-alive?" she stammered.

"I took you from them when you were four years old."

Cass's lip curled. "You kidnapped her."

"Aye."

"Where do they live?" Sephone pressed.

"I don't know." More green ribbons swirled, illuminating the clearing. "All the southern mountain villages look the same."

"Southern mountain villages? You mean I was born in—"

"Lethe, aye." His eyes lidded wearily. "Your father called you his little nightingale. That's all I remember. They were daft fools to trust me."

Cass raised his palm and the merchant shrank away. "Sorrow is more than a match for fear, little man, and my reservoir is only half-emptied. If you haven't learned your lesson already, I would suggest—"

"Nay, nay!" Cutter wailed, cowering. "I have learned it. Give me a moment."

He stammered out a series of disjointed explanations. How his men had told him of the powerful *mem* child living in a remote Lethean mountain village. How Cutter himself had traveled there, impressed by the young girl's abilities, even as his own were beginning to diminish. How he'd ingratiated himself with her parents by pretending to be a distant relative, using his memory gift to learn the necessary details that would complete the deception. And how, one night, he'd kidnapped her, telling the girl her parents had died suddenly from fever, naming him her adoptive father.

If Cass had used his gift again in that moment, even Dorian might not have objected. But at every word, Sephone came alive. Heedless of the blood still trickling down her face, she clutched her necklace.

"What were their names?"

"I don't remember. Look into my mind if you want." Once again, Cass's gift proved him truthful.

"I'm not going anywhere near your mind," she replied sternly. "What did they look like?"

"Your mother and older brother have the same hair as you, but they aren't *alters*. Your father is dark-haired."

"I have a brother?"

"Aye, a sullen little fellow who liked to throw rocks at sheep and birds."

"I'm surprised you remember that with such clarity," Cass remarked mildly.

"Believe me, the little wretch was unforgettable." Trembling, Cutter reached inside his coat pocket, withdrew something which gleamed copper, and tossed it onto the grass beside him. It was followed by an identical second object. Two arm cuffs, fashioned into serpents. Sephone froze when she saw them. "I told you that there were worse enemies out there than me, girl."

"How did you get those?" Dorian demanded. The arm cuffs had been in Sephone's satchel, left behind with Toria—

Cutter's eyes glowed mutinously. "Friend of yours, was she?" The corners of his mouth quirked. "She was the lucky one, executed on the spot by Draven. It's that Keon fellow I felt sorry for, sent to the arch-lord's dungeon to await further interrogation by the Eight."

Dorian felt the blood drain from his face. "You're lying."

"Am I?" Cutter glanced pointedly at the green ribbons drifting around his head. "More will die if the girl doesn't return with me. Perhaps the services of a powerful *mem* will be enough to sate Draven's bloodlust."

"She isn't going anywhere." Dorian's voice was taut. "What do you mean, '*more will die*'?"

"Like me, Draven is a man of deep ambition." The merchant had recovered some of his earlier composure. "He has his sights set on becoming arch-lord."

"You're telling me naught I don't already know."

"Oh, but there's more. When he has removed Lio, he'll move to attack Lethe, followed by Marianthe. He won't rest until Caldera is one united country under his rule. His rule as *king*."

Cutter paused, emphasizing the word. Caldera had sworn never to have another king, let alone a high king over all.

"You underestimate Arch-Lord Lio and the Council of Eight," Dorian said. "Calliope is well-guarded. And Lethe is a formidable enemy."

"As is Marianthe," Cass put in, sounding offended at the implication his homeland was a lesser target.

Cutter grunted. "Draven may not be an *alter* himself, but his interest in our breed runs deep. His army will not be comprised of ordinary soldiers."

Sephone's eyes narrowed. "How do you know all this?"

"You should know the answer to that, girl. I looked into his mind without him realizing. I'm very good when it comes to discerning ambition."

Dorian cocked an eyebrow. "For one apparently so powerful, you are very willing to incur Draven's displeasure by stealing something he wants. After this, he'll consider you expendable."

"Why else do you think I came back for what is mine?" He glanced pointedly at Sephone. "She may be the only one who is capable of defeating him."

"She doesn't belong to you."

"Doesn't she?" He patted his chest, and Dorian heard the crinkling of papers from within. "I beg to differ, Lord Adamo. I claim my property through official channels."

Dorian turned away from him to Sephone, noticing her wound was still trickling blood. "You should get that tended to. Cass and I will handle the merchant. Bear, would you accompany Sephone inside?" He expected them both to protest, but Sephone only nodded, as if in a daze. Bear lowered his crossbow and reached for her arm.

As she left the clearing, Cutter continued to track her with his eyes.

"Nice of you, Thane, to consider her feminine sensibilities before we kill him," Cass said with a savage smile, reaching for his knife.

Cutter stiffened, but Dorian held up his hand. "I'm not going to kill him."

When Cass still raised his blade, Dorian seized his arm. "Meaning, no one is doing any killing."

The *lumen*'s face darkened. "But if we kill him, she'll be free. If we let him go, he'll only hunt her down again."

"I won't be letting him go, either. But neither will I allow Sephone to remain a slave." Dorian levelled his staff at the merchant. "I want you to free her."

Cutter looked aghast. "Thanks to your kidnapping attempt and the resources I've expended tracking you down, this journey has already cost me a great deal. To free her would cripple me."

"Then sell her to me."

A calculating glint silvered Cutter's expression. "She's worth a significant amount of money, Lord Adamo. I'm not sure you could afford her."

"Perhaps you'll consider my considerable generosity in sparing your life before naming your price."

Looking mutinous, the merchant named a sum that loosed an explosive cuss word from Cass. Dorian named a more reasonable counter-sum—he refused to haggle over Sephone's life—followed by an icy glare. "I have every right to turn you over to Draven, merchant. Make sure you include that in your calculations."

Cutter turned sullen. "She's the strongest *mem* I've ever encountered. She is too rare—"

"You will find yourself another *mem* soon enough. In a legitimate business transaction, mind you. A freeman or freewoman."

The merchant glowered. "Fine. We have a deal."

"Once the papers are signed, you won't pursue us or harry us in any way. You will never speak to her again."

Cutter's eyes burned at them. "Agreed," he finally spat.

Dorian and Cass escorted him into the house, where they exchanged the necessary paperwork and then bound the merchant to a chair in their shared room. Cutter swore and struggled against the ropes, which held firm.

"You said you were going to release me," he snarled.

Dorian folded the papers and tucked them inside his tunic. "I never said anything about releasing you, Cutter. My representative here in Idaea will transfer the agreed funds to your nominated representative, but as for you, you're guilty of trespassing and assault. At first light, you'll be explaining your actions to the thane of Idaea."

Never mind that, wanted as Dorian now was, he would not be staying to deliver anything to the soldiers besides a tightly bound Cutter and a written account to pass on to the arch-lord and the Eight. He couldn't risk being captured. Not until his name was cleared.

"A word, Thane," Cass interjected, his voice oddly tight.

They closed the door on a string of colorful swear words.

Cass swung around to Dorian. "Congratulations on your new purchase. I'm sure Sephone will be glad to call you her master rather than her employer."

"It isn't like that." Dorian kneaded the back of his neck.

Cass's eyes narrowed. "Then you intend to free her?"

It had cost a small fortune to buy her. Even so, he would give her back her freedom in a heartbeat. He would have done it from the beginning if it were possible. Why, then, did he now hesitate? "As soon as I can."

"If you free her, she'll go to Lethe. She'll want to find her family."

The *lumen's* implication was clear. If he gave Sephone her freedom, she would abandon the quest for the Reliquary. She would abandon *him*. He couldn't decide which of the two consequences troubled him more.

But the truth was that she needed him as much as he needed her. She was dying. He might as well be. The Reliquary could save them both. Sephone couldn't lose sight of that, family or nay.

Dorian looked directly at the *alter*. "Once again, Cass, I ask for your discretion. Sephone doesn't belong to me any more than she did to Cutter. I will free her when I am able, I swear it."

He didn't know why he was making promises to the *lumen*—himself an escaped slave with no real interest in either of their predicaments. Perhaps he wanted Cass to understand his reasons. Perhaps he felt guilty for Toria's death and Keon's imprisonment. Or perhaps he wanted to prove to himself that his fervent vow was rooted in truth. He felt a wave of overpowering relief as the coveted green ribbons appeared between them.

"I will keep your secret, Thane," Cass replied with a half-mocking, half-rueful smile as he turned to depart. "But only because I know that sometimes the truth is far more painful than a lie."

Little nightingale. That was what my father had called me, according to Cutter, and this time I had Cass's gift to know it wasn't a lie. Was that why I'd been so drawn to the songbird?

The affection in the name was self-evident. It was a term of endearment given by a parent to a child who is their supreme delight and joy. My parents hadn't given me up because they were lacking in love or because they hadn't the ability to care for me. I'd been stolen from them. Perhaps the hole I'd felt in my heart my entire life was matched by a hole in theirs.

They were out there somewhere, in Lethe—my home country about which I knew virtually naught except that it was a nation which feared and detested the past. But they were alive. Possibly even searching for me, as I would now be searching for them. Loving me without any terms or conditions, simply because I belonged to them.

What would they be like? I wished I knew their names—my brother's name. If only I remembered their faces. Cutter had said that I shared my mother's and brother's hair color and that my father was dark-haired. But I knew naught else.

In my joy at learning my family was alive, I'd forgotten to ask about Regis, and to whom Cutter had sold him. But there was time yet. When Bear left me in the corridor to find the lady of the house, I headed for my room. Jewel was standing outside, looking distinctly unsteady on her feet. When she saw me, she whined.

"It's all right," I reassured her, moving aside Dorian's ruined handkerchief to expose my face. "It's only a bit of blood, and it's practically stopped bleeding."

She continued to whine, gazing past me in the direction of the atrium.

"What is it, Jewel?" I looked over my shoulder to the corridor, then back to the lady wolf. "We'll check it out together."

Jewel padded along beside me as I led the way. Lit by only a few lamps, the atrium was empty and silent, except for the water trickling into the pool from the fountain. I had gleaned enough from Dorian to understand that the house was some kind of inn for wealthy travelers, but besides us, there were no other guests. I'd only seen the man from our first day in Idaea, the woman with beads braided into her hair, and the young boy. And then only when they served us meals in the dining room.

Jewel stood still with her head raised, her ears flicking from side to side.

"Satisfied?" I asked, glancing down at the lady wolf. "Or are you just missing Dorian?"

Abruptly, Jewel looked to the entranceway and began to growl, hackles rising on the back of her neck. I stiffened. Cutter had determined our location. Lord Draven might not know Cutter had come after us himself, but there was every possibility he might have tracked the merchant and was now at the door.

I turned and raced back through the darkened house to our wing, only to smack into Cass in the shadowed corridor.

He grunted in surprise. "Seph, what are you—"

"We have to go *now*," I said urgently. Dorian was there, his quarterstaff fastened to his belt. His eyes flickered as he spied Jewel loping down the corridor, saliva dripping from her bared teeth. "I think Draven is coming."

This time, he believed me. Or, at least, he believed the wolf. Dorian gave a sharp nod, and the four of us sprang into action just as Bear reappeared with the lady of the house, the man who was presumably her husband trailing behind her. I ignored the woman's concerned glance at my face and sprinted down the hall to my room. I had few possessions, but there was my knife and the rabbit-fur cloak that concealed the memory potion Dorian had given me. I bundled everything into my pack and swung it over my shoulder.

Outside Dorian and Cass's room, Bas pushed himself away from the wall and straightened, an impressive array of throwing knives attached to a pair of baldric holsters crossed over his chest. Jewel paced fitfully at Dorian's heels.

"You could stay here and we could fight them off, my lord," the man was saying to Dorian. "This house is a highly defensible position."

"Nay, Farrow, I won't put you and your family in danger."

"Lydia is as good as any man with a bow," Farrow replied, glancing at his wife. "Better, even. She and I would protect you with our lives, Lord Adamo."

My eyes widened. Hunted by the arch-lord's soldiers or nay, the former thane of Maera commanded extraordinary loyalty from his subjects. Or were these people his friends? I glanced at Dorian and felt my gut twist, thinking of Toria and Keon. They had almost certainly been his friends.

"I thank you for your generous offer," Dorian inclined his head, "but you have a young son. We must take the fight far from here or else risk more innocent lives."

Bear and Cass disappeared into the room behind them and reappeared with a gagged, bound Cutter. His eyes blazed when he saw me, and I instinctively stepped back, remembering the fear. Only one man had ever made me feel as terrified as Cutter did, and he was Cutter's former ally.

Lord Draven.

"We'll take him with us. For now, at least," Dorian said, glancing at me. "We can drop him off to the soldiers on our way."

Farrow led us to the stables, where his son had made quick work of saddling our horses.

"Thank you," I said to the boy as he handed me my reins. "You're very kind."

"Ride fast, miss," he replied, bringing a smile to my face. I hadn't thought he knew the common tongue. He flashed a quick grin in return.

The men pushed Cutter into the saddle of a horse loaned from Farrow, his shouted threats partially muffled by the gag. His hands were tied firmly behind him, his legs free to grip the horse's back. Bear kept a tight hold on Cutter's reins as he mounted his own horse.

We'd barely ridden two hundred yards when another growl split the night—this time from the sky. Cass swore, and Dorian muttered a string of indecipherable words under his breath. Almost immediately, rain began falling, the force of it sweeping my hood from my hair and washing the blood from my face. I caught a flash of blue lightning in the distance, followed by a slash of jagged purple.

"Please tell me this is just another ordinary storm," I said to no one in particular.

"A pointless request when a *lumen* is present," Cass replied grimly, drawing his horse to a halt in the middle of the street. "But since you asked so ni—"

A ball of green fire tore through the air between us, so close it singed the hairs on my neck. My horse reared, and I scrabbled for a better hold on the reins, but the mare's momentum threw me backward, and I felt myself sliding. I hit the ground on my back, the air smacked from my lungs, though my pack bore some of the impact. Moisture from above and below seeped into my clothes as my horse returned to all fours, only to bolt.

And then there was chaos. I watched, horrified, as a succession of fireballs rained down on us. No bigger than an orange, they were nonetheless deadly when they encountered a target. The night flared to life as several roofs nearby caught fire in a blaze of green, blue, and yellow. Cass's horse reared as a ball of fire struck close by, but he kept his seat. Bas was forced to shed his cloak when a passing fireball set it on fire—an inferno that glowed gold. He yelped as he flung it into the pooling mud, proof that magical fire could burn as well as the ordinary kind. It took several minutes of heavy rain to fully douse the flames, and even then, a sickly, yellowish smoke rose in their wake that smelled like burning tar.

It wasn't the sky throwing fireballs at us. It was an *alter*.

I clambered to my feet and drew my knife as shadows crept toward us. Bear had dropped the reins of Cutter's horse and was frantically loading and shooting at the ghoulish shapes. Having recovered from his brush with flames, Bas threw his knives with abandon, and between him and his brother, I heard several screams that didn't belong to our party. Still, the circle of shadows advanced with the stealth of Nightmares.

By the light of several burning houses, I glimpsed a figure with his hood shoved back, exposing thick, rust-colored hair. Lord Draven. His features contorted in a snarl, he aimed a crossbow at Dorian, who was fighting to regain control of his horse after ducking to avoid a blue fireball. The sky rumbled overhead, an ominous sound I'd never heard so close.

"Dorian!" I screamed over the din. "Watch out!"

But it was not Dorian who ended up slumped forward, but Lord Draven. Dropping the crossbow, he bellowed and clutched at his forearm where a blade had sunk to its hilt. I traced the trajectory of the weapon to its source and gasped.

The man in the black hood stood in the shadows, another blade already in his hands as he took aim at our attackers. I couldn't see his eyes, or any of his features, but I felt his sharp nod of acknowledgement before he turned away.

The hooded man had saved Dorian's life.

Dorian wheeled his horse around and saw me standing in the mud. He kicked his heels into the stallion's flank, reaching down for me as he rode past. Sheathing my knife, I took his hand and he pulled me up behind him. I gripped his waist as he urged the horse forward. The combined efforts of the Mardell twins and the hooded man had forced our assailants to retreat, but the respite was only temporary.

"Ride!" he shouted to the others.

"Where's Jewel?" I yelled into his ear as crimson lightning tore the sky asunder. He whipped his head around, then, and turned the stallion in a circle, whistling for the lady wolf.

She came running from the shadows, blood dribbling from her fur and fangs. At the sight of the blood, I remembered Cutter and looked for his horse, but only Cass and the brothers were there.

"Cutter's escaped!" I exclaimed.

"I'm sorry, Sephone," Dorian said grimly. "We can't afford to go after him now."

He was right. The fireballs had ceased for the moment, but the street surrounding us was aflame, a tidal wave of people pouring from the burning houses. Pungent, yellow smoke filled the night with a foul odor. And then there was the lightning—

I gripped his elbow in acknowledgement of his statement, and he spun us around, heading for the outskirts of the city as Cass and the brothers followed at a gallop. Jewel had evidently found her second wind, for she kept up with us easily. Her gleaming white coat was a lantern in its own right as we outran the colorful inferno, the rain falling in vengeful torrents around us. I pressed the uninjured side of my face against Dorian's broad back while the wind lashed the other side, but nothing was worse than the pounding of hooves behind us that signaled Lord Draven's men were in pursuit.

Thankfully, Idaea was not a walled city, and its thane had chosen to concentrate his forces around the wealthier sections, leaving the outskirts poorly guarded. I saw only a handful of soldiers as we flew past the city's outbuildings.

We began moving downhill. I felt Dorian's heart rate quicken while my stomach plummeted. As luck would have it, the bridge spanning the icy River Memosine was further downstream.

"Nay, Dorian," I said in alarm as he steered the stallion toward the river. "We must head for the—"

He interrupted me. "We have to get out of the open. If we make for the bridge downstream, we'll be caught in the storm and possibly struck by lightning."

"But the ice won't be thick enough to walk on."

"The temperature is dropping rapidly as the storm builds. The river will freeze in time, trust me."

He was right about the temperature, at least: I was shivering uncontrollably. The rain faltered and, impossibly, snow began falling in spiraling currents. I huddled closer to Dorian. On another night, under different circumstances, I might have relished his nearness, the reassurance his presence provided.

But all I could think about was ice, creaking and groaning and cracking, splintering into fragments which stuck out like badly broken bones, crushing human flesh beneath their impossible weight. What a sickening twist of irony that I had been born with the gift of coating memories in ice when I couldn't abide the sight of it in reality.

We reached the riverbank and he dismounted, then reached up to help me. I stood beside the horse, watching numbly as Dorian carefully edged forward onto the ice, testing its thickness.

Cass wheeled his horse to a halt beside us, casting a nervous glance over his shoulder at our pursuers. At least ten riders were close behind, though it was impossible to tell if Lord Draven was one of them.

"Is he mad?" Cass stared at Dorian. Lightning cracked like a whip overhead.

"Dorian thinks the ice will hold."

Cass slid down his horse's side, his boots landing with a *thump* on the frozen ground. "I'd choose facing Draven over drowning in frigid water any day."

"I thought you said it was 'only a little water,'" I reminded him.

He tensed as vivid orange split the sky. "There wasn't a storm that night, Seph."

Dorian took ten steps across the ice, then returned to us. "The ice is thick," he said, snow dusting the exterior of his sodden cloak. "I can't feel or hear any fractures."

I eyed the frozen river. The ice certainly seemed thicker than the day I'd tried to cross the canal. But if I understood anything about ice, it was its treacherous nature. One never knew what lay beneath the slick surface. And out in the middle, where the ice would be the thinnest . . .

As the brothers arrived, Dorian grabbed his horse's reins and started across, moving cautiously. He'd chosen the narrowest section of the river, but my heart still beat wildly as I traced his tall form. It was only when he safely reached the other side that I let out the breath I hadn't known I was holding.

It was the carriage-bridge all over again.

"Go," I said to Cass. "I'll come after."

"I won't leave you by yourself, Seph."

"My motives aren't as noble as you think, Cass. You cross first and let me know if there are any thin parts."

He nodded, while Bear turned and began firing as the marauders advanced. The fireball thrower must have been injured back in Idaea, for no flaming spheres came at us through the thickening gray. The line of shadows faltered marginally, but then kept advancing.

Cass reached the other riverbank, followed by Bas, who made two trips to retrieve his brother's horse so Bear could continue fending off our pursuers. Jewel had made her own way across on sure-footed paws.

"Now you." Bear, still focused on the riders, was almost shouting over the thunderous roar from overhead.

"I—I can't."

"You can, Sephone. I expect a good bit of verse on the other side." He gave me a crooked smile. "Something rhyming with ice, perhaps."

That was easy enough. Dorian had decided to cross the river against my advice. The use of the Reliquary came at a terrible price. Lord Draven was a man ruled by shocking vice. I wondered what my chances were of surviving a frozen river not twice, but *thrice*.

"One foot in front of the other," Bear called to me. "Think about something else."

Paradise, perhaps. I smiled ruefully at myself and did as he instructed.

Dorian was right: the ice was thick, and freezing fast. But I still felt it shift slightly as I started across, the enormous sheets beginning to buckle after bearing the weight of several men and horses. Would it take Bear's weight?

Snow sheeted into my eyes as the storm became a blizzard, but the unearthly lightning continued to slash across the sky. The pain from the cut near my hairline had subsided, the blood freezing along the length of the wound. Hopefully, the combination of rain and snow would put out the fires back in Idaea.

I paused in the middle of the frozen river and made the mistake of looking down. Tiny fissures fanned out from my boots like worry lines as the ice shuddered beneath my weight. I instinctively dropped to my knees. This section of ice was thinner than the rest and liable to fracture. I would need to crawl the rest of the way.

If I *could* crawl. But my body was frozen, my mind as paralyzed as it had been in Cutter's grip. I was dimly aware that Bear was now making his way across the river, still facing the enemy. Blood dripped onto the ice from a crossbow bolt embedded in his shoulder. The snow fell in a shrieking whirlwind; I doubted the others could see us, since I could no longer see them.

The sight of the bodyguard's injury stirred me to action.

"Bear!" I inched my way toward him. "Get down! The ice is too thin to walk on!"

He obeyed just as a jagged blue column of light speared the river not twenty yards from where he crouched. The crack of thunder followed so quickly, there was no time to clap my hands over my ears. A high-pitched squeal rang in my eardrums as I winced from the pain, barely registering the ensuing popping sounds as a series of enormous fissures raced toward us.

The magical lightning had somehow shattered the ice. There was no more time. I got to my feet and looked for Bear. He was moving in my direction. I felt the ice shift and tremble as it splintered into pieces.

It is not ordinary lightning. The bolts seek the flesh of humans— especially alters.

"Go, Sephone!"

I turned and ran, leaping from fragment to fragment as each one lurched drunkenly beneath my boots. A man's voice rang out through the gray, calling our names. Through the snowstorm, I saw Dorian standing erect, leaning in over the riverbank, the others beside him.

I came to a halt on the edge of an enormous fragment, not six feet from where Dorian stood. Behind me, Bear wheezed, his blood continuing to stain the ice. I looked down and gulped, realizing why none of the others had come to our aid. The river had reasserted its dominance in the wake of the lightning, leaving a chasm of churning inky water between the bank and the ice fragment on which we stood. A gap of about six feet, too deep to wade and too fast-flowing to swim.

"You have to jump!" Dorian called to us. "Draven's men have reached the other side!"

One minute, I was trembling, my heart thudding painfully in my chest as lightning and thunder continued to crackle overhead. The next moment, I was impossibly calm. Warmth threaded through the cavity of my ribs, turning every muscle to steel.

Dorian's gift.

"You first," I said to Bear.

"Nay, Sephone. Ladies always jump first."

"You can help catch me on the other side. Besides, I went first last time."

Dorian gestured at us wildly. "There's no time! Go now!"

Bear grunted, backed up several paces, and took a flying leap. The fragment rocked to-and-fro in his wake, and I sank to my knees in the center, balancing it as water slid over the ice, making the surface treacherously slick. But Bear reached the riverbank safely, steadied by Dorian and Bas.

"Now you, Sephone!"

Not for the first time, I bemoaned my height—or lack thereof. Bear was several feet taller than I, and he had only just made the jump. But then, he was injured. I fought against the swirling doubt.

"I promise I'll catch you, Sephone!" Dorian shouted. "But you have to jump!"

I've got you, the brown-haired youth had told my semi-conscious younger self as he pulled me from the canal. *I've got you safe and sound.* Why had I only remembered that now?

I struggled to stand.

Stay with me, the boy had said as he worked on my unresponsive form. *Stay with me, little one . . .*

Dragging my eyes from the torrent of rushing black water, I fixed my gaze on Dorian. "You'll stay with me, then?" Every other sound melted away as I waited for his answer; the thunder, the shouts of men on the opposite riverbank, and the demonic whistling of the snowstorm faded into nothingness. We stared at each other.

His eyes suddenly widened in realization. He nodded. "Aye, Sephone, I'm staying."

I tamped down my fear and retreated as far as I could without tipping myself into the river. It wasn't much of a run-up, but there was no time to be choosy. I sprinted toward the edge and leaped into the air.

The next moment, I slammed into a male chest, feeling a pair of strong arms close around my back. Warm breath pulsed against my neck.

"I've got you, Sephone," Dorian said. It was only when I looked down that I realized he was standing knee-high in the freezing water.

He carried me from the river and set me down on the bank, but not before he bent and whispered three more words in my ear.

"Safe and sound."

At last he knew why Sephone Winter had been so willing to trust him from the first day they met.

Because it was not their first meeting, but their second.

It all came back to him as they galloped away from the fractured river, heading for the forest as snow fell blindingly around them. Dorian had almost forgotten his visit to Nulla as a youth, accompanying his father on a tour of the border towns and cities with several other prominent Memosinian and Lethean lords. Despite the growing unrest along the seam, it had proved to be uneventful, and he had found himself listless and bored. Until he'd looked out his window and seen the crowd clustered around the gaping hole in the frozen canal, gesturing at the girl thrashing within but doing nothing to save her.

For many minutes after he'd dragged her from the water, he'd been afraid he was too late. Her sodden body was frozen and lifeless as he held her tightly against his chest. Remembering how his older cousin had once resuscitated a woman after pulling her from a mountain spring, he'd laid her on the ground and begun the same procedure, using his gift with abandon, though he didn't know if it worked on the unconscious. When she'd come to, he'd been filled with even more joy than the day his parents told him he was going to be a big brother.

She was only a child—barely four or five years old. He'd wondered where her parents were and why no one had attempted to rescue the girl. She wasn't disfigured or sickly—quite the opposite. Not a pretty child, but certainly a striking one, with an undeniable sweetness to her face. Then a man with a shaven head had pushed through the crowd, his sharp gray eyes anxious and searching, then filling with relief as he saw the little girl.

Dorian's heart stuttered.

A man with a shaven head.

Cutter. It was the first time she had run away. It was him . . . *he* had been the one to return her to enslavement under Cutter. Sick at the thought, grim determination filled him that this time, the rescue would be complete.

He was thankful for the blizzard that shielded them as they raced through the trees, snow falling so fast it would cover their tracks. Hopefully Draven didn't have access to any more wolves. But Bear was injured, and Jewel was tiring, and Dorian could feel the moisture that had found its way into his boots beginning to freeze. If they didn't stop soon, they would all die of exposure.

Luckily, he knew where he was. He took the lead, grateful Sephone was riding with Cass so she couldn't feel his anguish at learning just how completely he'd failed her. A quarter-hour later, he dismounted in front of a large rocky overhang. The forest around them was a nondescript sea of endless white.

"Quickly now," he beckoned as the others rode up. "We don't know how far they are behind us." Though they would have difficulty crossing the river now that the lightning had shattered the ice into hundreds of pieces.

"I'm sorry, my lord," Bear offered humbly as he entered the cavern, leading his mount. "It was my fault the prisoner Cutter escaped back in Idaea. I lost track of him when Lord Draven attacked."

His brother was far less courteous. "Now will you agree to hire more help, my lord?"

"First things first, Bas."

As the others gazed up in wonder at the enormous, high-roofed cavern, naturally illuminated by a slit in the rock far above their heads, Dorian barked a series of orders: Bas to go in search of dry wood for a fire—he recalled that there was plenty strewn in the far reaches of the network of caves—which would give the fidgeting man something to do with his hands. Cass to see to the horses. Sephone to assist with Bear's wound.

The bodyguard was characteristically stoic. Sephone distracted him with a steady stream of banter while Dorian helped him remove his outer layers of clothing. She offered the use of her gift to gently guide his attention to happier memories, but Bear refused. The bolt had pierced his shoulder above his collarbone, and Dorian carefully inspected its entry and exit areas.

"Just pull it out, my lord. I can handle a little tugging."

"It'll be more than tugging, Bear." Even with courage, it would be agony.

Bear's expression was resolute. "I can handle it."

The bodyguard gave a muffled yell of pain as Dorian snapped off the arrowhead and extracted the bolt. Sephone knelt beside Bear, both hands clasping his arm in silent support. A few tears dropped onto his arm.

Bear reached out and patted her gloved hand. "That's the worst. It's over."

"I could help you sleep," she pleaded. "You will need sleep to heal."

He hesitated, deliberating, as Dorian finished bandaging the wounds. After they'd assisted him to a place beside the fire, now aflame, Bear finally acquiesced. "If you please, Sephone. And I thank you."

"I won't go too deep, I promise." She removed her glove. Bear settled himself beside Jewel, and the *mem* reached out and took his hand. Dorian watched as black tendrils—much like the ones marking her chest—sprang from her fingertips and sank beneath Bear's skin. Barely twenty seconds later, Bear's eyelids grew weighted, and he sank to the ground on the bedroll Bas had laid out for him. Less than a minute later, he was sleeping peacefully.

"Better than any painkiller," Cass remarked, while Bas's brows furrowed, his dark eyes tinged with uncertainty and suspicion.

Dorian faced Sephone. "Now you."

She looked at him, puzzled. "I can't use my gift on myself."

"Not the gift. Your wound."

"Oh, yes. All right." Sephone allowed him to lead her to the rock where they'd tended to Bear, the quiet conversation of the others fading away. After she'd seated herself, Dorian knelt and examined her face. The rain had washed the blood away, but the gash from Cutter's knife was still a fearsome wound. If they didn't get her to a physician soon, she would be scarred for life.

"We're only a few days' ride from Ceto," Dorian said. There was little he could do without the equipment to stitch the skin together, especially now the blood had clotted. "We'll find a healer there for you and Bear both."

Though she nodded, he saw another question in her eyes.

"Ask it," he urged her, knowing what she was going to say.

She searched his face. "Back at the river, you remembered."

He rocked back on his heels. "I don't know how I ever forgot, Sephone." He laid a hand on her arm. "I gave you back to him. To Cutter."

"Aye," she replied softly. "But you were only trying to help. You didn't know Cutter wasn't my father."

"You tried to run away, and I sent you back into slavery." His voice was flat.

"Nay, Dorian." Her eyes looked earnestly into his. "You saved my life. You gave me the courage to face my fate." She put a gloved hand over his. "And you gave me reason to hope that not all the world was cruel. To look for the good in people, even while surrounded by evil on every side."

"I would have taken you from there if you'd asked it of me." He couldn't shake the dismay, laced with shame.

"You were only a youth," she reminded him.

"And you were a child. I know my father would have intervened on your behalf."

"If he is half the man you are, Dorian, I know he would have." She smiled gently. "But it wasn't to be. And besides, Cutter wouldn't have parted with me. Despite his recent disappearance, he never will." Her smile vanished.

Hearing this, Dorian felt squeamish. He wondered if she knew the truth—if she would be angry he had presumed to buy her, or relieved she was free of Cutter at last.

Better to change the topic altogether. "You knew me from the beginning, Sephone, didn't you? Or rather, the second time we met."

"Aye, almost straightaway. When I realized who you were, I knew I could trust you implicitly. The same way I trusted you when you saved me from drowning."

"You knew me so quickly?"

"Aye," she said with certainty. "You hadn't changed in seventeen years. You have the same heart now that you did then."

He glanced at Bear, sleeping peacefully, and envy stabbed at him. His mind ached. His body ached. His very soul ached. But if Draven's men had found their trail, they would have attacked by now. What would be wrong with seeking a few hours of oblivion? He could face the nightmares better when he was stronger. Sephone was right. All he needed was sleep.

"Dorian?"

He glanced at her to find her face filled with concern.

"Do you remember who you were?"

He understood what she meant. "Aye, I remember." He was so weary. "I remember too much. That's why I need you to help me forget."

30

SEPHONE

"Aye, I remember."

My heart rose at the words, then swiftly plummeted as he reasserted his desire to forget.

He looked up and his tone was urgent, almost despairing. "Would you take it away, Sephone?"

I opened my mouth to ask what he meant, but he had seized my hand. Not the gloved one, but the bare one, and I plunged headfirst into his mind, drawn against my will to the memory he held out for my perusal.

My mental self faltered. Usually, I saw memories through the eyes of the person whose mind I'd entered, but this time, I saw Dorian as a younger man—twenty-five or twenty-six, perhaps—sitting beside a bed, holding a child in his arms wrapped in a lavender blanket. His wife looked on proudly as she reclined against the velvet headboard, her body sagging in exhaustion, but neither the dim lantern light nor the weariness of recent childbirth could conceal the exquisite beauty of her features.

I stepped back, hating to intrude on such a private moment. But Dorian beckoned me closer, inviting me to inspect the bundle he held. The perfect lips, the lemon-gold hair, the deep blue eyes.

Emmy Ashwood.

When I looked at Dorian again, his face was contorted in anguish. It was so out of place—a proud father visibly grieving the healthy child he held in his arms—that I could only stare at him.

"Please," came his voice, "take it away. It is torment to remember."

"This is a happy memory," I told him, glancing at Dorian's wife, who was watching her husband with adoring eyes.

"Nay," he refuted, "not anymore. This is one of my most painful recollections."

How could I deny such an ardent request? Back in the cavern, I gripped Dorian's hand more firmly, preparing to do as he asked. And then I felt it—a stirring warmth, like the touch of his gift. I looked past him and saw a current of molten gold, a gleaming river threading through the memory. I had seen many strange things in the minds I'd visited, but never this. Still, it wasn't difficult to realize what it was.

Dorian's love for his daughter. His wife.

As I gazed at the molten river of gold, I knew I could neither freeze nor cross it. Such great love was impossible to quench, even temporarily. Even now, I felt the heat of it, thawing my frozen body from my head to my toes. One could sit at the feet of such a love for a century and never grow cold. I imagined it filling the hollow place inside of me—a place I could not see, but nonetheless felt—and stoking the flames of long-deferred dreams. My love for my lost family. My love for Dorian Ashwood, a man whose heart I would never possess.

I let go of his hand and drew back, the bedroom immediately fading from view.

"I can't," I said, rising to my feet. "I'm sorry."

Dorian quickly stood also. "You can do it. I know you can."

When I said naught, he frowned.

"Or is it that you won't?" He glanced at Bear. "You were willing enough before."

"You don't understand, Dorian. I could put you to sleep as I did for Bear. I could numb your pain as I did at the carriage-bridge. But to try and extract a memory with both good and bad components, a memory at the heart of who you are . . ." I shook my head. "It is not that simple. It may even be impossible."

"You're the most powerful *mem* I've ever met," he replied, anger tightening his features. "If you cannot do it, nobody can. Or is this still about love?"

"Aye. And nay."

He stepped closer, grasping my bare wrist. I winced against the turmoil of his mind and the firmness of his grip. He wasn't himself.

"You're making no sense, Sephone. What else did you do to me at the river but take away my past?"

"That was different. You were under attack. I merely numbed the bad memories . . . as many of them as I could." I hauled in a deep breath. "I told you from the beginning, I won't manipulate any memory related to love. But especially not now that I have felt the strength of it in your mind. No power in the world can stand against such a force, Dorian. Lord Draven took Lida and Emmy from you, aye. But he couldn't take your love for them . . . who you are because of them. I can't take it either."

Was that what had drawn me, all those years ago? The molten current running through his mind? The love, compassion, and kindness he had for others, even strangers?

"You won't know if you don't try."

But, indeed, I had tried—several times—before Cutter finally agreed to let me work as I wanted. The recipients of those mind-bleedings—memory extractions that targeted the core foundations, the heart of who they really were—were never the same again. Even *alters* became shadows of their former selves. Many of them experienced a diminishing in the potency of their gifts or lost them altogether.

Doubt continued to stab at me. "What if those memories are tied up with your gift? I could rob you of your power."

He stilled, then shrugged. "So be it."

"The youth I once knew would never be so cavalier." I met his hard expression, trying to help him understand, even while my heart broke at the anguish in his eyes. "Without love, Dorian, you won't be the same man."

"You would condemn me to remember them forever?" His grip on me tightened.

"You do not know what you have."

"I think I know what I *had*," he replied rigidly. "Which is why I want to be rid of it."

I tried to tug my hand away as an increasingly familiar bitterness crept into my heart. "At least you had them, if only for a time. I don't even remember my family."

His dark eyes flashed. "Is that what this is about? That because I had what you've always wanted, you will not help me? Are we to compare our past misfortunes?"

"If it helps you realize what you're trying so hard to give up."

"Thane!" Suddenly, Cass was beside us. "Let her go," he demanded. "You're hurting her." When Dorian didn't reply, as if seized by an emotional trance, Cass grabbed both of our hands. Red and blue light darted between the hand that held mine, followed by only red light between his and Dorian's. Dorian jerked his hand away from my wrist.

He stared wildly at Cass. "What did you do to me?"

"You were hurting Sephone." Cass met his stare. "I simply allowed you to feel what she was feeling."

Dorian froze for a moment, then remorse filled his face. "Sephone." He turned anguished eyes to me. "I'm sorry." His hands dangled helplessly at his sides. "I don't know what came over me."

He might not know, but I did. It was the frenzy that sometimes possessed those who thirsted for the past, some of them so twisted by their cravings that they would kill for what they wanted, while others faded into living ghosts. Was that the fate which awaited Dorian should he successfully eradicate his memories? That he would wither away to nothingness, becoming a shell of a man like Lord Guerin? A man who was incapable of love or any human feeling?

Nay. I wouldn't let such a destiny befall the boy who'd saved me.

"Not wishing to interrupt your little argument"—tension underscored Cass's sardonic tone—"but I can think of several conversations we should be having right now. How we might evade this Draven fellow, for one. Why a mysterious hooded man saved your bacon and all our hides back there, for another. And while we're at it, I think we can all agree we need a pay raise after tonight."

"Naught in life is free," was Dorian's only reply.

"And here I believed you had a reputation for generosity, Thane. Well, one thing is clear." He glanced between Dorian and me. "Whoever this hooded fellow is—and whatever he wants from us—it's my guess that he knows one of you personally."

"You're a miserable lot tonight," Cass declared as he plunked himself beside Dorian. Sephone lay wrapped in her blanket next to Jewel on the other side of the cavern. The unmistakable scent of alcohol tainted the white plumes of breath that drifted from Cass's mouth with every word. "What happened between the two of you? She looked ready to run away before."

Dorian shot him a sideways glance. "Did she say anything to you?"

"Answering a question with a question, Thane? How very political of you. She's not going to leave you, if that's what worries you. She's rather naïvely loyal in that regard." He inclined his head quizzically. "I heard you saved her life as a child."

What had she said to the *lumen*? Or had he discovered it for himself? Perhaps he'd been eavesdropping on their conversation again. Returning the favor, he would say.

At Dorian's expression, Cass laughed softly, holding up a small flask and pointedly swishing the contents. "It's not an interrogation."

He chewed his lip. "Aye, I saved her."

"Earning her lifelong devotion in the process. No wonder she endures the constant threat of Draven for your sake."

"I swore I'd keep her safe. From Cutter and from Draven."

"As any good master would defend his most precious asset."

"I don't consider her an asset, at least not in the way you mean. I fished her from the canal in Nulla without any inkling of her powers."

Cass raised an eyebrow.

"And I didn't know she was a slave then, or I would have freed her."

"As you swore to free her tonight." Cass's eyes glinted in subtle challenge.

Dorian was silent.

The *lumen* stretched his arms and legs with feline grace. "Well, Thane, whatever your motivations, you've earned her trust. She'll never leave or betray you."

Dorian recalled the deep hurt in her eyes when he'd practically ordered her to take his memories of his newborn daughter. He wasn't so sure. Guilt tore at his insides.

"Still, you should reconsider her involvement," Cass was saying. "Me, I live one day to the next, taking advantage of every fair wind that comes my way. No one will mourn me if I die in your service, Thane. But Sephone, well . . . she has something to live for now. A family, a homeland, a better life."

If only Cass knew she might not live. But Dorian had given his word not to tell the *lumen*—a good instinct on Sephone's part. If Cass knew the truth, he might take advantage of her vulnerable state, even while considering it nothing more than another "fair wind" blowing his way.

"You heard that Cutter fellow," Cass said. "Draven will stop at nothing to kill you, and now he knows what she is, he wants her power for himself. I enjoy Sephone's company more than most women's, Thane, but the longer you keep her with us, the more danger she'll face. Back at the river . . ."

The *lumen* trailed off as if he knew he didn't need to elaborate. Dorian realized how close he'd come to losing her beneath the ice a second time. But what Cass didn't know was that Sephone wasn't only coming along with them for the sake of the Reliquary. She was coming for her own sake, too.

"She knows the risks," he responded. "And she wants to stay, at least for now. I have no choice but to bring her with us. Perhaps we will find her family along the way." *And a cure for whatever's slowly poisoning her, in the event the Reliquary cannot be found.*

Cass sighed, but nodded. "Very well, Thane. Have it your way. Or rather, have it her way."

An oddly companionable silence stretched between them.

Something occurred to Dorian. "'No one will mourn you'?" He

couldn't help the pity in his tone. Even with Lida and Emmy gone, he still had people who loved him.

An invisible dagger knifed his stomach, a belated counterpart to the blade which had nearly killed him. Aye, he had people who loved him. People like Toria and Keon, who'd paid dearly for their association with him.

A smile brightened Cass's face, and he glanced across the fire at the woman who'd rolled over to face them, her eyes closed, her gloved hands cradling her arms as if she sought to comfort herself in her sleep. The flames failed to reflect the brilliance of her hair, only revealed in the softest moonlight. "Perhaps Sephone would mourn me."

An unfamiliar emotion turned Dorian's stomach, and he forced a mirthless chuckle. "Sephone would mourn a dead squirrel."

"Ouch, Thane. Thanks." He tossed his head, and the black locks captured the firelight in metallic shades of green and purple. It was to Sephone's credit that she wasn't besotted with the man. She was too sensible to fall prey to passing infatuation. Or so he hoped.

Dorian lowered his voice, fearful she would overhear their exchange. "Sephone is still very young. In time, she will learn not to wear her heart on her sleeve."

And yet, was that not what he admired about her? Her company softened the horrors of the night, just as moonlight made caricatures out of shadows.

Cass quirked an eyebrow. "You mean, she'll become jaded and cynical, like us."

"Not cynical," Dorian replied icily. "Just informed."

What else is there to warm us in this frozen world besides love, Lord Adamo? Sephone's fervent words to him back in Iona.

Indignation rose to answer her. There was honor. Duty. Sacrifice. All the things which had prevented him from seeking an early end for himself after Lida's and Emmy's deaths.

I cannot take from you even the smallest fragment of that which I crave for myself . . .

For all Sephone had seen, she didn't understand what the world was truly like. But she would. He would help her. It was important for her to know.

"Informed, Thane? Sounds like politician talk again to me." Cass grinned. "Seems like Seph's heart is right where a woman's heart should be."

Spoken like a man who made a life out of a string of fleeting pleasures, not caring what beads were used and discarded along the way.

He shot a glare at Cass. "Ready for the taking, you mean."

The *lumen* held up his hands defensively. "Believe me, I have no designs on her." His face turned serious. "You might be surprised to know that I agree with you, Thane, on your summary of the world. It is a lost cause, a hopeless case. We simply diverge on what we have decided to do with that reality. But Seph . . ." He shook his head. "Though I think you underestimate her, the only thing she has left is hope, Dorian Ashwood. Whatever you decide to do with your own miserable lot, you must not take that away from her."

Startled by the *lumen*'s honesty, and his use of Dorian's name, Dorian was surprised into frankness himself. "Hope can be a torment, Cass. It will save her unnecessary heartbreak if she realizes the futility of her dreams early on."

"Perhaps. Or maybe she'll have better luck with the world than we have. But whatever her fortunes, you must agree it is far better to spend as much of one's life as possible in contented bliss than to discover what it is to survive a night in the bitter cold."

I'm not used to living without hope. Her words to him the night of her twenty-first birthday.

Perhaps Cass was right. And perhaps he was confusing hope with peace. Just because he'd had his chance at living didn't mean he needed to rob her of hers.

Cass gave a low chuckle. "Besides, maybe she'll discover what you and I were too blind to see. Maybe she'll find the happiness we were denied."

If she lived. Thinking ahead, Dorian listed his priorities in his mind. They weren't in any particular order.

Rescue Keon from the arch-lord's dungeons. Find Silas Silvertongue. Locate the Reliquary and heal Sephone. Avoid being arrested by Lio's soldiers. Evade Draven, while uncovering the proof

the Eight needed to arrest him for murder. And convince Sephone
that the Reliquary—and her gift—was his best chance to return to the
man he once was.

Perhaps not the exact man. Certainly not the boy who'd saved her
from the ice. That man had died with Lida and Emmy.

He would see to it that Lord Draven never hurt another living soul,
even if it cost him his own life. That was a worthy use of the breath
remaining in his body.

"You're elsewhere—lost in yourself," Cass remarked as if from a
great distance.

Dorian touched the bands at his throat. As usual, they lent him
courage. Focus. Purpose. He certainly wasn't elsewhere. Not in the
way he wished.

Not yet. But he would be.

He settled himself on his bedroll, reasoning that he should try and
get as much rest as he could, for the storm might last for days. But he
was still awake hours later when, across the dying fire, Jewel raised
her shaggy head, her ears flicking to the side, then flattening.

And a low growl rumbled from her chest.

ACKNOWLEDGMENTS

Writing a book is the smallest tip of a (largely invisible) iceberg of friendships, support, input, and guidance from so many people who have molded this book into the polished product that rests in your hands today. *Calor* owes its existence to an incredible team who have shown their wisdom, love, and expertise in a myriad of ways, from punchy critiques to putting on the kettle for tea to ooh-ing and ahh-ing with me over covers and character art.

A heartfelt thank you to my readers, who make this whole author gig possible . . . and to my street team/cover reveal team, for their love of and enthusiastic support for a book they hadn't even read yet! You guys are absolute champions.

For Paige and Dan—my first beta readers and wonderful friends, who read an early, very rough draft of *Calor* and gave invaluable feedback. Paige—thank you for being willing to challenge me to be a better writer . . . the way that you've helped to deepen and enrich the spiritual themes of this book (and especially the next) is absolutely priceless. Dan—you are a brilliant editor! I'm forever thankful to you, not only for the way your feedback has shaped this story, but for the excellent title suggestion when the initial title just wasn't working.

To Kirk DouPonce, for the stunning cover. When I first saw it, my jaw dropped and I couldn't believe that this magical, beautiful cover belonged to my story. Since then, I've looked at it approximately 105,451 times and each time I fall more in love with it than before.

To Marissa, for the character art—WOW! You have captured my characters so perfectly. Cass is certainly the dreamboat he was meant to be. Thank you for your incredible artistic talents!

To the amazing team at Enclave/Oasis Family Media: Steve, Lisa, Trissina, Jamie, and the rest working behind the scenes that I haven't "met" yet. Working with you all has been an absolute dream. Your professionalism, integrity, and solid Christian faith encourages and inspires me. You took this story and made it something that I could have never launched on my own. I've learned so much from you all. Thank you for your support!

A huge thanks also to my fellow Enclave authors who have welcomed me into the Enclave family and tolerated my silly sense of humor and rambling emails. A particular thanks to Cathy and Sharon—even though I've never met either of you, you are already so dear to me! I wish we could find a patch of sunshine, make a pot of tea, and sit and chat for hours. In the meantime, Messenger and Zoom will have to do!

A thousand thank-yous to my family and friends who have championed my writing and encouraged me at every twist and turn: Tracey, Jorg, Laura, Dave, Alice, Liam, Kathy . . . there are just too many to name. To my gorgeous, eight-year-old nephew Archie who, when he found out I was releasing *Calor,* dramatically exclaimed, "Let me guess, Aunty Jas— you've written ANOTHER book!" (Thanks, Arch, for always keeping me humble. ☺))

A special thanks to my mum and dad, Guido and Lucy, who deserve a commission for all the books they've probably sold on my behalf. Thank you for your wisdom, love, and generosity, and for building me up in my faith—I couldn't ask for better parents. And to my second set of parents, my wonderful in-laws Stuart and Maureen, who have been such an incredible support to me. It was only after I'd written the line "An iron fist in a velvet glove" that I realized it was one of Stuart's classic sayings! Full credit to your creative genius, Stuart—I'm only sorry I attributed this brilliant line to the villainous Cutter!

To my husband, my life partner and closest friend: as I've said before, you bow to no one (except God, of course). You are the Samwise Gamgee who shows his finest qualities in the wilderness; the unassuming but noble Aragorn who draws his sword to protect his friends (you don't have a sword, of course, but wouldn't it be cool if you did?); the Legolas with (admittedly much shorter and less conditioned) lovely blond hair and a smile that captured my heart the first time I saw it. Together we've battled chronic illness and cancer and the Housing Market . . . that last one was a terror. Thanks for sticking by me through thick and thin, even when there's been rather a lot of thin (to clarify, I'm not remotely thin . . . but you knew what I meant).

And finally, most importantly of all, to our all-powerful, all-loving God who puts our best and most "original" creations to shame, but graciously accepts our meager offerings anyway. To You be all glory, honor, and praise, now and forever. Thanks for lighting a creative flame in our world that never goes out, no matter how much we fiddle with it. And thank you, most of all, for never letting us go.

Jasmine

ABOUT THE AUTHOR

Jasmine's writing dream began with the anthology of zoo animals she painstakingly wrote and illustrated at age five, to rather limited acclaim. Thankfully, her writing (but not her drawing) has improved since then. Jasmine began writing her first proper novel at age fourteen, which eventually became her debut fantasy series, The Darcentaria Duology, which was published in 2021.

Jasmine completed her Bachelor degree in English Literature and Creative Writing in 2012. Also a qualified psychologist with undergraduate and postgraduate degrees in clinical psychology, Jasmine's dream is to write stories that weave together her love for Jesus, her passion for mental health, and her struggles with chronic illness.

When she isn't killing defenseless house plants, Jasmine enjoys devouring books, dabbling in floristry, playing the piano, eating peanut butter out of the jar, and wishing it rained more often. Jasmine is married to David, and together they make their home a couple of hours' north of Sydney, Australia. You can stalk her on social media or visit her official website at www.jjfischer.com, where she's always open to swapping good memes, talking about chickens, or whingeing about Luke Skywalker.